ASSASSIN'S WRATH: REVENGE

A LITRPG / GAMELIT PROGRESSION FANTASY NOVEL

JOHN ELIJAH CRESSMAN

MAVERICK-GAGE PUBLISHING

ISBN: 978-1-954524-25-5 (Paperback)
ISBN: 978-1-954524-26-2 (Hardcover)
ISBN: 978-1-954524-27-9 (Audiobook)
AISN: B0B23NNBK6

Any references to historical events, real people, or real places are used fictitiously. Names, characters, and places are products of the author's twisted imagination.

Front cover image by Daniel Castiblanco
Editing By TC Tunstall

Printed by Maverick-Gage Publishing in conjunction with IngramSpark, in the United States of America.
First printing edition 2022.
Maverick-Gage Publishing
Allentown, PA

info@maverick-gage.com
www.maverick-gage.com
John Elijah Cressman
www.johnecressman.com

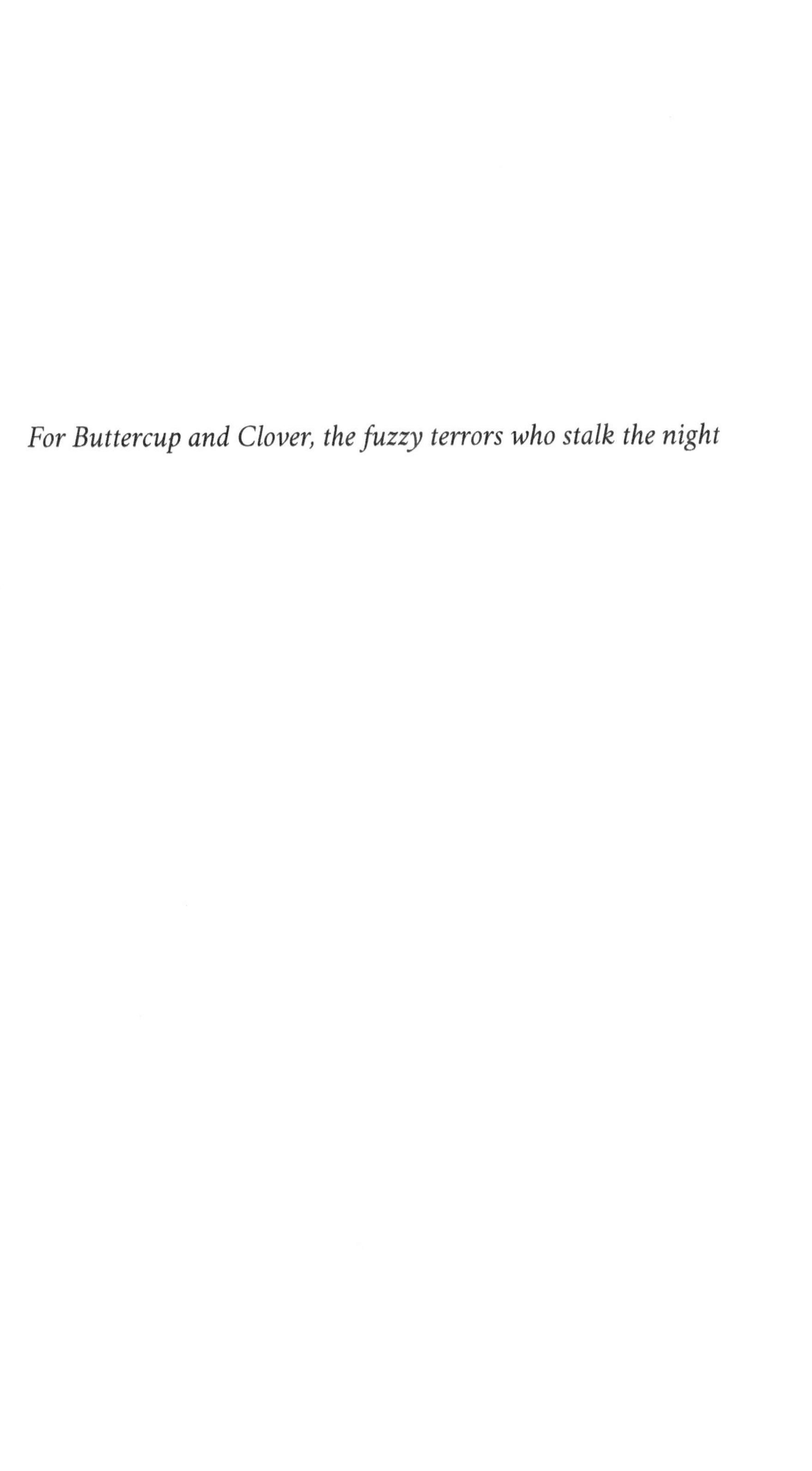

For Buttercup and Clover, the fuzzy terrors who stalk the night

CHAPTER 1

Deftly avoiding the Archmage's bat-like wings, Gage twisted the poison blade embedded in Ruy's back. The demonic channeler cried out and arched away from the blade. The flames around him died out as the poison did its work, robbing the Archmage of his magic.

Gage slid the blade out of him, ducking under the channeler's clumsy backhanded strike. He danced out of the man's reach even as Ruy Cernunnos fell to his knees. While the first poison robbed the Archmage of his magic, the second one shut down the man's organs.

The demonic Archmage stared at his impotent black-taloned hand, confusion scrawled across his visage. Ruy couldn't summon so much as a flicker of demon fire. He was completely powerless, and soon he would be dead.

Ruy collapsed to the floor, flailing his bulk upon the blood-covered tile in toxic convulsions. His gaze drifted to the stocky mage slayer standing over him, "Gods... take you... Gage!"

"I'm sure they will," Gage retorted with a snarl. "But they'll take you first."

Gage's face contorted with a mixture of hatred, anger, and grief. Ruy had sent assassins to kill Gage, but they'd made a fatal mistake. The assassins hadn't known, or perhaps hadn't been told, the extent of Gage's training. They hadn't been properly prepared to kill him. He survived. His wife and daughter hadn't. "I hope the demon you made a pact with roasts your soul for all eternity for Alani and Shaunna's deaths!"

Ruy coughed and blood sprayed from the Archmage's lips. With effort, the channeler sneered. "So self-righteous! Your hands... aren't clean in this either. Their deaths... are... as much on your hands as mine."

Vision going red, Gage kicked the demonic mage in the gut. "I walked away! I started a new life!"

The kick caused the Archmage to cough, spitting up blood, but the cough turned into a laugh. "Someone... like you... can... never just... walk away."

Gage reared back his leg for another kick, but he heard the inevitable sound of footsteps clattering in the distance. The sound of armored men running on the marble floor. More guards had finally made it to the top floor. To kill him.

Ruy heard it too. He laughed but it quickly turned into a coughing fit. "They're coming... you won't... escape."

"I'm not afraid of death," Gage retorted. He glared down at the dying channeler. "I'm not going to be tortured by a demon."

Paling, the channeler, seemed to consider Gage's words. The Archmage had made a pact with a demon to get his power. It had given Ruy mastery over fire magic. It was rumored that when a channeler died, his soul went to the demon he was bound to. Gage didn't know if it was true, but he hoped it was. It couldn't happen to a more deserving piece of garbage.

The Archmage coughed, then coughed again, this time bringing up more blood. He wiped the blood away with the sleeve of his expensive silk tunic. He chuckled. "You... you think this ends with me? You think... I... gave the order?"

Gage cast a glance at the doors, the sound of footsteps closer. He scowled down at the dying Archmage. "Lies won't save you. I know it was you."

"You think I... gave that order... on my own?" Ruy coughed. He was getting weaker. The poison from the dagger had almost completed its job. The Archmage's movements slowed, and he struggled to lift up his arm.

Bending down, Gage grabbed the man by his rich, gold-embroidered tunic and hauled him close. As he did, pain flared in the hand he'd burned when he'd stabbed Ruy through the flaming shield.

He knew he was breaking a number of rules by doing so. He knew to never get so close to a target, physically or emotionally. Even when they were wounded. No, scratch that—especially when they were wounded. He didn't care. He was beyond caring. The rules and the whole world could burn for all he cared.

He put his face close to Ruy's. There was one question

that had been eating at him since it had happened. "Why? Why did you come after us?"

"You know... why," he coughed.

Gage didn't know for certain, but he had a guess. Something was going on. Something mage slayers would be a threat to. But what? What did this idiot have planned? A revolt? An attempt at the Overlord?

The Archmage's blood-stained teeth formed into a smile. "This... is... bigger... than you know..."

Ruy's eyes started to roll back into his head, but Gage shook him. "Was someone else involved, Ruy?" he growled. "Who?"

Gage heard shouts now as the guards caught sight of the bodies Gage had left in his wake. They would be here any moment. He needed answers.

The once great Archmage's eyes glanced up at Gage with an unfocused gaze, blood loss and poison sapping his remaining strength. His lips moved and Gage leaned in closer to hear the channeler's last words. Nothing more than a rasping whisper. "The... Council."

Ruy's body went limp.

Gage stared into the corpse's vacant eyes. The Arch-mage, leader of House Cernunnos, was dead. Gage had killed him. His display flashed and he looked at the message.

Ruy Cernunnos dies.
You gain experience.
Quest Complete.
Vengeance is Mine—Part VIII

Get revenge by killing the man who gave the order.
Kill Ruy Cernunnos (1/1).
Reward: 9000 experience.
You gain 9000 experience.
You have received a new quest "Vengeance is Mine —Part IX"
You have learned that Ruy Cernunnos was not the only one responsible.
With his last words, Ruy Cernunnos informed you that the Council of Houses, together, authorized the crimes.
To gain vengeance, you must kill the remaining House leaders and the Overking.
Kill the Leaders of the Houses (1/7).
Kill the Overking (0/1)
Reward: 100,000 experience; Unknown.
Accept quest (yes or no)?

He thought a great weight would lift from his shoulders once the Archmage was dead. Gage thought he would feel better once justice had been served. He thought he'd feel something. But there was no joy, no happiness, no sense of justice. There was nothing. Nothing but the same rage he'd felt since his wife and daughter had been murdered.

Now that rage had a new target. The Council. Ruy had said the Council had ordered his death. But why? How was he a threat? It didn't make any sense.

And yet, if the Council had been the ones who had ordered his assassination, then they were equally responsible for Alani and Shaunna's deaths. He ground his teeth and looked down at the body of Ruy. If they were responsible, then they'd share Ruy's fate.

But to go up against the Council of Houses all by himself. Such a thing wasn't possible. Not anymore. With Ruy dead, the others would be wary. They would be on their guard. It would be impossible to get to them.

Gage saw shadows in the hallways and the sound of footsteps told him the men were about to burst into the room. In a moment, he would be fighting more of the House Cernunnos elite guard. Judging by the sound of the footsteps, there were at least a dozen—with more on the way.

He looked down at his burned hand. Gage was tired and wounded and had nearly no *Mana*. If he stayed and fought these guards, he'd likely die. While he had been ready to die only minutes earlier, he now knew more justice was due. He hesitated.

Cursing, Gage made his decision. There were other people who had to pay. He wouldn't go down in a blaze of glory. Not yet.

Gage hurried to the window leading out to the balcony. Like before, it was most likely trapped. If so, the trigger was on the floor tiles somewhere. Quiet as a shadow, he slipped through the glass doors, and hopped over the balcony tiles and onto the marble railing.

It was daytime, but dark clouds obscured the sky and the cool, moist air told him it would soon rain. His Shadow magic would be effective in the semi-dark, but not as good as at night. Gage would just have to make do.

He stood a hundred fifty feet above a moat. A long way down. Above him, men scurried around the battlements, obviously looking for the intruder. From inside, he heard guards clatter in. Then the shouting. He was out of time.

He checked his *Mana*. There was just enough for a single *Shadow Slide*. He'd have to make it count.

"The Archmage is dead! Find the assassin!" a strong, deep voice yelled. There was a hint of command, and Gage guessed it was a sergeant or captain.

Gage could use his Shadow magic to *Slide* to another rooftop, but the entire place was on high alert. They'd be searching everything. With only enough *Mana* for a single *Slide*, he'd have to wait for it to completely regenerate before he could attempt to escape the Keep.

"Search the room!" the commanding voice ordered. "The balcony door is open! You two, check it!"

Gage was out of time. He looked down, then at the nearby rooftops. Then he looked up. The guards would expect him to go down. A fact he learned early in his training. People always looked down. Occasionally they looked to the sides. They never looked up.

He picked a spot a hundred feet above him, then leapt off the balcony and activated his *Shadow Slide* ability. Instantly, he slipped through the shadows and up to a large statue of a gargoyle atop the Keep. He grabbed onto the stone statue and hoisted himself up and behind it.

Concealing himself behind the sculpture, Gage listened to the shouts from below and around the battlements. No one pointed up at him or called out his location. That was good.

He settled back, hidden between the gargoyle's wings, and waited for dark. Until then, he hoped he'd be safe in his hiding spot.

A bolt of lightning split the sky and thunder boomed across the city. A moment later, cold rain fell. Gage remembered his wife and daughter and how they'd sit outside to watch the thunderstorms. He pretended it was raindrops falling down his cheeks and not tears precipitated from memories.

CHAPTER 2

Just Over a Week Earlier

Gage crouched behind the spoonwood bush. His five-year-old daughter squatted at his side, silent as a whisper. He smiled down at the girl, Shaunna, noticing—not for the first time—how much she resembled her mother.

Shaunna had the same golden hair, pale blue eyes, and flawless skin as her mother. It was a good thing his daughter got her looks from her mother and not him.

Where his wife, Alani, was slight, he was stocky. While she had gorgeous wisps of pale blond hair, Gage sprouted a mop of coarse dark hair. Her flawless skin possessed an almost luminescent quality in the pale morning sun. His skin was tanned and weathered from exposure, and he bore the scars of his previous life.

He frowned at thoughts of his former profession and pushed the thoughts away. What he'd been and done before didn't matter. Now, only Alani and Shaunna mattered. Gage glanced down at his daughter and unconsciously scratched his thick beard again.

The deer his daughter watched through the bushes looked up, ears twitching. The twelve-point buck stared at the bush Gage and his daughter hid behind. The beast's ears twitched and its nose tested the air.

Gage smiled. No matter how hard the deer tried, it wouldn't smell either of them. Both he and Shaunna wore a special alchemical mixture called Dog's Bane. The mixture absorbed all body odors. In another life, he'd used it to sneak past beast-kin guards and sentries.

He hadn't seen a beast-kin in years, but, like the beasts they resembled, they all had an uncanny sense of smell. So acute was their sense of smell that most could track a man by his scent alone. That made sneaking up on them—or sneaking past them—very difficult. Unless you had some Dog's Bane.

After a full minute, the deer dropped its head down and resumed eating the apples Shaunna had set out for it.

Gage stayed still this time and watched the buck. As he did, he mentally brought up his game display.

Game display. It was how Gage thought of the writing that popped up in his vision when he mentally commanded it. The display reminded him of the stats on the video games he played as a child—back when he was on Earth.

Earth. His home. Or rather, his first home. How old had he been when the glowing portal had appeared and sucked him into this world. Ten? No, eleven.

Gage had thought it was a dream at first. But he never woke up. For months he kept expecting to wake up in bed back home, with his parents and his younger brother. But it never happened.

He'd stayed in this crazy, mixed-up world. A world the people called Darath. A world that orbited around a giant planet, one that reminded him of the ringed planet back on Earth. He strained to remember its name. Saturn! Yes, that was the one in Earth's solar system! Gage had learned about all the planets back in grade school—including Saturn, the planet with the majestic rings.

Flicking his eyes upward, Gage watched the ringed planet they orbited. He could also see three of the twelve other moons that shared the gas giant. And then, there were the three suns, low in the sky.

Technically, there were two suns and a black hole. Or rather, Gage thought it was a black hole. He'd learned about black holes in science class back on Earth and he thought the big black circle surrounded by a halo of light in the middle of the two suns was a black hole. Of course, it had been so long since he'd been in school, he wasn't sure any longer. It seemed a lifetime ago.

He moved his eyes back to the deer and willed his display to show him the creature's stats. Immediately, words appeared in the air in front of him. There wasn't much information, but with regular animals, there never was.

Deer
Level 5

Gage was impressed. The deer was level 5. It was rare to find herbivores above level 1 and carnivores rarely above level 7. Once, he'd spotted a huge level 10 grizzly bear, but it had been huge.

Glancing at the size of the buck and its huge antlers, he guessed it must be the leader of a herd. Perhaps it had defended its territory and fought off other males during mating season. That might explain it reaching level 5. There was no way for him to know and his display didn't tell him.

He had no idea how or why the messages appeared in his vision. When he'd first discovered them after waking up in this world, they reminded him of video games he'd played with his brother back home. The display even showed him stats on himself and other people.

It had been a shock to him to discover it and even more so when he discovered no one else had one. Over the years, Gage imagined many reasons for the display. He had no idea if any of his theories were right. He just knew that he'd never met another person with a display.

The deer looked up again, drawing Gage back into the moment. He briefly thought he'd unconsciously moved again, but the deer had finished the apples and was now looking for more food.

After a minute, the deer wandered off, doubtless in search of more food.

He relaxed and his daughter did, too.

"He was so big!" Shaunna said, looking up at him with wide eyes. "And he had big horns!"

"Antlers," he corrected.

His daughter cocked her head and then smiled. "Antlers."

"Cows have horns," he told her. "Deer have antlers."

"Antlers," she repeated with a nod. She looked in the direction the deer had gone. "It was really pretty."

It was Gage's turn to nod. The buck was impressive. He smiled. If his daughter hadn't been with him, and he'd had his bow, that buck's rack would be decorating his wall, and they'd have venison for a month.

"Can we find another one?" Shaunna asked, her big eyes pleading.

Gage glanced at the suns, which crept closer to the horizon. It would be dark soon and they were a good hour from home. He shook his head. "We should go. If we're not back by dinner, your mother will have a fit."

Shaunna pouted briefly then brightened. A large grin spread across her face. "Zoom me!"

"Zoom you?" he asked, feigning ignorance.

"Zoom me, daddy!" Shaunna nodded enthusiastically, holding her arms open wide for him to pick her up.

He chuckled at his daughter's insistence. She and his wife were the only ones within a hundred miles who knew of Gage's abilities. Shaunna just thought it was magic—like the hedge wizard in the village. Only he and Alani knew the truth.

His abilities were from his previous life. He rarely used them anymore—well, except for the Shadow Vision. Seeing in the dark was just too useful for him to ignore. Then there was his *Shadow Slide* ability, or "zooming" as his daughter called it.

The ability allowed him to move from one shadow to another in the blink of an eye. A wizard had once called it a limited form of teleportation. Gage didn't know and didn't care. He could do it and that was all that mattered.

Shaunna had learned about it when she'd fallen from a tree a couple of months ago. He'd been fifty feet away from her when he'd seen it happen. Gage hadn't even consciously thought about it. Some parental instinct had triggered the ability for him and the next thing he knew, he stood directly beneath his daughter, catching her.

Shortly afterwards, Shaunna started pestering him to "zoom" for her. Alani didn't approve but he did it anyway. Then, she begged him to "zoom" her too. When he finally relented and *Shadow Slid* with her, it became her favorite thing to do with him.

"Fine! Fine!" Gage smiled and shook his head. Reaching down, he picked up his daughter's small form and hugged her close. He bent down conspiratorially and whispered into her ear. "Just don't tell your mom."

Before she could answer, he picked a point over a hundred yards away and activated his *Shadow Slide* ability. As space warped around him and he shot to his destination, all Gage could hear was Shaunna's giggle in his ear.

CHAPTER 3

"Mama! Mama! Daddy zoomed me!" exploded out of Shaunna's mouth as they reached the yard. She gave her mother a wide grin and rushed to her arms as she began recounting the day in exacting detail.

Alani smiled at her daughter's story but flicked her eyes up at Gage.

He sighed. Gage knew that look. It meant his future included a stern talking to from his wife. He just wasn't sure if it would be about being late or about using his powers with his daughter.

Gage and Alani had talked before about his powers—many times. He'd never really been sure exactly how or why he'd gotten the Shadowmaster class as an option when he'd leveled up. He never really understood if it was some sort of demonic power—like warlocks and channelers, and that nagged at him.

He'd even been afraid to use the powers at first, but

little by little, he'd gotten more comfortable with them. Now, they were like second nature to him.

Alani had told him over and over that she didn't believe it was a demonic power. As she pointed out, he'd never made any sort of bargain with a demon. So how could it be a demonic power?

Her argument sounded solid, and it convinced Gage—mostly. There were still times when he wondered—wondered if these powers were from a demon, and if so, when would the demon come to collect its due?

Smiling, Gage shrugged at her and gestured at their daughter helplessly. It was hard to resist his daughter's charm. She was so much like her mother in that way. He'd do anything for them.

Alani rolled her eyes at him and then gave him a look that promised a further discussion before focusing her attention back on their daughter. Shaunna hadn't missed a beat and was telling her mother all about their encounter with the buck and how close they'd gotten to the great deer.

Gage started to turn to look in on their animals, but Alani shook her head as she looked up at him. "You can check on them later. Right now, it's dinner time. Both of you clean up before sitting down."

When neither Gage nor Shaunna moved, his wife made a shooing gesture. "Now, you two! Things are getting cold."

"Come on, pumpkin," he teased his daughter. He crouched down like he was about to run. "I'll race you to the well!"

"No zooming!" Shaunna giggled as she bolted for the well at the back of the house.

Gage didn't run after her right away. Instead, he took a step closer to his wife and wrapped his arms around her. She rolled her eyes at him, but he leaned in and planted a kiss on her lips. "Sorry."

"About being late or the zooming?" she snorted.

"Both," he replied with a lop-sided grin.

"You need to be careful," she told him, her face going serious. "What if one of the neighbors saw you?"

"There was no one around for miles," Gage assured her.

Alani frowned at him. "That's not the point. It just takes one person to see you and report you as a... you know..."

Gage nodded. He did know. If someone saw his powers and reported him as a warlock or channeler, there'd be an inquiry. There might even be a trial.

Warlocks and Channelers had once been put to death in all civilized areas. No one wanted someone in league with demons wandering around. It had been the law. All warlocks and channelers were put to death.

Of course, the demon pact wasn't the real reason. Gage had learned the real reason when he'd become the Master of Assassins for House Cernunnos. The law had very little to do with the pact with a demon and everything to do with the Houses maintaining a monopoly on magic.

The great Houses had strong wizarding bloodlines. They used that magic to rule the masses and wouldn't suffer any challenges to their stranglehold on the use of magic.

And because they had magic in their blood, they considered themselves the only true and legit source of magic. Hence, they had outlawed those who sought to get magic through pacts with demons. Or rather, that was how it HAD been.

Gage had learned that the Houses had been slowly losing the magic in their blood through years of inbreeding and assassination. It was now at the point that members of certain Houses were allowing those members who hadn't been born wizards to make pacts with demons to augment the Houses waning magic powers.

It started with House Cernunnos. They'd lost a number of prominent wizards to assassinations, and new wizards weren't being born. The previous Archmage of Cernunnos had authorized certain members of his household to enter pacts—including his own son, Ruy.

It worked. Ruy had become a powerful channeler and eventually replaced his father after his father was killed by a rival House assassin. When the other Houses realized what Cernunnos was doing—tilting the balance of power in their favor, they began doing the same.

Now, all Houses had channelers, warlocks, and even a few summoners—but very few wizards. Channelers and warlocks were no longer hunted and killed. At least not if they belonged to one of the Houses.

But that was in the cities. This was the countryside, far away from the big cities. They kept the old ways out here. They still put warlocks and channelers to death.

Gage wasn't a warlock or channeler, but these were simple folk. Alani was right. Gage needed to be more careful. If someone did see him using his power, they might report him to the constable, and then there would be trouble.

He wasn't afraid of the constable—or anyone in the village. The skills he'd acquired in his previous life made him more than a match for anyone in the village. Yet despite having the ability to kill every single person, he knew it wasn't an option. That part of him was gone. He'd left it behind when he'd started his new life with Alani.

If he was accused, he and his family would be forced to flee. They'd have to go to another village and start all over again. It wasn't a pleasant prospect. He'd finally made a life here—this was his home. Alani's home. Shaunna's home. He'd protect his home. No matter what it took.

"You're right," he told Alani, staring down into her blue eyes. "I'll be more careful."

His wife cocked her head at him, staring at him for a moment. "Something wrong?"

Gage flashed her a smile. "No. Just thinking about how lucky I am to have you and Shaunna."

Alani gave him a playful grin and nudged him with her elbow. "And don't you forget it."

She leaned up and gave him another kiss, but it was interrupted by his daughter's high-pitched voice.

Shaunna looked around the corner of the house and pouted. "Da! You didn't race!"

Alani gave him a knowing look and took a step back, gesturing for him to go after their daughter. "Well?"

Gage gave his wife a wicked grin and then turned to his daughter. He held his hands up and wiggled his fingers. "That's because I was looking for these... tumbling tickling turkeys!"

The tickling game was one of her favorites and always a good way to tire her out. He bolted for her, and she screamed in delight. Shaunna spun and sprinted back behind the house.

Running after her, it took him a good two minutes to finally catch up with her. He tickled her until she laughed so hard she cried. When he stopped to let her catch her breath, she jumped on him and tried to tickle him.

He wasn't really ticklish, but he pretended until Alani yelled for them to get to the table. Both of them shared a guilty look and then raced to the well. They brushed themselves off and washed their hands. After making sure they were presentable, he held her hand as he walked back around to the door, Shaunna skipping happily next to her father.

CHAPTER 4

The sound of horses outside their home interrupted their dinner. Gage exchanged looks with his wife. After dark and during dinner. Who would be calling on them at this hour?

Gage tightened his grip on the knife in his hand. It was only a dinner knife, barely sharp enough to cut the cockatrice he'd killed earlier, which Alani had prepared for their supper. While the knife gave him a small amount of comfort, he would have preferred a real weapon.

Not that he needed a weapon. He was perfectly lethal without it. Even if he hadn't used those skills in years. He had a new life. A full, normal life with Alani and Shaunna.

His family looked at the door in silence. It shook with a strong knock that echoed through the small house.

"Da," his daughter asked, bright eyed. "Who is it?"

Looking over at Shaunna, he forced a smile on his face. His daughter's dimpled face smiled up at him, curiosity showing in her blue eyes.

He smiled, struck again by how much she resembled her mother. In fact, they'd often remarked that she hadn't seemed to inherit any of Gage's traits at all.

"It's probably one of the neighbors. Maybe some of their cattle went missing," he lied to his daughter. He wished it were true, but some instinct told him it wasn't.

Alani gave him a dubious look. She was smart. One of the reasons he loved her. His wife knew it was highly unlikely for one of their neighbors to come to their farm after dark. Even less likely to ride over on horses. It begged the question: Who had come? And why?

He stood up from his chair. His wife's eyes flicked to his right hand, which still held the knife. The smooth skin of her forehead wrinkled. He kept the smile on his face, a smile which didn't reach his green eyes. "Both of you stay here. I'll see who it is and what they want."

With slow, deliberate movements, Gage strode to the door. He dropped his right hand down to his side and slightly behind him. With his left hand, he worked the latch and then pulled the door open.

A man stood in the doorway. A tall man, dressed in the gold and white robes of House Cernunnos. In his left hand, the man held a mundane torch. A hood was pulled down low, obscuring the man's face. Gage was instantly suspicious.

Sensitive to magic, Gage felt wrongness ooze from the man even before he noticed the red, taloned hands that marked him as a channeler. A channeler. Someone who had made a pact with an otherworldly being to get the power of magic. A person doomed to transform into an image of the demon they pacted with.

Gage narrowed his eyes. As he did so, he brought up his display seeing words appear in his vision just to the side of the stranger.

Onchu Lewis
Human
Channeler
Level 7

The information the display provided him gave him a slight edge over other people. Instantly, he could see a person's true name, race, class, and even level. It helped size up an opponent—even from afar.

Not only could he see statistics, his display also allowed him to make adjustments or choices to his stats, abilities and classes as he leveled up. He always thought it was a shame that neither his wife nor his daughter possessed one.

But they were both native to this world. His wife, Alani, was the daughter of natives. No one in her family had ever possessed a display. He had wondered about his daughter, Shaunna. Since she was his child, he hoped she would have a display. Alas, she didn't. It wasn't something that could be passed down. At least, not that he knew of.

Chiding himself for letting his mind wander, Gage focused on the stranger. He raised an eyebrow, while turning his body to hide his right hand and the knife it held. "Onchu Lewis."

Onchu was level 7. That was far above the average. Most people were level 1, with experienced fighters or craftsmen as high as level 5. It was rare to see anyone over level 10. The channeler was just over the high end of average. It made Gage instantly suspicious. It meant the man was not just a nobody but someone with at least some standing with the House.

The real question was: Why was this channeler here? His hand tightened on the knife as only two possibilities came to mind. Either they wanted him to come back, or they wanted him dead. If it was the latter, they'd sorely misjudged.

The man started and Gage smiled inwardly. He used this tactic many times to throw people off balance. Casually mentioning something that he shouldn't possibly know, like their name, seemed to unbalance people.

"You... know me?" the channeler replied, recovering quickly. "I see you stay informed. I am..."

"...a channeler from House Cernunnos," Gage replied, interrupting the man. He narrowed his eyes again. "What do you want?"

Onchu looked down at his hands. Most likely, he thought Gage had noticed them and made the connection. He cleared his throat. "May we go inside and speak?"

Gage frowned at the man. "No. We can talk outside."

"As you wish," the channeler replied and gestured for Gage to walk outside, past him.

Loath to turn his back on anyone from House Cernunnos, and a House Cernunnos channeler in particular, Gage shook his head and gestured for the man to go first. "No, I insist. After you."

The man chuckled softly. "They said you were cautious."

Gage didn't need to ask who. It was obvious his old

employer sent the man. If that was the case, Onchu knew all about him. Or rather, knew of his reputation and some of his deeds. There was no one alive today that knew ALL about him. Not even his wife.

Onchu walked out through his yard, to the dirt road that led back to town. Gage walked a few steps behind him. He kept the knife ready, as well as several special abilities he had from his own class and levels.

Luckily, the channeler couldn't detect him activating one of his most used abilities, *Uncanny Dodge*. He didn't need to look up the information for the ability, he had long since memorized it.

Uncanny Dodge
Type: Assassin
Cost: 10 Stamina / 10 Mana
Range: Self
Duration: 1 hour/level
Description: When activated, you automatically avoid the next attack that would do damage to you. Attacks that do no damage cannot be dodged. Expires after use.
Cooldown: 1 minute

Gage felt the ability activate as it drained a bit of *Stamina* and *Mana* from him. He knew from experience, there was no outward manifestation of the power. There wouldn't be until the power itself activated.

He also activated the improved version of the skill he'd acquired at a higher level. He knew the description of this ability by heart as well.

Improved Uncanny Dodge
Type: Assassin
Cost: 20 Stamina / 20 Mana
Range: Self
Duration: 10 minutes / level
Description: When activated, you automatically avoid the next attack that would do damage to you. This ability also prevents non-damaging attacks. Expires after use.
Cooldown: 5 minutes

With both of his *Uncanny Dodge* abilities activated, Gage felt slightly better. With them, even if he was surprised, he'd have a fighting chance. He just hoped it didn't come to that.

Looking past Onchu, Gage spotted the other horses he'd heard standing in the road. Six armored men stood near the horses, each wearing shiny suits of chain mail under tabards of the House Guard.

They were too far for him to use his display on, but he could tell from their stances and expressions that these were hard, experienced soldiers. He frowned but said nothing. His mind was already whirling, figuring out the best way to kill these men if it came to that.

He followed Onchu within ten feet of the road before stopping. "That's far enough. Now tell me: what do you want?"

The channeler kept walking for another heartbeat before stopping and turning. He smiled, but it didn't reach his eyes. It was the sickly-sweet smile of a shady merchant trying to sell people snake oil.

Gage tensed, ready to spring into action if he had to.

"Well, not to put too fine a point on it," Onchu replied, his cloying smile still smeared on his face. "I want you."

CHAPTER 5

Gage tensed, ready to kill the channeler. The shadows around him stretched out, anxious to do his bidding.

If this channeler and his escort had come to kill him, they'd picked the wrong time to do it. The night belonged to Gage.

Onchu stepped back, raising his palms. He must have sensed the violence Gage suddenly radiated. His crimson face paled. "Peace, Gage! I bear only a message from the Archmage."

Gage narrowed his eyes at the channeler. The shadows remained extended, pulsing with potential, but advanced no further. They no longer danced to the rhythm of Onchu's flickering torch. If the channeler noticed them, he didn't comment.

"What message?" Gage snarled, his voice low but hard. An unmistakable edge palpable with his words. And with good reason.

He'd "retired" from the Archmage's service six years ago, after serving House Cernunnos for twice that number of years. As their assassin. A very specialized assassin. Trained to kill magic users.

But he'd tired of the killing—and the politics. He hated politics. The political backstabbing of the Houses vying for a position closer to the Overking, the Grand Magus. In twelve years working for House Cernunnos, he learned to despise the royalty and their petty plans.

"The Archmage wishes to employ your services once more," Onchu replied, straightening himself and taking a more formal tone. "He wishes you to resume your former position with the House."

Gage snorted. His former position? Why not just come right out and say they wanted him to be their master assassin and kill more people for them?

Then again, the Houses loved to scry on each other, using magic to view a person or object remotely. Not many wizards could do that, but every House usually had at least one. Either that, or a hired wizard who could.

But none of that mattered. Gage was retired. Out of the game. His family was the important thing now. His "work" would endanger them, make them targets—a way to get at him. That wasn't going to happen.

"Not interested," he told the channeler flatly. "I'm retired."

"The Archmage is willing to compensate you well," Onchu countered.

Gage frowned at the channeler. "Not interested."

"You haven't even heard his offer—" the man retorted, his voice annoyed.

"Not interested," Gage interrupted, putting the edge back in his voice.

The channeler tried to press him, to convince him to take the offer.

Gage knew why. He knew the price of failure in House Cernunnos. His back bore the scars of his own early failures. He wasn't sure if they treated actual members of the House the same way, but he knew there would be a price to pay.

"The offer is extremely generous," Onchu blurted out. Gage thought he heard a tone of desperation. "And only for a limited time. Just a few jobs."

Gage shook his head but kept his eyes on the channeler. He put a bit more steel into his voice. "I said no."

"You don't understand..." the man argued, but Gage held up a hand.

Letting his arm relax to his side where the channeler could see the knife, Gage growled. "Do I need to carve the answer into your chest? The answer is no."

Onchu's eyes went wide as he saw the knife. He glanced over to the armored men by the horses. Perhaps he thought to call out to them. The channeler took an involuntary step back and his mouth worked silently for several seconds before he finally cleared his throat.

"Fine! Fine! I will tell the Archmage your answer," the man said, taking another step back. "But you know he won't like it."

"I don't care what the Archmage likes," Gage spat. "I served my time with the House. I'm retired now."

The channeler bit his lip, eyes darting around. He

grimaced and then spoke. "If you think you are keeping your wife and daughter safe by refusing, you are wrong."

A growl came from deep in Gage's throat and he took a step towards the man. His right hand came up with the knife even as shadows rushed towards him. "Are you threatening my wife and daughter?"

Onchu let out a high-pitched scream as he stumbled backwards. "No... no... no. Not us."

Gage stopped and narrowed his eyes at the channeler. He cast a quick glance over Onchu's shoulder at the armored men. He'd heard their heavy footsteps and the sound of swords being pulled from sheaths. All but one of them had started his way, most likely attracted by the channeler's rather unmanly scream.

"If you want to live and you want them to live, tell them everything's okay," Gage hissed.

The man swallowed and cleared his throat. Then he shouted out to the men. "Everything's fine. I don't need you. I... uh... just tripped in the dark."

Gage saw the men stop, but they kept a wary gaze in his direction. He wasn't sure if they noticed the strange behavior of the shadows. Most people didn't. At least, they didn't realize it on a conscious level. On an unconscious level, many people felt uncomfortable, as if something wasn't quite right.

"Are you sure, milord?" one of the armored men asked. The man was close enough for Gage to see him in his display.

Taraghlan
Human

Fighter
Level 6

Taraghlan was a fighter, probably either a guardsman or soldier. Of the armored men, he seemed to be the oldest. Looking closely at the man's pauldrons, Gage could make out the stripes and star of a captain.

"Yes," the channeler shouted back and made a shooing motion with his hand. "You may go back to the horses."

Taraghlan scowled. He glanced between Onchu and Gage before finally shrugging and turning around. He motioned to the others with his sword. "Back to the horses you lot."

Gage watched them sheath their swords and return to the horses. He flicked his eyes back to the channeler. The man stood there nervously, fidgeting with his taloned hands. Did he realize how close he'd been to death? Perhaps.

"Explain what you meant," he ordered the man. "Now."

Onchu looked around nervously and then cleared his throat. "Things have... changed... in the Houses since you left."

"What has changed?" Gage demanded.

"Well... uh... you know that the... um... wizard blood has... run thin—" the man started but ceased at a gesture from Gage.

"I was there for just over twelve years," he growled. "I know about the lack of wizards being born."

Gage did know. He knew all too well. The Houses ruled by their magical might. They had for centuries. At one time, all the leaders of the great Houses had been wizards—powerful wizards.

But that had changed in the last couple of decades. Less and less of the House children were born as wizards. Combined with the wholesale assassination of House nobles by competing Houses, suddenly the Houses had a shortage of magical talent.

He knew all of this, of course. He'd attended many meetings when it had been discussed. He'd overheard conversations from other Houses during the execution of his duties. A grave issue for House Cernunnos twelve years ago, it had worsened since then.

Desperate to maintain their level of magic, most—if not all—of the Houses had rescinded their ban on demonic pacts. They resorted to warlocks, channelers, and summoners to fill in their ranks and maintain their levels of magic. Onchu was proof of that. Twenty years ago, his sentence for being a channeler would have been death.

But what did that have to do with Gage now?

"Explain why I should care," he told the channeler.

"The balance of power is shifting," Onchu replied, seeming more relaxed with the familiar topic. "It may lead to war."

"Again," Gage said dangerously, narrowing his eyes at the man. "What does this have to do with me and my family?"

The channeler cleared his throat nervously. "The Archmage wants you to return before conflict breaks out between the Houses."

Gage snorted. "The Overking would never allow it."

"The Overking is old, and he has no magical heir. He will not be able to maintain control for long," Onchu replied. "Once he dies..."

The man trailed off, but Gage understood what he meant. Without a magical heir to pass his title to, the position of Overking would be up for grabs. It would be all out war as the Houses vied to fill the vacant position. An unfortunate situation, but one that no longer concerned him.

Gage shook his head. "The answer is still no."

"But..." Onchu started and then snapped his mouth closed as Gage glared daggers at the man.

"Thank you for stopping by," Gage said with not even a hint of sincerity. "Be careful riding back to town in the dark."

Gage turned around and strode back towards his house. Behind him, he heard the man shuffle back to the gate and speak quietly to the armored men. Reaching the door, he waited until he heard the horses riding away. Once they were out of earshot, he opened the door and entered his house.

His wife was there, worry thick in her eyes. "Who was that?"

Shooting a meaningful look at their daughter, he forced a smile. "I think it's time for Shaunna to go to bed. Then you and I can talk about it."

Alani knew about his past. Knew about his former profession. She knew it all and still loved him. He didn't know why, but she did. And he was happier for it. His wife read his face and then nodded. She turned to their daughter. "You heard your father. Off to bed with you."

After a few complaints, Shaunna allowed herself to be led into the bedroom and after a few minutes. Gage came in and helped his daughter into her nightclothes while his wife cleaned the table.

Shaunna climbed into her bed, the bed Gage had made for her the previous year when she'd outgrown her old one. He pulled the cover up and tucked her in.

"Good night, pumpkin," he told her and kissed her on the forehead.

His daughter smiled up at him with bright eyes. "Good night, da. I love you."

"I love you too, pumpkin," he replied with a grin. He reached over doused the candle next to her bed with his fingers and then stood up.

Leaving their daughter's room, Gage stopped at the door and glanced back at his daughter. She blew him a kiss and then closed her eyes. He smiled again and quietly closed the door. Gage walked to the dinner table and took a seat across from Alani.

"So, what was all that about?" she asked, voice low.

Gage opened his mouth to begin the explanation. That was when the entire house exploded.

CHAPTER 6

He felt the twisted magic just a moment too late to call out a warning. One moment, he was staring at his wife. The next moment, Gage's vision turned white as explosions rocked his small house.

The first fireball exploded just outside the house, blowing apart the wall and blasting through the windows. A moment later, a second fireball came hurtling into the house and exploded right in front of him.

The blast of both explosions washed over him, doing no damage as his *Uncanny Dodge* and *Improved Uncanny Dodge* triggered. Then a third explosion rocked him, lifting him off his feet and slamming him against the wall.

Unknown hits you with Fireball but you Dodge.
Unknown hits you with Fireball but you Dodge.
Unknown hits you with Fireball for 39 fire damage.
Wall hits you for 11 damage.

He'd snapped on his display as he had been thrown back and the jarring impact of smashing into the wall caused the words to bounce in his vision. He blinked and looked at the spot where Alani had sat a moment ago.

She was gone. The table, chairs and Alani had been completely incinerated by the fireballs. He knew from long years of conflict that it was too late for her. Feeling the rising anger, he pushed it down. He had to focus his attention on the one other thing that meant something to him—Shaunna.

Gritting his teeth against the pain of the burns, Gage pushed himself up. He had to get to his daughter's room. He had to get her out of here.

Shielding his face with his hand, Gage re-activated his two Uncanny Dodge skills as he rushed to the door of her room. He reached the door latch just as three more explosions shook the house.

Unknown hits you with Fireball but you Dodge.
Unknown hits you with Fireball but you Dodge.
Wooden door hits you for 9 damage.

His daughter's door exploded outward, hitting him and tossing him backwards. He landed in a heap on the floor with the door on top of him. Cursing, he pushed past the pain. He shoved the door off him and stared into the raging inferno that had once been a little girl's room.

His little girl.

Shaunna.

"Noo!" he screamed, his mind struggling to accept what had just happened.

White hot anger enveloped him as reality pierced his heart. Someone had just murdered his wife and daughter —and tried to kill him. He cursed under his breath. Whoever it was, they were going to pay—pay with their lives.

With adrenalin-fueled awareness, Gage felt the magic surge from three different places around his house. Even from a distance, he could feel the corruption in the magic. That meant warlocks or channelers. Three of them. Soon to be three corpses.

He had one more activation of his two *Dodge* abilities. After that, Gage would need to rely on his other abilities. Luckily, he had many other skills that were perfectly suited for handling magic users.

Gage activated both *Dodge* abilities again. He spun towards the entrance and, seeing the door had been blown off its hinges, Gage dove through. Behind him, his house rocked as three more fireballs hit it.

Using one of his *Shadow* abilities instinctively, he pulled the shadows over him. Gage's *Shadow Cloak* ability would make him impossible to see near shadows. At night, even with the roaring blaze next to him, he was invisible.

After sustaining heavy damage from the previous explosions, the house shuddered, creaked, and groaned. The structural damage from the series of explosions proved too much for his house. With a crash, the roof collapsed, taking one of the outer walls with it.

His wife—gone. His daughter—gone. His house—their pyre. Gage had nothing left. Nothing but the rage . A rage he would unleash on the murderer.

"I saw something come out of the front door!" a voice from his right yelled.

"Was it him?" another voice, this time from the left yelled out. "I don't see anyone."

On this world, there were many different races: elves, dwarves, catlings, foxlings, and more. Some of them could see as well in the dark as a human could in daylight. Gage was human. He had the normal sight of a human. Unless he used his *Shadow Vision* skill.

He pulled the shadows over his eyes, turning them black. The world dissolved into shades of gray. No light, no darkness—only gray. But in this achromatic view, he had perfect sight.

Gage moved away from the house, staying low and shrouded in shadows. He reached the tree by the road and examined the area. Movement to his left. A humanoid head peeking out from behind a tree.

"He might be in the barn!" A voice yelled from somewhere in the forest.

Watching the figure behind the tree, Gage saw a fireball appear in between the figure's hands. The figure pushed on the fireball, and it rocketed towards his barn. He caught the glows of other fireballs from different directions, all converging on his barn. A string of explosions and his barn and all the animals within it were gone.

Gritting his teeth in anger, he focused on the figure he could see. Even though he was unarmed, Gage didn't care. He worked better with weapons, but he didn't need them. He'd fought with anything and everything since he'd washed up in this gods-forsaken world.

Without hesitation, he *Shadow Slid*. The world blurred around him, shadows appearing—even in his black and white vision—stretched forward, washing him in unearthly cold. Suddenly, he was behind the man.

His target was dressed in a loose-fitting, dark tunic that tucked into pants. The man's head hid within a hood, but it couldn't hide the curved horns that protruded. A channeler then.

Channelers were ordinary folk who had no magical talent. These people made bargains with other-worldly entities. The person received magical ability in return for a connection between the entity and the channeler.

The connection didn't seem to influence the channeler's mind, but it did warp their body. Gage wasn't a sage nor a wizard. He didn't understand why they transformed or what dictated the type of transformation. Rumor had it that the channeler transformed into a likeness of the entity that granted the power.

The clothes the channeler wore were all too familiar. It was the uniform of a member of the Shadowed Fist—the assassin's guild. Gage knew it all too well. The uniform he used to wear himself.

And now the Shadowed Fist had come for him. He doubted it was personal. Gage hadn't broken any rules. He hadn't betrayed the Fist. No, they'd been hired to kill him. He was the mark. And because he was no longer an official member of the guild, he was fair game.

None of that mattered. It didn't matter that the person in front of him was a channeler. It didn't matter that the man had made a bargain or that he had power. It only mattered that he had murdered Gage's wife and little girl.

Fast as a viper, he struck out with both hands. He wrapped his hands around the channeler's horns. The man started, but it was too late. With a savage twist, Gage snapped the man's neck with a pop. The man's body went limp.

Lowering the dead channeler to the ground as quietly as possible, Gage searched the man for weapons. Despite the fact that the man had been a channeler, it was guild policy to always have a backup weapon—or ten.

His search quickly came up with two daggers and a small, gauntlet mounted crossbow. All were standard issue from the Shadowed Fist. All would be poisoned. Gage smiled and retrieved the two daggers. The crossbow he'd come back for.

"No one's moving, we got him," the voice that had been on the right called.

Unconsciously, he cringed. These two must be new recruits, or just idiots. You never called out. You never gave away your position. Gage looked down at the dead channeler, his head at an unnatural angle. Doing so usually got you killed.

But the one calling out didn't worry him. It was the third person. That last time, he'd seen three different fireballs from three different locations. That meant there was a third one. One who hadn't called out and revealed his location. A smart one.

The problem was, Gage wasn't sure where the third one had been. His magical sense wasn't precise. It was just a general feeling. And since the assassin hadn't revealed himself by speaking, he could be anywhere.

Gage wanted one alive so he could find out if they

knew who had hired the guild—and why. These men were just the arrow. Someone else had fired, and he meant to find out who. That meant he needed to keep one alive. But first, he had to find them.

CHAPTER 7

Gage waited several minutes in the dark. Watching and waiting. With his *Shadow Vision* active, Gage had no problems seeing the figure who finally walked into the open. This had to be the second speaker. If the third person didn't call out, he certainly wouldn't have just walked out into the open.

This assassin was hunched over and walked with a slight limp. Gage guessed the channeler's transformation wasn't going well. He would most likely be one of the less fortunate that died in agony when his body rejected the transformation into a demon. Or rather, he would have. Gage would spare him that fate.

In fact, the man would already be dead except for the third person. Gage had a rough idea of where the third channeler had been, but he could easily have moved since then. Depending on how good the assassin was, he could be nearly anywhere.

Gage decided to test the third man and see how

professional he was. Activating *Shadow Slide*, he appeared behind a tree that bordered the road. Years of experience came back to him, and he threw a dagger at the man's leg.

The blade sailed through the air and thudded into the man's thigh causing him to scream. Gage immediately *Slid* back to his original position and watched.

"Gods! Which of you did that?" the man yelled, clutching at the dagger. "Peadrus! Leitis! Which one of you did it! I'm not the mark you blasted idiots!"

A fireball flew from a point between Gage and the place he'd sensed the third person. In his *Shadow Vision*, he was able to clearly see the assassin's wide eyes just before the fireball exploded.

His vision went completely white for a moment as the fireball blotted out everything. Then it faded back into black and white. Gage blinked. The man was completely naked, but still alive.

"What are you? Idiots? I'm immune to fire! We all are you morons!" The naked assassin cursed. "But you burned away my clothes! I'll have your head for this! I'm not the blasted mark! Or are you trying to claim all the payment for yourselves?"

The furious man put his hands a foot apart and let a ball of fire form between them before launching his counterattack.

Gage snapped his head in the direction the fireball traveled. Knowing the explosion would momentarily ruin his vision, he closed his eyes until he heard the "whomp" of the fireball. He counted to one slowly and then opened his eyes. The fireball had cleared and he could see without any afterimage.

A smaller form darted away from the impact area. The third attacker. With a thought, he shifted from his position to a tree directly in the path of the fleeing figure. He had the dagger ready to stab the assassin through the heart but changed his mind at the last moment.

This was the "smart" one. Perhaps he would have more information than the other one—the loud-mouthed one who was obviously an idiot. Plus, it might take a little "persuading" to get them to talk. The one he'd stuck with the dagger was already poisoned. He wouldn't last long.

Making up his mind, he flipped the dagger in his hand and as the man ran by, he slammed the hilt into his solar plexus. The assassin stumbled back and dropped to his knees, sucking air.

Gage stepped behind the man, put him in a one-armed sleeper hold, and applied pressure. The man's hands came up, trying to free his throat. It was a natural reaction and Gage grabbed the man's slender left arm at the wrist. Like the other assassin, he had a small crossbow mounted on his bracer, but couldn't bring it to bear.

Feeling the beginnings of magic, Gage realized the man was either going to cast a fireball at point blank range or activate a fire armor ability that would wreath him in flame. Good thinking. It would have worked too. If Gage hadn't specialized in killing magic users.

Activating an ability called *Suppress Magic*, he grinned wickedly at the man's surprise. The magic extinguished before it even formed. Unfortunately, the ability also prevented his own magic and his vision faded back to normal. The world faded back into the muted colors of nighttime. Luckily, he didn't need to see in the dark to finish what he started.

He kept the pressure on the assassin's throat, cutting off the blood supply to his brain. In a few more seconds, the body went slack in his arms. Gage didn't trust the feeling of someone going limp. They could fake it to make him release his hold too early. He kept the pressure for a full ten seconds before letting go. The unconscious form slid to the ground and didn't move.

Gage reached down and patted down the body. He blinked in surprise as he felt soft breasts instead of the hard muscular chest of a man. This assassin was a woman. He frowned but didn't hesitate. He pulled the woman's sash off her while relieving her of three daggers. He then used the sash to hogtie her hands and ankles behind her back. He cut a piece from her robe and used it to gag her.

Once she was secure, he finished searching her. He found an unusual coin in one of her pockets—possibly a *Scrying* focus. Gage shoved it into the dirt, making sure it was completely covered.

Luckily, his *Suppress Magic* ability would have canceled any *Scrying*. He could only hope they hadn't already seen him. He waited until his *Suppress Magic* ability expired a few seconds later, then used his *Shadow Slide* to take them both to the top of a nearby tree. He cut off more of her robe, oblivious to her compromising outfit.

Using the pieces of cloth, he tied her to a large limb. When he was finished, he looked her over and nodded. She now dangled from the limb. If she tried to burn her way out of the bonds, she would fall fifty feet to the ground.

Satisfied she wasn't going anywhere, he glanced down at the road near his house. He saw the last assassin lying on the ground. No doubt the poison from the dagger was doing its work. Either that, or the man was playing possum, trying to lure Gage in.

Was the man smart enough to play dead? Gage doubted the idiot realized he was alive. Rather, the fool thought his friends had turned on him. Did he think they would come and verify that he was dead?

Gage decided to play it safe. He *Shadow Slid* down to the bottom of the tree, then *Shadow Slid* again to a tree near the man. The same tree he hid behind when he'd thrown the dagger. He watched the man in his black and white *Shadow Vision*.

He watched for two full minutes. The man's chest didn't move at all. This assassin seemed too inept to have mastered the ability to control his breath, but caution had kept Gage alive for longer than most assassins. He waited another two minutes, watching intently. The assassin's chest never moved.

Either the man was better than his actions indicated, or he was dead. Gage's instinct leaned to the latter. Wrapping himself in shadows just in case, he moved across the road to where the man lay.

Stopping a few feet from the body, Gage saw the large pool of blood. His eyes roved over the body until he saw the man had pulled the knife from the inside of his thigh. Gage shook his head. His throw must have sliced an artery, probably the femoral artery . As soon as the man removed the knife, he would have bled out in minutes without a tourniquet.

The man truly had been an idiot. He'd also been deformed. As Gage suspected, the man's back was a mass of red, scaled tissue—perhaps a malformed wing. He'd seen some channelers who had developed actual wings. Some of the wings were functional, allowing gliding or even flying over short distances.

Looking at the man's leg, he saw that the leg he'd hit with the dagger had been fully human. The other leg was scaled and ended in a cloven hoof. Gage shook his head. He had no sympathy for the man. The assassin had chosen his path.

Thinking practically, Gage reached down and took the dagger from the man's hand along with two other daggers lying in the pool of blood. The man's clothes might have been burned away, but the daggers were still intact—if a bit bloody.

Setting the daggers aside for later, Gage went back to the first body and stripped him. The man was slightly taller, but he'd make it work. He changed out of the remnants of his own singed clothing and donned the assassin's garb—including the crossbow.

Once he was dressed in the dead assassin's garb, he looked up at the tree where he had left the female assassin. He frowned. It was time to get some answers.

CHAPTER 8

Gage *Slid* back up the tree, landing on the branch adjacent to the tied-up assassin. The woman was conscious and glared daggers at him. He stared back at her, pushing all his anger and rage into it. They locked eyes for almost a minute, and she turned away first.

During that minute, Gage noted her appearance. She was a pretty girl, probably in her early twenties. The dark, four-inch-long horns sprouting from her head marked her as a channeler. But other than the horns, she looked fairly normal. The woman had no other mutations that he could see—probably fairly new.

Her eyes showed anger and defiance, but fear too. She hid it well, no doubt the Shadowed Fist training. But it was there if you knew how to look for it. And he did.

Reaching out, he removed her gag. "Don't bother calling out. The other two are dead."

Gage watched her reaction to the news. He specifically

mentioned two others rather than keeping it vague. If there were more, she might give something away. He hadn't seen any trace of others, but he'd been wrong before.

She took the news without giving anything away. There was no deception or hope in her eyes, like there would be if there were someone still alive who might rescue her. Instead, her expression was one of resignation.

She worked her jaw for a moment before snarling. "Just kill me. You won't get anything from me."

"I know," he said nonchalantly. "But you killed my wife and daughter. If you think you're getting a quick death... that option is off the table."

The woman's eyes widened slightly, and her mouth flinched. The movements were so small that he might have missed them had he not been looking for them. The news surprised her. Had they even known his wife and daughter were in the house?

Generally, the Shadowed Fist kept innocent deaths to a minimum. There were times when collateral damage was unavoidable, but it was considered unprofessional to kill any more than absolutely necessary.

He didn't think the Shadowed Fist would have given the order to kill his entire family. At least, not unless someone had paid to have Gage and his family killed. But who would do such a thing?

Gage felt the beginnings of magic being channeled again and he activated his *Suppress Magic* ability. Instantly, the magic faded, along with his own Shadow Vision. He blinked as his view returned to normal.

The assassin couldn't or didn't bother to hide her

surprise. Her eyes went wide. "My magic? How are you doing that?"

He guessed the woman had been about to either fireball them both, hoping to kill him before she fell to her death. Or she might have been about to activate her fire armor, burn through the bonds and fall. Either way, she probably guessed it would be a quicker death than what he had planned.

"How I'm doing it isn't important," he told her flatly. "It's only important that I can do it. So once again, if you think you're getting a quick death, you're mistaken."

This time, the fear in her eyes was plain. She must have thought she could end it quickly—die on her own terms. He understood that. Given the chance, he'd do the same.

Gage narrowed his eyes and put steel in his voice. "Just answer me this: was the contract just for me or for my family?"

Without his *Shadow Vision*, he could barely make out her features. From what he could see, the woman's face went defiant again but then she bit her lip slightly. She seemed to be considering her answer. But would she answer honestly? He watched her facial expressions carefully.

Finally, a look of resignation came over her. She looked almost apologetic. "The contract is just for you. We didn't know there were innocents in the house. They said nothing about a wife or child."

He made his face impassive while he considered her answer. Gage had seen no deception in her face, but he could have missed something in the dim illumination.

Keeping the same deadpan expression, Gage pressed

her for more information. "What did they tell you about me?"

The woman hesitated for a moment before letting out a little sigh. "Apparently, not enough."

Gage chuckled mirthlessly. "Did they tell you I used to be Shadowed Fist?"

She nodded her head. "That much they did tell us."

"Do you know who hired the guild or why I was to be killed?" he asked. He already knew the answer. The guild-master would never have shared that information. And yet.

It was her turn to chuckle. "You know we never get told that information."

"I do know," he replied, his face expressionless. "But I also know that sometimes we know anyway."

The assassin smirked. "True. But what incentive do I have to tell you, even if I do know? You're not going to let me go."

"True," he replied. There was no reason to lie. "You know I'm alive. You know what my next stop will be."

"The Guild," she hissed. She looked thoughtful. "What if I swear not to warn them? Swear not even to go back."

His *Shadow Vision* came back as his *Suppress Magic* ability faded away.

Gage shook his head. "I don't know you, lady. I don't know if your word is worth the breath it takes to speak it."

He thought for a moment. "But if you tell me some-thing useful, I'll let you go out on your terms."

"You'll let me kill myself?" She snorted. "So kind."

"Kinder than you were to my wife and daughter," he retorted harshly.

The assassin went quiet. She sighed, defeat in her face. "Even if I wanted to help you, I don't know anything. The job was to kill you. The guildmaster sent the three of us."

"You didn't find that odd?" He asked. In fact, it was odd. Nearly unheard of.

Assassins of the Shadowed Fist almost always worked alone. Only the wealthiest of clients could afford more than one assassin on a job. The only people with the means to hire two assassins were the banks, the most successful trading companies... or the Noble Houses.

He had no debts to any of the great banks and hadn't been involved with any trading companies nor gotten into their affairs. That left the Noble Houses. That was certainly a possibility. During his tenure with the guild, his assassinations had been almost exclusively members of the Houses.

The problem with that theory: no one but the guildmaster had known Gage had killed members of the Houses. It was a basic tenant of the guild. No one but the guildmaster ever knew exactly who had been assigned to a job. If it was one of the Noble Houses, how had they learned about what he'd done?

"It was a big job," the woman said, and he directed his full attention back to her. "We were getting double our normal fee."

Gage raised an eyebrow. "Double?"

"Now, I know why," she said bitterly.

A few times, with particularly difficult jobs, Gage had been given double pay. But never when working with someone else. It made no sense.

Three assassins, each getting double pay. Either the fee

was insanely high, or the Fist wasn't actually making any money on the deal. And that didn't make any sense either. The guild always made money. That was the whole point of the Shadowed Fist.

"That's all I know," she told him, and he believed her. Since that was the case, he had no more use for the assassin.

"Very well," he said, his face steely. "Then we're done here."

She nodded gravely. She opened her mouth and then closed it. Then, opened it again. "I am sorry about your wife and child. I really didn't know they were there."

Gage said nothing. There was nothing to say. His wife and daughter were still dead, regardless of what she knew.

The assassin squeezed her eyes shut and once again he felt the magic building. This time, he didn't try to stop it. Instead, he *Shadow Slid* to the bottom of a nearby tree.

Looking up, his vision went white as a fireball detonated where he had just been. His vision cleared just in time to see the woman hit the ground. She burned through her bonds and had fallen from her perch in the tree.

Despite seeing an experience message in his HUD, Gage was not one to leave anything to chance. He walked over to where the body lay on the ground. The assassin's naked form lay crumpled, her clothes having burned away in the fireball. The woman's neck and right leg lay at impossible angles. Her lifeless eyes stared up at him.

He bent down and checked her pulse, already knowing what he'd find. She was dead. He nodded. She'd died on her own terms. By her own hand.

Gage felt neither joy nor satisfaction from her death. She and the others had merely been daggers. He wanted the hand that had wielded the daggers. He wanted the client. That meant it was time to pay the guild a visit.

Reaching down, he closed the channeler's unseeing eyes. Even the dead didn't need to see what he did next.

The blaze from the house and barn would be visible for miles. Any of his neighbors who were outside would notice it, and come to investigate. It was dark, so they would come slowly—but they would come. That meant he didn't have much time.

He retrieved his hatchet from the shed, listening to the sounds of dying animals in the barn. He grimaced. For some reason, some of the animals in the barn hadn't all been killed by the fireballs.

Gage's first instinct was to let them out, allow them to get away from the fire. But he didn't. He couldn't. This needed to look like a house fire. Like everyone had perished inside the house.

If he let the animals out of the barn, it might raise suspicion. He felt bad for his animals. Gage had raised some of the sheep since they were lambs. He didn't want them to die. But he also couldn't create undue suspicion. His life depended on it.

He focused on his anger and rage, not letting the grief and anguish from losing Alani and Shaunna consume him. There would be time for that later. At the moment, he was in a time crunch.

Taking the hatchet back to the body of the first channeler, he cut off the man's horns and smoothed the skull the best he could. He then tossed the body into the raging inferno that was his house.

While the channeler may have been immune to fire in life, in death, his body burned just like a normal human. When the neighbors and townsfolk sifted through the ruins of his house, they'd find the remains of three bodies, not two. Unless his wife and daughter had been completely vaporized. The very thought rekindled his rage.

He focused on the task. The male body was all he worried about. If they found a man's body in the house, the people would assume it was him. That would be the story they told: There was a terrible fire and they'd found Gage's body, but his wife and daughter had been unrecoverable. Given that the roof had collapsed, it was a plausible story.

And the story was important. It wasn't his neighbors and the townspeople he was trying to fool. When the three assassins didn't return, the Shadowed Fist would send someone to investigate. He wanted to make sure that when they came, they found what he wanted them to find.

Gage needed the guild to believe he was dead for as long as possible. That would give him an edge. For what he had planned, he would need every advantage he could get.

Once the assassin's body was burning, he shoveled dirt over the spot where the mutated channeler had died. It wouldn't be perfect, and most likely animals would come sniffing around, but it should at least create confusion. It certainly wouldn't make sense for there to be a large pool of blood if everyone died in the fire.

He finished covering up the blood when he caught sight of light through the trees. Someone with a torch was coming. Probably Artair and his son from down the road. They were the closest neighbors. He only had minutes before they would be close enough to see him moving around.

Gage didn't replace the tools in the shed. He would need both the hatchet and the shovel for what came next. He hoped it wouldn't raise suspicion if someone noticed they were missing. Would his neighbors even notice? Gage would have noticed, but he'd trained to notice the little details.

Grabbing the body of the male assassin, Gage used *Shadow Slide* to take it a hundred yards into the woods. He then did the same with the female assassin. He was far enough away that whoever was coming shouldn't see him. Not with the light of the fire interfering with their night vision. But he wasn't taking any chances. He laid the bodies in some brush to obscure their profile.

Anyone who came would be focused on the house. On the fire. People were always fascinated by fire. Keeping behind a large tree, Gage watched as the light grew brighter and two men walked into the light of the fire.

As he suspected, it was Artair and his son, Cormac. The two came down the road and began calling out.

"Jardon!"

"Alani!"

"Shaunna!"

He frowned as they called out his alias, Jardon. He'd adopted the name when he started his new life. A life that was now gone. Stolen from him. Alani and Shaunna had been murdered, killed because of his past life.

Gage cursed silently. He had thought he'd put his old life behind him. But it finally caught up with him. And it cost him everything. Feeling his eyes moisten, he blinked them several times and tried to convince himself it was the smoke.

Artair and Cormac continued to yell their names. They tied off their horses and wandered around the area, continuing to call out. Gage watched the entire time, making sure they didn't find anything that would lead them to believe this was anything but a normal, tragic house fire.

The neighbors wandered around his homestead, calling out for Jardon and his family. Hearing the cries of the animals, the duo quickly made their way to the barn. They set the remains of his livestock free, trying to herd them into the nearby clearing near the small pond. Gage smiled and felt slightly better knowing his animals would be okay.

Fifteen minutes after they released his animals, Artair called Cormac. He spoke to his son for a few minutes, gesturing and pointing. They were too far for Gage to hear their conversation but he could guess.

When they were done speaking, Cormac got back on his horse and rode back down the road. Artair most likely sent his son to spread the word. He might even have sent him into town to get the constable. That was good. It meant they thought he was dead.

With his son gone, Artair found a tree near the road and leaned back to watch the fire consume the house. Watching the man for a few minutes to make sure he was fully engrossed, Gage wrapped himself in shadows and switched to his *Shadow Vision.*

Gage moved stealthily through the woods to the spot where he'd knocked out the female assassin. Keeping an eye on Artair, he searched the area for the woman's tracks. They weren't that difficult to find. She hadn't bothered to hide them.

Her trail led him around the house and merged with the footprints of the other two assassins. He retraced their path about a mile before he came upon three horses tied to a tree at the edge of a small clearing.

He scouted the area, looking for any signs of an additional assassin. Gage also checked for any traps the group might have left. They didn't seem experienced or competent enough, but why take chances?

Finding nothing of concern, he approached the horses. Gage had gained experience with animals over the past few years. With some soothing words, the horses allowed him to scratch them and examine them. All three bore different brands. That was smart. They couldn't be traced back to the guild.

Each of the animals had a small haversack and a water-skin tied to the saddle. He quickly searched it all. Unfortunately, there were no clues pointing back to the Shadowed Fist or giving any hint as to who had hired them. The haversacks contained only hard tack and oats for the horses, as well as a few changes of clothing.

Gage nodded in acceptance. The loose-fitting clothes he wore now were the traditional Shadowed Fist attire when carrying out an assassination. It wasn't an outfit worn openly. They'd worn regular clothes here, then changed before coming for him. That was good. It meant he now had a change of clothes.

Satisfied that he wasn't going to find anything else, he jogged back to the spot where he'd left the bodies. Using a series of *Shadow Slides*, Gage carried the two bodies back to the clearing. That done, he returned to the house.

Following the tracks and moving the bodies took a couple of hours, more people had gathered, watching his house burn. He recognized Manis, Iseabel, and their three children from further down the road. The widow Miared, who lived the opposite direction, also watched the conflagration.

They'd all come to help, or perhaps just to witness it burn. It didn't matter any longer. His family was dead. Jardon was dead. There was nothing for him here anymore. Gage would never come back again.

Turning his back on the place that had been his home, he headed to the clearing with the horses. As he went, he used a leafy branch to erase his own tracks and the tracks of the assassins—as if he was erasing his life with Alani and Shaunna. This time he didn't even pretend smoke stung his eyes.

CHAPTER 10

Gage reached the horses and spent another hour digging graves for the two channelers. Unlikely anyone would track him this far, but caution first. The beast-kin had sharp noses, and there were always a few of them in the Fist.

Once the dead channelers were buried and the area cleared of any trace, Gage replaced the loose-fitting Shadowed Fist garb with spare clothes the assassin's had brought. He used a combination of the two male channeler's clothes, since the female's clothes were too small for him.

The clothes were well made but not gaudy. They had been picked to blend into a crowd and not stand out. Gage smirked. At least they'd gotten that part correct. Glancing down at himself, he knew he'd be able to blend in with any villages he passed.

He scowled as he found a folded piece of parchment with the woman's clothes. Smoothing it out, he shook his head at the fairly accurate sketch of him. It seemed recent.

When he'd worked with the guild, he'd worn his dark hair short and kept a goatee. After starting his home with Alani, he grew the goatee out into a full beard and grew out his hair, usually keeping it pulled back in a ponytail.

The sketch in his hand depicted the beard and long hair. The question was, how had they gotten this sketch without him knowing? Had someone really been that close to him? Had an assassin been lurking around his home, and he'd been completely oblivious to it?

Gage shook his head. No. He didn't think so. He and his family had just been in Blarney last weekend for the first autumn festival, Lammas. Other villages had attended too. Hundreds of people. He glanced down at the sketch. It showed his shoulders and head, but he recognized the shirt collar. His one good shirt, the one he'd worn to the festival.

He cursed. Whoever made the sketch had been good. More alarmingly, they'd done it without his awareness. Gage's scowl deepened. He'd gotten sloppy. He couldn't be sloppy if he was planning to get revenge. Stopping his train of thought, Gage considered the ramifications.

Had he really decided to go after the person who ordered his death? The person responsible for the death of his family? His face hardened. Yes. They'd ripped his life away. The least he could do was return the favor.

As if waiting for his acknowledgement, his display blinked, and he saw that he had a new quest.

Vengeance is Mine—Part I

Get revenge for your wife and child's violent deaths by killing the man who ordered the assassination.

You have received a new quest "Vengeance is Mine —Part I"

Someone ordered your assassination and, during the attempt, killed your wife and daughter. You must infiltrate the Shadowed Fist.

Infiltrate the Shadowed Fist (0/1).

Reward: 10000 experience.

Accept quest (yes or no)?

Gage never really understood how the display worked or why the quests appeared when they did. Did the gods of this world hand out the quests? If so, why? And why only to outlanders? After all, he hadn't always gotten quests.

Quests had only started when he'd been pulled into this world. Pulled from his home on Earth. Earth. Yes, that had been his home. Gage barely remembered it now. He had been so young back then. He couldn't even say for certain what town he'd lived in back on Earth. Sometimes, he wondered if Earth had been a dream.

And yet, he remembered his parents. He chuckled mirthlessly. He didn't remember their names. To him, they'd always been mom and dad. But he did remember their faces—especially his mom's face.

But that family was gone as out of reach as Alani and Shaunna now. Gage gritted his teeth at the thought of their senseless deaths, and he turned his attention back to the quest. He needed to focus.

Yes, he would go into the Shadowed Fist. Gage would

find who had ordered his death and then he would hunt that person down and kill them. It wouldn't bring back his family. He doubted it would give him solace. But whoever it was had to pay. And pay with their life.

Hardening his resolve, Gage accepted the quest.

Breaking into the Shadowed Fist guild house would not be easy. The Fist hadn't survived for hundreds of years by being lax in their security. No, this would be one of the most difficult infiltrations he'd ever attempted.

His one advantage: he'd been a member of the guild. He'd been in the guild house many times. He knew their procedures. Or rather, he had known them. Some of them were bound to have changed since he left.

He glanced back down at the parchment. Of course, they knew what he looked like. Gage would need to change his appearance. He wasn't sure who else might have seen the sketch, but he wasn't going to make it easy on them.

Gage pulled a small steel mirror from the woman's pack. He studied his appearance, turning his head one way then the other. He couldn't remain the same, and he couldn't go back to the look he had when he was in the Fist.

There were many looks he could go with, but he needed to give them some thought. That, plus he needed a straight razor. Gage's razor was now buried with Alani's corpse.

Putting away the mirror and the sketch, Gage gathered up the rest of the items he'd accumulated. He put them into one pack and then moved the best saddle to the gray and black spotted mare the woman had ridden.

The gray was the best of the three horses, and he would keep her. He'd sell the other two in Blarney. The money would buy the supplies he needed.

The Shadowed Fist guild house was in Eastport, far to the south. It was a solid two weeks of travel on a good horse. He would need to follow the Blackwater River east to Jublin. From there, he could go south at the bridge to Daleford, then follow the coastal highway all the way down to Eastport.

It would be faster to take a barge from Blarney and float down the southern branch of the Blackwater River. By boat, he could make it in three days. He grimaced. That was, if he made it at all.

Gage shuddered. There weren't many things he was afraid of, but boats were one of them. Well, not the boat, per se. Rather, the waterspouts that formed unexpectedly.

The oceans were completely impassable because of waterspouts, and they formed in the lakes and rivers less often. It was rare, but it happened. Gage himself had witnessed it happen shortly after arriving on this world.

He and another kid from the orphanage, Tomas, had been looking right at it when the spout happened. Watching from the riverbank, Gage had seen the boat coming down the river. One moment coasting down the water, the next moment a waterspout had erupted directly beneath it, sending the boat hundreds of feet into the air. He could still remember the screams of the sailors over the roar of the spout. He'd sworn right then and there never to step foot on a boat. A promise he'd kept.

He scowled. Two weeks was a long time. By then, the Fist would know something had gone wrong. Most likely, the assassins had been told to ride to Jublin and send word via pigeon. Jublin was large enough that there might be a wizard capable of sending a message via portal.

Gage had no way of knowing which method they had intended to send their report by, so he couldn't guess how long until they were considered overdue. Or how long until the Fist would assume they had failed.

When he had worked for the guild, they'd used both methods to communicate his success. It had seemed completely random—and perhaps it was. He had to assume it was the shortest method—magic. That meant a day's ride from his farm to Blarney, and then three days to Jublin. A magical message would be there the same day. Four days.

He cursed. If he wanted to break into Shadowed Fist before they knew he was still alive, Gage would have to go by boat. Gage swore again. When he finally found who had ordered his death, he was going to make them pay for that too. What kind of sane person went on a boat?

CHAPTER 11

He reached Blarney just before the twin suns set that same day. After circling back around to the main road, well out of the way of his neighbors, Gage had ridden the horses hard. With three horses, he was able to cycle between them and keep up a breakneck pace.

During the trip, he'd kept his hood up to avoid any prying eyes. He'd passed two farmers that he knew. Both pulled carts behind old mares, most likely coming back from selling a crop in Blarney. While both men had looked up at the insane rider with three horses, neither had appeared to recognize him as he thundered past them.

At the outskirts of Blarney, he dismounted the horses and rubbed them down. He quickly checked their teeth and hooves, making sure everything was in order. Then Gage went to Elgar Guilliams, one of the three horse merchants in town. Elgar was fairly new to town, and he didn't know Gage personally.

Gage kept his hood up and disguised his voice. Despite never meeting Elgar before, there was no need to risk a passer-by overhearing and recognizing Gage. He needed everyone to believe he was dead. Someone recognizing him would upset his plan.

He haggled with Elgar long enough to not seem hurried and settled on a price for two of the horses and saddles. He thanked the horse merchant and immediately set off to his next stop.

He'd gotten a hundred gold Staters for the two horses. It was far less than he would have gotten in Jublin or Eastport, but he wasn't in Jublin or Eastport. Blarney just didn't have the market for riding horses that the larger towns had. Still, it was enough for what he needed.

At the docks, he found the river master about to close for the evening. Staring at the river, Gage nearly changed his mind. The memory of the sailors screaming came unbidden.

Once again disguising his voice, he spoke with Arvik Nool, the river master. "River master, I'm seeking passage to Eastport. Can you tell me when the next barge sails?"

While he knew of Arvik Nool, he'd never actually met him. The river master was an older man, thin with leathery skin from years outside, perhaps in his late fifties or early sixties. A scar ran down the left side of his face, from scalp to chin, passing over his left eye. Gage saw that the left eye was clouded, blind.

Gage knew the scar was left by a blade. He had a few himself. Judging from the age of the tissue, the man had lost it in a long-ago fight.

"River pirates," the man said, catching Gage off guard.

"Excuse me?" he replied.

"The eye," the man growled, voice like gravel. "I lost it in a fight with river pirates."

Cursing under his breath, Gage muttered an apology as he wiped sweaty palms against his pants. Gage hadn't realized he had been staring. He glanced out at the river and scowled. Part of him kept expecting a waterspout to explode out of the water, and it distracted him.

"Bah, everybody stares," the man huffed. "What was that you said about passage?"

"I need passage to Eastport," Gage repeated.

The river master looked him up and down. "Just you?"

"And my horse," he replied, gesturing to the edge of the dock where the gray was tied.

"You any good on a boat? Planning on working your way to Eastport?" the old man asked, raising the eyebrow over his right eye.

Gage shook his head. "I've never been on one before."

The man looked him up and down again, right eye narrowing. "Passenger only then? Must be in a hurry, eh?"

"Yes, passenger only," he answered, ignoring the man's second question. Gage wasn't about to reveal more than he had to. Anything he said, and anyone he interacted with, might give him away later—if someone from the guild came to investigate.

"Sixty staters," the man shot back. "For passenger only, plus a horse."

He didn't react, but inwardly Gage frowned. It was a steep price—more than most people in Blarney would see in a season. But thanks to his sale of the horses, he had the money. The fare would eat up a large chuck of it though. "Done."

Gage reached for his pouch and the river master held out his hand. "Ten to me now, the rest when you board tomorrow morning."

Chuckling to himself, he counted out ten gold coins and dropped them into the old man's hand. The real price for passage was fifty gold. The ten gold he was giving the river master was a town's share. The price of doing business.

Squinting at the gold with his good eye for a moment, the captain slid the coins away. "I'll let Captain Siany know you're coming. First light of the first sun, she sails. Make sure you're on dock. The captain makes the final call on who she lets aboard her ship."

"Thank you," Gage replied and turned to go.

"What's your name, stranger," the man asked to Gage's back. "So I can let her know who to expect."

He knew he'd have to eventually give someone a name and he'd already decided which one. The name he'd used since getting married, Jardon, was out of the question. He was supposed to be dead. He couldn't use Gage either, as that might give him away to the Fist.

Instead, he decided to sow a little extra confusion. Recalling the name he'd heard one of the assassin's yell out, he used it instead. "Peadrus."

"Peadrus," the river master repeated. "Very well, Peadrus. Make sure you're on time. Captain Siany won't wait."

"I'll be here," he replied and then walked back to his horse. Untying it, he walked the mare to the far east side of Blarney. There, just outside of town, was a small inn called the Scarlet Rooster.

He had chosen the Scarlet Rooster because it was the one inn he'd never visited during the time he'd been in the area. It catered to travelers and had a reputation as a place that got a bit rowdy. It was also the type of place that didn't ask a lot of questions.

Keeping his hood up, Gage went inside and immediately picked out the innkeeper, Bevan Gotch. A man in his mid-forties and a former army captain, Bevan was now nearly as wide as he was tall. He enjoyed his own cooking and his own brewing, but, according to the talk around town, he could still knock a few heads together when the occasion called for it.

Gage walked towards the innkeeper, who hoisted a small keg on his shoulder near the small bar. The dozen-and-a-half patrons in the bar looked up at him with passing interest, but most quickly resumed their libations and conversations.

He kept his head forward, but his eyes darted into every corner of the room, looking for anyone paying him too much attention. He saw two men from town looking him up and down and speaking quietly. He knew them— or rather, knew of them.

Ifan and Deri, two ne'er-do-wells that did odd jobs around the town. Rumor had it that they were tough characters and weren't above robbing the occasional traveler when they thought they could get away with it.

Ignoring the two men, Gage stopped in front of Bevan. "I'd like a room."

Bevan finished placing the keg on the counter and

then turned and wiped his hands on the stained apron that hung around his neck. He looked Gage up and down. Finally, he nodded. "Five chutes for the room, another chute for a meal and another for ale."

Gage had specifically asked for some of the money in silver chutes, but instead, he took out a gold stater and placed it in the man's palm. "If you have a razor I could borrow, I'd be much obliged."

The innkeeper looked at the gold in his hand and then narrowed his eyes at Gage. He nodded towards the stairs. "Room five, up the stairs and all the way back. I'll have my daughter bring the razor up."

"Can you bring the meal up to the room, too? And the ale?" he asked Bevan. "It was a hard day of riding and I just want to relax."

Bevan nodded and grunted, then turned away and waddled into the kitchen. Realizing the conversation had ended, Gage started for the stairs. As he reached them, he caught Ifan and Deri still watching him.

With a resigned sigh, he headed up the stairs to his room. He really was tired and would have preferred a good night's sleep. But judging how the two ne'er-do-wells had been eyeing him, he had a feeling his sleep would be rudely interrupted later. Gage scowled under his hood. So be it.

CHAPTER 12

The next morning, Gage led his horse out from the stable of the Scarlet Rooster. It was still dark, with the light of the morning suns still just a glow on the horizon. A low fog had rolled in from the river, creating the appearance of walking on a cloud.

As he passed the town square, the corner of his mouth turned up slightly at the sight of the two naked men. As he had suspected, Ifan and Deri had paid him a visit earlier that morning. They'd come just after midnight. Most likely, they thought he would be asleep, like the other patrons, and would be easy pickings. The two ruffians had been wrong on both accounts.

Gage was still angry—beyond angry—over the loss of his wife and daughter. He'd briefly toyed with the idea of killing the men. It would have been quick and easy. A slice across the throat or a stab through the ribs into the heart. But both of those methods would be messy.

He could have snapped their necks or strangled them. No mess that way. No mess that was, except for the bodies. But those could be easily disposed of; he could weigh them down and drop them in the river, or, if he wanted to use his *Shadow Slide* ability, he could take the bodies to a nearby farm and feed them to the pigs. Pigs ate anything.

Yet, he knew if two of the town's characters suddenly disappeared, it would be noticed. They might be ne'er-do-wells, but they were something familiar. Something expected. If they suddenly stopped showing up, questions would be asked.

Gage couldn't risk that. He couldn't risk it getting back to the Fist. He remained focused on his goal: finding out who ordered his assassination and making them pay for the death of his family.

Instead of killing them, he'd knocked the men unconscious with a series of nerve strikes the moment they'd opened the door. Once they were out, Gage had stripped off their clothes and used *Shadow Slide* to move them out into the town square.

Blarney didn't have stocks, like some of the larger cities did. So, Gage improvised. To make up for it, he tied them into a rather compromising position. Ifan had his arms tied around the tree which grew in the center of the square and Deri had his hands tied around Ifan's waist. He'd also tied the two men's ankles together and gagged them.

Ifan and Deri, who had probably been conscious for at least a couple of hours, saw him leading his horse. They strained against their gags and worked their arms, desperately trying to get his attention. The two wanted help. Wanted him to release them. Neither man recognized him as the one who had put them in that predicament.

Gage ran a hand across his shaved head and then down, along his smooth face. Even if the two men had gotten a good look at him last night—and even if they hadn't been drunk at the time—they wouldn't have recognized him. He barely recognized himself. And that was a good thing.

Before the two ruffians had attempted their breaking and entering, Gage had used the straight razor to shave his beard. After looking at himself in the mirror, he knew it would not be enough. Someone was sure to still recognize him.

That was when he had made the decision. Gage had hesitated briefly, but knowing the stakes, he chopped off his hair. It took him a while, but in the end, his head was completely clean-shaven.

When he had finally finished, he stared at himself in the small metal mirror. He saw a stranger's face. A face he barely recognized. That was good. If he barely recognized his own face, then he doubted many others would—especially not after the time that had passed.

Gage looked at the two naked ne'er-do-wells who were desperately trying to get his help. He feigned embarrassment, pretending he had just witnessed two men performing an obscene act in public. He brought his hand up to shield them from his view and hurried by.

He didn't feel bad for them. Someone would cut them

loose—eventually. He doubted either man would be arrested. The constable would most likely determine that the embarrassment they'd suffered was punishment enough and let them go. If not, a few nights in the dungeon was better than they deserved for their attempt to rob and probably beat him.

Putting Ifan and Deri out of his mind, Gage went straight to the docks. He walked the gray mare down the dock to the only barge there. Despite the early hour, sailors scrambled around the deck. They readied the boat for departure.

Reaching the edge of the docks, Gage paused. Very few things scared him. But boats and the possibility of being launched hundreds of feet into the air—yes, that frightened him. Gage knew the chance of it happening was actually very small, but it continued to gnaw at the back of his mind—one horrific scenario after another.

"You Peadrus?" A woman's voice called out and Gage spotted the speaker. Even in the dim light, he could make out the woman standing on the boat.

The woman was thin and wiry, wearing little more than a vest and short pants, with deeply tanned skin and short, cropped black hair. Each of her ears were pierced with numerous earrings and, like most of the men around her, every inch of exposed skin—except her face—was covered in elaborate tattoos.

Without conscious thought, he scanned her.

Siany Oster
Human

Sailor
Level 10

She looked to be in her mid-thirties and was level 10. It was level 10 in a profession, rather than a class, but it was still impressive. Remembering the cover name he'd given, Gage nodded. "Yeah, that's me."

The woman's eyes took stock of him. "You have the money?"

Gage nodded. "The river master said fifty gold."

"Ha!" The woman laughed. "He probably said fifty-five or sixty, the town got seven or eight and he kept the rest. Am I right?"

"Yeah," he replied, giving her a mirthless chuckle. "Something like that."

Once more, the woman's eyes ran him up and down. She frowned. "I will take you down river for fifty staters. But if we're attacked by pirates, everyone fights. Passengers too. Agreed?"

Gage had already decided on his alias last night. His Peadrus identity would be a charm merchant from Daleford, returning to Eastport to get more stock after selling out at the festival. It seemed fair enough, given the festival the previous week. If asked, he would say he came by caravan just before the festival.

Given his lack of recent knowledge of things outside of Blarney, it was the best he could do on short notice. The big flaw he saw immediately was that he was paying the insane price of 60 Staters to travel down river. No merchant would do that. But he had an answer for that too. He'd sold out early in the day, gotten drunk and missed the caravan.

It was a bit cliche but held a grain of truth. Since the trade caravans only hit the town once a month, it would have meant spending half his money on room and board —and wasting time. By taking the boat to Eastport and picking up more stock, he would make the festival in Jublin and hopefully earn back the money.

Or rather, that was the story he'd concocted. It was always better to have too many answers than not enough.

The woman was still waiting for his answer. Given that he was using a merchant persona, Gage made his face look uncertain. "I... uh... I'll fight."

The woman raised an eyebrow. "Do you actually have any weapons on you?"

Staying in character, he bit his lip. "I... uh... I came with the caravan, so I don't... really... have any weapons."

That wasn't true, of course. He still had several knives he'd taken from the assassins, secreted away in various pockets. But she didn't need to know that.

The woman rolled her eyes. "If fighting starts, find yourself something then, and try not to die. We won't have time to defend you."

Gage licked his lips and looked uncertain. Then he nodded. "I... uh... understand."

"Sure, you do. Sure." The woman laughed. "Now, get yourself and your animal aboard and give me the gold, so we can get on our way."

Staying in the character of Peadrus the charm merchant, Gage led his mare down the ramp and onto the boat. He didn't have to feign the nervousness he felt about being on the barge. That was real enough.

He handed the 50 gold staters to the woman, who snatched it out of his hand. She bounced the pouch of gold in her hand as if weighing it.

"I am captain Siany," the woman said with a grin as she made the gold disappear into one of her belt pouches. "Welcome aboard the *Riverbreeze*."

CHAPTER 13

Gage didn't relax at all the first half of the day. Instead, he stayed near the railing of the boat, staring out at the shoreline, ready to use his *Shadow Slide* ability at the slightest indication of a waterspout. Despite a mild spring day, by lunch he was drenched in sweat.

He wasn't sure why the idea of a waterspout terrified him so. It wasn't logical. Given everything he'd been through and everything he'd done in his life, he would have thought he was without fear. And yet, he couldn't shake the terror of suddenly being hurled hundreds of feet in the air.

Fear was not something he usually dealt with, and several times, he almost used his ability to leave the ship. He didn't understand why his mind obsessed over the possibility that they could be propelled skyward, but he couldn't dissuade it. He cursed himself for his weakness and tried to focus on his breathing.

Clinging white-knuckled to the railing the entire morning, he barely noticed as sailors moved around him, busying themselves with the operations of the boat. It wasn't until lunch time that Siany came to stand next to him with a plate of food.

"The price of the voyage includes the meals," she told him, thrusting the plate at him. In her other hand, she held a mug.

His eyes darted down to the grilled fish on the plate before immediately settling on the shore again. "I'm not hungry."

"Take it! You have to keep up your strength. You should drink something too." The captain thrust the plate at him harder. "You are sweating like a pig. You need to replenish your water."

"I'm fine," he growled.

Captain Siany barked a laugh. "The man hasn't moved from this spot since we left and is covered in sweat. Oh yes, that's my definition of fine."

Gage heard some nearby sailors chuckle as well, but he ignored them. He turned his head towards the captain, but kept his eyes fixed on the shoreline behind her—just in case he had to *Shadow Slide*.

"I'm not... comfortable... with boats," he said through clenched teeth.

"You picked the wrong way to travel then, my friend!" Siany chuckled. "We still have two and a half more days to Eastport!"

"Don't remind me," he snarled.

The captain leaned against the railing, her casual, relaxed posture in direct contrast to his own. "I've been doing this journey, up and down the river, for ten years. Other than pirates, we ain't ever had a problem."

"No waterspouts?" he asked, jaw tense.

"You see them occasionally," she said, nonchalantly. She shrugged. "Some are even close to the boat. But they don't cause a problem."

Tell that to the crew of the boat he saw destroyed in the blink of an eye. He didn't respond to the woman, and she shrugged again.

"You are obviously afraid of boats—or waterspouts," she said, trying to make eye contact. "Why did you book passage with me, if you knew you were afraid?"

"No choice," he retorted, trying to focus his mind on his persona's story. "I missed the caravan."

She raised an eyebrow, giving him a curious look. "How did you miss the caravan? They are a bit difficult to miss. Quite a production."

"Let's just say I partied a bit too hard after selling out," he replied, at least having the presence of mind to remember his cover story.

Siany nodded knowingly, a small smile coming to her face. "When I was just a sailor, I had a similar experience. I had agreed to a drinking contest against a dwarf."

Despite his situation, Gage smiled. Dwarfs had a well-earned reputation for being able to handle their drink much better than most of the other races in the world. Trying to outdrink one was a tough endeavor. Most non-dwarves knew better than to even try.

Gage whistled and arched an eyebrow. "Did you win?"

The captain furrowed her brow and shrugged. "I have

no idea. I woke up two days later with no memory and no job. My ship—as they say—had sailed."

"What'd you do?" he asked.

She smiled. "I signed up on the next ship. This ship, the *Riverbreeze*. Worked my way up to first mate and when the owner retired, I took over as captain."

"So, the story has a happy ending," he nodded, expression impassive. He remembered that she was a level 10 sailor. "You must have been pretty young when you started sailing."

"I started sailing when I was 12," she replied sourly. "Working as a captain's... cabin girl."

"You were a slave?" Gage scowled. He'd nearly been sold as a slave by the orphanage a few years after he arrived on this world. But he'd been scrawny back then and the merchant had taken his friend, Jeoff, instead. He'd run away the next day.

"Slavery." Siany snorted and looked off at the shore, her eyes faraway. "That was a better name for it. My parents thought it was an apprenticeship. Not that they really cared. I was the seventh daughter. I know now they just wanted to get rid of me."

Gage nodded gravely. What she had experienced was not uncommon. She had been handed over for an apprenticeship. Although it wasn't technically slavery, the conditions were usually similar. The main difference: the merchant or tradesman didn't actually have to pay for the apprentice. In fact, sometimes, the parents actually paid them to teach their child a trade.

While some apprenticeships were legitimate, many were just another form of slavery. The children were used and abused. If they didn't survive—there were always more parents who wanted to give their children a chance for a better life.

They were both quiet for a long time. Finally she broke the silence with a forced grin. "But now I have my own ship."

He glanced around at the boat. "Quite an accomplishment given your start."

"Yes, it is," she agreed. She looked down at the plate of food and the mug in her hands. She shoved both towards him. "And because I'm captain, I'm ordering you to eat. And drink!"

Gage looked down at the food and drink. He looked back up at her and took them from her.

"Make sure you eat it!" she ordered. "We do not waste food—or ale. Now, I have to get back to my duties."

With that, the captain spun and began barking orders to the sailors. Men and women who had been standing around suddenly burst into action, quickly carrying out the woman's orders.

The conversation with the captain had momentarily distracted him from the overwhelming sense of dread. Now that she was gone, his mind began to play through scenarios where he was suddenly catapulted into the air.

He downed nearly half the mug of ale in one gulp, suddenly realizing how thirsty he was. The warm liquid caused his stomach to growl and he quickly devoured the fish on his plate. By the time the captain passed him again, both the plate and the mug were empty.

"That's better," the woman said, stopping next to him. "You'll need your strength if we're attacked."

Gage raised an eyebrow. "You mentioned an attack earlier and again just now. Does that happen often?"

Siany uttered a curse before answering. "More often than we like. With the Houses neglecting their duties, piracy has been on the rise. We are getting attacked more and more."

He nodded. Even before he'd put his old life behind him, the Houses had become more concerned with waning magic and inter-House fighting than the care of their lands. It appeared it hadn't improved since then.

"Does this mean you're expecting an attack?" he asked.

For just a moment, the captain's forehead wrinkled in worry. She looked past him, down the river, before her expression became one of bravado. "I always expect an attack! That's why I've repelled all boarders so far."

He raised an eyebrow. "But you're worried."

She gave him a hard look, eyes narrowed. "Do I look worried to you?"

Not backing down, he returned her stare. "Yes, you do."

The two of them locked eyes, their stare becoming a contest of wills, but it was the captain who turned away first. She looked around the boat, at the sailors. Gage looked around too. Then he saw it. They were all on edge.

Cursing himself, he realized he'd been so obsessed with the possibility they'd be hit by a waterspout, that Gage hadn't even seen the mood of the people around him. The stiff movements, the wandering eyes, the nervous glances at the shore. The sailors were nervous.

"You are expecting an attack," he stated, daring her to contradict him.

Siany narrowed her eyes at him for a moment but then just shrugged. "You're a merchant. You know how it works. We just dropped off a shipment of goods for Blarney. We have the coin from the sale. It would be a good time to attack. Easier to move coin than goods."

Alert now and already pressing the idea of a waterspout to the back of his mind, Gage looked around, taking in his surroundings. There was no sign of anyone along either shore presently. He turned back to Siany. "Do you know when or where they will attack?"

The captain bit her lip and nodded. "The best place to attack would be at Mournehead."

Mournehead was the place where the Blackwater River forked. The Blackwater continued to the east and ran past Jublin before hitting the ocean at Daleford. The south fork became the Mourne River and went past Dingley, all the way to Eastport.

He didn't know anything about piracy, but it made tactical sense to hit up boats at what was effectively a crossroads. Gage scowled. "And how long until we reach Mournehead?"

She flashed him a mirthless smile. "Tonight."

CHAPTER 14

Gage pushed his obsession with being blasted by a waterspout to the back of his mind. He'd seen real concern in the captain's face and heard it in her tone. She was actually worried about the possibility of being ambushed by pirates.

He wasn't worried. Not about the pirates. Given he was level 20, his various classes, and unique skill set, Gage would most likely be able to take out all of the pirates single-handedly. The problem was, he doubted he could do so without giving himself away to the crew.

If the crew saw him using his abilities, especially his shadow abilities, his cover would be blown. The Peadrus-the-charm-merchant charade would be over. The sailors would spread the story once they hit port and word would quickly find its way to Shadowed Fist.

He didn't think anyone at the guild knew of his abilities—he'd never revealed them to anyone. But the guildmaster, Aeg Derg, was a crafty old man. He could have worked it out or even had someone shadowing Gage.

He cursed silently. It was precisely what he didn't want. If word got out, and Aeg Derg did know about his abilities, the cat would be out of the bag. Gage couldn't have the guild knowing he was coming. He'd be walking into an ambush.

And yet, he had to help the sailors. Gage couldn't let pirates attack the ship, kill the crew, and scuttle the boat— or try to take the boat to a different port. He needed to get to Eastport—and he needed to do so discreetly. That meant he needed as many sailors to survive as possible. The dilemma was how to help the fight without giving himself away.

Gage brought up his character sheet, something he hadn't done in a long time.

Name: Gage Cross
Race: Human
Class: Rogue 5 / Assassin 5 / Witch Hunter 5 / Shadow-master 5
Strength: 17
Agility: 39
Hardiness: 18
Intellect: 20
Intuition: 13
Charisma: 14
Health: 30
Mana: 40
Karma: 20

When he'd first arrived as a kid, all his attributes had been 7's and he'd had a class of *Commoner*. It hadn't taken him long to figure out what most of the stats did—or at least, guess at what they did. He'd realized early on that his *Hardiness* stat corresponded to his *Health*. He'd put his first few stat bonuses in *Hardiness* so he could stay alive longer.

After he'd run away from the orphanage, forcing him to live on the streets, he'd quickly realized that he wasn't the biggest or strongest. That meant Gage needed to be the quickest and the smartest. By stealing to survive, he'd gained the *Rogue* class. With each level of *Rogue*, he received an *Agility* point, plus an extra point to place wherever he wanted. He'd put the next five points into *Intellect*.

He'd spent years on the street, in various gangs, improving his *Rogue* skills and leveling up. Compared to the other gang members, he leveled up quickly because of the quests he received.

Although he hadn't understood where the quests came from or why they came, he did know that it gave him an edge, an edge he was happy to exploit to quickly rise through the ranks and eventually be recruited by the thieves' guild.

Shortly after Gage had reached level 5 in *Rogue* he'd been approached by the Shadowed Fist. He'd killed men before—when he had to—but he didn't have any real desire to join the assassin's guild. He'd said no.

The next evening, everyone in the thieves' guild was dead except for him. The Fist had come again and asked if he wanted to join. The message was clear: He could join the assassin's guild or he could die with the others. Not much of a choice.

Gage had joined the Fist and they'd trained him in the art of assassination. While he still didn't agree with killing people for no reason, he soon found he was good at it. Whether it was natural skill or because of his display and the quests, he quickly rose through the ranks. He'd even been able to change classes to Assassin.

While his first year of assignments were mostly petty thugs, as his skills increased, so did the visibility of his targets. He went from killing members of rival thieves' guilds and corrupt merchants, to taking jobs that involved members of the Houses—some of them mages.

Wizards and other magic-users commanded incredible magical power. But they weren't gods—despite what the Houses tried to convince the masses. Provided you were able to take them unawares or get past their magical defenses, they died just like everyone else.

The Houses continued their secret wars on each other, ordering assassinations made to look like accidents—or making it appear as if a different House had done it. After a year of almost exclusive contracts to kill House mages, Gage had leveled up and received the option for *Witch Hunter*.

Given the nature of his most recent work, and the extra challenges involved in killing mages, Gage had switched classes yet again. He became a wizard killing machine, given contract after contract for House wizards.

That was, until the Houses finally got tired of losing their magic-users. As if by some mutual agreement, the Houses all approached the Shadowed Fist and contracted out their own "master of assassins," for which they paid handsomely.

Nearly each House put an assassin from the Fist on retainer to work directly for the House. Not only did the master eliminate rivals, they also provided security to foil other Houses' assassination attempts.

It was while working for House Cernunnos that Gage had received the option, yet again, of switching classes. This time, it was a class he'd never heard of before, the class of *Shadowmaster.*

Unsure what the class was, he'd done some research at the Cernunnos library and Shadowed Fist library before he'd finally decided to switch classes. Evidently, he wasn't the first person to have the option of *Shadowmaster*— though he realized those without a display called it many things: Shadow Walker, Shadowdancer or something similar.

Once he'd begun to use the *Shadowmaster* abilities, he'd never looked back. It was the closest to being a wizard he'd ever been, and in the dark, around shadow, he might even be more powerful than a wizard—especially with the magic-neutralizing poison he could make.

Yet, even if he could make magic-neutralizing poison, it wouldn't help him against normal brigands and pirates. No. He needed to come up with a way to help while avoiding notice? To do that, he needed more information about how the pirates would attack.

Gage looked over at the captain, who was staring off at the shore as well. "How will they attack?"

Siany blinked and looked at him. "I'm sorry, what did you say?"

"You said they will attack tonight," he repeated. "How will they attack? I mean, it will be dark, right?"

"True," she said. "But we use torches at night so we don't run ashore. They'll be able to see us coming. They'll come in small boats and board us. Then we fight."

He nodded. That made sense. The pirates would probably have a beast-kin, with their excellent night vision, in each canoe, guiding it to the ship. That would allow them to travel without lights and sneak up on the ship.

Gage had already seen two beast-kin sailors on her ship, a monkey-kin and a dog-kin. Like all beast-kin, they had the ability to see in the dark. No doubt, they were great for helping to prevent the boat from going aground at night.

"You have some beast-kin on board," he said aloud. "Couldn't they steer the boat without having to use torches."

The captain raised an eyebrow. "Not a bad idea... if they didn't have their own beast-kin. They'd still smell us and when they got here, my other sailors would be blind."

He nodded. Gage had suspected as much, but he wanted to get confirmation before he thought about other ideas. "What about hoisting your sail right before and simply outrunning them?"

"Ha! If only it were that easy." Siany snorted. "They call it Mournehead because of the ships that have run ashore or beached on the rocks at the branch. We actually have to rig the sail and slow ourselves to navigate the turn."

"Is it more risky to try and fight them?" he shot back.

"Even in the day, when we could see the rocks, I would be hard pressed to navigate us through there," she replied.

"In the dark... well, let's just say I'd rather take my chances with my blade. Sorry mister merchant, it's going to come to a fight. And you're going to have to help if you wish to survive."

Siany put her hands on her hips. "You're a traveling merchant. You must have been in a fight before. Bandits? Robbers? Highwaymen?"

Gage guessed a merchant would have been in some altercation at some point. It would make sense that his Peadrus persona would have fought off an occasional bandit. He nodded. "I've been in a couple of scraps. But mostly I got lucky. That's when I started going by caravan."

The captain gave him a hard look but then shrugged. She bent down and pulled a long knife from her boot. She held it out, hilt first. "Here, take this. And let's hope you get lucky again tonight."

He reached out tentatively, like a merchant would, and took the knife. His expert hands instantly felt the poor balance of the blade and his eyes caught the dull edge. But Peadrus wouldn't have noticed either, so he smiled. "Thanks! I'll do my best."

She rolled her eyes. "Just try not to stab me or any of my sailors. Oh, and try not to die."

Keeping in character, he bit his lip and put a worried look on his face. "I'll... I'll try my best."

Siany spun and padded away. Gage's sharp ears caught her parting words. "Sure you will."

He smiled inwardly, knowing that she—and the rest of the crew—had completely bought into his merchant persona. None of them would expect any serious help from him and would most likely stay away from him when the fight happened.

That was good. He needed them to steer clear so he had some room to work. Gage looked down at the dull blade in his hand. He was already formulating a plan that just might allow him to help and keep up his persona.

CHAPTER 15

The twin suns, and the black hole between them, dipped under the horizon. As the last light faded, the enormous planet the world revolved around—Aaru became more prominent on the horizon, along with several of the many moons that also orbited the planet.

With night arriving, the mood on the ship soured. The sailors became agitated and glanced frequently at the shore. The back-and-forth banter that the crew had shared disappeared, replaced by an uneasy silence.

Torches flickered on tall poles scattered around the ship. The light reflected and refracted across the dark water of the river, creating an eerie glow of shimmering illumination which sparkled across the water. It wasn't enough for normal human eyes to see the shore, but it was enough for them to spot any approaching attackers.

Gage moved to the darkest part of the ship, near the rear. Hidden in the shadows, and faced away from the sailors, he activated his *Shadow Vision* and the world went black and white.

With his *Shadow Vision*, he had no difficulty seeing the shoreline. He saw things moving, but they were creatures of the night, not pirates. Gage scanned up and down the shore but spotted nothing that indicated the presence of anything other than the animals who normally inhabited this area: alligators, river cats, otters, and the occasional bear or wolf.

His sharp ears caught the captain's footsteps as she approached and he switched off his *Shadow Vision*. He didn't react to her approaching presence. After all, Peadrus the merchant wouldn't be so aware. He'd be worried right now about the pirate attack. Gage waited until she spoke and then jumped a bit, feigning surprise.

"We're still a couple of hours from Mournehead," the woman said. He spun at her words, putting a look of shock and surprise on his face, tinged with a bit of fear. Gage wasn't playing the Peadrus role as a coward, but any normal person would be worried about an impending pirate attack.

Siany rolled her eyes at him and Gage laughed nervously. "Sorry, you... surprised me."

"You need to pay more attention," the captain scolded him. "If I were a pirate, you'd be dead."

Dropping his eyes and putting on a contrite expression, Gage nodded. "Sorry."

"Don't be sorry," she growled. "Pay more attention! We are coming up on Mournehead. They will attack at any time."

"We slowed," Gage said, having noticed the speed of the boat decreasing for the last ten or fifteen minutes.

The captain nodded. "We have to make the turn into the southern branch. I told you before. Too risky—even if we are expecting an attack."

"How do they know we're coming or what time to expect us?" he asked the woman. Gage had already guessed the answer, but he wanted to hear what Siany thought.

In his experiences with the thieves' guild, he knew there were many ways to get the information on easy marks. Some were more elaborate than others—like breaking into a merchant's business and reviewing their shipping logs. But the easiest and most common was simply to pay someone off.

A dock worker or the river master himself would be slipped a few gold for any information. For that matter, it didn't even have to be a dockworker, it could be anyone who could keep any eye on the dock. Gage suppressed a wry smile. He wouldn't put it past Ifan and Deri to be lookouts for the pirates.

No matter who it was, the question remained: how did they get word back to the pirates. A pigeon had to be trained to return to a specific place. He doubted there was a nest of pigeons sitting somewhere in Mournehead. The army had to have searched the area before. Surely they would have found them.

That meant the messages were being relayed by fast horse—or by magic. Given the terrain, he doubted even a fast horse would have beaten the *Riverbreeze*. That left magic. And if it were magic, then there must be a wizard or other magic-user among the pirates. That would complicate things.

Siany looked out at the river. She shrugged. "I don't know. The word is that they seem to know which ships to target and when. They go for ships with easy to move cargo or those like us, who are returning with profits."

"Why even fight?" he asked, trying to stay in character. "Just hand over the profits."

The captain glared at him. "Maybe you can do that. Give up your profits. But I can't. These aren't my profits. They belong to the trade companies who contracted me. If I don't turn these over, they'll take my ship as collateral."

From his time in the thieves' guild, Gage was aware of similar situations. In fact, the guild had created a "protection" business for shipowners in port to make sure their goods or services went undisturbed. It had been quite lucrative, until the Fist had wiped out the thieves' guild.

Before he could respond to her, one of the sailors from the front of the boat called out. "Captain, we've got movement in the water!"

Siany spun and hurried away towards the speaker. Alone again and knowing everyone would be focused on the water in front of the barge, Gage reactivated his *Shadow Vision*. The shades of nighttime colors and torchlight on the water faded to gray. Looking forward, he could see six canoes approaching the front.

Doing a quick count, he saw that each canoe held four people. Just as Siany had said, at least one beast-kin sat in the bow of each boat, directing them towards the ship and around any obstacles.

"Bows!" Siany yelled and the sailors quickly grabbed short bows.

Her voice carried across the river and the men in the canoes reacted as well. The pirate at the front of the canoe put his oar across his lap and brought up a large shield. He held it in place while the three behind him continued to paddle.

The captain raised her saber and then dropped it. "Loose!"

The five or so sailors who had bows, released their arrows with a twang but they either flew wide or thudded into the shields. Siany raised her saber again and then dropped it. Another volley of arrows flew. The second wave of arrows had a similar effect. The canoes continued moving closer.

The crew's attention was focused on the approaching battle. Gage realized this was his opportunity to act without being seen. He scanned the shore, looking for what he needed. When he found it, he activated *Shadow Slide*.

One moment, he was on the ship. The next moment, he was on the shore, grabbing hold of a large, scaly form which immediately began thrashing in his grip. Gage looked out at his target destination and *Slid* with his new friend.

Traveling between light and darkness, Gage appeared at his chosen destination, a point about twenty feet above one of the canoes. As he felt himself starting to fall, he released his unwilling passenger and *Slid* back to the shore. There, he spun and watched as the alligator plummeted into the canoe with a crash.

Pirates screamed as the enraged alligator began to twist, snap and bite at anything within reach.

"Gator! Gator!" one of the men shouted.

Seeing how his plan had worked, Gage searched the shore for another alligator. Finding one, he quickly did the same thing with the second reptile. He dropped it on a second canoe. Once more, the men in the canoe screamed. This time, either the men or the alligator caused the canoe to capsize, spilling everyone into the water.

Gage wanted to do it again, but he was low on *Mana*. Even in the dark, when his shadow abilities were at their strongest and cost the least amount of *Mana*, he could only *Shadow Slide* so many times before running low.

Running along the shoreline, he managed to get within range of the ship. He activated his ability, *Sliding* back to the *Riverbreeze*. He arrived back on the deck just in time to hear the captain shout. "Loose!"

Siany's shout was followed by the twang of bows. This time, he heard shouts of pain in the water as arrows found their marks. With two of their six canoes under attack or capsized, the others were in disarray. They're shields weren't quite at the right angle and some of the pirates took arrows.

"They're turning around!" the monkey-kin called out. "They're heading back to shore."

A cheer went up from the crew, but Gage was far from happy. Looking down at himself, he realized he was wet and dirty from appearing on the shore and grabbing the alligators. He frowned. There would be questions if people saw him now. Or at least, suspicions. He couldn't afford either.

Looking over the railing into the dark waters, his frown deepened. He knew what he needed to do. First, he slammed his head into the railing, hard enough that it would leave a lump. Then, with a resigned sigh, he jumped into the water.

"Help! Help!" he yelled. "Man overboard!"

CHAPTER 16

"Tell me again," Siany said, giving him a look of disgust. "How did you fall overboard?"

Gage was back on the deck with the captain and several of the sailors looking down at him. They'd thrown him a rope and managed to pull him aboard just as they cut over into the southern branch.

"I was heading to the front to help," he said, one hand on the lump on his head. He didn't have to fake the pain, his head actually hurt. Gage realized he might have hit it a bit too hard. At least it was convincing. "I don't know what happened next. I think I slipped and hit my head. The next thing I knew I was in the water."

Siany shook her head. "Just be glad you grabbed that mooring rope. If not, we would have left you behind."

He nodded, the motion flaring the pain in his head. Gage let it show on his face. "We're safe then?"

"We're safe, although I'm not sure how," the captain

replied. She frowned and looked past him into the darkness. "But we're about a mile past Mournehead now."

Gage, playing the part of the curious merchant, cocked an eyebrow. The motion pulled the skin around the lump on his head and he allowed himself a flinch. "What do you mean, you're not sure how?"

"Gwawl said he saw alligators attacking some of the pirate's canoes," she replied, still looking out into the darkness. "But that doesn't really make sense. Alligators wouldn't be that aggressive to something so big."

"Gwawl?" he asked.

"The monkey-kin," she replied. "He's got great night vision."

Gage nodded. "We're lucky those alligators were aggressive."

"Yeah," she said in a faraway voice. "Lucky."

"Captain!" a voice said from the back of the ship. "We have canoes behind us."

The captain snapped out of her thoughts and spun to the voice. On the starboard side of the stern, near one of the torch poles, Gage saw Gwawl standing on the rail, looking behind him. He was pointing into the darkness.

Siany rushed over to the monkey-kin and stared out into the dark waters behind the *Riverbreeze*. She turned back to him, her brow furrowed. "Are you sure?"

"Three of them," Gwawl replied with a nod. "And they're gaining."

Gage thought he'd heard the man wrong, and apparently so did the captain. She looked at him like he was crazy. "They can't be gaining."

Gwawl didn't back down. He just nodded grimly. "Sorry captain, but they are. I don't understand it either."

"You're absolutely sure?" Siany asked the monkey-kin.

The man nodded again.

The captain uttered an impressive stream of curses before spinning around. "All hands to the stern! Prepare to repel boarders!"

Gage was already on his feet and moving to the stern. He had a bad feeling he knew why the canoes were moving towards them—and catching up to them. Reaching the railing, he leaned over and activated his Shadow Vision. He was taking a chance, but he should be far enough over the railing that the crew couldn't see his eyes.

The world went black and white, and his vision sharpened. Glancing out into the river, he spotted the three canoes—no, not three—four canoes, gaining on them. He squinted at the canoes. The men on them weren't even paddling.

Magic. It had to be magic. He focused his attention on the canoes, opening up his awareness. He felt it. Water magic. A mage was using water magic on the canoes to propel them through the water. And the magic-user had to be in one of the canoes.

Given his experience with mages, he guessed the person was in the fourth canoe. Generally, mages preferred not to be on the front lines. They would stay back and use their magic from the safety of the rear.

He cursed under his breath. He could take out the mage, but not without alerting the crew. The "I fell into the water" explanation would only raise suspicions if he tried it again.

"Captain," one of the sailors said. "How are they catching up to us?"

There were mutters of "magic" and "sorcery" from the other sailors. They didn't sound pleased. If anything, they sounded downright afraid.

Gage didn't blame them. The empire's power had been built with magic. The Houses had magic and used it to subjugate the masses and keep them in fear of magic. They also kept the common people ignorant of magic to keep them afraid of it.

In that way, the Houses really weren't much different than the gangs and thieves' guilds he'd been a part of in his younger years. They ruled through fear and intimidation, and the occasional demonstrations of power. He'd seen it firsthand with his time as master of assassins for House Cernunnos.

"Captain, we can't fight a wizard," one of the crew said and there were murmurs of agreement.

"We don't even know that it is a wizard," Siany countered, though her tone was unconvincing. If anything, it held a note of resigned defeat.

"We could surrender," another sailor said. "Just let them have the profits."

The captain glared at the man, and he shrank back but the other men mumbled agreements.

Gage found it interesting that most people would fight against overwhelming odds, so long as there was no magic. Sword against sword or fist against fist and they were ready to defend their goods, their property, their family, or their honor. Add magic to the mix, and they were ready to surrender.

Siany had already said that giving up their profits was tantamount to giving up her ship. The traders who contracted her would seize her ship to make up for their losses. She and the crew would be out of jobs.

While the sailors would most likely find new berths quickly, he doubted anyone would trust a captain who gave over her profits or cargo without a fight. It would effectively end her career. But it just might save the lives of her crew. Which would she choose?

He was watching Siany's face when he felt magic being channeled. It was a familiar magic, fire magic. As he suspected, it came from the fourth canoe—the one in the back. Though his site was in black and white, he could see fire forming in the hands of a robed figure, standing on the canoe.

Without a conscious thought, he activated his *Uncanny Dodge* and his *Improved Uncanny Dodge*. He also switched back to normal sight just as the fireball was released. He followed its path with his eyes, ready to jump into the water.

After a second of watching the fireball's trajectory, he knew it would explode over their heads. It hadn't been aimed at them. It was a warning shot. A few seconds later, it detonated above them into a brilliant yellow-orange explosion.

The sailors screamed and cowered. Even Siany's bravado was momentarily shaken. Chances were none of them had seen this level of destructive magic close-up before. They were, understandably, afraid.

"Drop Anchor! Surrender your vessel and your cargo," the mage's voice called out. It was high pitched and nasally but held an undertone of arrogance, "and we will spare your lives. Resist, and I will burn you to cinders!"

The cowed sailors began immediately shouting their surrender and some moved to the anchor. Siany recovered, drew her sword and began yelling for quiet. "I'm the captain! I'm the one who decides whether we surrender!"

Gage saw by the woman's face that she had already accepted her fate. Like the sailors, she knew that fighting a mage with fire magic while on a ship made of wood was a bad idea. A very bad idea.

She was going to surrender. Siany was a good woman and she'd turn over her cargo rather than let her crew be killed.

He scowled and shook his head. Gage needed to get to Eastport, and he needed to get there quickly. The fastest way to do that was on the *Riverbreeze*—under the control of captain Siany. He simply couldn't let the pirates take it or destroy it.

Cursing under his breath, Gage knew he would have to deal with the wizard and the pirates himself. His earlier disruption had been meant to allow them to outrun the pirates without giving himself or his power away.

Because of the mage with them, it hadn't worked. They'd persisted. Now, he had no choice. Gage would have to deal with the pirates—personally.

Pushing his way through the sailors, he reached Siany and grabbed her forearm. Gone was the weak and timid merchant persona. It was time to be the old Gage. It was time to be master of assassins. The master of shadows.

Siany felt his grip and spun to face him, her face flushed in anger. She tried to pull away, but he kept his vice-like grip on her arm. He moved his face close to hers and activated his Shadow Sight, letting his eyes go completely black.

The captain's face went from anger to shock and fear in a heartbeat, and she froze, staring into the pools of inky blackness. The woman wouldn't know what he was, she'd only know it was magic.

"We need to talk," he hissed, close to her ear. "I can get you out of this, but only if you do exactly what I say."

CHAPTER 17

The men from the canoes reached the *Riverbreeze* a few minutes later. They were a variety of humans and other races—there were even a few halflings among them. One by one, they climbed aboard and looked around at the empty deck.

"Uh, where is everyone?" asked a burly man who was missing several of his front teeth.

It took several minutes, but finally the stern of the boat was full of men, elves, dwarves, halflings, and beast-kin, dripping water onto the deck. The group parted as a final figure, an elf in robes, floated up over the railing and landed gently onto the deck.

The elf was perhaps five feet tall and appeared slender despite the voluminous robes he wore. His hair was straight, dark, and long, pulled back off his face to cascade down his back. In his hand, the mage held an ornately carved staff with a glowing blue crystal embedded in the top. A wizard's staff. The thing he used to focus his magic.

The wizard wore a scowl as he surveyed the deck. He turned to a mangy dog-kin next to him. "Where are they?"

The dog-kin sniffed the air, moving his head up and down and then side to side. He pointed to the hatch in the middle of the ship. "They're still here. Down there."

"Idiots," the elf spat. "If we didn't need this ship, I'd burn it all down right now. As it is, we do need this floating junkyard to move the slaves down river." The wizard gestured to the hatch. "You lot, go down there and kill every last one of them."

A man and a bear-kin who were closest to the hatch, took a step towards it. After a single step, both men coughed and sputtered, clutching at their throats. A moment later, the two dropped to the deck, blood spraying from their necks. Their movements slowed and finally stilled completely.

The other men, including the wizard, were looking around, weapons at the ready.

"What in Hel's bottom was that?" one of the halfling's screeched in a high-pitched, child-like voice. "What just happened?"

"They just died," a dwarf said. "Choked on something!"

"They didn't just die or choke on something, you idiot," the mage growled in his nasally voice. "Look at the blood. Someone just killed them."

"How?" demanded one of the men. "I didn't see nothing."

Spooked, the pirates continued to look around the deck. The beast-kin sniffed the air while the others darted glances around the various crates, supplies and masts around the boat—searching for the person who had killed their companions.

"Probably a knife or one of those throwing blades," the wizard retorted angrily. He pointed to a dwarf and a cat-kin near the bodies. "Check their throats, see if there's a knife or something."

The dwarf and cat-kin moved forward and bent down to examine the bodies of the dead pirates only to fall face forward into the deck, bodies twitching.

"Jasper! Ranal!" one of the men exclaimed. "They're dead!"

"It's ghosts!" another shouted. "Or river spirits!"

"It ain't no ghost or spirit. It was a knife or something," the dog-kin next to the wizard said. "I heard it this time."

"So," sneered the wizard. "One of the crew is good with knives. Let's shed a bit of light on this situation and see if we can ferret him out."

Four balls of pale blue light erupted from the crystal on the mage's staff and quickly spread out to the four corners of the boat, illuminating the deck with a pale, ghostly light.

Unlike torchlight, these orbs of light didn't flicker. The shadows created by them didn't flicker either, but neither did they reveal the presence of anyone. And then the shadows began to move.

The shadow of the mast began to twist and stretch into the shape of a giant serpent. The shadowy serpent stretched towards the rear of the deck, as if angry at the intruders for entering its territory.

"What in Hel's panties is that?" screamed one of the men, scrambling backwards. Most of the men moved back, pushing into each other. Even the wizard looked taken back.

"That's... that's not real," the elf sputtered, lowering his staff.

The giant shadow serpent suddenly darted to the starboard side, slithering towards the side of the ship. The men leaned over and watched the thing slither all the way to the deck and then over the deck and into the darkness.

"What just happened?" the dog-kin barked. "What was that?"

"It was just a..." the elf wizard started to say and then a dark patch of shadow appeared behind one of the men and yanked him over the starboard railing. There was a brief scream from the man, but it cut off with a gurgling choke just before a splash.

"It's the snake!" screamed one of the pirates, pushing further away from the starboard side.

"Ahh... ugh..." Another man disappeared from the port side with a scream and then went quiet just before there was a splash.

The pirates, shouting and mumbling in fear, backed into the center of the deck, facing outwards with weapons ready.

"It's pulling them into the water!"

"The snake is eating them!"

"It's a ghost snake!"

The panicked men pressed into their small circle, crushing the wizard in the middle until he finally growled and burst into flame. The men screamed and moved away from him, but still didn't approach the railings.

"Idiots!" roared the wizard, his entire form wreathed

in flame. The flames that cloaked him were referred to as elemental armor and it could appear as nearly any element—earth, fire, air, or water.

Some forms of elemental armor were better suited for certain situations. For instance, if you wanted to keep someone from touching you, fire armor was good. If you wanted something that acted as armor, then earth armor was a good choice. Water armor, in the form of ice, protected against fire and fireballs, while air armor made it nearly impossible for the person protected to be hit by arrows or thrown weapons.

The wizard stepped towards the railing and held his staff up. "If it is a warlock or channeler—or if it's an actual creature—my water elemental will find it and kill it!"

With a flash of blue light from the mage's staff, water began coming up over the railing and forming into a puddle in front of the elf. The puddle grew quickly until a shape began to take form as the water consolidated into what appeared to be a huge dolphin made completely of liquid.

"Go and find whatever is attacking us! Kill it..." the wizard ordered but gasped as the watery dolphin seemed to lose cohesion and collapsed back into a puddle that ran across the deck.

At the same time, the flames surrounding the wizard snuffed out and the blue-white glow coming from the crystal on his staff dimmed and went out completely. When that happened, the balls of light he'd conjured earlier winked out of existence, plunging the area into darkness.

A large splash sounded near the back of the boat and the pirates cried out in fear. The sudden disappearance of the light left most of them temporarily blind—their night vision completely gone.

The beast-kin and a few others who could see, watched a dark shape climb effortlessly onto the deck from the river. It seemed to flow over the railing and drop into a ball on the deck.

Backing away, the pirates whined and cried in fear, unsure what this dark entity was going to do or who it might kill.

The elven wizard seemed the most panicked. He stared wide-eyed at his staff, at the dull blue stone at the top, in fear and confusion. When the shape dropped down a few feet from him, the elf turned his head slowly towards the shape.

Before anyone could react, the shape darted forth and slammed into the elf. The small elf was lifted off his feet, a gurgle coming from his throat, as his staff dropped to the deck with a clatter. His arms and legs jerked for a moment before the shape let the wizard drop bonelessly to the ground.

"It ain't no monster!" cried one of the beast-kin, this one with the gray fur, long pointed nose, and worm-like tail of a mouse. A rat-kin. "It's just a man!"

Pulling his dagger out of the wizard's throat, Gage turned towards the men. He grinned wickedly at the remaining pirates. There were nine of them left—and half of them could barely see. Not bad odds.

He'd used his *Suppress Magic* ability on the area to

dispel the water elemental. It had also suppressed the wizard's magic, as well as his own Shadow powers. At the moment, he was just a normal man. Albeit, a highly trained and experienced, normal man.

Not wanting to give the pirates a chance to recover and organize, Gage let loose a blood curdling scream and launched into them.

In the first few seconds, he took down four of the pirates. One simply turned and jumped overboard but the remaining four began to react.

Gage side-stepped a clumsy thrust of a short sword and answered with a dagger to the chest. Two others, the rat-kin and the mangy dog-kin would have scored slices across his arm and his ribs but his *Uncanny Dodge* and *Improved Uncanny Dodge* kicked in and he avoided the blows completely.

Rat-kin stabs at you but you Uncanny Dodge.
Dog-kin stabs at you but you Improved Uncanny Dodge.

He managed to push the rat-kin in the way of a big burly man's club, hearing a crunching sound as it impacted the small beast-kin's head. But then felt a sting of pain as the last man's dagger sliced across his leg.

River Pirate slashes you for 8 damage.

Ducking down and spinning between the pirates, he brought the dagger in his left hand across the back of the large man's hamstring. Gage's dagger sliced through muscle and tendon and the pirate collapsed onto the deck, hands reaching for his ruined leg.

You critically slash River Pirate for 27 damage.
River pirate is hamstrung.

Continuing his spin, he came up behind the man with the short sword and his other dagger slipped between the man's ribs and into his heart. The pirate stiffened and then collapsed. Leaving only the dog-kin standing.

You critically stab River pirate for 31 damage.
River Pirate dies.
You gain experience.

Wide-eyed, the beast-kin stared at Gage, its long tongue hanging out of its mouth as it panted in fear.

Gage stood, staring back at the dog-kin. Maintaining eye contact with the beast-kin, he casually dropped to one knee and stabbed the burly, hamstrung man through the eye. The man's body jerked and then went still.

You critically stab River pirate for 32 damage.
River Pirate dies.
You gain experience.

The dog-man yelped and turned to run. Then his body stiffened as Gage's dagger thudded into the back of his neck. The dog-kin yelped and then collapsed to the deck, body twitching.

You critically stab River pirate for 37 damage.
River Pirate dies.
You gain experience.

Looking around to make sure there were no other survivors, Gage bent down and wiped his remaining dagger on a pirate's shirt. Then began searching the bodies.

CHAPTER 18

Four hours later, the ship was on its way to Eastport. But now it had thirty extra people milling around the deck.

Having overheard the men's talk of slaves, Gage knew that—with the wizard dead and most of the pirates dead—the remaining pirates had no chance of moving the slaves. They'd use them until they became tired of them, then kill them.

Despite his desire to get to Eastport as quickly as possible, he knew his late wife would want him to rescue them. Alani, the daughter of a merchant, had briefly been a slave when the House of Ra had suddenly declared a vendetta on House Cernunnos while she and her father had been conducting business in Waterford.

The two of them had been rounded up and sold into slavery, along with many other Cernunnosians. They'd been slaves for nearly a year before the political assassinations on both sides had finally caused them to call a truce.

Gage had been a big part of those House Ra assassinations. In fact, taking the guise of a returning slave was how he'd made his way back north into Cernunnosian territory. That was where he'd met Alani.

She was unlike anyone he'd met. She was the most positive person he'd known with a strong sense of inner peace. Even in the face of having been a slave for over a year, losing her father and even losing their trade business during their absence, she focused on helping others and overcoming her own conditions.

Alani had no idea what she was going to do when she returned or how she would make a living, but she never gave up. No matter the hardship, she not only kept her own spirits up, but went out of her way to keep others from succumbing to despair.

And while he'd been instantly attracted to her physically, it was her positive outlook and willingness to help others—even when she had nothing—that made her even more attractive. That level of positivity and kindness was something he had never seen on this world.

While he courted her in secret, away from the Fist and from House Cernunnos, he watched as she had set up a shelter for former slaves from the conflict—especially women. She'd given them food and shelter while they found jobs and got back on their feet.

The shelter had taken donations to keep it going and even after they'd been married, he'd never told her that he'd been the large anonymous donor that had nearly single handedly kept the shelter going.

Gage smiled sadly as he looked out at the slaves. Alani would have wanted to help every single one of them. Part of him wanted to help them, more in her memory than his own inherent kindness, but he'd done his part. He'd rescued them from the stockade and killed every single surviving pirate.

He frowned. They hadn't really been pirates. The slaves had been survivors of the latest caravan out of Blarney. The one that had left right after the festival. The men he'd killed had been nothing more than common bandits. They'd turned to piracy for no other reason than to obtain a ship to transport their "cargo" downriver.

"I don't suppose you're going to tell me how you did that?" the captain said, coming up to lean against the railing next to him. She glanced up at his eyes and shivered. "Or exactly what the hell you are."

Gage kept looking at the slaves and said nothing. He pulled the hood he'd acquired from one of the dead pirates lower. The less the newcomers could describe him, the better.

"You don't seem crazy enough to be a warlock," she said. Siany looked him over, checking out his hands, feet, and head. "You don't have any of the... ah... signs of a channeler."

The captain paused, giving him a chance to chime in. When he said nothing, she shrugged. "Fine, keep your secrets." The woman bit her lip and looked down at the deck. "Listen, I owe you."

"You don't owe me..." he started to reply but she held up her hand.

"This ship is all I have," she said, her voice breaking. "If they would have taken the profits, I would have lost her. You saved the ship. You saved me..."

Siany looked uncertain, a far cry from the confident woman he'd seen so far. She reached out and put a hand on his bicep. "Maybe I could, you know, show you my appreciation down in my cabin. I don't care what you are... you saved the *Riverbreeze*."

Gage looked down at the woman. She'd made herself vulnerable, making an offer like that. Then again, she was a strong, attractive woman. He doubted many men in their right minds would turn her down.

He shook his head. "That's not necessary."

"Maybe not," she said with a smile, her confidence seeming to come back. "But it would still be nice."

"It's not going to happen," he replied, a little harder than he had anticipated. He frowned at himself. He usually had better control of his emotions. It was just too soon after Alani's death. He couldn't even think of being with another woman.

"I'm sorry," the captain said, dropping her hand and taking a step back. "I just thought that..."

"It's not you," Gage interrupted. He grimaced, hating to give away any more information, but also not wanting to alienate the captain. "I... I lost someone recently. Someone very close to me. It's just... too soon."

Siany bit her lip but then nodded. She leaned back against the railing again. "That whole story you told me before about being a merchant was nothing but fish guts, wasn't it?"

He nodded but said nothing.

The captain's eyes flicked towards him and then back at the former slaves. "Whatever happened, it wasn't an accident, right?"

Gage glanced over at the captain, eyes narrowed. "What makes you say that?"

"Before, you were... I don't know... playacting? You're good. I bought it. We all did," she said, furrowing her brow. She glanced over at him, briefly meeting his eyes before looking away. "But now you're not playacting. I think... I think this is the real you."

"And?"

She bit her lip again. "You look like... you look like a dangerous man. A man who wants to do violence."

"How do you know that this isn't my warlock persona?" he asked.

Gage had told the captain to spread the word that he was actually a warlock and had used his magic to kill the pirates. Warlocks were feared because of their unpredictability and their tendency to talk to things that normal people couldn't see.

Siany shrugged. "Maybe it is a persona. But I get the feeling it's really you."

He'd dropped the Peadrus role once he'd revealed himself. He hadn't really taken the time to figure out the new warlock persona. With no persona to wear, he'd inadvertently reverted back to himself.

Once his thoughts had turned to Alani, he realized he'd made a mistake. Gage had let too much of himself show through. He was rusty. He needed to be more careful.

He took a deep breath, held it, then let it out. Gage relaxed his face, putting on a crazy-eyed expression and relaxing his posture. He twitched his eyes slightly, giving him the look of someone who appeared to be a few eggs shy of a full basket.

The captain rolled her eyes and winked. "Fine. Be that way. But the offer is still open—crazy eyes or not."

"The less you know about me and the less you're around me," he told her. "The safer you are. Make sure your men stick to the story."

"Right, crazy warlock," she sighed. "Half of them believe you really are some warlock—or some dark wizard. The other half think you're a..." The captain lowered her voice and made a warding sign, "Shadowed Fist come to kill them all."

Gage purposefully didn't react to the woman's statement. But he was surprised that the men had come to that assumption. Or was he?

The Fist had cultivated an image of mysterious killers who could do the impossible. In fact, Gage himself had helped to reinforce that image not too long ago. Should it be any surprise that the men would think that he was some legendary killer from a shadowy organization after he'd single-handedly dealt with over a dozen pirates and a wizard.

He gave Siany a hard look. "It's important that your crew tell no one about me. Very important."

"Will someone come looking for you?" she asked, eyebrows piqued.

"If they tell the story," he said, "people may show up— bad people—and torture every single one of you to get information about me."

The captain gawked at him, her eyes roving his body once more. "Who are you?"

"I'm no one," he told her. "I was never here."

"I'll keep the men on the boat while we're in Eastport,"

she said. "But there's the slaves you rescued. There will be questions."

"If anyone asks," he told her. "You fought off the pirates, one tried to trade information about the slaves for his life and you rescued them."

"But the slaves..." she started.

He shook his head. "I made a point of telling them that I was leading them back to the ship while the rest of you hunted down the remaining pirates. They certainly wouldn't believe one man could take out the eight pirates that guarded them."

"So, no credit and no reward for rescuing them?" she asked.

"It's all yours," he replied. "You're the captain."

"You're a frustrating man," she told him, though her tone had a playful edge to it. "Has anyone ever told you that?"

Gage thought back to Alani and some of their conversations. She told him the same thing. He smiled sadly. "All the time."

CHAPTER 19

Gage spent the remainder of the voyage avoiding the others. It wasn't difficult to do. Once he adopted the persona of Peadrus the warlock, even the slaves he'd rescued gave him a wide berth.

During the last few years in House Cernunnos, as the wizard blood had thinned, he'd been exposed to more and more warlocks. He'd had no choice; since the Houses' power was based on having enough magic to stay in control, they'd turned to making pacts with demons to give them power. They'd become warlocks, channelers and summoners.

He used his experience with warlocks to create his new persona. Like the warlocks he'd been around, he mumbled loudly to himself and occasionally yelled things out as if he were having an argument with an unseen person.

Real warlocks claimed they were talking to their "patron" demon—and that the demon was talking back to them. Whether they were talking to a demon or the power had caused them to go crazy and they were talking to themselves, people tended to avoid them. That fact worked to his benefit in this case.

At this point, he was certain even the crew had bought into his warlock persona. All except for Siany. She knew the truth. Or rather, she knew he wasn't a warlock. He was certain she had no idea what he really was. No one truly knew what he really was. Perhaps not even him.

Bringing up his display, Gage looked at his classes.

Class: Rogue 5 / Assassin 5 / Witch Hunter 5 / Shadowmaster 5

His *Rogue* class was common. Gage had seen many people with it by examining them in his display. People with the *Assassin* class were rare outside the Fist, but he'd seen quite a few of them in his career. Several dozen, at least.

Witch Hunter was rarer. Much rarer. He'd only met one other in his lifetime, his mentor, Aeg Derg. The man was a higher-level *Witch Hunter* than Gage. A high-level assassin, too. But he didn't have Gage's final class—*Shadowmaster*.

He had never really been certain why he'd suddenly gotten the choice for the *Shadowmaster*. Gage had gained level 15 and there it was, one of the options. The description had sounded interesting and seemed to lend itself to his line of work.

Shadowmaster

Your love and use of shadows and darkness has given you the unique ability to manipulate shadows,

become a shadow yourself, and even travel through the realm of shadow.

Given the nature of his work as an assassin at the time, it had sounded like a perfect synergy with his other abilities. Little had he known how right he would be. The class granted him a form of magic—something he'd never had before.

He hadn't told anyone, not even Aeg Derg, about the shadow abilities. If Gage had learned one thing since being brought to this world, it was not to give away all your secrets. Not to anyone.

Frowning, he thought of Alani. She knew his secrets. The ones that mattered. Maybe not every person he'd ever killed, but she knew what he was and his abilities. She knew his fears.

Gage didn't have many fears. Being abducted and cast into a strange world, having to carve out a living on the streets, and becoming an assassin had purged him of most fears. He didn't even fear death any longer.

His biggest fear before meeting Alani was that his *Shadowmaster* class really was some form of warlock—and at some point, he'd go mad, just like they did. It was a big fear of his. He didn't want to go crazy. When he died, he wanted to die as himself—as Gage.

Alani hadn't believed he was any sort of warlock. She hadn't believed his powers came from demons. She hadn't known where his powers came from, but she thought he had too good a heart for them to come from demons.

And he'd believed her. Mostly.

There had always been that nagging doubt in the back of his mind that one day he'd start hearing demons. But the more time he'd spent with Alani—and then his daughter—the less he'd thought about it.

But now his wife was gone. Her and Shaunna both. Ripped from him for some reason he didn't understand.

Gage's frown turned into a scowl. He would find out why. He would find out who. And they would pay. Of that he was certain. It didn't matter who it was. If there was one thing he'd learned during his time as a Master of Assassins for House Cernunnos, it was that no one was untouchable.

Siany approached him at his normal spot at the back of the ship. As she'd done several times in the last few days, the captain walked to his side and turned to lean against the railing. She didn't look up at him, but stared out at the crew and former slaves scattered around the deck.

"We're only a few hours or so away," she said, shielding her eyes from the twin suns.

"I know," he replied quietly. He'd recognized some of the villages they'd passed and had been mentally ticking down the time to arrival.

"Been to Eastport before, I take it?" she asked, her head tilting slightly towards him.

Gage said nothing. The less she knew, the safer they both were. It hadn't been an idle warning he'd given the captain earlier. If the Shadowed Fist thought she knew something about their dead assassins or him, they'd torture every last morsel of information from her.

He didn't want that to happen. Gage liked the captain. She was strong, like Alani had been. In the end, she had been ready to turn over her boat, rather than risk her crew. It was something his wife would have done.

The personas he had adopted weren't just for his own safety. Sure, he needed the element of surprise if he had any hope of infiltrating the Fist. But he also didn't want the death or torture of any innocents on his conscience.

"Remember what I told you." His eyes flicked towards her. "If anyone asks about me, I was just some crazy warlock who killed a bunch of pirates."

The captain sighed. "Is that really how you want to be known? I mean, you saved those people. I'm sure some of them would be willing to give you some sort of reward."

"I don't need a reward," he replied softly.

Siany turned towards him then, looking into the shadows of his hood. "What do you need?"

Gage stayed quiet. The answer was: Revenge! He needed to find the person who ordered his death and watch the life drain from their eyes.

He couldn't tell her that—he couldn't tell anyone that. That knowledge alone might be enough to doom them both. It might be enough for the Fist to know he was coming. Enough that they'd kill the person they'd learned it from, just for knowing. Gage wouldn't risk that. He couldn't risk that.

The captain let out an exasperated breath and leaned back against the railing again. "Fine, keep your secrets."

"It's better that way," he told her.

"Better for who?" she asked.

"For everyone," he replied.

Gage caught a glance of her biting her lip out of the corner of his eye. Her brow was furrowed and several emotions played across her face.

"Was there something else?" he asked.

Siany started and looked up at him. She frowned. The captain hesitated, as if searching for the right words. After a moment, she glanced around to make sure no one else was near. When she spoke, it was barely louder than a whisper. "Are you a warlock?"

He turned his head slightly towards her. "It doesn't matter if I am or if I'm not. If anyone asks, you tell them I was."

"Is that what you'll tell the harbormaster?" she asked, eyebrow raised.

Once again, Gage said nothing. The truth was, he would use his *Shadow Slide* ability to get off the ship before they reached the docks. It was harder during the day, but there was always darkness—even in the day. And despite the ability's name, he didn't need actual shadows. The ability only needed darkness at the start and stop of his *Slide*.

She sighed. "You're not planning to talk with the harbormaster, are you? Are you going to jump overboard?" She held up her hands. "No, don't tell me. I don't want to know."

He nodded. "It's best that way."

"So you keep telling me," she replied snarkily.

"It's the truth," he replied simply. And it was. But the less she and her crew knew, the better.

She rolled her eyes. "Fine. I'm going to make preparations."

The captain started to go and then stopped. She spun around. "Will I see you again before you... do whatever you're going to do?"

Gage said nothing and after a moment, she moved in.

Leaning up, she kissed him lightly on the lips and then backed away. "If I don't see you, thanks for what you did back there."

She waited for a response, but he stayed quiet. After a minute, she sighed. Turning, she strode away and began barking orders to her men.

CHAPTER 20

As the next few hours flew by, forest became farmland, farmland became villages, and villages became a city. The closer they moved towards Eastport, the more abundant the signs of civilization became. Gage stared at the moving landscape with detachment, his mind already working on plans to infiltrate the Fist.

He did pause plotting briefly as the spires of Eastport came into view. Gage knew those spires belonged to House Cernunnos. More specifically, the spires belonged to the House Keep, a huge castle that was the seat of House Cernunnos's power.

Seeing them, Gage felt a sense of nostalgia. It had been years since he'd been in the Keep. That had been his "home" when he was the House's master of assassins. It felt like a lifetime ago now.

Gage scowled as he thought about his old life and wished it was still behind him. His scowl deepened at the reminder of the circumstances bringing him back to Eastport.

Vengeance drew him back, pure and simple. Gage would find the person who ordered his death—the one responsible for the murder of his wife and daughter. Once he found them, he would kill them. Slowly. Very slowly. And painfully.

The spires loomed closer, and Gage gathered his belongings into the backpack he'd taken from the dead assassins. He shrugged the backpack onto his shoulder. Glancing around to make sure no one else was looking, he moved to the port side of the boat.

The suns were high in the sky, leaving few shadows across the deck. For now.

As if on cue, the river went around a bend, and the *Riverbreeze* came about, the city wall rising to either side of them. The city folk called this portion the Riverwall. At only twenty feet tall, it was shorter than the main wall that encircled Eastport. It was still tall enough to prevent any sort of river invasion.

The stone of the walls was worn, having been built hundreds of years ago. Along the river side, mold and vegetation grew lush, giving them a slimy green coating. Rumor was that they'd tried to keep them clean when the wall was first built but had given up and let the vegetation take hold.

The boat floated between the two walls, and a long shadow dragged across the *Riverbreeze's* deck. Gage smiled. It was what he'd been waiting for. Scanning the walls, he looked for an equally shadowed area at the top.

He found one just west of the towers that dotted the

wall every fifty feet. He glanced around to make sure no one saw. His eyes found Siany, at the wheel of the ship, barking orders to her crew. He liked the captain. He hoped the Fist didn't come asking questions.

Pushing those thoughts out of his mind, he waited until she looked away. He scanned the shadow of the tower and picked his spot. Gage activated *Shadow Slide* and instantly appeared on the wall.

A surprised guard yelped but Gage toggled on his *Shadow Blend* ability, making him effectively invisible as long as he remained in the shadows.

Gage brought up his display so he could monitor his stats.

Mana: 34

While *Shadow Slide* used a fixed amount of *Mana*, *Shadow Blend* continued to drain mana while active. The more light there was, the more it cost. It was an ability suited for the night—not for broad daylight.

Left on, the ability would continue to drain his Mana. If he didn't keep an eye on his stats, it could drain him completely dry. When that happened, he'd fall unconscious. In most situations, that would mean capture— probably death.

The guard, a young man with barely any chin whiskers, stared into the area where he'd just seen Gage. The man was still wide-eyed with shock and fear. The young man blinked and stared into the spot where he'd seen someone just a moment before.

Mana: 33

Eyes darting left and right, the young guard seemed to realize he still held a halberd and slowly began to bring it down but then stopped. He craned his neck, looking where Gage was squatting. The guard bit his lip and then glanced left and right, possibly seeing if any of the other guards had seen him react to nothing.

The young man laughed nervously. Straightening, he leaned his halberd back against his shoulder, turned, and continued his walk along the wall to the next tower.

Mana: 32

Gage watched him go, waiting until the guard was a dozen paces away before moving to the opposite side of the wall. Glancing down into the city, he spotted a shadowed alley and *Slid* into it.

As soon as he appeared in the alleyway, he moved behind a pile of broken crates. He looked up and down the alley to make sure no one was looking and then toggled off *Shadow Blend*. He felt the draw on his Mana disappear and glanced at his stats again.

Mana: 25

His Mana sat just over half, but it would regenerate. He shouldn't need to use his shadow abilities now that he was in the city. He'd been a Rogue, then an Assassin, long before he was a Shadow Master. He knew how to blend into cities.

He mentally re-adopted the merchant persona. The only difference was, Gage wouldn't use the name Peadrus—not in Eastport. This was the home of the Shadowed Fist and Peadrus had been the name of one of the assassins. He had no idea whether the name had been real or not, but even an alias might be known.

Gage used the name on the boat in an effort to plant a bit of confusion. If someone from the Fist questioned anyone from the *Riverbreeze*, they would find out that someone calling himself Peadrus had been aboard. They might assume the assassin was still alive, possibly the sole survivor, and would be reporting in. That might just give him the time he needed.

After mentally going through several options, Gage decided to go with the name Robart. It had been the name of Alani's father. It was a name that no one from the guild would associate with him.

Robart the merchant, recently returned via caravan from Jublin via Daleford. Since he didn't know exactly when the last caravan from the north had come through, he needed an excuse in case questioned. He quickly decided that Robart had a drinking problem and drank his profits away at a tavern over the last few nights.

Nodding to himself at his new persona, Gage walked out of the alley. He changed his gait and his posture, adopting the shuffle of someone recovering from a hangover. He would even occasionally let out a moan of pain and rub his forehead. To the casual observer, he would appear as just another random drunk.

He joined the crowd moving along the main street the alley intersected. This area was known as the Northern

Slums, an area controlled by the Brassy Gentlemen. At least, the Gentlemen had run the district when he'd left Eastport. It was possible one of the other thieves' guilds had taken over.

The Gentlemen was one of the three thieves' guilds that operated in Eastport. Barely a gang, they were more thugs than thieves, running protection rackets, prostitution rings, and dealing in drugs. They were tough but not subtle.

As he headed south towards Tradetown, Gage kept a sharp eye out for the tell-tale signs of the Brassy Gentlemen—a red bloody dagger over a black circle. It wasn't hard to spot.

Gage spotted the symbol carved into the sides of some of the businesses and houses he passed. Most likely, those buildings were under the "protection" of the Gentlemen. In other words, they paid the guild to protect them—from the guild.

He also spotted the Gentlemen's sign tattooed on the wrists, hands, and arms of tough looking men. The men were dirty and poorly dressed, the very opposite of the true gentlemen from which their guild name was derived.

After passing a small group of the guild members, Gage caught a glimpse of them from the corner of his eye. They had fallen in step behind him. He sighed to himself. The men had obviously decided that his persona of a merchant recovering from a hangover was an easy mark.

He pretended to stumble and as he did, he saw that the men already had weapons in their hands. They planned to either beat him senseless or kill him and rob him. That was their bad luck. While he did his best to keep innocents out of any House conflicts, he had no problem dealing with those who marked themselves as predators.

Gage recovered from his fake stumble and then ducked into an alleyway to his left. It was time to show these petty thugs who the real predator was.

CHAPTER 21

The shadowed alley provided a perfect environment for his abilities, but Gage only wanted to teach these men a lesson, not kill them. If he revealed his powers, word would spread and could get back to the Fist. No. He'd deal with these men without his Shadowmaster powers.

Once again pretending to stumble, Gage deliberately moved to his left as he heard the footfalls of the men enter the alleyway.

"Ey! You there!" one of them cried out, gesturing at Gage with a small club.

Gage turned to the men, swaying slightly to maintain the illusion that he was not quite sober. As he caught sight of the men, he scanned them with his display.

Abatt

Human

Brigand

Level 2

Costerro
Human
Brigand
Level 3

Risteard
Ratling
Rogue
Level 2

Mairead
Human
Brigand
Level 2

Getting a better look at the four of them, he noted one was a ratling. Unsurprisingly, he was the shortest of the group, his furred body and rat-like face hidden by a cloak and hood. Of the group, he would be the fastest. Ratlings were naturally more agile than humans.

Another of the brigands, who he'd mistaken for a teen with a young face, Gage could now see was a woman, her small breasts giving her away. She bore knife scars on her face. They looked too deliberate to be accidental or the results of fights. He guessed someone had cut her face as some sort of payback, or perhaps a lesson. But what sort of lesson?

The other two were both men and were parodies of each other. One, Abatt, was taller and extremely slender.

The other man, Costerro, was shorter and stockier, almost overweight. Despite being almost comical opposites of each other, Abatt and Costerro each carried daggers and appeared to know how to use them.

"Hey, Abatt," the short man sneered. "What do we got here?"

"Looks like someone who hasn't paid taxes," the taller man responded in a deadpan tone.

The woman and the ratling moved around to either side of Abatt and Costerro. They sidled along either wall of the alley in an attempt to circle around Gage. It seemed a practiced move, probably something they'd done many times. Both carried clubs.

"Tasses?" Gage slurred, keeping up his drunken persona. "Wah tasses?"

"This here is our neighborhood," Costerro replied with a snake-like smile. "And you have to pay a tax if you want to walk through it."

Gage swayed a bit, keeping a wary eye on the two brigands working their way to either side of him. He pulled his money pouch from inside his shirt and shook it. "How mush is tasses?"

Abatt licked his lips and flashed a grin at Costerro. The shorter man grinned too.

"What you have in your hand should cover it," Costerro replied, gesturing at the pouch with his left hand. His right hand remained down at his side, still holding the dagger ready. He paused and cocked his head. "Unless you have more?"

Shaking his head in an exaggerated fashion, Gage waved his hands in the air. "Dis is alls I gots."

He could see all four of the brigand's eyes following the money pouch as he waved it around in his arms. No doubt they thought they were in for a quick score. Easy money. Or so they thought.

Abatt smirked. "I'm not sure if we can just take his word for it. We should search him, just to be sure."

"Yeah, I think you're right, Abatt." Costerro's smile turned wicked. He made a slight nod with his head as he brought his dagger up. At the same time, Abatt brought his own knife up.

In what appeared to be a practiced move, both the woman and the ratling stepped behind him and moved in. They raised their clubs, moving in to try and bludgeon him unconscious.

Gage dropped the money pouch and it hit the cobbled alley floor with the sound of clinking coins. Almost as one, the brigands looked down at the money pouch. That's when he struck.

The ratling was coming from his right and Gage spun and grabbed the creature's furry right wrist—the one holding the club. He used his other hand to come up behind the ratling's neck. He used his own momentum, and that of the ratling, to shove him into the woman.

As the two became entangled, he twisted the ratling's wrist and caused it to squeal in pain. Snatching the club from its trapped hand, Gage brought the club down on the back of the ratling's head.

You critically crush Risteard for 26 damage.
You have performed a Sapping Blow.
Risteard is unconscious.

Sapping Blow was an ability he'd acquired early in his career as a rogue. With it, he was able to render his opponent unconscious. Since he didn't want to kill these brigands, it was a good alternative.

The ratling's body went limp and dropped to the floor. Mairead, the female brigand, was forced to step back or be pulled down with the ratling. As she did, Gage stepped with her. Closing in, he trapped her club with his right hand and brought his own club up with his left hand. He slammed the club into the base of her jaw, lifting her off her feet and throwing her several feet back.

You critically crush Mairead for 21 damage.
You have performed a Sapping Blow.
Mairead is unconscious.

The scarred woman thudded into the alley wall and her club dropped from useless fingers. She slid down the wall into an unmoving heap on the cobblestones.

Gage spun around to face Abatt and Costerro. The two men had started forward but now backed away a bit, cowed by the bodies of their fallen comrade. Both men's eyes widened. They'd expected an easy mark and now it was down to just the two of them.

Before the men recovered, Gage darted forward. He aimed himself at Abatt, the taller man, who brought his knife up defensively.

Side-stepping the knife, Gage brought his club down on the man's thin wrist. With a crunch, Abatt's knife dropped from his fingers and he grasped his broken wrist with his other hand.

You crush Abatt for 6 damage.

Before the man could even utter a curse, Gage spun around him. Using his momentum, he brought the club across the back of Abatt's skull.

You critically crush Abatt for 23 damage.
You have performed a sapping blow.
Abatt is unconscious.

The skinny man dropped to the cobblestones like a sack, unconscious but alive. That left only one more brigand.

"Abatt!" Costerro yelled and rushed at Gage.

Gage waited until the man was committed, Costerro's clumsy thrust heading towards his chest. At the last moment, he side-stepped the blade and struck out with the club at Costerro's head.

You crush Costerro for 6 damage.

Costerro stumbled. He'd expected to meet resistance when his knife found its mark in Gage's chest. The lack of any target and the sudden blow to his head, sent the larger man off balance and crashing into the wall.

Moving in quickly to close the gap, Gage grabbed Abatt's fallen dagger.

Moving sluggishly, Costerro spun and tried to bring up his dagger.

Gage slammed the club down on the man's wrist once,

then twice, before Costerro's knife fell from his numb fingers.

You crush Costerro for 7 damage.
You crush Costerro for 6 damage.

Before the brigand could reach down to pick up his dagger, Gage had closed in and had his dagger up to the man's throat. He smiled at the man—the smile of a true predator. "We need to talk, you and I."

Costerro swallowed, the action causing a red line of blood to form where his throat met the dagger's edge. "What... what you want to know?"

CHAPTER 22

His conversation with Costerro didn't last long. Gage confirmed his suspicions. All three thieves' guilds were still in operation and, for the most part, their holdings hadn't changed.

One thing that did surprise him was the fact that Costerro had mentioned that the guilds were recruiting mages—warlocks, channelers and even summoners.

When Gage had left, the Houses had been replenishing their ranks with non-wizards, but they were still rare and only allowed in the Houses. To find they were now becoming so common that thieves' guilds were recruiting them was disconcerting. He didn't trust people who made pacts with demons.

Gage pushed the thoughts of demons and warlocks out of his mind and continued towards his destination. It took him nearly an hour to make his way to the North Bridge. Crossing the bridge, he went south through the Docks

District, then continued to the merchant district known as Tradetown.

The merchant district hadn't changed much since Gage had last been in it. A few shops, taverns, and inns had changed names—one or two that he remembered had closed and were boarded up.

The smells of livestock, cooking food, leather and weapon oil coupled with the bright colors of silks and dyed armor to assault his senses as he entered the main street. In addition, vendors lined the streets with small, portable booths, their goods displayed. They called out to passersby who mostly ignored them.

"Meat on a stick!"

"Armor! Weapons!"

"Best leather goods you can find in Eastport!"

"Warm honey rolls!"

Deftly avoiding the sellers and merchants vying for his attention, Gage made his way further south, into the heart of Tradetown—the Bizarre. The Bizarre, as it had come to be called, was a huge market in the center of the merchant district.

It had started out as only a single empty lot at the intersection of two main roads but had grown over the years to encompass ten square blocks. It was now the home of hundreds of merchants from up and down the coast. One could buy nearly anything there, especially the strange, unusual, and exotic.

Gage entered the massive collection of booths, tents and stands. He knew the cutpurses and pickpockets would be out in force. The throng of people in the Bizarre provided a tempting target, and it was neutral ground for the three thieves' guilds.

When he'd lived in the city, the guilds went to war over the lucrative area from time to time. It was usually short lived before the town guard stepped in. While the guard may look the other way for certain vices and ignore the petty theft, they acted when taxes were at risk.

Keeping a careful eye out as he moved between the booths, Gage spotted pickpockets with the tattoos of the Brassy Gentlemen. He also caught a few pickpockets and cutpurses with the red sashes of the Crimson Brotherhood. Then there were the dark hoods of the Ravens.

Thanks to his conversation with Costerro, Gage knew the Crimson Brotherhood controlled most southwest Eastport, including the Dairy Quarter, also called the Blood District. More importantly, they controlled the Docks. They had their hands in the loading and unloading of every ship that made port in the city. The Brotherhood also had control of the slaughterhouses in the Dairy District.

The Ravens, on the other hand, mostly stuck to the east side. They operated more like the type of thieves' guild he'd been a member of in Daleford. They specialized in larger, specialized jobs in the Gold district and the Gardens, or noble district. The jobs were riskier, but also more rewarding.

Gage pushed the nostalgic thoughts from his head and focused on his task. He needed items. Specific items. One did not simply infiltrate the Shadowed Fist guild hall unprepared. Or rather, one didn't infiltrate the Shadowed fist unprepared and expect to leave alive.

And he wasn't ready to die yet. He had work to do, and someone to kill. That meant Gage needed to be prepared. As much as he could, he needed to stack the odds in his favor.

Going from booth to booth and merchant to merchant, Gage slowly found the items he needed. He haggled as much as he could, but in the end, he was no match for the bargaining skills of an experienced merchant. He was certain he'd paid more than he could have. So be it.

He managed to purchase the items he needed—all except one. The one thing he couldn't find was Cichiadamon, sometimes referred to as Bitter Petal. Then again, he hadn't really expected to find it in the Bizarre.

Bitter Petal was a rare herb that came from the southern deserts and had unique properties. The plant's leaves were extremely bitter. Even a tiny bit was enough to ruin an entire pot of stew. Only the most skilled chefs could hope to make a meal that brought out the herb's unique flavors while not causing the dish to be too acerbic. Most people had no use for it, so there was no demand. That meant, no supply either.

Unfortunately, Cichiadamon was the main ingredient for a special type of poison that he'd learned to make from Aeg Derg, as part of his Witch Hunter training. While not exactly like his Shadowmaster ability, *Suppress Magic*, the poison had a similar result.

Draiocht-neim, sometimes called Wizard's Folly, would drain a person's *Mana* almost instantly. It also prevented them from regenerating *Mana* until it wore off.

It was very useful against mages, since without Mana, they couldn't cast spells.

Few people knew of mana draining poisons. The great Houses kept it that way. Their control of the masses was built upon their use of magic. If it became common knowledge that there was a way to rob the ruling class of their power, there might be a general rebellion. The Houses weren't about to risk an uprising.

Having worked as the master of assassins for Cernunnos, Gage knew that the patriarch of the House, Archmage Ruy Cernunnos, was aware of draiocht-neim. In fact, the Archmage had a small section of Cichiadamon growing in the garden on his estate.

Ruy's estate was not in the House Keep. The Keep would be nearly as difficult to get into as the Fist guildhall. No, the Archmage's estate was in the Gardens—the noble district. There were a few city guards and some estate guards, but they wouldn't be a problem.

Gage would go tonight, sneak onto Ruy's estate and get some of the Bitter Petal. He'd use that along with the other herbs he'd bought to make the draiocht-neim. Once it was brewed, he'd infiltrate the Fist and find out who had ordered his death.

Unfortunately, a midnight herb heist from the Archmage's estate pushed his timetable back. By the time he retrieved the Cichiadamon and brewed the poison, it would be morning. Daylight meant his Shadow Master abilities would cost more and he'd be able to use them less.

He growled in frustration. Gage couldn't afford to break into one of the most dangerous places in the city with less-than-ideal circumstances. He would need to wait until tomorrow night. He cursed silently but there was nothing to be done about it.

There had been a time when he wouldn't have needed the mage toxin. A time when there were no wizards in the Fist, and certainly not any warlocks or channelers. But times had changed. The three assassins who had come after him had all been channelers. He had to assume there would be more in the guild itself.

His decision made, Gage headed east to Riverwalk. The district bordered the west bank. More upscale than the merchant district, and therefore more costly, River-walk lay closer to the Pearl Bridge—the only Bridge that led across to the Gardens.

Gage pushed through the late afternoon crowd and went to the eastmost part of the Riverwalk—the part that bordered the river itself. He purposefully chose an inn he'd never frequented before. There was no use in taking a chance that someone might recognize him from the old days.

He settled on a three-story inn called the Rainbow Trout. It was one of the few inns allowing Gage a good view of the Pearl Bridge and part of the Gardens. He could watch the guards' routines before venturing out to relieve the Archmage of his Bitter Petal.

The Rainbow Trout charged 5 gold Staters a night for a room. After paying for two nights in advance, he was left with only 2 gold and a handful of silver. If he couldn't get the information in the next two days, he'd either have to move to a more affordable inn or figure out a way to make more money.

But that was a problem for another day. At the moment, he needed to get everything prepped before dark, then do some reconnaissance of the Gardens once night had fallen. His Shadow Master abilities were powerful, but they weren't infallible. It was always better to be prepared.

After paying the innkeeper, Gage went up two flights of stairs to room seven on the third floor. Once he was safely in his room on the third story, Gage unpacked the items he had bought and began setting up a makeshift alchemy lab.

Gage couldn't start brewing the draiocht-neim until he had the Bitter Petal, but there were a few alchemical substances he could make before sundown. Substances that would be extremely useful tonight.

CHAPTER 23

Gage crouched just outside the wall of the Cernunnos estate, hidden in shadows. The gigantic planet this world orbited, as well as several moons, cast a dim illumination. It wasn't enough for the average human to see well, but there were more than just humans on this world.

Turning, he looked down the hill at the rest of the sprawling city. This side of Eastport was on a slope. It steadily rose at an angle until terminating abruptly in a two-hundred-foot cliff. With a cliff on the ocean side and the inner wall on the river side, the inner city was very secure. Unless you were Gage.

He'd used his *Shadow Slide* ability to slide to the top of the river wall, then over it, and into the eastern part of the city. From there, he'd kept to the shadows until he'd made it to the Cernunnos estate.

Now, as he surveyed the estate, he was glad he'd taken the time to prepare. As he'd anticipated, the estate guard consisted of at least a dozen beast-kin. Dog-, wolf-, and jackal-kin to be precise. With their superior sense of smell, any unfamiliar scents would be picked up immediately.

Rubbing his fingers together, Gage felt the greasy remnants of the atalydd-arogl, or Dog's Bane, on his hands. A special blend of herbs, flowers, fruit, and charcoal, the alchemical mixture would suppress his own scent for a time. Effectively, it made him invisible to scent.

It was the same substance he'd used on himself and his daughter when they'd been out to look at the deer. The memory was bittersweet, knowing he'd never get to see her again. He pushed the thought away and focused on his task.

Earlier, he'd stolen a cloak from an off-duty estate guard and wore it now. Combined with the Dog's Bane, he hoped any scent the beast-kin might smell would be the familiar scent of the guard. With any luck, he hoped his presence would go completely unnoticed.

He shivered in the cool night air. Looking down at himself, he shook his head. He was completely naked except for the guard's cloak and a loincloth he'd fashioned from a piece of the cloak's lining. He didn't even have shoes.

Gage also didn't have any weapons. In fact, the only thing he did have was a small bundle in his arms that was made from a large piece of the cloak he'd stolen. The bundle shifted in his arms occasionally, but he kept a firm but gentle hold of it.

While the Dog's Bane would work on his skin to suppress his scent. It could also be used on clothing, but he didn't want to waste it. Not when he didn't have money to buy more ingredients. He looked down at himself. It wasn't the first time he'd done a job almost naked. So, mostly naked, he watched the guards go by and memorized their routines. Just like old times.

He was taking a chance with the cloak, but it was a calculated risk. Theoretically, if the beast-kin were keen enough to realize that the scent of the off-duty guard shouldn't be there, he might have a problem. But in his experience, it was unfamiliar smells that attracted their attention, not out-of-place familiar smells.

If they did notice the off-duty presence, he counted on the familiar scent to spur the beast-kin to investigate first and not immediately raise the alarm. That would give Gage the option of dealing with the beast-kin quietly.

The courtyard guards passed by about thirty feet inside the wall. With his *Shadow Sight*, he could see that just like the last time, there were three guards—two humans and a wolf-kin.

Despite the beast-kin not needing it, all three guards carried torches. They passed his position without showing any indication they either saw or smelled him. As they went by, Gage started a mental countdown.

Gage had ten minutes before the group completed their circuit. He wanted to be out of the estate before they made it back around. If not, he'd have to wait until they passed before trying to jump out.

Having already picked his spot, he activated *Shadow Slide*. The landscape shifted around, and Gage appeared thirty feet inside the estate fence. Glancing slowly around him, he double-checked no one else was around.

He paused and looked further into the courtyard. He'd spotted two roving patrols before—an outer patrol and an inner patrol. Currently, he was between the two. The garden with the Cichiadamon grew next to the house. Once he got past the inner patrol, he would be free to make his way to the garden.

Gage counted down in his mind. As he reached three, two, one, the inner patrol came around the corner of the estate maintaining a distance of about fifty yards from the house, walking along a stone path through the statues and hedges.

This group of guards had two beast-kins, a dog-kin and a jackal-kin. Like the other group, all three of them carried torches. With the light from the torches and the fact that they would pass within ten feet of him, Gage was forced to use his *Shadow Blend*. He couldn't take the chance that one of them would see him.

He held his breath as they passed, keeping still despite being wrapped in shadows. They passed him and Gage started to relax. Then, the jackal-kin slowed.

The beast-kin raised his head and sniffed the air, turning one way, then the other. The remaining patrol members slowed as well. The dog-kin began sniffing the air as well.

"You smell something?" the human asked.

"I... I thought... I thought I smelled someone," said the jackal-kin, shaking his head. "But it's nothing."

The dog-kin stopped sniffing and shrugged, then the patrol moved on. They continued their circuit around the estate and disappeared around the corner.

Gage waited until they were completely out of sight

before breathing a sigh of relief. He picked his spot in a section of statues near the estate and activated *Shadow Slide*. Once more, the world blurred around him, and he was suddenly next to a statue of a robed man in a very heroic pose.

Gage dropped *Shadow Blend*, first making sure he hadn't missed any guards. Even at night, it constantly consumed Mana. He needed to be judicious with his Mana in case he needed a rapid escape.

Gage crept from statue to statue until he reached the Archmage's garden near the house. Mixed in with the roses and other flowers a small section of herbs sprouted. Among the herbs, was the Bitter Petal.

He slipped silently into the garden area. Unlike the rest of the estate, which was carpeted in thick, well-kept grass, the garden was rich soil. As Gage stepped into the garden, he felt his foot sink slightly. He cursed. He was leaving tracks.

He used his free hand to grab a handful of his tattered cloak. With each step he took in the cool, moist earth, he brushed the dirt with his cloak and smoothed out his tracks. He wanted no evidence of his passing at all.

Moving more slowly than anticipated, he made his way to the area where he knew the Cichiadamon grew. With his *Shadow Sight*, he easily picked out the large leaves of the plant and plucked a dozen of them.

No sooner had he gotten the twelfth leaf when he heard voices coming closer. Cursing, he crouched lower and used *Shadow Blend*. Hidden, he turned his head and cursed again as he saw the inner patrol walking his way.

"I tell you," the dog-kin said. "I saw something move."

"Are you sure?" the human asked, waving his torch one way, then the other. "We're off our patrol route and you know how the sergeant gets."

"I saw something," the dog-kin repeated.

The group walked closer and although Gage was practically invisible, the closer the beast-kin came to him, the more likely they were to catch a whiff of his true scent. It was time for his backup plan.

Setting the bundle in his arms on the ground, he unwrapped it. Slapping it on the butt, he watched as the rabbit hopped away, directly towards the guards. It stopped about fifteen feet from them and abruptly changed directions and darted off to the side. It ran directly towards the shrubs, where it disappeared.

"What was that?" the man cried out, waving his torch around. "I think I saw it too!"

The jackal-kin laughed, his head following the motion of the rabbit. "Roddat, the mighty guardsman... just found a rabbit."

"A rabbit?" the man asked, turning his head to look at the dog-kin.

The dog-kin looked slightly embarrassed and then shrugged. "I saw movement."

Even as the men were chatting, Gage used the opportunity to *Slide* to one of the statues. He kept *Shadow Blend* up as he turned back and made sure the guards had not noticed. When he was certain they hadn't, he *Slid* to the shrubs.

He crouched between two of the bushes and dropped his camouflage. He checked his *Mana*.

Mana: 23

He still had a decent amount of *Mana*, but he had several jumps to make to get back to the inn, including a long one across the river. It would be close.

Making sure the outer patrol was nowhere in sight, he *Slid* just outside the wall. From there, he crept into the shadows and made his way slowly back to the water's edge, pausing to make sure no one was around.

When he was certain there were no guards or passersby, he picked the open window of his room in the inn and *Slid* one last time. With a thud, he appeared in the room. He flinched at the noise, hoping it hadn't woken anyone.

Gage listened for a full minute. There was no sound, other than the sound of his breathing. Finally relaxing, he stripped off his cloak and loincloth and put his normal clothes back on.

Snatching up the stolen Cichiadamon, he quickly got to work brewing the draiocht-neim. The magic killer.

Brewing the anti-magic toxin, draiocht-neim, was a time consuming and exhausting task. The ingredients had to be added in just the right order, in just the right amounts, and at just the right times. In addition, depending on what stage you were at in the preparation, the mixture required different temperatures.

If any of those things were not right, the batch would fail. Gage learned this again the hard way with the first batch. His alchemical skills were rusty, and he didn't lower the temperature enough after adding the Bitter Petal.

Luckily, the remaining two other batches were successful. He now had six vials of the blue-green liquid. It was much more than he should need. After all, how many warlocks or channelers could the Shadowed First really have?

For a single mage, his Witch Hunter abilities were usually more than adequate. Using his *Suppress Magic* ability, Gage could negate all magic in an area for a short period of time. While that included his own magical abilities, his physical prowess had been more than a match for any wizard without their magic. Gage had no idea how many warlocks or channelers the Fist might have recruited, but he planned to be prepared for them.

With his alchemical preparation done, Gage disassembled his makeshift alchemical lab and hid away the vials. He still had hours before dark and it was time to do some reconnaissance of the Shadowed Fist headquarters.

He let out a breath as he thought about the guild hall. Once the temple of Hoenir, the silent god, the building had been taken over by the Fist almost thirty years ago when he fell out of popularity. The guild had moved in, offered to buy the large marble building, and the priests of Hoenir had quietly accepted and disappeared into the smaller towns.

Even now, most people still thought the temple of the god of secrets was a legitimate place of worship. It was not. All the priests were members of the Fist. They spent some of their downtime, playing the roles of priests to keep up the appearance. Gage had done the same during his time in the Fist.

Luckily, the priests were known for their vows of silence. The Shadowed First hadn't pretended to preach the teachings of Hoenir or led recruitment of converts. Instead, they just walked around the temple and meditated in front of a statue of the silent god. Or so it seemed.

In actuality, any "priest" walking around was actually on guard duty. Although it had been extremely rare throughout the history of the guild that one of the Houses tried to shut them down, there had been attempts.

Gage opened his pack and brought out a bundle he had purchased from the marketplace. It was a pale blue robe. The pale blue of the priests and priestesses of Njorour, god of the sea and of rivers. Given Eastport's livelihood came from the river, he was a popular deity.

Njorour was also the god whose temple was directly adjacent to the temple of Hoenir. With the robes and his shaven head, Gage should easily be able to pass as a priest of the river god. The disguise should allow him to surreptitiously keep an eye on the Fist for a few hours.

Wrapping himself in his cloak to cover the blue robes, Gage left the inn. He walked the opposite direction as the temple district, or district of lights as it was known. When he was several blocks away, he ducked into the alley and slipped off his cloak. He folded the cloak as he walked and slipped it under his robes. When he emerged from the opposite side of the alley, he walked out as a priest of Njorour.

He quickly circled back around and made his way across the Pearl bridge and back into the eastern part of the city. The guards gave him only a cursory glance before turning their attention elsewhere. He moved past the Gardens, gave the House Keep a wide berth, and skirted past the Gold District.

The Gold District, or luxury district as it was referred to, was the playground of the rich. It was an area that catered to the vices of the nobles and the very wealthy. It was said that nearly any vice could be satisfied there—for a price.

Gage kept just outside the luxury district. While a priest of Njorour might go unnoticed elsewhere in the city, very few men of worship had the coin necessary to enjoy the delights of the Gold District. And no one who frequented it wanted to be preached to.

Because of the wealth nearby, the area was much more heavily patrolled by the city guard. Gage knew from his time with the Fist that the captain of the guard was slipped extra gold to make sure that the best—and most discreet—guards patrolled the area.

Unlike other areas, who tolerated the thieves' guilds in other parts of the city, the Gold District had a zero-tolerance policy. If the guards caught a thief in that district, they were free to enforce their own judgement on the person. The punishment usually consisted of a severe beating, but if another thief was found dead in the gutters, no one complained.

All thieves knew this. They knew it and ignored it. The possibility of great reward was just too tempting in the luxury district. There were simply too many rich pockets to pick and full purses to cut.

As he moved uphill along the outskirts of the district, Gage heard music, yelling, cheers, and sounds of merriment. He shook his head. It was the decadent lifestyle he'd never understood.

Gage scowled. He'd had exactly the kind of life he'd wanted. An amazing wife. A beautiful daughter. A peaceful life.

Someone had taken that all away from him. Stolen that life from him. Destroyed it forever. And now, very soon, he would return the favor.

Noticing a few passersby glance at him with looks of concern, he remembered his outfit and sighed. He guessed priests of Njorour didn't walk the streets scowling at people. With effort, he relaxed his face and put on a slight smile.

He hurried to the district of lights and made his way through the various temples. There were the most popular temples, Odin, Thor, Frigg, Freyja, and Njorour. There were also some of the less worshiped gods and goddesses. All were welcome in the temple district—even Hel and Loki.

Gage didn't worship any of the gods or goddesses. He knew the truth. There were no gods. There were only wizards pretending to be gods. Odin, Thor, Frigg—he knew of them. They were wizards in the north, the House of Aesir.

Gods. Gage snickered. He'd killed Thor years ago, in the service of House Cernunnos. He'd returned, only to find out another wizard had taken Thor's place. Since the common folk never saw their "gods" up close, none of them knew.

In fact, House Aesir went to great efforts to make sure there was always a successor. The word was, they'd continued the line for hundreds of years, always having a pantheon of "gods" their people worshiped. It was how they controlled their people.

He shook his head. It was sad and pathetic—and it was coming to an end. He hadn't been to the north in a long time, but like the other Houses, Gage guessed they were suffering from the same problem—lack of wizard blood. How long would it be before their "gods" began growing horns, wings, or worse?

Pushing the thoughts of the false gods from his mind, he moved through the temples. Navigating the various places of worship, he reached the temple of the ocean god directly adjacent to the seaside cliff with an amazing view of the ocean and the massive water spouts. Next to it, was the rather worn looking temple of Hoenir, the guild hall for the Shadowed Fist, flush against the cliff.

He stopped and stared at the temple. It had been years since he'd laid eyes on the place, but memories came flooding back to him. The place had been his home for a long time. And now he was going to break into it.

Shaking his head to clear the nostalgic memories, he turned back to the temple of Njorour. He put a fake looking smile on his face—the same fake looking smile the other priests walked around with. Then, he strode forward and entered the temple.

Almost immediately, an older priest intercepted him, glancing up and down at him. "I do not recognize you, Brother...."

"Brother Armann," Gage filled in helpfully, mirroring the priest's fake smile. "Newly arrived from Roundstone. I've come to worship at the temple."

Roundstone was a small town a bit north of Eastwood, about halfway to Daleford. Gage happened to remember there was a temple there from a job he'd done for the Fist. The temple there was little more than a converted inn and nothing like the sprawling building here, but he hoped it would pacify the man's suspicions.

"Ah yes, Roundstone," the priest nodded, his smile

showing a bit of contempt. "How is the... temple... in Roundstone, these days?"

"We're doing quite well," Gage responded with mock enthusiasm. "We've gotten quite an increase in offerings lately. Why, just before we left, Jerthro and Elli donated a cow."

"A... cow," the man said. His face contorted as if he had just eaten something sour. "How wonderful for you. Well, I won't keep you from your worship here at the real temple of our sea lord."

"Thank you," Gage said and nodded to the man before continuing to the far side of the temple, nearest the wall.

When he had found the right spot, he knelt. Mirroring the other worshippers near the sea wall, he lifted his arms up to the sky. Unlike the others, while Gage's head was pointed up at the sky, his eyes roved the Shadowed Fist's guildhall—watching.

CHAPTER 25

$\mathcal{J}$ust before midnight, later the same day, Gage crept towards the temple of Hoenir. After watching the guild hall until sunset, he'd made his way back to his room at the inn. There he'd changed his clothes, strapped on his weapons, and made his final preparations.

He wore the Shadowed Fist uniform he'd taken from the assassins under a long, dark cloak. Once he entered the guildhall, it would allow him to blend in if there were others around, hopefully.

Gage stopped just outside the walls of the Shadowed Fists' lair and peered over. He was using *Shadow Blend* to stay hidden, but he remained wary. Despite covering himself and his clothes in Dog's Bane, he knew the alchemical concoction was not foolproof. He'd spotted at least two beast-kin among the "priests of Hoenir" and if they caught wind of him, they would raise the alarm.

Using his *Shadow Sight*, he scanned the courtyard.

There were significantly less people now that it was nearly midnight. Even assassins had to sleep. Despite the rumors and stories, there wasn't an assassination every night. Usually.

He watched the area for several minutes before ducking down behind the wall and deactivating his *Shadow Blend*. He was dressed from head to foot in loose fitting dark clothes. The clothes weren't a uniform black, like some assassins wore. Instead, they were different shades of dark gray to break up his silhouette.

By force of habit, he checked his *Mana*.

Mana: 14

Even at night, using *Shadow Blend* continuously drained his *Mana*. Unsure how much he'd need to use his abilities, Gage waited silently for his *Mana* to regenerate. While he was hidden in the shadow between a tree and the wall, he nevertheless kept his senses alert.

As soon as his *Mana* was full, he scaled the wall and dropped into a crouch on the opposite side. Gage remained still for several minutes. His shadow covered eyes roved the area, tracking the three assassins that moved about the courtyard.

From watching them for the past half hour, he knew two of them were human, both average height and build, much like himself. That was perfect for an assassin since it made you forgettable.

The third was also human, but she sported a set of ram-like horns that protruded from the side of her head. She also had a tail that darted back and forth as she walked. The woman was a channeler, reminding him of the assassin he'd interrogated.

None of them carried torches. Unlike the estate guards, who carried torches, the assassins were relying on their night adjusted eyes to catch movement instead. That was both good and bad.

Without the light ruining their night vision, the guards would see large movements further away. At the same time, they lost the ability to distinguish small movements and see details—even up close. That was good. It worked in his favor tonight.

Gage waited until the trio were facing away from him before creeping to a line of statues that ringed the main temple. He was familiar with the marble statues, having passed them many times when he'd lived at the temple.

The statues were of huge angelic men and women in different poses. All had the feathery wings associated with beings from the higher planes. Some of the wings wrapped around the figures while others were outstretched. They were all different but did have one thing in common – every one of them covered their mouths.

Hiding behind one of the statues, whose wings obscured his profile, Gage watched carefully as the three figures followed their predictable routes. It was the same patrol pattern he'd observed earlier. It was amateurish but he wasn't going to complain about small favors.

He wondered if they were amateurs, or rather, were they new recruits? From his earlier reconnaissance, he'd been surprised to find that he hadn't recognized any of his former guildmates. Gage would have thought he would see at least one familiar face. But he hadn't. Everyone he'd seen had been a new face.

One thing he had noticed from watching the men and women going in and out of the temple: more than one of them was a channeler, like the woman on patrol. Gage had seen horns, tails, and other deformities, all tell-tale signs of a channeler. He'd also thought he'd seen a warlock, judging by the conversation the person held with empty air.

Gage had counted a half-dozen of the mages who now appeared to be part of the Shadowed Fist. Given he'd already killed three others, he guessed that nearly half of the twenty or so assassins who used to be based in the temple were now mages of some sort. Why so many?

While he would like to have sat and pondered the new changes, he didn't have the time. Gage had memorized their patrol pattern and as the three assassins moved away from the temple, he saw his opportunity.

With practically no thought, he *Shadow Slid* from the statue to the pillars that supported the temple. As soon as he materialized, he went completely still. His eyes darted from assassin to assassin to see if any of the three guards had spotted him.

The two men continued their previous paths, turning at the cliff and walking the perimeter. Neither seemed to notice him. The female assassin stopped in her tracks, turning her head one way and then the other.

Gage cursed silently as the woman turned around. With his *Shadow Sight,* he could see her brow furrow as she cocked her head to the left and right. She'd heard something, he realized. But what?

He was certain he hadn't made a sound. Had there been a crunch of dirt or stone as Gage materialized? He didn't think so, but something had spooked the woman.

Keeping absolutely still, Gage held his breath as the woman stared towards the space where he hid. His dark clothes should mask his outline, but he couldn't afford to take any chances. He activated *Shadow Blend*.

The female assassin glanced his way but didn't seem to be looking at him specifically. He saw her head sweep back and forth. She was definitely looking for something in his direction. But what? There was no way she should be able to see him at that distance. So, what was she looking at?

Silently, he cursed again as he stared at the woman. Could she be seeing him? She shouldn't be able to, not with his *Shadow Blend* active. Had her demonic transformations given her enhanced senses?

Intent on the woman, he didn't notice that the two men had stopped their patrol. One of them called out in a hushed voice. "Glesni! Is something wrong?"

The channeler didn't say anything for a moment. Instead, she continued to stare at Gage's hiding spot. Despite his *Shadow Blend,* he was starting to grow a bit alarmed. Why was she still staring at him?

Finally, the woman spoke. "I... thought I felt something."

Gage's blood went cold. Could this person sense his shadow magic? Was that possible? No one had ever sensed it before. He corrected himself. One person had. Or rather, one other warlock had, years ago.

Until this point, he'd thought that had been a fluke.

Now he wasn't sure what to think. If this woman could sense his powers, she had to be another warlock. A warlock with shadow magic. There was only one thing he could do. Gage moved deeper into the shadows and deactivated his *Shadow Blend*.

He also deactivated his Shadow Vision, blinking as his eyes adjusted to the darkness. He still had his night vision. Thankfully, unlike normal light, the magical vision didn't ruin it. He only needed a moment before his eyes adjusted.

"You felt something?" the other man called out. "What?"

In the dim light, Gage saw the woman cocking her head again. He didn't move. Instead, he simply stared back at the silhouette of the woman, ready to take all three of the assassins out if he needed to.

After what seemed like an eternity, the woman shrugged. Without his magical vision, he couldn't see her expression, but he did hear her respond.

"I guess it was nothing," she said. "Just spooked, maybe."

"You sure?" the man from his right called out. He was a few steps closer than he had been, judging by his voice and had probably been on his way to the woman.

"Yeah," she replied. "We'd better get back to our patrols."

Gage turned his head slowly, tracking the three assassins as they went back to their patrol routes. Once they were out of sight, he crept towards the temple's entrance. There was still a mission to accomplish.

CHAPTER 26

Gage paused a few feet from the steps leading to the large wooden doors of the temple. Torches were set on either side of the door, casting flickering shadows across his hiding spot between two of shrubs that lined the small walkway to the entrance.

He hadn't reactivated either of his Shadow abilities and Gage felt naked and exposed. Although he'd continued to practice his stealth abilities over the last few years, it was mostly when hunting. It had been years since he'd needed to hide from humanoids, especially well-trained humanoids, without his powers.

How the woman could sense his use of abilities, he didn't know. Gage could sense other magic, but that was due to an ability he'd received from his Witch Hunter class. It was an ability that had upgraded as he progressed through the class.

Sense Magic III

Type: Witch Hunter
Cost: None (Passive)
Range: 100 ft.
Duration: Special
Description: Your training to counter spellcasters has heightened your sensitivity to all forms of magic. You can now sense the use of most magic within 100 feet. Note: This sensation only tells you the presence, type, and general strength of the magic. It does not allow you to sense the actual intention of the magic.

From talking with wizards, and the occasional warlock or channeler, they had no such ability. They seemed to be able to sense only the type of magic they had learned, in the case of wizards. Channelers and warlocks could sense only the single type of magic they'd gained from the demon they'd made the pact with. Summoners couldn't detect magic at all.

By that logic, the female assassin had to be a channeler who had received shadow magic from her patron demon. That was rare. Very rare. Only one warlock he'd met had been able to sense his shadow magic.

The person had been a mark. The warlock had formed a new gang and was using his magic to make headway into the thieves' guild's territory in Daleford. The guild-master had been on the brink of losing the thieves' guild. In desperation, he'd hired the Shadowed Fist to take care of the warlock.

When Gage had made his move, the warlock sensed him coming and managed to flee into the shadows. The sudden revelation had taken Gage by surprise. Their game finally ended only because the man became overconfident. The warlock allowed Gage to get close enough to use his magical suppression ability, nullifying the man's magic and allowing Gage to finish the job.

This time was different. The woman hadn't been the mark, and, luckily, he hadn't been close to her when she'd sensed him. He'd had to drop his Shadow Blend and his Shadow Vision, but that was more of an annoyance than anything else. A premature annoyance.

He was always going to have to stop using magic as soon as he entered the building. Gage had known that all along. The channeler wasn't the only person in the Fist who could sense his shadow magic. There was one other person.

Aeg Derg was a *Witch Hunter* too. His old mentor had the same magic sensing ability Gage did. That meant, the guildmaster would detect his shadow magic if Gage used it too close to the man.

His old mentor wouldn't know the magic was Gage. Once he had become a *Shadow Master*, he had been extremely careful to never use his magical abilities around the Shadowed Fist guildmaster. But Aeg Derg would still be forewarned that someone with unfamiliar magic was in the temple. That was all it would take to raise the alarm.

Gage frowned. Like most of the temples perched on the cliff, the guild hall of the Shadowed Fist had many underground levels. At the bottom level was the guildmaster's office. That was his goal. He'd never make it if the place went on alert—even using his powers.

Aeg Derg was his biggest threat. The man was a *Witch Hunter* too, with the same abilities Gage had—plus some.

Not only could his old mentor sense Gage's magic, he could suppress it.

He needed to get to the office and to the ledger book. Other than asking Aeg Derg himself, there was no other way to find the person who had hired the guild to kill him —the person who was ultimately responsible for his wife and daughters death.

His mouth became a hard line and Gage stared at the door intently. Behind that door lay one of the most dangerous infiltrations he'd ever done. But Gage had to make it. He needed to find that person. Find them and make them pay.

Gage took a last glance around the courtyard, making sure the sentries didn't have a line of sight to him, and then stripped off his cloak. He bundled the garment up and slipped it in the branches of the shrub where it should go unnoticed.

He darted to the two large, wooden doors. Reaching down for the large metal ring attached to the door, he swung the left door open just enough for him to slip inside. He let out a breath and stepped inside.

Keeping his face towards the door and his back to the foyer he'd just entered, he pulled the door shut.

"Damian?" came a voice from behind him. It was a man's voice, but held a "Is that you?"

Gage assumed Damian was one of the two men outside, patrolling the courtyard. With his back turned, and the hood covering his head, the sentry couldn't see his face. He could reply affirmatively, but there was a good chance his voice would give him away.

He decided to use the name of one of the assassins

who attacked him. Gage turned, keeping his head ducked and his face hidden in the shadows of his hood as he walked towards the sentry sitting on a simple wooden chair near one of the large pillars that lined the entryway. "No. It's me, Peadrus"

Continuing his casual stride forward, Gage scanned the sentry.

Amren Prosser
Human
Brigand / Assassin
Level 5 / Level 2

Amren Prosser. The sentry had a last name. It meant he either came from a minor noble house or a well to do merchant house. Gage briefly wondered what had turned the man into an assassin. Not that it mattered. The man was in his way.

The man cocked his head as Gage casually strode towards him, squinting into the shadows of his hood. "Your back? I heard..."

Gage walked just within reach. Just as he got within range, he struck out at the man's solar plexus.

You critically crush Amren Prosser for 23 damage.
Amren Prosser is stunned.

Amren grunted quietly as the breath left him. His mouth worked as he tried to suck in a breath to replace the air, but his stunned solar plexus wasn't allowing his lungs to work. Instead, he just opened and closed his mouth.

Wasting no time, Gage slipped behind the man, wrapping his left arm around the man's throat and pushing against the back of his neck with his right arm. As he did, he also lifted up slightly, increasing pressure on the man's carotid arteries. The man struggled briefly before lack of blood to his brain caused him to go limp.

Amren Prosser is unconscious.

Releasing the pressure so he didn't kill the man, Gage quickly dragged the man away from his post and into a small alcove, which had originally been a cloak room, just off the entryway. Judging from the few cloaks which hung from marble pegs, it was still used as a cloak room.

He stopped then and listened for any sign that someone had witnessed the attack. When he heard nothing, Gage quickly stripped the man, tied him up and gagged him. Next, Gage took a few cloaks from the pegs and covered the man's body. The lump of cloaks lying on the ground wouldn't fool someone taking a close look at it, but it should pass a casual glance at the alcove.

Gage stripped off his own garments, rubbed a new coat of Dog's Bane on himself before donning Amren's clothes. He hadn't encountered any beast-kin, but Amren's clothes would help mask his own scent with that of a familiar one. He hoped.

Pulling his hood low over his head, he glanced around the entryway and then stepped out. He headed back towards the rear of the entryway and into a large chapel. It was empty. There hadn't been worshippers for decades.

He walked to the raised dais that contained a ten-foot-tall statue of the god of silence. Glancing around the chapel to make sure he hadn't missed any other sentries, Gage ducked behind the statue.

Located just past the statue of Hoenir were marble steps leading down into the underground levels of the temple which had been carved from the cliff itself.

Gage didn't even pause. He knew the risks. There was only one way in or out of the underground complex, and he was looking at it. If he was discovered, he'd have to fight his way back to this spot. So be it.

Hands close to his weapons, Gage descended the staircase.

CHAPTER 27

As he went down the stairs, Gage left the smooth marble of the temple behind. The underground area was rough granite, like a mine shaft. Having not been down under the temple in years, it was both familiar and alien at the same time.

Gage stopped midway down the steps as he spotted the flickering light of a torch at the bottom. He pressed himself against the wall and stared down.

The torchlight didn't move, and no shadows passed the bottom of the stairs. He proceeded cautiously, guessing it was a mounted torch. Slowly, from step to step, he angled himself so he could see around the corner of the stairwell.

As he had thought, there were torches to either side of the steps. Peering around the wall of the stairwell, Gage glanced first right and then left. From his previous time in the guild, he knew the left passage led to the sleeping areas for the assassins. The right side led to the mess hall.

Straining his ears, he couldn't make out any voices in

either direction. He wasn't surprised. It was after midnight. Assassins who had jobs were out. Those who didn't were sleeping. Gage frowned as he glanced down both sides of the passageway again.

When he had been at the guild previously, there was always another guard stationed on this level. He saw no sign of anyone. Of course, the guard could be in one of the dark areas, watching the torchlit stairwell from the shadows.

Gage needed to go right. Just before the mess hall was the stairway down to the next level. The problem was, there was no way to do that and remain unseen.

If someone was in the shadows, there was no way to sneak past without using his shadow abilities. Gage realized the two torches to either side of the stairs had been placed there purposefully. They completely illuminated the area around the bottom of the stairs. It left no way for a person to come down the steps and not be seen.

Gage smiled. If he couldn't hide in the shadows, he'd hide in plain sight. After all, he was wearing the garb of the Shadowed Fist. With the hood pulled down, the guard wouldn't be able to see his face. He might be able to fool the person long enough to get close. There was only one way to find out.

Stepping into the torchlight, Gage stopped and pretended to yawn. He kept his head pointed straight ahead, so any guard would not be able to see his face. After his yawn, he turned towards the mess hall.

He kept his head down, ensuring his face was shadowed. Gage walked tiredly, slightly slumped over and shuffling his feet. To any onlookers, it would appear he was dead on his feet and about to lie down somewhere and go to sleep.

His face away from the torches, his eyes began to adjust to the shadows again and Gage strained to see in front of him. He was still struggling when he saw movement in front and to the left of him. He brought up his hand to his mouth and yawned again.

"Amren?" a female voice whispered from the darkness ahead.

Nodding his head, Gage mumbled something incoherent as he yawned again.

"You know you're not supposed to leave your post," the female voice said softly but sternly. "If the guildmaster finds out..."

The voice stopped and he heard sniffing. Gage swore silently. A beast-kin. He continued forward, closing the gap between himself and the source of the voice. He kept the slow, tired pace but slightly lengthened his stride.

Gage's eyes were adjusting and he could just make out the shape of the small form in front of him. She was slight and a good foot shorter than he was. He thought he saw feline ears in the dark, but he couldn't be sure. Luckily, she was close enough to scan.

Mati
Catling
Thief/ Assassin
Level 5 / Level 1

"Amren, did you spill something on..." the sentry began to ask but she trailed off. Most likely, her superior eyes had seen his face from her lower vantage point. She started to take a step back, her eyes going wide and mouth opening to raise the alarm.

He didn't give the catling the chance. Closing the distance with a single stride, he struck out at the guard with an open hand to the throat. He had no desire to kill her—or any of the assassins in the guild—but he also couldn't alert the entire place to his presence.

The members of the Shadowed Fist had been family to him for many years—up until he'd left and started a real family. Despite that, he still had a certain amount of respect and fondness for the members of the guild. He wouldn't kill unless he absolutely had to.

The strike hadn't been enough to crush her windpipe, but it had been enough to cause her to choke and wheeze as she struggled to get her breath.

You critically crush Mati for 9 damage.
Mati is choking.

Reflexively, her hands came up to her damaged throat and he struck out hard to her solar plexus, doubling her over.

You critically crush Mati for 14 damage.
Mati is stunned.

Slipping behind the catling, he brought his elbow down on the back of her head, knocking her unconscious.

You crush Mati for 6 damage.

Mati is unconscious.

The small form went limp, and he caught her before she could hit the floor and make a sound. He held her for a long moment, listening for any sound of anyone else who might have heard the brief struggle. There was nothing.

Scooping up the catling in his arms, he carried her into the mess hall, stopping just outside the doorway to make sure it wasn't occupied.

There were no meals scheduled until breakfast, but occasionally an assassin would come back from a job and take something from the pantry before going to bed. He'd done that himself many times.

At first glance, the room appeared empty. Gage's eyes washed around the room, making sure he hadn't missed anyone.

Confident the room was empty, he carried the small assassin to one of the pantries. He bound her arms and legs and then gagged her. After checking her bonds twice, he locked her inside the pantry and retraced his steps back to the stairway down.

Gage sighed softly and shook his head. He'd disabled two assassins. All hopes he'd had of sneaking in and out, unnoticed, were gone. When the assassins got loose or were found, they'd know someone had infiltrated them.

Aeg Derg was no fool. If he didn't already suspect that the three assassins had failed, finding out someone had infiltrated the guild hall would be all the confirmation he needed. The question was, what would the guildmaster do?

He'd hoped to slip in, peek at the ledger, and slip out. His plan had been to kill whoever had hired the Fist to assassinate him before the infiltration had even been discovered. That wasn't happening.

Whoever had hired him had to be someone in one of the Houses. They'd probably discovered he'd been responsible for some member of their House and wanted to get back at him. The problem for him was—that didn't narrow it down.

Gage had carried out many contracts against House wizards. The Houses were constantly hiring various assassins to send a message or remove a particularly troublesome mage from another House. He'd lost track of how many contracts he'd personally completed.

He'd still find out exactly who it was when he saw the ledger. But now the guild might warn the person before Gage could get to them. Once they discovered he had been here, Aeg Derg would know it was him. He would be honor bound to inform the client.

Staring down the second staircase, Gage scowled. It wouldn't matter even if they did warn the person. Whoever ordered his death—the person responsible for killing his family—was going to die. If he had to kill every single person in that House, he would get the person responsible.

Hardening his resolve, Gage quietly started down the stairs.

CHAPTER 28

There were no torches at the bottom of the stairs to the second floor. In fact, there were no lights of any kind that Gage could detect. He paused halfway down as it became too dark for him to see.

When he'd lived in the guildhall, years ago, there had always been torches at the bottom of the staircases. The torches helped the members navigate the stairs and served to illuminate the hallway at the bottom of the stairs. Seeing those torches missing instantly made him suspicious.

From his time in the guild, he knew that this level consisted of a training area to the right and another living area to the left. Given the living area, Gage found it very odd that there were no torches illuminating the stairs. How were the assassins on this level supposed to see if they got up in the middle of the night to go relieve themselves?

It didn't make any sense and that made Gage wary.

Had his presence been discovered? Had someone heard him disable the guard upstairs? Was there an ambush waiting for him?

Cursing silently to himself, he once again wished he could use his shadow abilities. His *Shadow Vision* allowed him to see in absolute darkness, better even than a beast-kin at close range. Without it, in the dark, he was as blind as the proverbial bat.

Gage crouched down, completely still. He listened for any sounds in the inky blackness. There was nothing. No sounds of people talking, nor any sounds of activity. Not even the faint rustle of clothing.

He mentally recalled the layout of the floor. Gage knew all he had to do was follow the wall to the left. The stairs down were only thirty feet away. It should be an easy walk to the next staircase if he used the wall as his guide. Even in the dark, he should be able to make it—so long as there was no ambush waiting for him.

Cursing silently, Gage realized he was running out of time. Eventually, someone would notice the missing sentries. When that happened, everyone upstairs would be awakened to search the place. He would be forced to use his powers to escape.

If that happened, he'd never get another opportunity to find out who hired the guild to kill him. At least, not without killing half the guild—maybe all of the guild. He'd also have to face his old mentor, Aeg Derg. Even if he wanted to kill the man, he wasn't sure he could.

Gage made the decision to press forward. He needed the name of the person responsible. He felt his anger rising as he thought about the last moments with his family. He needed to make them pay. Nothing else mattered. If he had to kill everyone who got in his way, then so be it.

He dropped down to all fours and began to slowly crawl down the steps. Still paranoid, he gently probed each new step for any tripwires. The guild hadn't set any traps when he'd lived here—but times changed.

With his time in the thieves' guild, Gage had gotten experience finding and bypassing traps. It was a skill that had come in useful when doing heists. But while merchants tended to set traps around their goods to prevent theft, the Shadowed Fist had never needed traps. No one in their right mind broke into the assassin's guild.

Gage chuckled to himself. He was breaking into the assassin's guild. Did that mean he wasn't in his right mind? Probably not. But he had a purpose. A mission. Without stopping, he continued down the stairs.

When he reached the bottom of the stairs, he paused and listened again. He hadn't found any traps or tripwires on the way down the stairs, but he searched the floor around the staircase anyway. There were none.

Silently, he stood up and slid one of his daggers from its sheath. Holding it ready, he listened again. When he heard nothing, he slid his head around the side of the staircase so anyone in the hall would be able to see him, and then quickly slipped it back.

There was no twang of a bow string and no whistle of a flying dagger. There was also no sound of an alarm being raised or the rustle of clothes as someone came to investigate. Once again, there was nothing but silence.

He cursed silently again. Gage realized the uncertainty

was causing his pulse to rise and his breathing to come quickly as his unconscious mind readied itself for a trap or ambush. He felt a sheen of sweat on his brow. It was something he hadn't felt since he'd put the Shadowed Fist behind him. Fear. Excitement. Uncertainty.

With conscious effort, he forced himself to relax and slowed his heart rate. At the same time, Gage took deep breaths until he was back in control.

He was tempted to use his Shadow Vision to see if there was someone waiting for him. Unfortunately, he was only a single floor above Aeg Derg's chambers. Using any of his abilities at this point would give him away.

Gage waited another minute before crouching low and moving around the corner. He kept his left hand touching the wall. Using the wall as his guide, he padded along. He heard nothing at all.

After thirty feet, his hand reached the edge of the wall that signaled he had reached the staircase to his left. A quick glance down showed him the flickering light of torches at the bottom of the steps.

He cocked his head at the torchlit floor below. He felt the hairs on the back of his neck rising. Something wasn't right. Why were there torches down on the guildmaster's level but no torches on the training level? It didn't make any sense.

The situation should have been reversed. There should have been torches on the training level for the assassins sleeping there to see. Aeg Derg's floor shouldn't be lit at this time of the night. His old mentor would just light an oil lamp if he got up in the middle of the night.

Gage swore to himself. This whole situation felt

wrong. It felt like a trap. If this was a job, he would have backed off and done more reconnaissance. Given that he'd already rendered two assassins unconscious, he knew leaving and coming back wasn't an option. If he wanted the information he was seeking, he had to go forward.

Stepping onto the stairs, Gage withdrew another dagger. With weapons in both hands, he descended the staircase, one step at a time. He continued until he was a half dozen steps from the bottom.

Crouching low, he watched the torch lit hallway. There was no guard, but he hadn't expected one. There was no point in having a guard on this floor. Normally, no one would be able to reach this floor without raising an alarm. Of course, no one expected an ex-assassin to infiltrate the guild.

He silently padded to the bottom of the stairs. Weapons ready and body coiled like a viper ready to strike, he slipped his head partially around the corner, looking left and right, before retreating into the stairwell. The corridor was empty.

To his left, he'd seen the reinforced wooden door that led to Aeg Derg's bedchamber. The door was closed. To the right, was a longer corridor that ended in another closed wooden door. Gage knew the door to the right led to the guildmaster's office. It was where he'd find the ledger.

Casting another glance into the hallway, Gage took a longer glance in both directions. His eyes searched the shadows, looking for any sign of a guard or traps. The hairs on the back of his neck were still warning him that something didn't feel right but there was no sign of anyone. It looked safe.

Gage slowly stepped from the stairs into the hallway. He paused, alert for any sound or movement. There was nothing but that nagging feeling; something just wasn't right. He just couldn't put his finger on it.

He turned to the right, towards the study. Slowly and silently, he crept down the hallway to the thick wooden door. Reaching it, he put his ear to the door and listened intently. All quiet.

With a quick glance behind him, Gage reached for the iron ring attached to the door. Taking a deep breath, he slowly pulled the door open. The well-oiled door swung towards him.

There was light inside the guildmaster's office. He cursed. Someone was in there.

Before he could close the door, he heard a familiar voice from inside the room. "Come in, Gage. I've been expecting you."

CHAPTER 29

Gage froze, door only partly open. Hands tightening his grips on his daggers, he growled softly. The entire thing HAD been a setup.

He glanced behind him. Gage half expected members of the Shadowed Fist to come pouring down the steps and out of the guildmaster's bedroom. No one appeared. There weren't even sounds of people coming down steps or racing to the door. Were the assassins waiting in Aeg Derg's office?

Slowly, he swung the door open. He readied himself to use his Shadow abilities, even though he knew his mentor could suppress them the same way Gage could suppress other mages. He reached for his magic and found it hadn't been blocked—yet.

As the door opened, Gage recognized the familiar office of the guildmaster. It hadn't changed at all in the years he'd been gone. The walls were still lined with bookshelves, all filled with books on many topics, as well as hundreds of years of ledgers.

Each ledger contained the details of each and every contract since the founding of the Shadowed Fist. It was all encoded, of course, to prevent anyone outside the guild from reading the guild's contracts. Standing in front of the desk was the smiling form of his one-time friend and mentor, Aeg Derg.

"Gage," the guildmaster said with a nod. "It's good to see you again."

Anger flared inside Gage at the man's casual demeanor. Aeg Derg had sent assassins to kill him. Assassins who had killed his wife and daughter instead. And now, the older man spoke casually, as if none of it had transpired.

"Master," Gage responded, though it came out as a growl. He struggled to keep his anger in check but some of it bled out.

His old mentor's eyes widened briefly at his harsh tone. Aeg Derg chuckled, and Gage nearly attacked the man right then. Laughing at the death of his family

Gage's knuckles went white as his grip tightened on his daggers.

A seasoned assassin himself, Aeg Derg noticed Gage's tension. He frowned and furrowed his brow. "You're not upset at the three novices I sent, are you? I'm sure you handled them without breaking a sweat. I mean, I assume they're dead. Right?"

Gage took an involuntary step forward, his body tensed. When he spoke, his voice came out as a hiss. "They killed my wife and daughter."

Aeg Derg rocked back as if struck, his face going white. "No!"

"Yes!" Gage snapped. He nearly took another step towards the older man but mastered himself just before. Still, he held his daggers in white knuckled grips.

"Gage," the man responded, his face crestfallen. "I.... I didn't know. They never should have...." Aeg Derg looked up at him, almost pleadingly. "You know our rule. No innocents unless the contact calls for it."

The man's facial expression and tone conveyed nothing but sorrow and regret, but Gage knew his old mentor was an accomplished liar—it came with the business. It was impossible to know whether Aeg Derg felt remorse or if it were a show for Gage's benefit.

"They fireballed my house," Gage stated flatly. Some of the anger had faded at the old man's words—but not all of it. "It killed them instantly."

The guildmaster's face grew red. "They did what?"

"They fireballed my house—with me and my family in it!" Gage retorted.

"Those morons!" Aeg Derg shouted. "If they weren't dead—I assume they're dead?" The man looked to Gage for confirmation.

He nodded curtly.

"If they weren't dead," his old mentor growled, "I'd kill them myself. That was not part of the plan. I told them specifically to take you when you were alone."

Gage chuckled mirthlessly. "Thank you so much for that."

Aeg Derg waved his comment away. "They were no

match for you. I knew that. Why do you think I sent them?"

"What do you mean?" Gage asked. Was his old mentor saying he had sent those assassins after Gage, knowing they would fail? "If you knew they would fail, why did you even bother sending them?"

The guildmaster smiled grimly, the expression not reaching his eyes. "You know the rules. We received a contract. All contracts must be fulfilled."

"But you knew they wouldn't succeed," Gage countered.

Aeg Derg raised a finger. "True. But the contract was executed. Assassins were sent." The guildmaster winked at him. "And when they fail to check in a few days from now, I will know they failed."

Gage thought he was beginning to understand. He raised an eyebrow. "And then what?"

"Contractually," the old assassin replied. "I would be obligated to send another assassin after you—provided the contract was still valid."

"Why wouldn't it still be valid if I'm still alive?" Gage asked. Contracts remained valid until the mark was dead —or the client cancelled the contract. Did Aeg Derg think the client would cancel the contract just because the first group of assassins failed?

The guildmaster shook his head disapprovingly. It was the same disapproving look he'd received when he'd failed a lesson so many years ago. "Have you forgotten so quickly?"

"It's been five years," Gage snapped. "Remind me."

Aeg Derg shook his head again and made a sound.

"Who is the one group we do not honor contracts against?"

Gage frowned. There was only one group of people the Shadowed Fist never went after—members of the guild itself. "But I'm not a member any longer."

"We could remedy that," the guildmaster said with a predatory grin. "If you agree to join us again, I can cancel the contract."

Finally understanding, Gage felt his anger surge again. Aeg Derg had sent novice assassins after him, knowing they had no chance, all to lure him back to the guild. He glared at the old man. "My wife and daughter are dead because you wanted me back in the guild!"

The guildmaster sighed. "No. Your family is dead because those novices violated our rules. They were innocents. They never should have been hurt."

"But they were hurt!" Gage growled, and he stepped towards the man.

Aeg Derg held his palms up. "You have to believe me, I would never have put them in harm's way. In fact, I was trying to protect them—and you."

"By sending assassins after me?"

His old mentor shook his head. "Novice assassins you could deal with in your sleep. No one was meant to get hurt—except for those three."

"You could have warned me," Gage spat, thinking of his family. Had he known assassins were gunning for him, he would have sent his family away.

"You know I couldn't do that, Gage. Not even for you."

"Rules," Gage snorted.

Aeg Derg nodded. "Rules. If we don't adhere to our own rules, the Houses will lose faith in us."

"And because of those rules," Gage shot back. "My family is dead!"

The old man seemed to grow even older under Gage's stare. He shook his head sadly. "Your family is dead, ultimately, because someone took out a contract on you. It should have been you, but instead they got your family."

His old mentor's words reminded him of the reason he'd broken into the Shadowed First to begin with. "Who! Who put out the contract on me?"

Aeg Derg shook his head and made a disappointed sound. "You know the rules. I can't tell you that."

"Unless I re-join," Gage growled. "But then, I couldn't go after the person."

"Not unless there's a contract on them." The guildmaster confirmed. He paused and then shrugged. "Which I will tell you there is not."

Gage laughed mirthlessly. "So, join back up and I'm safe, but I can't go after the client." His old mentor opened his mouth to respond, but Gage already knew the answer. "I know... rules."

"Rules," the old man confirmed with a nod.

He knew it was useless to argue with Aeg Derg over the rules. The man might be a cold-blooded killer, but the guildmaster didn't waver in his adherence to the letter of the rules—even if that occasionally violated the spirit of the rules.

"I can't," Gage said after a long silence. He tightened his grip on his daggers. "Does this mean we have to fight?"

It was his mentor's turn to chuckle. "There's no rule

that says the guildmaster has to carry out the contract—even if the mark is right in front of him."

Gage relaxed slightly. "Then give me the name and I'll be gone."

Aeg Derg shook his head. "You know I can't do that." Gage opened his mouth to protest but his old mentor held up his hand. "Rules are rules. I cannot divulge the name of a client to anyone—especially someone outside the guild."

The guildmaster shot a glance at an open book on his desk. Gage followed his eyes and saw that it was a ledger book. Aeg Derg faked a yawn. "I'm tired and it is past my bedtime. I'm going to sleep now. Do see yourself out." He gave Gage a meaningful look.

The guildmaster walked past him and Gage stayed tense and alert for any sort of deception. He turned as the old man walked to the door, keeping his eyes on Aeg Derg.

His mentor stopped at the door but didn't turn his head towards Gage. "Those three assassins I sent are due back tomorrow. If I don't hear from them, I'll have to assume they failed and send another."

Gage grunted in acknowledgement. The guildmaster was telling him he had a day, maybe two, before he could expect another assassin. "You know I'll kill them."

Aeg Derg nodded but still didn't turn around. "Rules, Gage. The contract must be honored. Procedures followed."

Without another word, the aged assassin opened the door, walked through and then closed it behind him, leaving Gage alone.

He stared at the door for nearly a minute before

turning around. Gage padded over to the large wooden desk and stared down at the open book.

There was a slip of parchment, seemingly used as a bookmark but there was writing on it. Gage picked it up and scanned the writing. The heading said "Safehouses" and a list of addresses followed.

Gage quickly committed the addresses to memory and then replaced the parchment before looking at the ledger. His eyes skimmed the details on both pages and realized the book was open to the pages about the contract on him. Reading the passage, his breath caught in his throat.

The man who had taken the contract out was none other than the Archmage himself, Ruy Cernunnos. The leader of House Cernunnos and the most powerful man in the province.

Quest Complete.
Vengeance is Mine—Part I
You have infiltrated the Shadowed Fist and discovered the name of the person who hired assassins to kill you.
Infiltrate the Shadowed Fist (1/1).
Reward: 10000 experience.
You gain 10000 experience.
You have received a new quest "Vengeance is Mine —Part II"
You have discovered that Ruy Cernunnos ordered the assassination which resulted in the death of your wife and daughter. If you wish to avenge your family, you will first need to find a way to infiltrate the Cernunnos Keep.
Find a way to infiltrate the Cernunnos Keep (0/1).

Reward: 5000 experience.
Accept quest (yes or no)?

Even as his display updated the quest, Gage cursed and accepted the quest. He'd come too far to turn back now, even if it was the Archmage.

CHAPTER 30

Gage slammed his fist down on the heavy wooden desk, rattling ink bottles and quills. He cursed again as he re-read the name just to be certain. Ruy Cernunnos, the head of House Cernunnos and its current Archmage.

He had worked for Ruy and House Cernunnos as their master of assassins, on loan from the Shadowed Fist. He'd killed dozens of rival mages for the man and been privy to nearly all their secrets.

The Archmage hadn't been happy when he'd retired. He hadn't been happy that he was leaving the Shadowed Fist and would no longer be bound by its code of secrecy. He'd been afraid Gage would sell the information he knew. In the end, only a personal meeting with Aeg Derg had convinced him Gage would not be a threat.

The Shadowed Fist enforced its code of silence, even if someone left the guild. No one revealed details of jobs or secrets they learned when contracted out to a client. If they did, the guild would silence them—permanently.

Gage swore again. Was that why Ruy had come after him? It made no sense. Any secrets he would know would be years old. Why wait so long to come after him? Or was there another reason? Could it be something personal? But why? What had been so important that his family had to die?!

He read the entry in the ledger again.

Client: Ruy Cernunnos
Target: Gage Cross
Price: 10,000 gold
Deadline: Samhain

Just his name, Samhain, and the amount: 10,000 gold! It was a small fortune and an amount normally reserved for minor house mages—not ex-assassins. It seemed an extravagant amount for Ruy to pay to have him killed.

Why did Ruy want him dead so badly? And what was the significance of Samhain? Gage wracked his brain, trying to recall any secrets he might have overheard that would still be relevant and worth paying so much money to have him killed. Nothing came to mind—especially nothing related to Samhain.

Samhain was a yearly holiday for honoring one's ancestors. It was supposedly a time when the barrier between the living and the dead was weak and one's ancestors returned for the night as spirits. It was a night when one could speak with the dead. Or so the people said.

Gage had never seen any spirits return during Samhain. He'd never seen any spirits, period. It was just another holiday everyone celebrated to take their mind off the troubles of the world. It was no different than Yule, the Winter Solstice, or Ostara—the Spring Festival.

He stared down at the coded ledger entry for several minutes, as if staring longer would impart some other information. It didn't. He now knew who, but not why.

Backing away from the guildmaster's desk, Gage shook his head. He'd gotten all the answers he could from the ledger. He didn't know why the Archmage of House Cernunnos wanted him dead—nor did he really care. Ruy was responsible for his family's death and Gage would make him pay.

He padded to the door, opened it, and stepped into the hallway. When he exited the study, his old mentor was across the hall. Aeg Derg leaned causally against the door to his bedroom, arms crossed over his chest. The man met Gage's eyes as he walked towards the steps. "You've seen the ledger."

It was more a statement than a question, but Gage nodded as he closed the door to man's office.

Even in the dim light of the flickering torches, he could see his old mentor raise an eyebrow. "Are you sure you don't want to reconsider my offer?"

Gage frowned and walked down the hall. He stopped next to the staircase and stared back at the old assassin. "He was responsible for the death of my family. I can't just let that go."

"I know." Aeg Derg nodded, his face impassive. "You understand the ramifications of taking revenge?"

"The House will come for me," Gage replied.

"Not just House Cernunnos," the old man noted. "The entire Council will want your head. Even if you wanted to rejoin the guild at that point, I couldn't protect you."

Gage shrugged. Once he killed the man responsible for his family's death, did he really care what happened to him anymore? He wasn't sure he did. He just needed to kill the Archmage first. He looked to his old mentor. "You'll send someone else after me?"

His mentor gave a slight shrug. "Rules are rules. A contract is a contract. You know the score."

Gage nodded. It was the answer he'd expected. Aeg Derg might not want to, but he would follow the rules. He'd keep sending assassins after Gage until they succeeded—or until the contract was terminated. So be it.

He gave Aeg Derg a nod good-bye. "Master."

The old assassin returned his nod. "Gage."

"It would not be safe to attempt to return to the guild," Aeg said as Gage turned to go up the stairs.

He paused and glanced back at his old mentor.

The old man continued. "I've recently found our security to be a bit... lacking. If you were to return, you would find it much more difficult. Even your—shall we say—extraordinary abilities would not allow you undetected entry."

Gage smirked. He'd always wondered if the guildmaster somehow knew of his Shadow abilities. Given the man's words, it seemed as if he did. He wasn't surprised and chuckled to himself. Aeg Derg always seemed to know things he shouldn't.

"I won't be back," Gage told the man. He turned to go

but before he could take a step onto the stairs, his mentor spoke again.

"Yes," Aeg Derg continued, scratching his chin. "In fact, in a week or so, I may have to revisit the security on our safehouses as well."

He paused, looked back at the guildmaster, and cocked his head. Had he just heard what he thought he'd heard. Was his old mentor basically telling him the safe houses they had scattered around the city would be available for the next week?

"A week?" he asked, eyebrow raised.

"Or so," the man replied with a nod. "I'll want to revise security here first. Obviously, that will take priority. That should take... hmm... about a week..."

"A week, then." Gage nodded.

"Or so." Aeg Derg nodded, his face an expression of mock seriousness. "The safe houses will need to be completely moved in a week. It would be the only prudent thing to do after a breach. And speaking of a breach... will we find that some of the members on guard died during the breach?"

Gage shook his head. "No. I disabled them and tied them up. By now, they've regained consciousness and are probably trying to free themselves."

Aeg Derg gave a nod of approval, perhaps appreciation. The guild had already lost the three assassins his mentor had sent after him. Likely, the guildmaster was hoping he hadn't lost any more.

The question reminded Gage of the dark living quarters of the second floor. "Is the second floor living quarters being used? It seemed dark for a floor that should be occupied."

The guildmaster frowned. "It's been empty for some time. We lost quite a few of our number after you left. They've been difficult to replace."

Gage raised an eyebrow. "No new protege?"

"Not since you." The guildmaster chuckled mirthlessly. "Although there is one prospect. She just needs a bit more experience. If she survives..."

"Then do her a favor," Gage said. He narrowed his eyes and put some steel in his voice. "Don't send her after me."

"The thought never crossed my mind." Aeg Derg smiled and chuckled slightly. The smile faded from his face as he looked at Gage with sadness in his eyes. "I'm afraid they don't make them like you anymore, my boy."

"Nor like you, old man," Gage replied.

The corners of his old mentor's mouth turned up, but the smile didn't reach his eyes. He nodded to his former protege. "Gage."

"Master," Gage nodded back.

Without another word, Gage turned and hurried up the stairs. He quickly retraced his steps and a few minutes later, on the ground floor of the temple.

Gage paused at the door of the guild house and glanced around. His return to the temple and his meeting with Aeg Derg had stirred memories within him—memories he had been trying to suppress since he'd started a family with Alani.

And now, he was going to use his skills to kill the most powerful man in the province—or die trying. He needed to get back to the inn and make plans. After all, he had his revenge to plan and an Archmage to kill.

CHAPTER 31

Gage easily left the Shadowed Fist guild house without notice, slipping between the sentries as they continued their patrol. He paused briefly just outside the courtyard and watched the three sentries on patrol. His attention focused on the woman he'd seen before—the one who seemed to be able to detect his use of Shadow magic.

Was it possible this was the woman Aeg Derg had mentioned? Was she already learning to become a Witch Slayer? Was that why she'd sensed his magic? Or did she somehow have access to Shadow magic?

Either was something that would serve her well as a member of the Shadowed Fist. If she were to possess both, she would easily become one of the top assassins in the guild—just as Gage had.

He took one last look at the slender woman and then turned away. It didn't matter. He would never return to the guild house, and they would never meet. Gage's expression hardened. If they did meet, it would be because she had been sent to fulfill the contract.

Slipping from shadow to shadow, Gage waited until he was several blocks away before activating his *Shadow Vision*. Once he was able to see in the dark again, he carefully surveyed the area around him to make sure no one was following him.

Gage trusted Aeg Derg—to a point. The old assassin had been his mentor and they'd become close—probably the closest thing to a father figure he'd had since coming to this world. Given their earlier conversation, he didn't think the guildmaster would send someone after him already.

Then again, it didn't hurt to be cautious. He hadn't lived this long by being reckless. Gage made a series of *Shadow Slides*. He did long ones, short ones, and even doubled back. Only once he was certain no one was following did he finally head south to the Rainbow Trout inn.

Sliding back into his room through the open window, Gage paused and scanned the room for any sign of intruders. The room was dark, but his *Shadow Vision* penetrated even the darkest corners.

Confident the room was unoccupied, he turned back to the windows. Gage pulled the faded shutters closed. He used a piece of twine to tie them together and attached a small, crude bell he'd bought earlier. He then went to the door and did the same tying a length of twine around the latch and attaching a second bell to it.

The concept was simple. If someone attempted to open either the window or the door, the bells would alert him. Even if someone cut through the twine, the bell would sound when it fell. It wasn't foolproof, but it was the best he was able to do with the resources at hand.

His room as secure as he could make it, Gage stripped off his garments and slid into the bed. Gage had many things to think about and consider, but they could wait until morning. For now, he pushed everything to the back of his mind and forced himself to relax. He needed as much sleep as he could get to face the busy day tomorrow.

* * *

THE NEXT MORNING, Gage was tired but forced himself to get up and pack his belongings. He left the Rainbow Trout and headed southwest to a safehouse in the Blood District.

Named for the many slaughterhouses that populated the district, the Blood District was not the ideal place to stay. Unfortunately, his choices were limited. The safehouses were all in out-of-the-way areas, where assassins could lie low.

Every member of the Shadowed Fist was given a list of safehouses to memorize before each job. If the job went bad or they were seen, they were to go to a safehouse, rather than back to the guild. It was one of the most important tenets of the Fist: an assassin never put the guild at risk.

Once an assassin made it to the safehouse, they waited until someone was sent for them. Sometimes, that was to bring them back to the safety of the guild. Other times, the guild cut the person loose. Permanently.

Gage had only needed a safehouse once in his career.

He shook his head as he remembered the incident. It was when he was just being trained as a *Witch Hunter* and had gotten an assignment to kill a warlock who was starting to cause trouble in House Cernunnos.

Every warlock eventually goes crazy, supposedly from the demon's voice in their head. Some just take longer than others. What they did in their insanity varied.

This warlock, an old man named Torcall, was a member of House Cernunnos. He had once been a respected scholar, but the longer he lived with his powers, the more insane Torcall had become.

Eventually, he had been driven to believe he could bring the demon he'd made a pact with into this world by breeding with women—and he pursued the goal with forceful disregard for the women involved.

After covering up the first half dozen, the House decided to remove the source of their irritation and quietly hired the guild to do the job. Aeg Dern had assigned Gage.

Everything had gone well; he killed the warlock quietly and without being seen. Gage had been about to leave Torcall's room when a trio of town guards had burst in to arrest the errant warlock for raping a woman earlier in the evening.

They'd seen Gage and he'd been forced to kill all three of them. He'd then arranged the bodies so it appeared that the guards had killed Torcall while trying to take him in, but not before he'd used his magic to kill them.

Torcall specialized in air magic, and it had been tricky to arrange things plausibly. In the end, he could only hope that the scene he created was chaotic enough that the investigators bought it.

But he'd killed someone other than the target. He'd killed innocents—at least, as innocent as any town guardsman was.

Unsure what to do, Gage retreated to one of the safehouses he'd memorized and waited. He waited for three days, unsure if someone was coming for him—to "retire" him. It had been a very long three days.

Finally, Aeg Derg himself had shown up at the front door. Gage had been certain the guildmaster had come to put an end to him. He'd nearly run from the man when he saw him at the door—as if it would have done him any good.

The old assassin had simply shaken his head at Gage and said "sloppy" before leading him back to the guildhall in silence. The entire walk back to the temple, he'd been certain his mentor meant to kill him. But he hadn't.

When they'd finally reached Aeg Derg's office, the guildmaster went behind his desk, retrieved a small bag of coins and put it on the desk—Gage's payment. He did so without a word and then immediately began looking through the ledger.

After several minutes of silence, Gage realized his mentor wasn't going to say anything else. He walked forward, took the money, and then walked out of the office.

The next day, Aeg Derg said hello when they passed and acted as if nothing had happened. The two of them never spoke about it again and Gage never killed another innocent.

Gage shook the memories away as he reached the address of the safehouse. In this case, the safehouse was on the second floor of one of the countless slaughterhouses that made up the Blood District. This one specialized in lambs and he could hear the doomed creatures inside the building, waiting for their turn to die.

Ignoring the dying livestock, Gage climbed up the narrow stairs. There was no latch on the outside so, making sure no one was watching, he slipped his dagger between the door and the frame, lifted the inside latch, and pulled the door open.

He scanned the large room quickly, making sure another assassin wasn't already here and that no squatters had taken over the room. After deciding the place was empty, Gage went inside and set his pack down on the small, wooden table. He rigged bells on the door and the two windows and then searched the room for the stash.

Gage found it in a loose floorboard, retrieving some nondescript clothing, two unadorned sharp daggers, and a small leather pouch of coins. It wasn't much, but it would be enough for him to buy some supplies, as well as food for the next few days.

A few days would be all he needed. By then, he would kill the Archmage and be out of the city—or he'd be dead.

Gage visited the other two safehouses, removing each location's emergency supplies. His small investment of time netted him two more small pouches of gold, some additional daggers, and a few more sets of clothing. It wasn't much but every bit helped.

He stopped at the market on the way back. Gage picked up some bread, jerky, apples, and a small hand cask of ale. The food and drink were nothing special, but all of it would keep for several days—and a few days was all he needed.

During his travel to the safehouses and the market, Gage had noticed more slaver press gangs in alleys. He'd even spotted some out in broad daylight. Twice he'd recognized the tell-tale signs of the thieves' guilds, but the other times there were no signs. That meant they were freelancers or mercenaries.

Seeing the gangs made Gage think back to his own encounter with the thieves' guild in the alley. Had that been their end goal? Rob him and then sell him into slavery? He frowned. Had he known they were slavers, he might not have left any of them alive. He continued back through the Blood District, even as he thought about his earlier encounter.

Passing an alleyway, Gage heard a woman's voice cry out softly. "Help me!"

He paused. Gage looked down the alleyway and saw some forms in the shadows. He was tempted to use his *Shadow Vision* but decided not to. There were people on the street, and if they saw his eyes go black, it would just cause undue attention.

The woman cried out again. This time, her voice sounded pained.

Growling to himself, he stepped towards the alley. The old him might have kept going—focusing on his mission. But years with Alani had changed him—or maybe just reminded him of who he had been before coming to this world.

Walking into the alley, Gage moved towards the forms in the shadow of the buildings. He made it halfway down the alley before using his *Shadow Vision* to peer through the darkness.

As his vision faded to black and white, he spied a woman being cornered by two large ruffians at the far end of the alley. A quick glance told him the girl was in her early twenties. She was pretty if a bit dirty. She looked over at him hopefully as she caught sight of him. Luckily, the shadows hid his black eyes.

"Help me, stranger!" The woman cried out and her

words caused the two men to turn their heads and squint down the alley at him.

Some inner instinct warned him that something didn't seem right about the situation. He started to take a step back when he heard the crunch of gravel behind him. Gage glanced over his shoulder to see two more men coming into the base of the alley, blocking his retreat.

The two men pinning the woman suddenly released her and turned to face him. Both pulled small clubs from their jerkins. Behind him, the two newcomers did the same. Instead of running away, the woman just leaned casually against the wall, crossing her arms over her chest.

Gage smirked. He'd just fallen for one of the oldest tricks in the book. The woman, or sometimes a child, would pretend to be in trouble and call out. They'd lure some do-gooder into the alley and then rob him—or, given what he'd seen so far in the city, probably sell him into slavery.

Taking in each man in turn, Gage scanned them in his HUD.

Brys
Human
Brigand
Level 7

Rhain
Human
Brigand
Level 6

Griff
Human
Rogue
Level 7

Irfon
Human
Brigand
Level 7

All were higher level than he'd expected. Certainly much higher level than the low-life thugs he'd encountered when he'd first come to the city. Gage glanced at the girl, his eyes widening slightly as he read her description.

Cristyn
Human
Summoner
Level 9

A summoner! Gage cursed under his breath. His eyes darted around the alley, searching for her familiar. Summoners always had their familiar with them—some of them could even summon several familiars. Although, when they could summon more than one familiar, they were always smaller creatures.

As he searched the alley for the familiar, he activated his Evasion. Some familiars were extremely dangerous with otherworldly powers. He cursed again for getting caught in such an obvious ploy.

"Oi!" called out Brys, a bearded man with an ugly,

jagged scar down his bare right arm. The brigand was the largest of four men. He was probably the leader of the band, though if the summoner's familiar was dangerous enough, she might well be in charge.

"Give over your coin and come quietly," Brys told him, taking a step towards him. "Or there's going to be trouble."

Gage glanced behind him again, still searching for the familiar. There was no sign of it. He didn't sense any magic, so it wasn't hidden by magic. So where was it?

"That's right," said Griff, one of two thugs behind him. Griff wasn't the tallest of the lot, but he was even broader than Brys. "We got you surrounded."

"What's wrong with his eyes?" Rhain asked, squinting at Gage.

Despite wanting to keep a low profile, Gage knew he needed to deal with these men quickly. The familiar changed things. He had no idea where the summoner's familiar was, how many there were, or what their capabilities could be. Those were odds he didn't like.

Gage dropped the small sack with his food and the hand keg. He watched the men's eyes glance down at the two items and smile. Moving faster than the men could see in the shadowed alleyway, he launched two daggers at the two men in front of him, Brys and Rhain.

You critically pierce Brys for 42 damage.
You critically pierce Rhain for 39 damage.

"I... I'm hit," Rhain said, gaping at the dagger protruding from his chest.

Neither hit was a killing blow, and the blades hadn't been poisoned, so the two men weren't out of the fight. With their level, it would take more than a single strike to bring them down. Gage had known that when he'd attacked. He just hoped it would slow them down enough for him to finish off the other two.

Sliding two more daggers from their hiding places, he spun and rushed the two men at the entrance of the alley.

Although momentarily surprised at his rush, the two men recovered quickly. As he neared, the taller of the two, Irfon, swung his club at Gage's head.

Irfon crushes you but you Evade.

Despite ducking under the blow, his Evasion kicked in and the blow completely missed him. The miss caused Irfon to overbalance himself. Gage spun around and buried a dagger in his solar plexus, and then struck the other dagger through his ribs and into his heart. Irfon looked down dumbly and then collapsed to the ground.

You critically pierce Irfon for 35 damage.
You critically pierce Irfon for 41 damage.
Irfon dies.
You gain 70 experience.

Gage grunted as pain exploded in his left shoulder and his entire arm went numb from the shock of Griff's club slamming into him.

Griff crushes you for 16 damage.
Griff hits you with Crippling Blow.

The dagger fell from numb fingers and Gage allowed the momentum of the blow to push him away from the stocky brigand. As he was pushed away, he tried to move his arm. It didn't respond at all.

Having been hit with *Crippling Blow* before, he knew it would be several minutes before the ability wore off and he could use his arm. He cursed. He thought about using another charge of Evade, but hesitated. The familiar was still out there, and it was an unknown. He decided to wait.

"You like that?" Griff asked with a wicked grin. "I got more where that came from."

Now at a disadvantage, Gage knew he didn't have a choice. He couldn't use his arm and he still had no idea where the summoner's familiar was. He had to use his Shadow abilities.

The sadistic smile still plastered on his face, Griff took a step towards him to finish him off. Gage waited until he started his swing before *Shadow Sliding* behind the man. He spun and slid his dagger into the man's back, between the fourth and fifth ribs once, then twice. He added a twist on the second stroke.

You critically pierce Griff for 42 damage.
You critically pierce Griff for 49 damage.
Griff dies.
You gain 70 experience.

Griff stiffened and started to turn around. The thrusts had pierced his heart, but his brain didn't know he was dead yet. He tried to raise his club, but his arm only started to move before the club fell from dead fingers and Griff collapsed to the ground.

Gage spun just in time to see Brys's club coming down at his head. He just managed to side-step the blow, but it glanced off his already injured left shoulder.

Brys crushes you for 11 damage.

Grunting in pain, Gage forced himself to counterattack and drove the dagger up beneath the man's jaw, through his mouth and into his brain. His body jerked before collapsing.

You critically pierce Brys for 44 damage.
Brys dies.
You gain 70 experience.

Even as Brys collapsed, Gage had to throw himself to the side to avoid a crushing blow from the last man, Rhain. Unfortunately, that meant he hit the alley wall with his injured shoulder, causing pain to shoot down his arm and up his neck.

Rhain yelled and came back at Gage with a wild swing. Gage easily ducked under it, slipped behind the man while sliding his dagger across the back of the man's hamstrings.

You critically slash Rhain for 11 damage.
You critically slash Rhain for 9 damage.
Rhain is hamstrung.

His tendons cut, the man stumbled towards the wall

and Gage gave him a push—with his dagger. His blade slipped through the man's ribs and ended his life. His body hit the wall before falling in a heap.

You critically pierce Rhain for 44 damage.
Rhain dies.
You gain 70 experience.

Trying to ignore the pain in his shoulder, Gage spun towards the final figure—the summoner. He was about to take a step forward when something leaped down from the top of the building at him.

CHAPTER 33

Gage threw himself to the other side of the alleyway and rolled out of the way as he activated another charge of his Evade. Grunting in pain as he rolled over his injured shoulder, he heard something heavy land next to him. A new message seemed to appear immediately.

Fanged Beast lashes at you but you Evade.

A clawed tentacle flashed past his face, narrowly missing him. Gage didn't hesitate. He activated his *Shadow Slide* ability and *Slid* to the end of the alley. Spinning around, he saw the summoner's familiar bounding towards him.

The creature bore down on him with incredible speed. As it closed the distance with great loping strides, Gage could make out the demon in excruciating detail. Its body resembled that of a great hunting cat. The difference was, this familiar was much larger than any mountain lion or bog panther.

Not only was its body larger, it also had two huge fangs jutting from its maw. Gage blinked as a childhood memory hit him like a hot poker. It was a memory of his time before he'd come to this world. His time back on Earth.

His parents had taken him to a building with large stuffed animals—a museum. The demon's large fangs reminded him of something he'd seen that day. A name popped into his mind: Saber-toothed tiger.

But unlike the Saber-toothed tiger from Earth, this creature had four long tentacles erupting out from its back. The tentacles were as thick as his forearm. Worse, the writhing tentacles were tipped with three curved claws.

Gage doubted he—or any human, elf, or even beast-kin—could outrun the demon. He doubted he could kill it now. He snorted. He wasn't sure he could kill it even if he was prepared. The long tentacles gave it a greater reach and if he got in close, there were the claws and teeth to deal with. His only hope would be poison.

There were poisons that killed demons. Because of their otherworldly origin, their bodies were immune to most normal poisons. He'd found that out the hard way. He still had a scar along the right side of his back to remind him.

He'd survived the encounter and fulfilled the contract —barely. When he returned and healed, he'd taken time to research demon poisons. The knowledge hadn't come easy, or cheap. In the end, he'd learned of two poisons that worked against otherworldly creatures. Both were difficult and expensive to make—and he had neither with him now.

With the beast bearing down on him and still unable to use his left arm, Gage knew he had no chance against this demon. But he looked beyond the beast to the summoner. No matter how strong the summoned creature was, all familiars had the same weakness: The summoner.

Gage saw the woman, her eyes wide as she stared down the alleyway at him. She'd seen him *Shadow Slide*. To her, it would have been nothing short of magical teleportation. As far as he knew, no one could travel magically without creating a portal. No one except him.

The beast stalked closer, and Gage waited until the last second. Just as the demon saber-toothed cat rushed within tentacle reach, he activated *Shadow Slide*.

While he knew that his *Slide* looked instantaneous to others, it was never quite that way to him. Gage actually saw himself moving to the location—traveling in a straight line to his destination.

As that happened, the world seemed to blur past. Shapes elongated briefly and then he was suddenly at his destination—and everything snapped back the way it should be. It was very disconcerting at first. Now, he'd long since gotten used to it.

When he *Slid* from one spot to another, intervening objects and people couldn't see or touch him. To them, one moment he was in one spot and the next moment he was somewhere else. Until now.

As the alleyway elongated and he moved down the alley, he caught a glimpse of the demon cat's eyes. They followed him. He was so stunned by the cat's ability to see him that he missed the clawed tentacle until it sliced across his left calf.

Fanged Beast lashes at you for 13 damage.

Gage gasped in pain and surprise, unable to comprehend what had just happened. Something had just seen—and attacked him—in the middle of a *Slide*. How was that possible?

Still reeling from the pain and shock, he materialized next to the summoner, Cristyn. She yelped as he appeared next to her. She fumbled for a knife at her belt, but he was faster. Weight on his right leg, his hand darted up so the blade of his dagger was at her throat.

If he killed her, the familiar would disappear—banished back to whatever hell or universe it came from. The summoner was the creature's link to this world and without that link, it couldn't maintain its presence. And yet, he hesitated.

Cristyn stared at him wide-eyed as the edge of his dagger rested against her throat. She was terrified. She most likely depended on her familiar for protection and, given its size and speed, no one got this close to her.

Behind him, the demon cat roared, and he spared a quick glance to see it charging towards him. He had no doubt that it would tear him to shreds if it reached him. And still he hesitated.

Hesitation meant death on the streets. The old Gage wouldn't have hesitated. He would already have killed the summoner and ended the threat. So why was he hesitating?

The woman had the same blue eyes as his daughter. The blue eyes that had looked up at him through many bedtime stories. He cursed and moved his face close to her. "If I see you preying on the innocent again... I won't hesitate. And next time, even your demon cat won't save you."

With that, he glanced behind her, into the next alley over. He picked a shadow there and *Slid*. Then he immediately Slid to the next alley and then the next. He continued sliding until he was out of *Mana*.

By that time, he was ten blocks away and hopefully out of range of the summoner's familiar. He knew from studying up on them that there was a limit to how far a summoned creature could move from its master. If it tried to move beyond that, it lost its connection and was banished back to whatever place it had been summoned from.

Gage searched along the path he'd followed. Even with his *Shadow Sight,* there was no sign of the summoner or the beast. He watched for almost a full minute, before slumping against the wall and then sinking to the floor of the alley.

He cut a piece of cloth from his cloak off and used it as a makeshift bandage. He wrapped it tightly around his shin but had to wait several more minutes before the *Crippling Strike* wore off and he could use his left arm to tie off the dressing.

There was still no sign of the summoner or her familiar, so he limped to the entrance of the alley and then joined the bustle of people on the street. He kept his eyes and other senses alert for danger and made his way back to the market.

The wound to his leg ached and his left arm still throbbed. Despite this, he knew he couldn't go back to the safe house just yet. Gage had things he needed to buy now.

Gage had been forced to abandon his food and drink when he'd fled the summoner and her beast. He'd also left three of his daggers at the scene. He cursed himself for being rusty. In the old days, he'd never have been caught so unaware.

And now, Gage would have to spend some of his precious money to replace the daggers and the food. He also needed to buy some herbs so he could brew a healing draught. It would take a day for his arm to be better, and even longer for the wound in his leg, without it. That was time he didn't have.

After finding all the items he needed at the market, he took the quickest and shortest path back to the safehouse. He kept a wary eye out for the summoner and her demon cat, but they were nowhere in sight.

When he finally reached the safehouse, he checked it thoroughly to make sure there was no one waiting for him. Satisfied it was clear, he set some bell traps on the doors and shuttered windows. He then changed the bandage on his leg and collapsed onto the bed.

He'd brew the healing potion later. For now, he needed rest.

CHAPTER 34

It was dark when Gage awoke. He groaned as the pain from his shoulder and his leg hit him. Since leaving the guild, he hadn't been in a real fight until the assassins had shown up at his doorstep. He'd lost much of his edge. He'd gotten sloppy. And now he was paying the price.

Cursing, he pushed himself up into a sitting position in the bed, activated his *Shadow Vision* and scanned the dark room. He spotted nothing out of the ordinary. Everything was as he had left it.

Gage swung his feet off the bed and stood. Or rather, that had been his intention. Instead, he sat back down heavily on the bed as his injured leg collapsed beneath him. He cursed again. The leg injury was still throbbing.

His thoughts went back to the demon cat in the alley. How had it seen him in the *Shadow Slide*? And how in the three suns had it been able to injure him during a Slide? It was surprising and disturbing.

He didn't know how late it was and he had things to do. Gage pushed himself back up but kept the weight off his left leg this time. He hobbled over to the small table and collapsed into the simple wooden chair.

Pulling his haversack over to him, he began unpacking the alchemical bottles he'd brought from the inn. Gage needed to brew a healing potion. Without a healing draught, he had no chance of doing the reconnaissance of the House Keep.

Luckily, the healing potion was one of the few things he'd continued to make after his retirement. There were always injuries around his farm, and with just him and Alani working it, neither could afford to be out of commission.

He smiled sadly. Once Shaunna had come along, he'd always kept several vials in the house. His daughter had been a fearless daredevil. She'd sustained more than her fair share of bumps, bruises, cuts, and scrapes. One sip of the healing potion and they were gone within seconds.

His smile turned into a scowl as he felt the loss of his daughter—and the loss of her mother. Gage would never see either of them again. And it was because of Ruy Cernunnos. He narrowed his eyes and clenched his jaw. The Archmage would pay soon enough.

Pushing his pain and anger aside, he focused on making the healing potion. Slowly and carefully, he assembled his makeshift alchemical set. Gage ignored his stiff shoulder and the pain in his leg. He worked methodically, putting components together until he was ready to brew his healing potion.

Gage ground the herbs up with the small mortar and pestle he had procured.

With that done, he added them to solvents that would extract the properties he needed from the herbs.

Each herb went into a separate vial and he poured each through a series of filters to remove the residue. To activate his purified extracts, he heated them on small charcoal burners until they turned the proper color.

One at a time, he slowly stirred them into a larger beaker over medium heat. Bringing the potion to a boil, he held the temperature for several minutes, until the solution reduced by half, before removing the burner and allowing the potion to cool.

He examined the light green tincture. Despite its pleasant color, he knew the concoction tasted like something from a pig's trough. It also burned worse than the strong dwarven spirits. Unfortunately, there was nothing to be done about it. He stared at the liquid for a moment longer and then downed half the beaker.

You have used Major Healing Potion.
You are healed for 38 Health.

As expected, the healing drought burned going down his throat. The concoction scorched his throat, all the way down to his stomach. The burning radiated out from his belly and spread across his entire body. He gritted his teeth against the fiery sensation the alchemical potion produced as it worked.

After nearly a minute, the burning subsided and he immediately noticed the pain in his shoulder was completely gone. He rotated his arm and was pleased to find it was back to normal. He did a few stretches to confirm before moving on.

Gage reached down and removed the bandage from his leg. Where there had been deep gashes, there was now new pink flesh. Given the shape of the pink skin, he guessed the wound would leave yet another scar. The potion couldn't prevent scarring—he knew that from experience. But at least the wound itself was healed.

Extending his ankle, he worked the injured calf. It was a bit stiff but there was no pain. Gage stood up and gingerly put weight on the leg. The leg supported him. He took a few careful steps, making sure he hadn't lost any mobility.

He smiled. The healing potion had done its job. Gage stomped his feet several times, testing the leg's response. Next, he sprinted from one side of the small room to the other, skidding to a halt when he reached the wall. In each instance, his leg held up with only the slightest stiffness when he dug into the stop.

Confident his leg and arm would support his endeavors tonight, he strode back to the table. He took the remaining healing potion and poured it into a drinking horn he'd picked up in the market. He'd take the potion with him—just in case.

Gage's stomach growled as he corked the container. Glancing at the sack with his bread and jerky, he realized he hadn't eaten. Pulling the sack to him, he ate a bit of bread, an apple, and a piece of jerky.

Finishing his quick meal, he retrieved his night clothes and laid them across the bed. He stripped down and used the last of the Dog's Bane on himself and his clothes. He guessed the House Keep would have beast-kin too, so he masked his scent.

He then dressed in his nighttime garb and strapped on the few daggers he had remaining. Gage frowned as he thought about the weapons he'd lost earlier. That brought back thoughts of the demon cat and its strange ability to see and attack him during his *Slide*.

Shaking his head to clear his thoughts, Gage glanced down at the daggers strapped and hidden around his body. He wasn't expecting a fight—quite the contrary. If he was spotted by any of the fortress's guards, let alone had to engage one, the place would go on high alert. If that happened, the chances of him making it to the Archmage would plummet drastically.

As the previous master of assassins for House Cernunnos, Gage had been involved in the security for Cernunnos Keep. He hadn't been completely in charge of it. That duty had belonged to Horas Sorbar, the Captain of the Keep Guard.

Horas Sorbar was an older man, a former Army officer, and veteran of many campaigns against the other houses. With the Houses always skirmishing over borders or perceived threats, there was never a shortage of fighting.

Gage had given Captain Horas advice from an assassin's point of view. He'd pointed out obvious holes that an assassin from one of the other Houses might utilize. The man had never really cared for Gage, or assassins in general, but had listened to him and made any changes he'd agreed with—which had been most of them.

But that had been years ago. Things would have changed. For all he knew, Horas wasn't even Captain of the Keep Guard any longer. Not that it mattered. Gage wouldn't let Horus or anyone else stop him from killing the Archmage. Ruy Cernunnos had to die.

Satisfied with his appearance and his weapons, Gage used the windows to check the area around the safehouse with his *Shadow Vision*. He wasn't expecting anyone but part of him half expected to see the demon cat looking back at him.

He shivered. The demon cat was the last thing he wanted to come face to face with. Not without some of the demon poison. Unfortunately, he didn't have the money for the ingredients—not at the moment. For now, best to avoid it and focus on his mission.

There was no demon cat staring back at him. In fact, there was no one at all. He glanced up at the sky. Judging by the moons and the position of the planet in the sky above him, it was well after midnight. It was late—or early, depending on how you looked at it. All normal people were sleeping.

Gage wasn't normal. Plus, he had a mission. Right now, that mission demanded that he scope out the fortress and find a way inside.

Once he re-familiarized himself with the layout and memorized the patrols, he'd plan the assassination. Tomorrow, the day after at the most, the Archmage would get what was coming to him.

CHAPTER 35

*I*t was only a few hours before sunrise by the time Gage crept to the outside of the Cernunnos fortress. His nap and the brewing of the potion had taken much of the night and now he only had a short window to accomplish his agenda.

As he remembered, the fortress was surrounded by a thirty-foot-tall stone wall. Precious few handholds were present for anyone attempting to scale the wall and get inside the compound. But that wouldn't stop Gage.

Picking the darkest section of the wall, Gage waited until the guards who patrolled the wall had passed and then *Slid* onto the wall. As soon as he appeared on the parapet, he ducked low and activated his *Shadow Blend*.

He checked his stats.

Health: 30
Stamina: 51
Mana: 35

At the moment, he was down 5 *Mana* from the *Shadow Slide*. Because of the darkness, his abilities would cost less but *Shadow Blend* used *Mana* for each minute it was active. If he left it on, it wouldn't be long before it drained him. He needed *Shadow Slide* to get back out, so he'd have to keep a close eye on his stat.

Gage glanced in both directions along the wall. The patrol to his left was over a hundred yards away. From his earlier observation, he knew it would turn back in fifty-seven seconds. It would then take them ninety-one seconds to make it back to his breach point. He'd need to be gone by then.

He scanned the buildings inside the walls. Gage recognized the largest structure, the castle, instantly. As the master of assassins, he'd spent most of his time in the castle. Even after all these years, he still remembered the layout. He also remembered the guard patrols. Or rather, he remembered what they used to be.

From his experience with Captain Horas, he guessed the patrols schedules and routes were changed every month. It was a smart move, but it would make things more difficult for Gage. He'd play things by ear once he got into the castle.

First, Gage needed to know the movements of the outside guards. Once he knew their timing, he could plan his exact route to get into and out of the castle.

He chuckled mirthlessly to himself. Was he really more concerned about getting to the Archmage and killing him than he was with escaping? His wife and daughter were gone. His happy life was gone. Did he really care what happened to him after he killed the Archmage?

Pushing his morbid thoughts away, Gage continued to count silently in his head. Forty-three seconds before the guard turned. He looked over the courtyard, picking out possible scouting spots.

Despite the near invisibility *Shadow Blend* offered, he couldn't keep it up indefinitely. Gage needed a place where he was hidden and wouldn't need his special ability to be active. Someplace hidden from normal view but someplace high enough that he could scope out the entire courtyard. He also needed a place that wasn't patrolled. It took him another twenty-six seconds to find the right spot.

The barracks were near the castle, just to the left of it. It was a two-story, stone building that housed the hundred or so guards responsible for the security of the keep. Like the castle, the barracks had turrets.

Gage knew from his previous experience that the squat towers were ornamental. There was no ladder or stairway that led to the top of them. Not only that, but because of their location and the lack of accessibility, they were completely in shadow. The perfect place. Unfortunately, they were just out of range of his *Shadow Slide*.

Twenty seconds.

Scanning the area below him, Gage looked for a spot about halfway between the wall and the barracks. He saw the perfect spot only to discard it as he saw light coming from the side of one of the smaller buildings. A moment later, a group of two soldiers came around the corner carrying torches.

Fifteen seconds.

Gage glanced around the other buildings, looking for a

shadowed area where he could Slide. His eyes darted from location to location until he finally settled on a shadowed area on the roof of the forge, directly behind the chimney.

Ten seconds.

Another patrol was walking near the forge, a human and a catling. They turned onto the small street that ran parallel to the forge and would walk in front of it in less than thirty seconds. He cursed silently. The patrol on the wall was about to turn. He was out of time and had to risk it.

Mentally picking his destination, Gage *Shadow Slid* to the chimney. Doing so, suspended his Shadow Blend and he knew he would be temporarily visible to any beast-kin who might look his way. He just hoped no one was watching.

He *Slid* to the space next to the chimney. As he landed on the crest of the roof, one of the slate shingles shifted beneath his sudden weight. He had intended to re-activate *Shadow Blend* as soon as he landed but Gage was forced to grab the chimney as his perch became precarious.

The tile slipped out from beneath his foot and began sliding down the roof. As it did, the sound echoed around the courtyard. Gage cursed again as he glanced from the patrol on the wall to the guards below him. Both were turning to look his way.

Knowing he only had a moment to act, Gage glanced up to the closest turret on the barracks and activated *Shadow Slide*, instantly moving a hundred yards away. On top of the turret, he ducked down and listened to the commotion following the fallen shingle.

The wall guards hurried closer to the forge while the

patrol on the ground waved torches towards the roof and squinted at where the tile had come loose.

Gage peeked over the side of the turret, carefully staying hidden in the shadows. He checked his *Mana*.

Mana: 23

He would need at least 15 *Mana* to get back out of the fortress. That didn't leave him much to waste on *Shadow Blend*. Unfortunately, because of the commotion, other guards gathered. He couldn't risk a beast-kin's stray glance in his direction. He activated *Shadow Blend*.

Thanks to his *Shadow Sight*, Gage could see in the darkness. Unfortunately, his Shadow abilities gave him no special powers to hear the guards' conversations. He could only watch as the guards searched around the forge and then in it. Two other patrols showed up to assist with the search.

Their search took ten minutes, and by the time the guards resumed their normal patrols, he was starting to get low on *Mana*. He brought up his display.

Mana: 3

Gage swore under his breath and deactivated Shadow Blend. He would need to wait for his *Mana* to regenerate before he could leave. For now, he was stuck inside the fortress—all because of a loose shingle.

Pushing his frustration to the back of his mind, Gage remembered he had a mission to complete. From his place in the shadows, he quickly picked out the guard patrols. It was easy. They all carried torches, making them easy to mark.

There were twelve patrols in total, including the four on the walls. One by one, he memorized their patrol routes and then counted out how long it took each patrol to complete their route.

Luckily, the patrol routes were simple, but it had been a long time since he'd used his memory for this sort of thing. By the time he'd memorized all the guards' movements and times, he had a headache.

Gage knew the suns would be rising shortly and escaping the fortress undetected would become much more difficult. He checked his *Mana*.

Mana: 40

He smiled. During the time it had taken him to memorize the patrol routes, his *Mana* had completely regenerated.

With the guards' movements and an improved layout of the courtyard, he *Slid* to a shadowed section between the forge and the building next to it, then *Slid* up to the wall. He activated *Shadow Blend* briefly while he picked a spot outside the fortress and then *Slid* off the wall and to the safety of the city.

He looked back at the fortress. Gage now knew the information he needed to get over the wall and to the castle. Now, he only needed to get some ingredients for a few poisons and some more Dog's Bane, then he'd be ready to pay back the Archmage.

With a last glance up at the keep, Gage turned and

made his way through the streets and alleyways back to the safehouse. By this time tomorrow night, Ruy Cernunnos would be dead—and Alani and Shaunna would be avenged.

CHAPTER 36

By the time Gage returned to the safehouse and changed into normal clothes, the suns were up. He took his remaining money to the marketplace, herb shops, and even the few underground sellers, that still remained, until he found everything he needed.

During his travels around the city, he kept a wary eye out for the summoner and her demon cat familiar. Even though he was healed, he had no desire to run into the pair. Gage made a mental note to buy the ingredients for the demon poison as soon as he had the funds. Right now, he barely had enough to buy what he needed for his mission.

Gage ended up visiting several herb shops and apothecaries before getting all the ingredients. He finally found the last one, but it took nearly all his remaining funds. Leaving the apothecary, he looked down at the few coins in his hand. One silver and two copper.

The amount would barely cover a cheap room and a

meal at an inn, but it didn't matter. Gage had enough food to last him until tonight. It was all he needed. Tonight, Gage would break into the fortress and kill the Archmage. He didn't know what would happen after that and he didn't really care—as long as Ruy died.

Pushing the morbid thoughts from his head, Gage quickly returned to the safehouse. Given the number of slaver gangs he'd seen, he remained alert. He still chided himself for falling into the summoner's trap the previous day.

He thought back to the female summoner. Gage still wasn't sure why he'd left her alive. There'd been some-thing about the eyes that had reminded him of Shaunna. Gage felt his throat constrict at the thought of the daughter he'd never see again. A daughter he'd never "zoom" again.

Gage steeled his resolve and comforted himself in the knowledge that the man responsible for their death wouldn't see another sunrise. Picking up his pace, he hurried back to the safehouse.

Twelve hours later, Gage prepared to take a short nap. He'd spent the entire day brewing the various alchemical substances he needed. The first thing he'd created was a vial of Draiocht-neim, the poison that reduced a person's *Mana* to zero almost instantly. It rendered even the most powerful magic user helpless in seconds since, without *Mana,* they couldn't cast magic.

The irony of using the Draiocht-neim, or Wizard's

Folly, was that it was a formula developed by House Cernunnos and known only to their most trusted agents. As the former master of assassins for the House, Gage had been one of few entrusted with its secret.

Gage had learned other poisons with similar properties. He might even have been able to find the ingredients for them. Instead, he was going to use their own poison against them. And not just against them, but against the Archmage himself. He smiled again at the irony.

Draiocht-neim by itself would not kill a person, only prevent them from using any spells or powers that required *Mana*. To make sure that a single strike would take care of his enemy, he needed to combine the Wizard's Folly with something else.

He chose to combine the Draiocht-neim with Widow's Tears. While not the deadliest poison he knew how to make, it was the most deadly poison he could afford to make on his budget. It would have to do.

Gage checked the other vials. First, was the antidote for Widow's Tears. Aeg Derg had taught him that very important lesson many years ago: Before you make any poison, always make the antidote. Too many poisoners had been felled by inadvertent contact with their own poisons.

He'd also created another batch of Dog's Bane to absorb his scent and prevent any beast-kin from noticing him as he made his way into the castle. It would be foolhardy to go into any guarded structure without safeguarding against the beast-kin's scent ability.

Finally, there were also two more healing droughts. While he'd mapped out the guard patrols in the inner courtyard, he couldn't know what to expect inside the fortress. His hope was that he could *Shadow Slide* all the way to the Archmage's office. If not, he might have to fight his way all the way to the top of the tower.

The fortress guards weren't local town guardsmen. Each one was a professional soldier who trained daily. While there were few people who could best him in one-on-one combat, the guards wouldn't hesitate to gang up on him and use their numbers to their advantage. If that happened, a few healing potions might mean the difference between life and death.

Normally, he would also have brewed at least one *Mana* potion. Gage had always carried one on his missions. Unfortunately, the ingredients were expensive. Very expensive. They were also notoriously difficult to brew—much like Draiocht-neim. While Gage could have managed to brew it, he just didn't have the coin. He'd have to make do.

Gage looked over the beakers once more. Given his limited resources, he was happy with his limited selection of potions. He made sure all his burners had been extinguished before grabbing an apple, some jerky, and a mug of ale.

He thought of Alani and Shaunna as he ate. Gage knew that some of the religions in the world taught about an afterlife, but he'd never really paid them much attention. He'd never seen any true gods in the world. Only wizards, warlocks, and channelers who thought themselves gods.

Still, Gage hoped there was an afterlife. He hoped his wife and daughter were there now. Then, after he killed Ruy Cernunnos, maybe he would join them. He frowned.

Did the afterlife allow assassins? He hoped so, if only for a moment, so he could see Alani and Shaunna one more time.

Finishing up his meal, he reset and rechecked all his alarms and then laid down in the bed. He tried to push thoughts of the upcoming mission out of his mind. He mostly succeeded. Instead, his mind went to thoughts of the afterlife.

Gage drifted off into a restless sleep. In his dream, he could see Alani and Shaunna across a meadow. They beckoned him, but when he tried to run to them he never got any closer. They were always the same distance away. Gage jumped, crawled, ran, walked, and, even though it made no sense, swam towards them, but they remained the same distance away. Then he heard a bell toll.

Waking up suddenly, his hand brought up the dagger from underneath his pillow. Instinctively, he activated his *Shadow Vision* and the world went from black to shades of gray. Gage glanced around the room. He looked for the source of the noise—the sound of a bell. For the briefest moment, he thought he saw something outside the window by the door, through the shutters. Yet, when he focused on it, there was nothing.

The ringing. The bell. Had it been one of his alarms? His eyes darted around the windows and door, but there were no intruders or anything disturbed. But there had been that shadow or silhouette—just briefly. Had it been an intruder or just him seeing things.

Slowly, he slipped out from beneath the wool blanket. He stood up, still wary. Gage strained his ears for any hint of an out of place sound. There was nothing. Had he really heard one of the alarms? Or had the bell been part of his dream?

He padded around the safehouse and checked the door and all the windows. When he got to the shutters where he thought he'd seen someone, he thought the bell was not quite in the same place he had set it. Had someone tried the window, heard the bell, and run away? Had it been some petty thief?

Finally, he lowered his dagger. If it had been someone poking around the safehouse, they were gone now. Real or imagined, the alarm had woken him and he knew there was no way he'd fall back to sleep.

He glanced out the shutters at the sky. The suns were just sinking. He'd only gotten three hours of sleep. Sighing, Gage set down his dagger and looked over his night clothes and the potions. If he couldn't sleep, he may as well get ready.

He decided to have another snack first. He grabbed some of his food and poured a mug of ale. He looked at the sparse meal in front of him. It wasn't much, but it very well could be his last meal.

Eating his food mechanically, he finished quickly and then set about dressing and applying the poison to his daggers. He did so slowly, taking extra care with the poison and making sure the antidote was within easy reach.

Once the daggers were prepared, he applied the Dog's Bane and then slipped back into his night clothes. He then strapped on his daggers. He filled small ceramic vials with the potions and antidote.

He tied the healing potions to his belt. He used a

special knot he'd learned that would keep the vial secure but pulling the twine a certain way would release the vial and drop it into his hand. He'd used the method many times before and it worked well for *Health* or *Mana* potions.

He put the Widow's Tears antidote in a vial with a larger cork stopper. This, he affixed to his right hand, just beneath the sleeve. If he needed, he could quickly bring his wrist up to his mouth, pull the stopper out with his teeth and then drink the contents.

Once the potions and antidotes were in place, Gage was ready to go. He was ready to kill the Archmage.

CHAPTER 37

It was after midnight when he made his move.
Gage watched the guards on the wall for nearly an hour to make sure they stayed to the same schedule he'd memorized. Certain the patrols were the same, he knew it was time to put his plan into motion.

He couldn't see the internal patrols, so those would need to wait until he was inside. He had already had a plan of exactly when and where to jump. He just had to hope the internal patrols were on the same schedule.

Switching off his *Shadow Vision*, Gage looked up and cursed silently. The sky was clear tonight, allowing the light from the half dozen moons in the sky above him to bathe the city in pale luminance. While beast-kin and elves would see as well as daytime, with all of the moons full, even humans would have decent night vision this night. He'd have to take extra care.

Since Gage didn't know the makeup of the internal guard patrols, he had no idea how many beast-kin there were or which patrols they were a part of. Until he physically verified each patrol, he had to treat them all as if they had beast-kin.

Gage switched back on his Shadow Vision and the world became shades of gray. He turned his attention back to the wall. He'd already spotted a beast-kin with each of the two wall patrols—a tiger-kin and a dog-kin. He waited until both were at their furthest point from his *Slide* point before activating his *Shadow Slide*.

The landscape blurred by, and he was instantly on the wall. Having already picked out his next *Slide* point the previous night, he *Slid* again and blurred to the roof of the smithy. He'd barely landed before he *Slid* to another roof, and finally to the barracks turret, just like the night before. As soon as he arrived on the stones of the turret, Gage ducked down and listened for any alarm.

As he listened, he silently looked at his stats:

Health: 30
Mana: 16
Stamina: 59

His *Mana* was down by 24. The extra light from the moons had increased the *Slide* cost to 6 *Mana*. Gage made a mental note of the fact so he could manage his *Mana*. He needed enough to *Slide* back out of the keep. Best to let his *Mana* regenerate before the next *Slide*.

Despite keeping his ears open, he wasn't expecting an alarm. His *Slides* had been fast and precise, and they'd been on the roofs of the buildings. One thing common among even the best guards, they rarely looked up. It was a fact that he'd exploited many times. He listened for any tell-tale shouts from the guards to see if he'd gotten away with it this time.

After a minute of not hearing an alarm, Gage peaked over the edge of the turret. He quickly noted the positions of the patrols. They were all right where he expected them —give or take a few seconds. No two patrol times were ever the same.

Gage watched the patrols for another minute before turning his attention to the main keep. He was familiar with both the inside and the outside of the keep from his time as master of assassins. He knew the entire layout by heart.

Mana: 19

Glancing up, he saw the balcony leading to the Archmage's office. He and Ruy had spent hours on the balcony, discussing plans away from the prying ears and magical scrying. Gage growled quietly as memories of his previous life washed over him. He'd served House Cernunnos for years—and they'd turned on him. He cursed Ruy and he cursed the great Houses.

He moved his gaze from the office balcony to an equally large balcony just to the left. It led directly to Ruy's sleeping quarters. He'd only been in the channeler's bedroom a few times, checking it for security issues.

The Archmage's bedchamber was an enormous room, dwarfing the man's office. It had a gigantic bed where Ruy entertained his many playthings—whores and courtesan's whose love of money or prestige outweighed their revulsion for his demonic appearance.

Gage cocked his head. As a channeler, Ruy's pact with his demonic patron slowly warped his body to resemble an actual demon. From what he'd learned through sages, the more a channeler used his magic, the faster his or her body transformed to resemble their demonic patron.

The last time Gage had seen the man, the Archmage's skin had turned a deep red. Ruy had also grown jet black horns and claw-like fingernails and toenails. Without regular trimming, the claws grew several inches, preventing him from wearing shoes and giving his hands a bestial appearance.

Mana: 20

But that was years ago. He couldn't imagine the Archmage had slowed down his use of magic since Gage had left. What other transformations might have happened to him in the intervening years?

He gritted his teeth. It didn't matter. After tonight, there would be no more Ruy. The Archmage would pay for coming after Gage—for coming after his family. He'd pay with his life.

Glancing up at the sky, Gage guessed it was about 2am in the morning. He glanced from the office balcony to the bedroom balcony. Both had glass doors, an expensive luxury that only people like House Cernunnos or extremely well to do merchants could afford.

Mana: 22

There was no light from either door. Given the time of night, it wasn't surprising. Gage had met the Archmage at all hours of the day and night when they had been at war with one of the other Houses, but he knew the man preferred to retire early with his retinue of companions. Tonight appeared to be one of those nights.

He knew that Ruy would be alone with his women. The channeler never allowed any guards into his bedroom. It was a security risk Gage had pointed out multiple times, but the Archmage ignored him. He liked his women and what went on between them, private.

Gage went over multiple scenarios in his mind as he waited for his *Mana* to regenerate. He came up with a contingency for each one. It was always best to be prepared for as many scenarios as possible.

Continuing his mental preparations, Gage thought about the women who were most likely with the Arch-mage. He had no desire to kill them. They were most likely innocents, whose only crime was desperation or bad taste in men.

He should be in and out without any of the Archmage's companions even waking up. But if it came to it, he would knock them unconscious, rather than kill them. He wasn't Ruy. He didn't order the death of innocents.

Mana: 34

Feeling the anger welling up inside him, Gage forced it down. Now was not the time to be hot-headed. It was the time to be cold, calculating and in control. It was time to be the assassin again.

Gage felt a twinge of guilt at the thought. He'd promised Alani his old life was behind him. He'd told her he would never go back. And now, here he was, about to kill the head of House Cernunnos.

For a moment, he considered walking away. But only for a moment. Then he remembered the last time he'd seen his wife. He'd been staring right at her when the fireballs exploded and she burned alive. His daughter had died in her sleep, hopefully she had felt nothing. And he'd never gotten a chance to say goodbye to either.

Gage felt the muscles in his jaw tighten and his heart thumping in his chest. Once more, he pushed his anger down and checked his stats.

Mana: 40

His *Mana* was full. It was time.

Gage peeked over the turret and checked the patrols. When he was confident they were exactly where they should be, he turned back to Ruy's bedroom balcony.

He unsheathed two daggers and checked the blades to make sure the poison mixture was still on the blades. In the shades of gray that his Shadow Vision gave him, it was difficult to see but he could make out the slight discoloration around the edges of the blades. The poison was there. Everything was ready.

Lifting his head back towards the balcony, Gage gripped both daggers tightly. He picked a spot just to the side of the glass door. Gritting his teeth, he triggered *Shadow Slide*.

Instantly, he blurred forward across the space that

separated the balcony and the turret. Gage appeared at the exact spot he'd aimed for. So far, so good.

Even as the thought entered his mind, he sensed magic. At the same time, he heard a twang and felt something wrap around his right leg. Gage felt something grab him and wrap itself around him!

CHAPTER 38

$\mathcal{A}$t the same time an invisible force wrapped itself around him, Gage's *Shadow Vision* faded, leaving him blinking. He wasn't sure if there was some sort of unseen creature or if it was *Air* magic wrapping him in tight bonds. Either way, it didn't matter. He'd triggered some sort of trap or guardian and he needed to retreat.

Reflexively, Gage activated his *Suppress Magic* ability to cancel magic in the area. If it were *Air* magic or a creature using magic, his magic dampening ability would temporarily block it.

He blinked as nothing happened. Gage tried again. Still nothing. The ability wouldn't activate. He felt an unfamiliar panic rise. It had never failed him before. Ever.

Feeling panic starting to build, he quickly brought up his HUD.

Health: 30
Stamina: 58

Mana: 34

His stats all looked exactly the way he would expect. He'd used 6 *Mana* to Slide to the balcony. Everything else looked fine. Then he noticed a blinking message at the bottom of his HUD.

You are suppressed.
Suppression
You are unable to use any magic or magical abilities while under the effects of suppression.

Gage's blood went icy cold. Suppression was the effect he normally felt when he activated his own *Suppress Magic* ability. Someone or something was using the same effect on him.

Just to be sure, he tried activating his *Shadow Vision* again. Nothing happened. Looking over his shoulder, Gage tried to Slide back to the turret. He cursed silently when the ability didn't activate. None of his magical abilities worked.

He had blundered into some sort of magical trap. He swore. How many times had he told Ruy of the dangers of the balconies. And the Archmage had done nothing. Now, when Gage tried to exploit the weakness, he found that someone finally took his advice and trapped them.

Still able to move his head, he glanced down at the thing around his leg. It appeared to be some sort of stone or metal circle connected by leather cord. A bola? In the dim light, he managed to catch the slight blue glow of multiple crystals embedded in the balls. Chymera stones!

Cursing, he realized the bola was some sort of enchanted item—an enchanted item with the ability to suppress magic, just like his ability. Gage frowned. He'd heard of items such as these before. They were extremely rare and difficult to make, and very expensive.

Even to someone like Ruy, the Archmage of House Cernunnos, it had to be a massive expense. Why use such a rare and expensive item as a trap on his balcony? Gage scowled. Unless he knew Gage was coming and knew his abilities. He swore again.

Had Aeg Derg told Ruy he was coming and revealed his abilities? He gritted his teeth in anger and frustration. Had the old man really betrayed him? Gage wouldn't have thought so, but now he wasn't sure.

Angry now, he struggled against the bonds of *Air*, despite knowing it was pointless. He was certain it was *Air* magic. It didn't feel at all like a creature. There wasn't the feel of limbs or even tentacles, just solid, unbreakable *Air*. It might be part of the bola's enchantment, or it might be another enchantment.

As he continued to struggle, Gage saw a light appear in the Archmage's bedchamber through the glass doors. A glowing ball of flame hovered in the air, illuminating the room and enormous bed inside.

Now with normal vision, Gage blinked at the sudden light, and it took his eyes a moment to adjust. When he could finally see, he could make out numerous bodies lying on the large bed. Most of the shapes were women, naked or in sheer nightclothes. They all appeared to still be sleeping.

The one person who wasn't sleeping was the obese,

red-skinned man who was looking directly at him—Ruy Cernunnos. The Archmage was even larger than the last time Gage had seen him, although it hardly seemed possible.

Ruy waved at him and then called out as he rolled off the bed. As the large man pulled a silk bundle from a table next to the bed, Gage saw four elite guardsmen come into the room with pikes ready.

The guards looked around the room in confusion, some of their eyes lingering on the naked women in the bed. Ruy finally rolled his eyes and pointed at the glass doors. Immediately, the men caught sight of him and rushed towards the glass doors.

Slowly pulling on silk night pants over his corpulent form, Ruy called something to the men and they stopped just outside the door. The men glanced from Gage to Ruy, seemingly unsure what to do. Still, they waited while the Archmage tied the silk pants around his enormous waist.

Finally getting the silk pants to stay up, Ruy waddled to the door. The hovering ball of flame followed him. Ruy was still grinning. As he got closer, Gage could see that the Archmage had changed in other ways since he'd last seen the channeler.

Ruy's skin appeared to be a darker shade of red. His eyes were completely black, much like Gage's eyes when he was using Shadow Vision. The man's obsidian horns had grown from a few inches to almost a foot in length. Additionally, it appeared the man no longer bothered with trimming his nails and sported six-inch claws on all fingers and toes.

While those changes were somewhat surprising, they

weren't the biggest change. As the man's obese form shuffled closer, large, bat-like wings unfurled behind him—stretching and extending before folding themselves up behind him.

Wings on channelers were not unknown. He'd seen several before. Some channelers could even use them to fly. While Ruy's wings were large, possibly a wingspan of twenty or more feet, Gage couldn't imagine them being powerful enough to lift the overweight Archmage.

Ruy stopped at the door and waited. When nothing happened, he gave meaningful glares at the elite guards until one of them opened the door for him. The Archmage didn't step out onto the balcony but stood just inside the room and grinned at Gage.

"Gage!" Ruy cried in delight in a strangely high-pitched voice that seemed at odds with the man's enormous face. "So good to see you again."

The Archmage looked around the balcony, his brow furrowing and the smile faltering. He shook his head. "Not quite the fish we were hoping to catch, but a welcome surprise anyway." Ruy stuck his head through the doorway and looked back around the balcony and the courtyard. He frowned.

"No one else with you, then?" the channeler asked. He shrugged, not waiting for an answer and pulled his head back inside. "A shame, but no matter."

The man's fake smile returned and he looked at Gage. "Well then, don't just linger on the balcony. Come in! Come in!"

Ruy gestured to the elite guards as he stepped back. "Pull him inside, but don't step onto the balcony."

The closest two guards looked onto the balcony with confusion. There were at least five feet separating them from Gage. They murmured to each other before finally using their pikes to hook Gage and pull him close enough that they could grab him with their gauntlet clad hands. In the process, his hood fell down, revealing his shaved head.

"I like the look," Ruy snickered, rubbing his hand across his own bald head.

Gage didn't bother replying. Rumor was the man once had a full head of dark hair but it had completely fallen out once the demonic transformation had begun.

Ruy's smile dropped as he sighed and shook his head. "I was hoping that you would have come back to be our master of assassins. I did send Onchu to make the offer, but he hasn't returned yet." The Archmage's eyes dropped to the daggers still clutched in Gage's hands. "Given the way you entered and the daggers in your hands, I assume the answer was no."

"Which does beg the question, why wasn't the contract on you fulfilled?" Ruy asked, rubbing his chin. "Perhaps Aeg Derg is losing his touch."

"He sent three assassins." Despite not being completely sure if Aeg Derg had betrayed him, he still felt compelled to defend the man. "They're dead. I'm not."

The Archmage looked impressed. "Three against one. Impressive. But you always were the best."

"The best? They killed my family!" Gage snarled. "I'll kill you, you son of a demon!"

Ruy snorted and looked Gage up and down. "Aww. Your family was killed and now you want to kill poor, old

Ruy?" The man's black eyes narrowed. "Or is there some other reason? Perhaps... someone put you up to it?"

The Archmage came closer to Gage, well within striking distance.

"Your grace!" one of the guards snapped and reached out a hand to prevent Ruy from getting too close to Gage. The guard understood the danger of getting too close to an assassin like him.

Ruy's face screwed up in anger and with a gesture from the Archmage, the man was enveloped in fire. He screamed and clawed at himself as the fire burned him. The pungent smell of burning flesh filled the room and after a few seconds, the guard stopped screaming and dropped to the floor in a smoking heap. "Anyone else wish to stop me from doing what I wish?"

None of the other guards replied, but they all took steps back, a few of them glancing at the still smoking body of their former companion.

"Good," Ruy hissed and turned back to Gage. The Archmage moved within a foot of him and stared down into his eyes.

"Go ahead, Gage," the man taunted. "Strike me down. That's what you do, right? Assassin."

Looking at the mocking face of the Archmage, Gage strained against the *Air* magic, desperately trying to stab Ruy. One cut was all it would take. But he couldn't move. Couldn't break the bonds of *Air*.

In desperation, he tried *Suppress Magic* again. Nothing. He tried *Shadow Slide*. Nothing. None of his powers worked. He cursed and swore as he put his entire effort into moving.

Gage strained with the effort of trying to escape the bonds, but he didn't even budge the *Air* restraints. Finally, he slumped. Defeated. He had failed. He'd come this far only to be captured by the Archmage.

"What's wrong?" Ruy said in a mocking tone. "Gage can't get his revenge?"

"Just kill me and be done with it!" Gage spat.

"Kill you?" Ruy chuckled. "Oh, we'll get to that. But first, I have some questions for you."

"Questions about what?" Gage demanded.

"All in good time." Ruy's fake grin dropped and he spun to his men. "Take him to the dungeon. I'll be down later."

"Yes, your Grace!" the men replied in unison. They moved forward, picked up Gage and began carrying him out of the room.

As Gage went through the door, Ruy called out. "Be seeing you, Gage."

CHAPTER 39

The guards carried him out the door before promptly dropping him on the floor. Unable to move, Gage grunted as he hit the marble. Luckily, the *Air* magic binding him took the brunt of the force but it still knocked the wind out of him.

Two of the guards were human, the third was a beast-kin. Some sort of pale catling, possibly part puma or mountain lion. As he tried to catch his breath, Gage scanned all three guards.

Salas
Human
Fighter
Level 13

Brandubh
Human
Fighter

Level 13

Katain
Beast-kin
Fighter
Level 14

They were all higher level than typical guards, but Gage didn't recognize any of them from his former time with the House. He found that odd but, at the moment, he had other things to worry about.

"Filthy assassin!" snarled Brandubh and spit in Gage's face.

Bound in magic as he was, Gage barely managed to turn his head enough so the spittle hit his cheek and not full in the face. He memorized the man's face. If he got out of this, he'd pay the man a visit.

"Enough!" Growled Katain, who appeared to be the leader. He gestured to the two humans. "Take this one down to the dungeon and then come back for Reggus."

"Poor sod." Salas shivered, casting a glance at the still smoking corpse in the bedroom.

Brandubh shrugged indifferently. "Perils of the job."

Salas shook his head and then turned back to the other human guard. "Well, then. Brandubh! Grab his feet and let's get him down there."

"Send Uallas and Ruair back here as you pass," the catling told the two men and then spun around, walked over to the bedroom door, and pulled it shut. He then turned around and stood at attention.

Salas and Brandubh bent down, grabbed him by the

legs and shoulders, and hauled him through the Arch-mage's office to the double mahogany doors at the far end. Salas, at Gage's shoulders, banged on the door with his foot until it opened.

A red-faced guard pulled the door open from the opposite side and peeked in, pike at the ready. His eyes opened wide when he saw Gage "Ey! What's this then, Salas?"

"Assassin got caught in the wizard trap on the balcony," Salas replied. "Archmage knows him. Wants us to take him to the dungeon."

"The dungeon, eh?" the guard replied with a whistle. "Looks like he's in for a fun time."

"Sergeant says you two should come in and help him guard the Archmage until we get back," Salas told the other man.

The red-faced guard opened the door wider, revealing a second guard, another beast-kin. The part-hyena guard squinted menacingly at Gage.

Gage scanned both of the new guards.

Uallas
Human
Fighter
Level 13

Ruair
Beast-kin
Fighter
Level 12

The two new guards were as unfamiliar to him as the first group. It was increasingly odd that he wasn't recognizing any of the elite guards. Before he left, he'd known all `the elite guards that protected Ruy by name. Now, he wasn't recognizing any of them.

Ruair chuckled, sounding like the hyena he resembled. "To the dungeon, huh? To get some of Archy's special attention."

Uallas flinched, and Brandubh and Salas exchanged looks. Uallas elbowed the beast-kin in the ribs, clanging off his metal breastplate. "I told you not to call the Archmage that. If he hears you..."

"He's in the bedroom." The beast-kin scoffed, "He can't hear nothing except the moaning of his whores."

Uallas clenched his jaw and lowered his voice. "Who knows what his demon ears can hear."

"Best watch your mouth," Salas growled. "He just fried Reggus."

Uallas and Ruair blanched. The beast-kin shook his head. "Reggus? He's going through us like we're candy. There aren't going to be any of us left soon."

"If you don't keep your voice down," Brandubh hissed. "There might be one less mangy dog around."

Ruair pulled back his lips and growled at Brandubh, but Katain's voice sounded from the opposite side of the study. "What's the problem over there?"

"Now you've done it," hissed Uallas, elbowing Ruair again. "Come on!"

Uallas and Ruair hurried past and Gage lost sight of them as he was carried through the doorway.

Brandubh and Salas carried him down the familiar

halls, towards where he knew the stairs to be. As they did, he passed more guards but once again, failed to recognize any of them. He found it stranger and stranger than there seemed to have been a complete turnover of the elite guards.

Gage thought back to how casually Ruy had killed the guard, Reggus. What had Brandubh said? Perils of the job? Was Ruy indiscriminately killing off his own men whenever he felt like it?

The Ruy he'd know had been cold and calculating, completely ruthless. But he'd never squandered his soldiers' lives. To him, they'd all been assets. Sure, sometimes assets had to be sacrificed for the greater plan, but Ruy had always done so in a shrewd way.

He frowned. Had Ruy changed that drastically in the last few years? Was it his transformation?

It was common knowledge that eventually warlocks went insane, talking to people—or demons—who weren't there. They generally had more power than channelers, but that power came at a price. The price being the warlock's sanity.

From what Gage knew, a channeler's power came at the cost of a physical transformation. Generally, their mental facilities weren't affected. But few channelers grew so far into their transformation as Ruy. Could the transformation have affected his brain? Could he be taking on the mental attributes of his demonic host?

Gage was contemplating the possibility when they reached the stairs. The two guards stopped, pausing as they looked at the winding circular staircase leading down.

After a moment, Brandubh scowled. "I don't feel like carrying him all the way down. Let's toss him down and let him roll to the dungeon."

"Toss him?" Salas retorted, eyes wide. "Are you mad? You want to join Reggus?"

"What?" Brandubh replied, furrowing his brow. "He's an assassin. We're going to kill him anyway."

"Yeah," Salas agreed. "But the Archmage didn't kill him outright, did he? He knows this one. He wants to give him the special treatment if you know what I mean."

That brought a smile to Brandubh, a smile that turned to a sneer as he looked down at Gage. "Lucky chap! It's the special treatment for you."

Salas shrugged. "We can at least set him down for a spell."

"Now you're talking," Brandubh said with a wicked grin and let Gage's feet fall to the ground.

"Oy!" Salas growled. "I meant SET him down, not drop him."

Brandubh shrugged as Salas set him down on the gray stone floor.

Gage thought back to Salas's statement. The special treatment. He knew what the "special treatment" was. Torture. He'd known what was in store for him the moment Ruy had ordered him to the dungeon.

Tortured purely for the Archmage's pleasure. After all, he had no information Ruy wanted. Gage would be tortured until he died or until the Archmage tired of him. Neither was a pleasant prospect.

But that was assuming they could get him into a cell. At some point, they'd have to take the enchanted bola off him. Once it was off and his magic was no longer suppressed, he could use his *Shadow Slide* ability to escape.

Knowing the layout, he should be able to get out of the dungeon and back up to Ruy easily enough. Once he was face to face with Ruy again, he'd stab his daggers into the man's black eyes.

Gage just needed to wait for the opportunity. Bide his time. Wait for them to take off the magical restraint. He just needed them to make one mistake.

After a few minutes, the two guards picked him up and carried him down the stairs. They stopped at each landing and set him down briefly before continuing to the next landing.

Each time he was set down, Gage tested the *Air* magic. Unfortunately, it was still just as strong as the first time.

Still, he waited for his opportunity. They'd take off the restraint once he was in the cell. Then he would act.

After what seemed like an eternity, they finally made it to the dungeon. Brandubh and Salas stopped at a thick, iron bound door and set him on the floor. The ground here was rough stone, old and filthy.

Salas wrapped on the iron door with the hilt of his dagger until they heard the sound of a locking mechanism being manipulated. A moment later, the door opened and a huge, burly man with rotted teeth looked out at them.

This man, Gage did know. Arteen, the dungeon master and head torturer. The big man looked between the two guards and then looked down at Gage. He flashed him a broken smile that had a sadistic mirth to it. "Gage."

"You know this assassin?" Salas asked, glancing between Arteen and Gage.

"Used to be the master of assassins here," Arteen replied with a nod. "Not so mighty now, are you?" The man's broken smile became a truly evil grin. "I reckon I'll be enjoying this."

Brandubh chuckled down at Gage. "Looks like you'll be in good hands."

"Yeah," Arteen agreed and gestured for the men to follow him.

Once more, Gage was hoisted up as Brandubh and Salas followed the man into the wide hallway and past two more guards. They were guarding one of the cells, but the door was solid and Gage couldn't see who was in it.

The two guards followed the torturer as he turned down a passage to the right, another hallway opening into a large open area filled with implements of torture. There were more cells on the walls and the dungeon master gestured to the one against the far wall.

"Okay then," Arteen said, turning around. "Let's get him in a cell."

"He's got one of those enchanted thingies on him," Salas pointed out. "It's what's keeping him restrained."

"We can remove it once we get him in the cell," Arteen said and then walked over to the door of one of the cells. He fished through his keyring, grunted, and selected the key to open the door.

The two guards carried him in and then dumped him into the cell. Salas reached down to undo the enchanted bola. Gage tensed, ready to make his move.

"Are you daft?!" Arteen roared, shoving Salas away. He glared at the confused guard. "You never take those things off a conscious prisoner."

Arteen raised a thick leather-bound club, aimed at Gage's temple. Gage activated his Evasion ability, but something was off. Before he could bring up his HUD, the dungeon master brought the club down on his head.

Pain exploded in Gage's head and everything went black.

CHAPTER 40

Gage blinked at the bright sunlight streaming across the meadow. He felt the warmth of the triple suns on his body and heard the sound of the river to his left. He sat up and looked around. He furrowed his brow. He was at the swimming hole near his home.

He shook his head, trying to clear it. This was wrong. Gage was in a dream. He frowned, head still muddled. Or had he just been dreaming?

"Da! Da!" The familiar voice caused Gage to jerk his head around. The voice belonged to his daughter, Shaunna.

"Shaunna?" He exclaimed, looking around for the sound of the voice.

"Come in! Come in!" the little voice giggled.

Heart racing, Gage leapt to his feet. His head whipped towards the sound of his daughter's voice. She swam in the river, splashing in the shallow water with her mother. Alani! Shaunna! They were alive!

Gage blinked. No, they were dead. This was a dream. Or was it a memory?

Something was very familiar about the scene. He was sure this had to be a memory, but if so, it was the most vivid memory he'd ever experienced.

Yes, he remembered this now. It was a few months ago, at the end of summer during a hot spell. He'd taken Alani and Shaunna to the swimming hole over lunch. They'd brought a blanket and had a picnic before swimming. He'd laid down for a nap and...

"Honey!" Alani called to him, beckoning him to the river. "Come on, sleepy head!"

He definitely remembered this. He'd taken a nap, swam with them for a bit and then they'd gone home where he'd finished repairing the fence around the barn. He tried to remember everything, but his head throbbed.

This wasn't real. It couldn't be real. They were both dead. He'd seen them die in the explosion. He remembered that too, right? He cursed. Why was it so hard to think?

Gage looked back down at the blanket where he'd just been lying. No, not lying. He'd been napping, just like in his memory. Had Alani and Shaunna dying just been a dream? Or rather, a nightmare! A terrible, terrible nightmare!

Or was he in a dream now?

He looked around, furrowing his brow. Everything was confusing. He brought his hands up to rub his forehead. His head pounded.

He remembered being captured at the House Keep. He'd been dragged down to the dungeon. Arteen hit him on the head. He was unconscious and dreaming this.

Or had he dreamed the entire episode? His wife and daughter dying. Going to the city. Breaking into the Keep. Getting captured. Had it all been a dream from his nap?

Was he somehow reliving a memory? If this was a memory, had his head hurt the first time? He couldn't remember.

"Gage?" Alani called out, her voice tinged with concern. His wife looked worried and pulled Shaunna close to her. She looked around the woods and then looked at Gage. "Is something wrong?"

His heart melted as he saw them. He wished so many times that he could see them again, and now they were here. Only, he wasn't sure where here was. Or when it was. He was confused.

His head hurt. He couldn't think. He knew it had to be a dream, despite him wishing it weren't. A moment ago, he was in the Cernunnos dungeon. He remembered that. He remembered getting hit. He must have been knocked unconscious. And now he was dreaming. Or remembering. Or both.

He paused. Or was he dead? Perhaps Arteen had killed him and he was in the afterlife. He grimaced. The throbbing in his head made it so hard to think. Would his head hurt in the afterlife?

"Gage, you're starting to scare me," Alani said. She held Shaunna in her arms now and waded out of the river in her short clothes, clutching their daughter to her chest. "Tell me what's wrong!"

His breath caught. She looked as beautiful as ever. Alani looked just like she had the last time they'd gone swimming. And his daughter was right there.

"Da okay?" Shaunna asked. His daughter looked scared, as if she were about to break out crying at any moment. Her blue eyes flicked from Alani to Gage, unsure what to make of the situation.

Alani was coming closer now. What he wanted to do was run to them and hug them both and never let go. But what if this was a dream? Or a memory? Or the afterlife?

He stopped. Did it matter what this was? His wife and daughter were right in front of him. Why waste the opportunity to see and feel them again?

Gage took a step towards his wife and daughter, intending to sprint to them and wrap them in a bear hug, but even as he moved forward, things shifted.

The forest, the river, and his wife and daughter faded away, replaced by another all too familiar scene.

Gage was back in his house. He knew it was impossible. The house had been destroyed—burned to the ground by the assassins. And yet, here he was. Standing at his daughter's door, looking at her getting ready for bed.

He winced, as pain flared in his head. He cursed the pain. He just needed a moment to gather his thoughts and figure this out.

"Da?" his daughter said, looking at him in concern. "Da okay?"

Gage didn't know what to say. He knew what was about to happen. The assassins were about to fireball his home and kill Alani and Shaunna.

Pain blossomed in his head and yet he knew he needed

to stop the assassins. Any moment now, they were going to fireball his house. He had to stop them.

Spinning, he flinched at the sudden lancing pain but pushed it to the side.

Alani looked at him in concern. "Honey?"

"Grab Shaunna!" he ordered. "Get her out of here. Someone's about to fireball the house."

His wife's eyes went wide. "What do you mean?"

"Get Shaunna and get out! Now!" he repeated, moving towards the door. Agony flared through the front of his head as he stumbled, managing to catch himself against the wall before he fell over.

"Gage!" Alani called out. "What's wrong?"

He could barely open his eyes, the pain in his head was so intense. He clenched his teeth. He hissed. "Get Shaunna out of here!"

"Da?"

Overcome with the pain in his head, Gage sank to the floor. He turned his head, causing explosions of agony throughout his skull. He cursed and tried to push himself up. He had to get them out of here.

He turned towards his daughter's voice and saw her standing in the doorway, looking at him.

"Mama is Da okay?" his daughter asked.

"Go to your room," Alani told her daughter. "Da will be fine."

"No..." He muttered between clenched teeth. The pain was overwhelming now. It felt like his entire brain was on fire.

Fire. He needed to warn them. He needed to save them. "Get... out..."

He couldn't keep his eyes open, no matter how hard he tried. Even the small amount of light from the candles in their home seemed to burrow right into his brain.

"Gage," his wife's voice said. "What's wrong? What is it?"

Gage opened his mouth, but no words came out. The pain in his head was overwhelming everything else. He made one last effort. "Get... Shaunna... out..."

The pain in his head was all he knew. Gage couldn't even be sure he'd spoken the words aloud.

Then he felt magic being used and forced his eyes open just in time to see the entire room, including his wife and daughter, disappear in a blinding flash of fire.

He felt the fire burning him away. Burning his head. The pain was unbearable and he cried out.

CHAPTER 41

Gage gasped awake, unsure what was happening. He opened his eyes to blackness. He winced at the throbbing pain in his skull.

Groggy, Gage blinked his eyes open slowly again, but everything was still dark. He activated his *Shadow Vision*, or rather, he tried to activate it, but nothing happened. He cursed.

Bringing up his HUD, he looked for any status effect. He swore as he read the effect.

You are nullified.
Nullification
You are in an area that prevents any magic, magical abilities, or special abilities.

Nullification. Gage cursed again. He'd thought the room looked familiar. Whether intentionally or unintentionally, they'd brought him to the room normally reserved for enemy wizards. It had some sort of enchantment that completely nullified magic and even special abilities like his *Evasion*.

Everything had been a dream. His family next to the river, his attempt to save his family; it had all been a dream. He really had been captured trying to kill the Archmage and now he was in a wizard cell.

Gage was no stranger to this particular cell. He'd been present during many "interrogations" of enemy wizards or magical assassins. Just being in the room and not having access to his abilities had made him feel uneasy when overseeing the questioning. Now, the roles had been reversed—he was the prisoner.

As the grogginess wore off, Gage realized he wasn't lying on the ground. He was chained up against the wall. When he tried moving his arms, the metal of the shackles dug into his wrists. He tested his feet and cursed. He was spread-eagle against the wall of the cell. And judging from the cold, damp stone against his back and legs, he was naked.

In the darkness in front of him, a jingling sound, a lock mechanism being worked. A moment later, the door opened. Light flooded into the room from the hallway. Squinting against the sudden brightness, Gage recognized the hulking shape of Arteen.

The dungeon master stalked forward, a sadistic grin on his face. He stopped in front of Gage and looked him up and down. Without warning and with a speed Gage didn't expect from such a big man, Arteen punched Gage in the gut.

Arteen slams you for 4 damage.

Gage doubled over at the sudden blow. Or rather, he tried to double over. The shackles on his wrists and ankles bit into his flesh and prevented him from moving more than a few inches. He flinched at the pain and glared at the hulking man.

"Good, you're up. I'll let the Archmage know." Arteen snickered. He turned to leave but then stopped and looked back. "I'll be back."

The giant slammed the door behind him, once again plunging Gage into darkness. He heard the jingle of keys and working of the lock mechanism, and then, nothing. He was alone again—in the dark.

A minute later, he heard the outer door to the dungeon open and close. Arteen was going to inform Ruy that he was conscious. No doubt, Ruy wanted to oversee Gage's "questioning" personally. But what did the Archmage want to know? Any information he might have would be years old.

Perhaps there would be no questions. It was possible Ruy just wanted to watch Gage tortured to death. It wouldn't be the first time the channeler had simply wanted to revel in his enemy's suffering before he died.

Gage steeled his resolve. He'd been captured and tortured by a House before. Earlier in his career. Before he'd claimed the title of Shadow Master.

That time, he'd held out for days before the torturer had become overconfident. The sadistic beast-kin, part hyena, hadn't bothered to shackle Gage's legs. He'd come in by himself one night to inflict some extra pain. Unfortunately for him, he had gotten too close. Gage had swung his legs up, wrapped them around the torturer and snapped the beast-kin's neck.

He'd then managed to lift the keys off the man's body with his feet, transfer them to his hand and unlock the shackles. After he'd freed himself from the cell, he'd killed a guard, dressed in the man's uniform and managed to get out of the keep.

Testing his current shackles, Gage knew that wasn't a possibility. Both his hands and feet were shackled this time. Not only were they shackled, but his arms and legs were pulled taut. Even if he were to somehow manage to get the keys, there wasn't enough slack in the chains to allow him to unfasten the locks.

Arteen was good at his job. Too good. Gage wasn't going to make it out of his cell without help. Considering he wasn't part of the assassin's guild any longer, nor affiliated with any House, there would be no help.

Gage accepted the fact that he was alone, and he'd die alone. But he wouldn't be allowed to die until he'd suffered. How much and how long he suffered would be completely up to the Archmage. Ruy would keep him alive until he became bored, then he'd have him killed.

It wasn't a pleasant prospect, but Gage accepted it. He'd failed and now he wouldn't get revenge on the man responsible for his family's death.

He thought of Alani and Shaunna then. Gage wished he'd gotten to spend more time with them. He wished he'd gotten to see Shaunna grow up. He wished he'd had the chance to say goodbye to them, but even that was denied.

Once again, he thought about an afterlife. Is it possible

he'd get to see them again? If there was a place for good people to go after death, he knew Alani and Shaunna would be there. He frowned.

If there was a place for good people after death, surely he wouldn't go there. He was an assassin. He had killed more people than he could remember. If there really was a good place, he knew he wouldn't be welcome there.

Nothing to do but endure the punishment Ruy dished out until he was allowed to die. Gage set his jaw. He would accept whatever came, knowing that at the end, there might be a chance he would see his family again. Just a chance.

A noise interrupted his thoughts. The outer door opened and then closed, muffled voices approached, and keys jingled at the lock.

The door opened, and he squinted against the light. Blinking in the sudden illumination, Gage made out two large men in the doorway. Arteen and Ruy.

"Gage!" Ruy said with sadistic glee. "I can't tell you how much I've been looking forward to this."

Staring at the Archmage stoically, Gage said nothing.

"Nothing to say?" Ruy frowned. "No clever quip or retort?"

The Archmage stepped into the cell, stopped, and shivered. He looked around, his face twisting in disgust. "I hate this room. I hate being cut off from my magic."

"You have no magic yourself," Gage responded. "Just demon magic."

Ruy smirked. "So, you do have some clever quips after all."

The Archmage made a slight gesture with his head and

Arteen stepped forward and slapped Gage across the face, rocking his head to the side.

Arteen slams you for 5 damage.

The man was strong! Gage saw stars and tasted blood. He spit the crimson mess at Ruy. His aim was off and instead of striking the Archmage in the face, the spittle struck the channeler's black robe.

Ruy looked down, his face flushing an even darker red. He glanced at Arteen and then down at the spittle.

A look of disgust and annoyance flickered on the dungeon master's face, but it was gone quickly. He wiped the spittle off the Archmage's robe, turned and slapped Gage across the face with the spit covered hand.

Arteen slams you for 4 damage.

"You always did have spirit," Ruy chuckled as Gage tried to clear the stars from his vision. The Archmage shook his head. "But right now, there are questions I need answered, and you're going to give me answers. I think you know what I want to know."

Working his bruised jaw, Gage glared at the channeler. In fact, he had no idea what the Archmage wanted to know.

Ruy took a step forward and looked Gage straight in the face. "Who is helping you?"

Gage frowned and furrowed his brow. Ruy wanted to know who was helping him? That made no sense. No one was helping him.

A sudden realization hit Gage then. Did the Archmage suspect Aeg Derg had let him into the guild house and essentially told him who had put the contract out on him. Aeg Derg had been a mentor to him and a friend, despite allowing the contract to go forward on him.

Aeg Derg had seemed genuinely angry to learn the assassins he'd sent had killed Gage's family. He'd done his best to make sure Gage wouldn't be harmed by sending novice assassins after him.

And now, Ruy wanted Gage to betray him.

Arteen slams you for 5 damage.

Another slap by Arteen snapped him back into the moment.

Ruy snarled at him. "Tell me the name of the wizard who helped you get onto the balcony!"

Gage blinked. Ruy thought a wizard helped him onto the balcony? He didn't have to fake the look of confusion on his face. "Wizard? What wizard? Maybe I climbed onto the balcony."

The Archmage's face contorted in fury, making him look more and more like the demon he was becoming. "The trap wouldn't have been triggered without magic! Tell me the name of the wizard who created the gateway for you! Was it a member of my own House? Tell me!"

Suddenly, the Archmage's question made sense. Gage's *Shadow Slide* was a magical ability and had triggered the trap. Ruy knew nothing about his Shadow Master abilities, so he assumed a wizard had created a portal for him to use to get to the balcony.

Given the channeler's question, he must suspect someone in his own House. It was an interesting tidbit— one Gage could exploit to sow doubt and confusion before he died. Maybe he could even provoke Ruy into killing him faster.

Gage grinned at the Archmage. "Your own House hates you so much that they helped me to kill you. Kind of sad really."

Ruy's face became even more enraged, the color almost purple as his mouth worked but no words came out. Then, suddenly, his face went calm and he smiled.

"You think you will make me angry enough to kill you quickly, before I get the name," Ruy said in an oddly calm tone. "Oh no, Gage. You will give me that name. And then —only then—will I allow you to die."

The Archmage stepped forward and ran his clawed hand down Gage's chest, leaving deep furrows in his flesh. It was all he could do not to cry out.

Ruy Cernunnos slashes you for 3 damage.

Stepping back, the Archmage looked at the bloody slashes and smiled. He turned to Arteen, who was also smiling. "Give him a healing draught. We can't have him dying or passing out on us. The fun has just started."

Chuckling maniacally, Arteen spun and left the room in search of the healing potion.

Gage steeled himself. He knew he was in for a world of pain. He just had to endure it until he could provoke one of them into killing him.

CHAPTER 42

Gage snapped his eyes open. He thought a sound had awakened him, but now it was quiet. He blinked his eyes, taking in a bit of the room. A strange room full of strange items. And yet, there was a sense of familiarity. It tickled his brain, but he couldn't recall.

The last thing he remembered was another beating from Arteen. He must have passed out and this was another dream. Gage frowned. Wherever he was, it was nothing like the cell he'd been in.

He laid in a small, odd bed. The blankets were even stranger, covered with designs of small men in different action poses. It was like no artwork he'd seen. He found himself grabbing the blanket and pulling it over his head, despite not consciously doing it.

He closed his eyes. Gage was so tired. He just wanted to go back to sleep.

"Gage!" A woman's voice called from outside the room.

His heart thudded in his chest; he recognized that voice. He hadn't heard it in decades, but he still knew it.

"Mom?" he tried to say, but nothing came out. He didn't seem to be in control of his body. He struggled to make himself move or talk as memories came cascading back to him.

He shot up in his bed and stifled a yawn. Unbidden, Gage slid his feet to the floor. He reached down, picked up some clothing, and dressed.

This was a memory, he realized—or a dream that mirrored a memory. This was a memory of him before he had come to this world. It was his room. It was the room he'd lived in back on Earth—with his family.

"Gage!" His mom called again as he pulled his shoes on. "Hurry up! You're going to be late for school!"

Gage blinked. School. Yes. He remembered school. It had been so long ago, but he remembered school. He'd gone there to learn things. He frowned, forehead creasing as he tried to recall specifics about what he'd learned at school. It was difficult. Gage hadn't thought about school, or his previous life, in years.

Try as he might, he couldn't remember any of his teachers or friends from school. He was certain he'd had friends but when he thought of them, no faces popped into his mind.

The door opened and a short, blond woman stood in the doorway. He recognized her immediately. It was his mother. She looked so young to him now. How old had she been when he'd disappeared? She looked to be in her early twenties, maybe even younger.

His mom pointed out of the room. "Gage! Get down there and eat your cereal before the bus comes!"

His younger self rolled his eyes and grabbed the backpack containing his schoolbooks. As he did, Gage caught a glimpse of himself in the mirror. So young. He'd been so young when he'd been taken.

Realizing which day he was remembering, Gage frowned internally at the eerie sense of déjà vu. This was the day he'd been sucked into a different world. A world with three suns—or two suns and a black hole.

Running past his mother, his younger self hurried down the wooden steps to the first floor, grabbing onto the banister at the bottom and swinging himself into the hall leading to the kitchen. His younger version jumped into a chair at the kitchen table and shoveled in spoonfuls of a colorful, crunchy food.

Gage wanted to look around the room and commit everything to memory, but his younger self controlled the action and focused only on gulping down his breakfast. They both heard Mom coming down the steps—much slower than he'd come down.

She walked into the kitchen and stood over him, arms crossed over her chest. "That's the last time you stay up playing video games on a school night."

His younger self looked up at his mother. "But mom..."

"No buts! No cuts! No coconuts!" she snapped and then glanced up at the clock on the wall. Clocks. He remembered those! They were like the gnomish clockworks, only much smaller and more nicely decorated. She growled. "Your bus will be here any moment! Get out there!"

Grabbing the largest spoonful he could and shoving it into his mouth, the young Gage slid out of the chair and ran for the door. Yanking it open, he ran outside and slammed the door behind him, cutting off his mother who was yelling for him not to slam the door.

His younger version raced down the loose stone driveway to the road, just as a large bright yellow vehicle came around the curb. Gage remembered this. It was his school bus!

Chewing his last bite of cereal, his younger self swallowed it as the bus slowed to a stop in front of him. The doors opened and he walked up the steps, looked around the bus and slipped into an empty seat at the back.

Gage remembered these rides. His family lived out in a rural area, and he was one of the first stops in the morning and one of the last in the afternoon. His younger self had always liked it that way—it gave him more time to play video games.

As if reading his older self's thoughts, the younger Gage pulled a handheld game console out of his backpack and turned it on. He chose his game and began playing it.

He'd remembered the concept of video games but forgotten the specifics. He watched through his younger self's eyes as he played some game involving tiny monsters that fought each other.

His younger self was completely engrossed in the game, so Gage couldn't really tell what else was happening, other than the bus was continuing its route. It stopped every few minutes and one or more children boarded the bus and took their seats.

Even though he knew what was coming, Gage wasn't

sure when it was going to happen. His memories of the incident were vague now—lost to the intervening years. But when it finally happened, he instantly knew what it was.

One moment, his younger self was pounding his fingers on the buttons of the handheld game, the next moment, the screen went black. At the same time, the noise of the bus's engine died, and it coasted to a stop.

The younger him smacked the side of the video game a couple times until he realized the commotion on the bus. There was a general murmur of confusion and alarm from the other kids, and young Gage looked over at the blond boy in the seat next to him.

"What's going on?" His younger self asked the kid. If Gage had ever known the boy's name, it was lost as well.

"Bus broke down, I think." The kid shrugged, looking down at something in his hand. Gage struggled to recall what it was, but without success.

"My game died," Gage said to the boy.

"That's weird," the boy replied, cocking his head and holding up his phone. "My phone died too."

A phone! The concept struck Gage like a blow. A mobile phone! He had played games on his own mobile phone too. Before he'd gotten the game console for his birthday. He remembered he could also use it to talk to people. He'd completely forgotten about them.

Suddenly, the dull morning light became intense and filled the bus, forcing his younger self and the other kids to shield their eyes. Nearly simultaneously, the bus creaked and lurched slightly backwards.

There were shouts of panic from the kids on the bus

and even some crying. Above it, he heard the bus driver shouting. "Everyone! Off the bus!"

The bus lurched backwards again, and scared kids jumped into the aisles to get off the bus. Gage was in the back and couldn't make any headway as the kids in front of him waited their turn to get off the bus.

When the bus lurched again, followed by a strange sound of metal scraping, the blond boy next to him turned and looked at the back door. Gage looked too. It said Emergency Exit.

"Let's go out this way!" the blond boy said, his tone shaking.

The bus shuddered, as if pulled back by invisible hands. Gage didn't think it was a good idea to go out the back. After all, the bus was being pulled back somehow. It was best to go AWAY from the direction the bus was being pulled.

The blond boy didn't seem to consider it, or he was too panicked. He pushed open the door, immediately causing an alarm to sound.

At the same time, the blond boy was pulled out the door by an unseen force. The boy screamed. "Help me! Something's got me!"

Gage didn't think, he just grabbed the boy's arm and yanked as hard as he could. The boy came flying past him and hit the girl in line in front of him, who was staring aghast at the open door.

Unfortunately, yanking on the boy had left Gage off balance. As he struggled to regain it, something tugged at him—pulling him towards the door. His arms windmilled as he tried to regain his balance, but the force pulled him out the door. The blond boy reached for his hand but missed.

The next thing he knew Gage fell out the door. Only, he didn't fall to the ground—he fell UP. He floated towards the bright light, unable to do anything but watch it get closer.

Then, a high-pitched sound went right through him. He covered his ears with his hands, but it got louder and louder even as the light got bright and brighter. And then... nothing.

Gage awoke from the dream. More likely a memory—the memory of him being pulled into this world. Unfortunately, he didn't have time to process what he'd remembered. Arteen was there, sneering at him. The dungeon master immediately began punching him.

He passed out several times from Arteen's abuse, though he didn't have any other strong dreams. Each time he awoke, the beating or whipping began again until he fell unconscious. A few times, the burning sensation in his body told Gage he had been revived with a healing potion.

Arteen was a seasoned professional with years of experience. Gage knew the torturer would take him right to the brink of death and then bring him back with a healing potion as many times it took to break him.

The routine alternated between the beating and the times when Arteen would loosen the chains and drop him to the floor. He'd then cover Gage's head with a burlap sack and pour water over it, creating the sensation of drowning. Those times took all his willpower to remind himself that he wasn't drowning, that this was all part of the dungeon master's job.

Even the dark cell was purposeful. The lack of any natural light and the complete darkness prevented Gage from keeping track of the passage of time. He had no idea how much time had passed since he'd been captured.

During the sessions, the dungeon master never asked a single question. And Gage never volunteered information. It wouldn't matter if he had.

Arteen's job wasn't as an interrogator. He was a torturer. The dungeon master's job, and Gage had to admit he was very good at it, was to inflict pain without killing the person.

Gage had seen this all before. Arteen would cause physical pain to wear him down mentally until he broke. The man would keep punishing Gage until he would literally do anything to stop the pain.

Most men broke eventually. At that point, most were milked for any and all information the Archmage wanted before they were killed. On rare occasions, they might actually try brainwashing the person to become a spy for House Cernunnos.

There were both mundane brainwashing techniques and then there was magic. Mental magic was an extremely rare sort of magic that allowed the wizard to invade a person's mind. A wizard powerful in Mental magic could find almost any information in a person's mind—given enough time.

In the right situation, they could also manipulate a

person's memories. The wizard could erase or suppress old memories. They could also implant new memories—like memories of believing they were a double agent.

Gage had seen it done twice, by a wizard named Guaire Cernunnos. Guaire had been a cousin to Ruy, and a true wizard. He'd been on track to be the next Archmage when he was assassinated by a rival House. Or rather, that was the official story.

It had happened right before Gage had become the master of assassins for House Cernunnos. One of the first things he'd wanted to do was investigate the assassination and find out which House had ordered it.

The new Archmage, Ruy, had ordered him to forget the assassination and focus on shoring up the Houses defenses—presumably so no more of their magic users were killed. Since Ruy was Archmage, Gage did as he said and dropped the investigation. At least, that's what he told Ruy.

Curiosity had gotten the best of him and Gage had privately done his own investigation. He'd found Guaire had been killed in a locked room with no windows or entrances, other than the guarded entrance. When he went to question the guard on duty at the door that night, Gage found the man had died in a brothel fire a week after Guaire.

Against his better judgement, and in defiance of the laws of the House, Gage had opened Guaire's tomb, which was located in the House mausoleum. He'd checked the dead wizard's body and found traces of Draiocht-neim in the wound.

Draiocht-neim, the unique poison of House Cernunnos. Gage knew it had been an inside job and the person who stood to gain the most had been Ruy, the new Archmage. He could never trace the murder directly back to Ruy, but since then, he'd seen plenty of evidence of the man's ruthless nature.

But Guaire, House Cernunnos's one and only wizard who knew Mental magic, was dead. That meant the House didn't have any other masters of mind magic. At least Gage wouldn't have to fight off a mental attack in addition to the physical torture.

A sharp blow to his left kidney brought Gage's attention fully to the present. He flinched and coughed, tasting the now all too familiar coppery taste of blood.

Arteen backed up and grinned. Then, he backhanded Gage across the head, causing his head to rock to the side and stars to dance before his eyes. Before he could recover, he was hit again—and everything went black.

Gage awoke to pain and realized he'd been slapped. Blinking his eyes open, he saw Arteen grinning at him. Behind the torturer stood Ruy. The Archmage wrinkled his nose in disgust at Gage—or perhaps it was the stench of the cell.

"Ready to talk yet, Gage?" Ruy asked, his face still screwed up in revulsion.

Gage said nothing. He just glared defiantly back at the Archmage.

A backhanded strike rocked his head to the left and he

saw stars. As he blinked his eyes to clear the stars, he turned his glare to the dungeon master.

Ruy scowled. "I will have the name of the wizard who helped you."

"Maybe it was a warlock or channeler," Gage replied. He was hoping he could at least spark some additional paranoia in the Archmage.

"Don't be an idiot." Ruy sneered. "Portal magic is one of the few types of magic demons can't do themselves, so obviously, they can't grant it to others. Not that you would understand the subtleties of magic."

Gage cursed himself quietly. He hadn't known channelers and warlocks couldn't do portal magic. So much for stoking the man's natural suspicion.

Arteen grinned even more wickedly and glanced from Gage to Ruy. "We could start breaking things or cutting things off."

Ruy seemed to consider the idea. He looked Gage up and down and snorted. Finally, the Archmage shook his head. "Too risky. I need him alive until he gives me that name."

"How do you know it's just one?" Gage said, flashing the man a mocking smile. His first tactic hadn't worked, but perhaps he could still stoke the man's paranoia. His Bluff skill was maxed out, so if he made a somewhat convincing argument, Ruy should believe it.

The Archmage cocked his head, eying Gage suspiciously.

Seeing the Archmage take the bait, Gage continued. "You don't really think I could have gotten to your balcony with just a wizard helping me, do you? Someone had to know your schedule and know the guard patrols, so we would know exactly when to transport to your room."

Ruy stepped past Arteen, the dungeon master letting himself be pushed out of the way by the equally large channeler. The Archmage got right into Gage's face, grabbing his throat in a beefy, clawed hand. He brought his face within a few inches of Gage's and when he spoke, his voice was a hiss. "You will tell me the names of everyone who helped you!"

Having been waiting for someone to get close enough, Gage struck out with his forehead, head bunting the Archmage in the face and hearing the satisfying crunch as his nose broke.

You critically crush Ruy Cernunnos for 9 damage.

Gage saw the message in his display as Ruy stumbled backwards, holding his broken nose and trying to stem the blood flowing down his face. He was happy to see that his high dexterity still functioned, allowing him to at least get the critical hit in, even in the Nullification enchantment.

His joy was short-lived as Arteen moved in faster than a man that large should be able to move and began pummeling him in the face and body. Gage's consciousness slipped away with each blow.

"Stop! Stop!" Ruy yelled in a nasally voice. His left hand was still clamped over his nose, but he reached out with his right hand and yanked Arteen back. "I need him alive!"

Arteen whirled on the Archmage with his arm raised and, for a moment, Gage thought the torturer might strike the man. Ruy must have thought so too because he took a step back.

The torturer seemed to realize what he had been about to do and let his arm fall to his side. He cast a glance back at Gage that promised plenty of pain later.

"Go get me a healing potion," the Archmage ordered. When Arteen didn't immediately move, Ruy's face went an even deeper scarlet. "Now!"

"Yes, your Grace!" Arteen paled slightly and hurried out of the room, leaving Ruy and Gage alone in the cell.

Ruy held up his right hand, still covered in blood from his broken nose. He nodded. "Well played. I underestimated you."

The Archmage took a step closer to Gage but this time, stayed a good arm distance away. He nodded. "You were the best, Gage. You never should have left. You should never have joined the others against me."

Gage glared but said nothing. Mentally, he wondered who these "others" were. Other Houses? Or was there someone in his own House trying to take him down?

"You think you will be able to hold out against the torture." Shrugging, the Archmage smiled. "Knowing you, you actually might be able to do it."

Arteen came back into the room holding a small vial. Ruy turned, snatched the vial and downed the entire contents. Instantly, the bleeding stopped. There was a crunching sound and the Archmage flinched as the nose reset itself.

"That's better," Ruy replied, letting the vial drop to the

floor. He used his sleeve to wipe the blood away from his face. He looked down at the blood and then up Gage and smiled.

"Maybe you can hold out against the torture..." Ruy started but Arteen interrupted him.

"Your Grace, I'll make him..." The dungeon master blurted, but a glare from the scarlet faced Archmage caused the words to die in his throat. Arteen dropped his head and stared submissively at the floor.

"You think you will hold out, but you will not." Ruy turned back to Gage, his voice harder. "Tomorrow, a mental mage will be arriving. I've summoned them back from some negotiations with... well, nevermind who they were with. They will get me the information I need, whether you want to give it or not."

Gage furrowed his brow. Was the man bluffing? House Cernunnos hadn't had a mental mage since Guaire. There hadn't even been any potential for mental mages. "Nice try, Guaire is dead."

"Guaire? No, you are right. That pain in the arse is long dead." Ruy raised an eyebrow and then chuckled. "No, you wouldn't have met our new mental mage, Sibeal. She came into her powers after you left."

What the Archmage was saying made no sense. Without being trained by another mental mage, wizards didn't just stumble into their powers. It took years—decades usually—for a wizard to master a new form of magic. Certainly, it would take longer than five or six years.

When Gage said nothing, the Archmage continued.

"Sibeal is the House's new master of Mental magic. She's a channeler."

This time, Gage couldn't hide his surprise. A channeler? A channeler who used Mental magic? He'd never heard of such a thing. This had to be a bluff. And yet, if it was, Ruy was very convincing.

"Despite her rather... striking... transformation," Ruy told him and couldn't suppress a shiver. Gage saw Arteen shiver too and he wondered just what type of demon this Sibeal had bonded too that would make the torturer shiver. "Sibeal has been very useful in extracting information... even if it doesn't leave much of the subject's mind left."

"If you and the others think they'll stop the..." Ruy started but then stopped, consciously snapping his mouth shut. His black eyes flicked from Arteen to Gage, he put on a fake smile. The Archmage looked at Gage and chuckled. "No matter. Enjoy your sanity for the short time you have left with it."

With that, Ruy spun and waddled out of the room, leaving Gage alone with the torturer.

Gage expected the torturer to immediately resume the beatings, especially considering what he'd done to the Archmage's nose. Instead, the dungeon master looked at him and shook his head. Then, without a word, he left the room. Arteen shut the door behind him, leaving Gage in the dark to contemplate his fate.

CHAPTER 44

Gage waited until he heard the outer door of the dungeon slam before he activated his display. He was still amazed it even worked. Through the years, he'd always assumed it was some sort of magic. The fact that it worked inside the Nullification field had both surprised him and dispelled that theory.

Between the beatings and bouts of unconsciousness, Gage really hadn't had a chance to think about the display and what it might really be. At the moment, it didn't matter. He needed to find something in his display.

He paged through various screens until he found the list of his class abilities. He brought up the description of an ability he'd acquired through his Rogue class.

Elusive Mind
Type: Rogue
Cost: None
Range: Self

Duration: Permanent
Description: Your personality has become as elusive as a shadow. Mental abilities and effects find it difficult to latch on to your slippery mind. Even effects that manage to penetrate your defenses cannot hold you like they would others.
Cooldown: N/A

Over the years, he'd read the description many times and had never really understood the ability. Nor had he used it—at least, not to his knowledge.

Mental magic was rare. Most Houses only had a single wizard who practiced it, if that. Those wizards were in high demand for the House, keeping them busy with negotiations, meetings with other Houses, and similarly important things.

To his knowledge, Gage had never encountered one. Then again, would he have known if he had? Would he even know if they had used their Mental magic on him or if his *Elusive Mind* ability was ever activated?

Gage blew out a breath. A channeler who could somehow do Mental magic was on her way and would be here tomorrow. A channeler who had been summoned from an important negotiation, or so Ruy had let slip. The Archmage had been very careful not to mention who the negotiations were with. Gage was curious, but at the moment, he had other things to worry about.

Then there was the line he'd let slip about the others. Ruy thought he was helping others, but Gage had no idea who these others were or why the Archmage thought he might be helping him.

Was there some sort of plot to overthrow him as Archmage? It wouldn't surprise Gage if there were multiple plots. It was just everyday House politics. The members were always plotting against each other, always jockeying for position. It was one of the reasons the Shadowed Fist and the other assassin guilds existed.

It was also the reason why there were so few wizards left. For every wizard born, two were killed through House in-fighting or by other Houses. The birthrate just couldn't keep up. There were too many assassinations.

Now, more than half of the Houses members were channelers or warlocks—or rather, it had been half when he'd left. It might be an even larger percentage now. That meant, it was only a matter of time before the wizard blood became a rarity or disappeared completely.

Gage frowned, realizing he'd gone down a tangent. He wasn't sure what the decreasing wizard bloodlines would have to do with any sort of plot against the Archmage.

The fact was, he was at a severe disadvantage. He'd been out of the game for so long, he no longer knew what the current politics of the Houses were. Gage had no idea who might be plotting against Ruy or want the Archmage dead—other than himself, of course.

Whoever it was, they must be either a wizard, channeler or warlock. Gage didn't believe the trap he'd blundered into had been set for him. It had been meant for someone with magic—magic other than his Shadow magic.

Ruy had immediately assumed a wizard had helped him. He'd believed that Gage had come onto the balcony via a portal and that only a wizard could have opened one for him.

Another tidbit Ruy had let slip was the fact that demons couldn't create portals, and by extension, neither could channelers or warlocks, who received their magic from their host demon. Gage wasn't sure how he could use that information—especially if he was stuck in this cell.

That brought him full circle, back to the Mental magic channeler, Sibeal, his *Elusive Mind* ability, and the magical Nullification field.

If no magic worked inside the cell, then they would have to move Gage out of the cell for the Sibeal to work her Mental magic on him. Once he was out of the cell, he should be able to use his Shadow abilities to *Slide* out of any restraints they put him in.

Normally, it would be super easy, barely an inconvenience. But if Sibeal could somehow read his mind, then she might warn them of what he was about to do, or worse, use her Mental magic to somehow stop him. He just didn't know enough about that type of magic.

Theoretically, he could use his own *Suppress Magic* to block her Mental magic, but that would also prevent him from using his Shadow magic. That meant he'd have to go toe-to-toe with Arteen, naked and weaponless—and without his abilities.

Gage didn't like the odds. He might be able to kill Arteen, but not before he, or Sibeal, called out. He'd passed two guards on the way in. No doubt, if they heard cries for help, they would come running. That would further decrease his odds.

He could hope that Arteen or one of the guards would kill him, allowing him to die with his sanity intact. That was preferable to having his identity and personality stripped away by Sibeal.

No. Gage didn't want the easy death. He wanted to get out of this dungeon and kill Ruy Cernunnos! He'd do it with his bare hands if he had to. Once the Archmage was dead, then Gage could die. But first, he needed to get out of this cell, escape the dungeon and make his way up to Ruy.

He was betting everything on his *Elusive Mind* ability protecting him from Sibeal's Mental magic long enough for him to escape whatever restraints they put him in. Gage hated relying on unknowns. He just had no choice.

Gage thought back to the layout of the room just outside his cell and the various items he'd seen when he'd come in. He'd also gotten a few glimpses of the room outside each time the door was open. He carefully considered each item he remembered and how he could use it as a weapon.

When he made his move, he would only have seconds to *Shadow Slide* to a weapon, kill Arteen and then kill the channeler. He needed to make every second count and that meant coming up with multiple scenarios with each item. If not, he'd be dead. Or he'd end up back in the cell.

Luckily, planning out his fights was something he excelled at. He was good at planning out precise moves but could also improvise on the spot when things went wrong. It was one of the reasons he was still alive.

Once he killed Arteen and Sibeal, he'd try to recover his items. He knew from his previous experience that the dungeon master kept the items he took from prisoners in a storage area until the prisoner died. Then he sold them.

Assuming his items were still there, he could then dispatch the two guards he'd seen in the hallway, escape the dungeon, and make his way back up to Ruy's office or bedroom and kill him.

If his items weren't there, he'd take whatever he could use and go after Ruy. There had been plenty of torture implements he would happily ram through the Archmage's heart. It would just make things a bit more difficult. Either way, Gage had a plan. As soon as he was removed from the cell, he would act.

With his plan made, he went back to creating scenarios in his mind on exactly what he would do. He was still going over the scenarios when he heard keys rattling and the door opening.

The hulking form of Arteen filled the doorway and even in the dim light, Gage could see the cat-o-nine-tails in his hand. The leather whip had nine long, leather cords that were knotted in a way that they would leave small scratches on the victim—like a cat.

A glint of something blue caught his eyes and he recognized Chymera crystals. The crystals were rare and valuable and were used by wizards to channel their power. They were also used to make magical items—like the enchanted bola used to restrain him.

The presence of Chymera crystals embedded in the whip meant it was enchanted. Given what a normal cat-o-nine-tails was used for, Gage guessed it was enchanted to cause additional pain. He steeled himself for what was to come.

He looked around the room, remembering its Nullification effect. For a brief moment, he held hope the room would nullify the item's enchantment. Then, he remembered the bola. It had kept him bound, even when they'd brought him into the room. He cursed. The room must only affect people.

Arteen grinned wickedly at Gage's oath. He lightly slapped the cat-o-nine-tails against his other hand. As he did, blue sparks flew. He yelped and flinched his hand away. "Loki's balls, that hurts. But you'll find out for yourself soon enough.

"I've been saving this," the dungeon master said with a sadistic grin. "I thought I'd bring it out later, but it won't be any fun if Sibeal mangles up your mind."

Gage said nothing. He glared defiantly at Arteen and steeled himself for what was to come.

The dungeon master snapped the cat-o-nine-tails in a quick motion, causing a loud crack to echo through the dungeon. Arteen's grin became demonic. "Let's get started, shall we."

CHAPTER 45

Gage thought he was ready. He'd endured previous torture and then the dungeon's master's early beatings. He'd always had a high tolerance for pain but the agony he felt when the cat-o-nine-tails struck him was indescribable.

The enchantment didn't just increase the pain, it added new kinds of pain, too. The cords that struck his flesh burned with fire instead of the sting of leather. And the burning lingered even after the lash was pulled away. He cried out involuntarily.

"Finally," Arteen said with smug satisfaction. "I get a rise from you."

Gage snapped his mouth shut, not daring to open it. The pain burned at his skin, but he felt something else too. The pain seemed to burrow into him like tiny insects made of lava. At the same time, he felt something drawn out of him and into the whip.

With effort, he brought up his HUD.

Arteen whips you for 1 damage.
You are drained of 1 Stamina.
You are drained of 1 Mana.
You are drained of 1 Karma.
You are afflicted with Agony.

Agony
This enchantment directly stimulates nerves to cause long lasting pain without permanent physical damage. Can be stacked up to 10 times.

Reading the words, he cursed. The enchanted cat-o-nine-tails did only a small amount of damage, but it inflicted some sort of status effect called Agony. He'd never seen that one before, but given the pain he was feeling, he thought it was well named.

He didn't like the sound of "stacking" up to 10 times. Did that mean he'd experience ten times the pain? Gage gritted his teeth.

What worried him almost as much as the stacking was the draining effect it had. With one blow, it had drained a point of *Stamina*, *Mana* and even *Karma*. He wasn't even sure what *Karma* was or how it was used. None of his abilities used *Karma* and he'd never actually seen his *Karma* go down until now.

"You like that? First strike ain't too bad." Arteen chuckled mockingly and shook the hand he'd smacked with the weapon. "It does take a bit to go away."

The dungeon master nodded, looking down at the cat-o-nine-tails. "Most people can even take two or three before the screaming starts." Arteen stopped talking and cocked his head, looking Gage up and down. "I give you five at the most."

The torturer cracked the cat-o-nine-tails again. "Let's see, shall we?"

Arteen grinned and slapped the weapon against Gage's chest.

Arteen whips you for 1 damage.
You are drained of 1 Stamina.
You are drained of 1 Mana.
You are drained of 1 Karma.
You are afflicted with Agony (x2).

Gage stopped from crying out but the burning sensation burrowing into him seemed to double. He gritted his teeth. He decided he really didn't like stacking status effects.

Arteen whips you for 1 damage.
You are drained of 1 Stamina.
You are drained of 1 Mana.
You are drained of 1 Karma.
You are afflicted with Agony (x3).

Another strike, this time against his abdomen and the pain intensified even more. He felt like something was eating his insides and he struggled against the chains.

The fourth strike came against his left thigh and the fifth against his right thigh. It was taking all his willpower not to cry out. He was clenching his teeth so hard, he thought they might crumble. He stared defiantly at the dungeon master.

Arteen nodded appreciatively. "Not bad. I thought you might lose it on the fifth one."

The torturer was holding the cat-o-nine-tails down at his side. Without breaking eye contact, Arteen brought the cat-o-nine-tails up between Gage's legs.

Shock and pain finally broke through his will and ripped a scream from him. He tried to angle his body to prevent the dungeon master from striking him there again, but the chains kept him spread eagle against the wall and unable to stop the next several strikes—all to the groin.

As the Agony hit ten stacks, Gage could barely manage coherent thought. There was nothing but pain.

Each time a stack timed out and went away, Arteen seemed to know and hit him again, keeping ten stacks of Agony on him constantly. This went on for what seemed like hours to Gage, until he finally, mercifully blacked out.

* * *

GAGE COUGHED AWAKE, feeling the familiar burn of a healing potion. He checked his stats:

Health: 30
Mana: 1
Stamina: 30
Karma: 1

The potion had restored his *Health* and some of his

Stamina but left his other stats at minimal levels. He cursed inwardly. If Arteen continued this until the channeler arrived, Gage would have no *Mana* to use his Shadow abilities.

Arteen took the vial from Gage's lips and shoved it back into a pouch at his side. He nodded. "I have to admit, you lasted longer than I thought."

Gage said nothing. There was really nothing to say. He could see it in the torturer's eyes. There was nothing he could say or do to stop the man from continuing. Arteen was doing it for the sheer joy of inflicting pain. He was a true sadist.

"Feeling better now?" The dungeon master asked. He licked his lips. "Because there's lots more where the first session came from."

Not waiting for Gage to reply, Arteen slammed the cat-o-nine-tails into the left side of Gage's head, causing incredible burning pain to eat its way towards the center of his brain. He couldn't even be sure whether he had cried out.

He closed his eyes as the dungeon master rained blow after blow, first against his head and then against his groin again. The pain was so intense, Gage could barely think and after only a few minutes, he slipped back into unconsciousness.

Arteen once again revived him with a healing potion and Gage coughed and sputtered into consciousness. He blinked. It was difficult to think, and his entire body ached despite just being healed. At the moment, he was just happy the pain was gone.

The dungeon master, who had been holding his head

up to pour the potion down his throat, let his head fall and slipped the empty vial back into his pouch.

Gage thought the man would immediately begin the torture again but instead, Arteen felt around his pouches, stopping to open a few of them before frowning.

"Bad luck. Out of healing potions," the dungeon master muttered. He looked from the cat-o-nine-tails in his hand to Gage and then back. Arteen seemed to be considering whether or not he should torture him without having a healing potion.

Part of Gage didn't care. He almost hoped the sadistic torturer would do it and just kill him. He might not get his revenge on Ruy, but if Arteen killed him, Gage knew Ruy would punish him severely—possibly even kill him. He smiled at the thought.

"Oh, no," Arteen said, shaking his head at Gage. He must have thought Gage's smile was about the possible end of their session. "Don't you worry. Our fun isn't done. I have some more healing potions in the office."

Arteen turned to go but stopped and looked back. "You stay here. I'll just go get them and then we can start the fun again."

Chuckling to himself, the dungeon master left the room, turned and locked the door. As he did, Arteen whistled happily to himself.

Gage listened to the man's off tune whistling fade away on the way back to his office. With mental effort, he brought up his status. He saw exactly what he expected.

Health: 30
Mana: 1

Stamina: 1
Karma: 1

The enchanted cat-o-nine-tails had stripped him of all his stats except for *Health* and *Stamina*, which had been restored by the healing potion. He cursed.

At the moment, even if he were somehow able to escape, the only ability he'd be able to use was his *Shadow Vision*, which didn't require any *Mana*. He wouldn't be able to use any of his other Shadow abilities.

He had to hope that Arteen gave him some time to regenerate his stats before the channeler arrived. If not, he had no chance to *Shadow Slide* out his bonds and escape.

Gage heard the torturer's whistling returning and hardened his resolve. He heard the key go into the lock of his cell door but just before the door opened, a banging echoed through the dungeon.

Someone was at the main entrance. Gage felt his blood go ice cold. Was it the channeler already? Maybe he'd been unconscious longer than he'd thought. Or had the channeler arrived early? Either way, he had no *Mana*. There was no way he could enact his plan in his current state.

CHAPTER 46

*A*rteen stopped whistling and then the keys jingled again as they were removed from the door. The sound of the banging on the outer door of the dungeon came again and Gage heard Arteen mutter a curse.

"I'm coming! I'm coming!" the torturer growled. "Ruining my fun...."

He heard the muffled sounds of Arteen still grumbling to himself as he slowly faded away. Gage cursed. He looked at his stats.

Health: 30
Mana: 3
Stamina: 3
Karma: 3

In the intervening minutes, he'd managed to regenerate a couple points of his stats, but it wasn't enough to use his abilities. Gage had to hope that by the time they removed him from the cell, he would have enough *Mana* to use his *Shadow Slide*. If so, he should be able to *Slide* out of his bounds.

He smiled, despite the pain, remembering the first time he'd actually *Slid*. Gage had been experimenting and had managed to *Slide* out of his clothes. Luckily, it had been dark and no one had seen him. *Sliding* out of restraints shouldn't be a problem.

After he was free, he had a chance. He would need to immediately use his *Suppress Magic* ability to disable the Mental magic channeler, then procure a weapon from whatever torture implements were at hand.

Once the channeler's magic was negated, Gage would have to take down Arteen as quickly as possible—all while naked and armed with only an improvised weapon. Gage chuckled mirthlessly. Piece of cake. What could go wrong?

A far away clang told him the outer door to the dungeon had been opened. He checked his stats again. Even as he looked at his display, he saw another point regenerate in each of his stats.

Health: 30
Mana: 4
Stamina: 4
Karma: 4

In the dim light of the dungeon, his Shadow abilities would cost less *Mana*, but not knowing if it were day or night out, he didn't know how much less. If it were night, he might be able to *Slide* with as little as 6 *Mana*. If it were daytime outside, he'd need several more points.

The clanging of the outer door told Gage it had been shut. If it was the channeler, she and Arteen would be returning in less than a minute. It should give him time to regenerate another point.

Gage began to do the mental calculations in his mind. By the time he was unchained and pulled out of the cell, it would be at least two or three minutes. He should have enough to do a single *Shadow Slide*—barely. He just needed to be ready.

The sound of muffled voices warned him that the dungeon master was returning. He heard two voices and one of them was definitely female. The channeler!

This was it. Gage took a deep breath and tried to relax his mind. He would only get once shot at this. If he failed and the Mental magic channeler managed to get into his mind—he had no idea what abilities she might have and what she might be able to do to him.

He waited as the voices got closer.

The voices stopped moving abruptly and grew louder. They were still too muffled to understand, but the tone was unmistakable. They were arguing about something. But what?

Gage frowned. He could only make out two voices. There was a male voice, which was obviously Arteen's voice. The other voice was higher pitched. Despite it being muffled, he thought it was a female voice. Given who they were expecting, he assumed it had to be Sibeal. But what could they be arguing over?

Did Arteen want to finish his "fun" before the channeler started? She was early. Or at least, Gage thought she was early. Was the dungeon master really that desperate to torture him? Gage didn't know and he didn't care. The delay worked in his favor and he checked his stats.

Health: 30
Mana: 6
Stamina: 6
Karma: 6

After a final burst from the female, the voices died out. Gage strained his ears but there was no further talking. Moments later, he heard the jingling of keys outside the door. The sound of the key being turned in the lock echoed in the silence of his cell and then the door creaked open.

Blinking against the sudden torchlight that flooded into the room, Gage saw two figures silhouetted against the doorway. He was familiar with the larger of the two silhouettes. It was Arteen, of course.

The second figure was shorter and much more petite. As his eyes adjusted to the new light level and the new silhouette came into focus, it was obvious by the curves the figure was a woman. Blinking a few more times, Gage frowned.

The woman in front of him didn't appear to be a channeler. She had no visible mutations typical of channelers: No horns, claws, or any other visible signs of demonic transformation. Stranger yet, she was dressed in the uniform of an elite soldier.

She was a thick woman, but thick with muscles from

working out and practicing swordplay. Her hair was blonde but cut short so she could wear a helmet without her hair getting in the way. A scar decorated the right side of her face, running from her ear to the middle of her cheek.

Bringing up his display, he scanned the woman, trying to get additional information about her.

Terina
Human
Fighter
Level 13

Gage's frown deepened but he was also confused. This wasn't Sibeal. The woman wasn't even a channeler. She was just a run-of-the-mill fighter, like nearly all the other elite guards. Why was she here?

Neither of the figures moved for a long moment. Finally, Arteen growled. "Well, go on then!"

He felt himself tense. Was this really the channeler then? Could she somehow use her magic, even in the Nullification field? If they didn't take him out of this room, his entire plan was useless!

Terina snorted and stepped back from the doorway. She put her hands on her hips. "I was sent to deliver the message, torturer. Not do your dirty work. Now, get on with it so I can report back to his Grace!"

The dungeon master loomed over the shorter woman, fixing her with a glare. Gage was actually impressed that Terina didn't even flinch. The big man towered over her and was probably twice her weight. The warrior woman just returned his glare.

"Fine. I'll tell his Grace that you refused a direct order." Shrugging, the woman started to turn away. "I'm sure he'll understand."

Terina made to turn back towards the entrance, but Arteen held out a beefy hand in front of her. "I didn't refuse nothing."

The giant of a man stared daggers at the woman for a moment longer and then turned and stepped out of the room. Arteen disappeared around the corner for a moment and then came back with a large, curved knife. As he stepped past the woman, the dungeon master took the opportunity to glare at her once again.

Entering the cell, his expression changed to one of sadistic glee. "Bad news for you, Gage. It seems they found the traitor wizard without your help. I guess we'll be getting our answers from him instead of you."

Gage furrowed his brow. Who was this traitor wizard they were talking about? He hadn't had any help—especially not from a wizard. So, who had they captured?

Arteen stared at Gage and licked his lips. "You know, I could slit your throat."

The dungeon master ran a thick thumb down the blade of his dagger. "It's not really that sharp, so it'd be slow cutting.

"Nah," Arteen said with a shake of his head. "Still too quick, even if it would be slow going." He made a horizontal gesture with the knife. "No, I'm going to gut you. It won't be quick and it won't be painless—and I'll enjoy every moment of it."

Terina let out an exasperated breath. "I don't have all day! I'm supposed to report back to his Grace once he's dead and he'll be down here later to check the body."

It was Arteen's turn to furrow his brow. He looked over his shoulder at the woman. "Coming down here to check the body? Why?"

"I don't know!" The woman spat back. "He doesn't tell me why he does things and I'm smart enough not to ask!"

Arteen snorted. "Yeah, people who question him tend to get burned."

Terina said nothing and after a brief pause, Arteen turned back to face Gage. He shrugged, his previous smile gone. "It looks like, once again, I am denied my joy."

The dungeon master took a step forward, blocking out the light from the doorway. "End of the road for you assassin."

Gage watched as Arteen brought the curved blade up. He cursed the gods for not being able to get his revenge on Ruy. At the same time, he hoped that, in death, he might see Alani and Shaunna again.

The dungeon master was bringing the knife up towards his throat but suddenly stiffened. "Ow! What was that?"

Arteen's face contorted in anger. He started to turn around but then stumbled. Gage watched as the man swayed on his feet. The dungeon master stumbled right, then left, as if dizzy. The dagger fell from his fingers as he held his hands out for balance.

After a moment of that, he fell to his knees. Gage saw his eyes roll into the back of his head and then he fell face first onto the stone floor.

Gage looked from Arteen's body to the woman. It wasn't the same woman. Not at all. He looked around the room, craning his head to see outside the cell. There was no sign of the bigger, warrior woman.

The new woman was slender, with pale skin and dark hair, she was nearly the opposite of the woman who had just been there. There were no scars on her flawless face, though she wore makeup like a high-born lady—or a courtesan.

In her hand was a thin pin, a little smaller than a knitting needle. There liquid beaded at the end of the pin, Gage guessed it was blood. She'd jabbed him.

The new woman looked down and shivered. She dropped the thin pin on the ground and stepped back. "He wasn't lying. That stuff really works fast."

CHAPTER 47

Gage blinked. He looked from the body of Arteen to the new woman, at Arteen again, and finally back to the woman. She was still looking down at the body of the dungeon master. He wasn't completely sure what had just happened. He also wasn't sure what happened next.

He didn't recognize the woman but given the way the woman had dispatched Arteen, Gage suspected she was an assassin. He had a lot of questions. Who was she? Which assassin's guild was she working for? Why had she killed Arteen? And most importantly, what did she plan to do with Gage?

The dark-haired woman moved to Arteen's waist and fished around until she found his set of keys. She stood up and looked Gage over. Her gaze lingered below his waist long enough to make him blush. It had been a long time since any woman other than Alani had seen him naked.

"Ahem." Gage cleared his throat and the woman looked

reluctantly up at him. There was no embarrassment or apology in her face.

"Name's Heather," she said with a smile. "The old man sent me."

Gage's brow furrowed in confusion. Aeg Derg sent her? That seemed unlikely. Mentor or not, he'd never risk the guild to help him out. Was this some sort of trick?

Something else suddenly occurred to him. "Wait, I thought your name was Terina!"

The woman's head snapped towards him, eyes narrowed in suspicion. "How do you know that name? I never said it in front of you!"

He knew he couldn't explain how he used his display to analyze people and get their name, class, and level. No one else he'd ever tried to explain it to had any clue what he could see. Most thought he was a bit mad.

"Wait!" Heather's eyes went wide and her mouth fell open. "Can you read me in your HUD?"

Gage blinked. "My what?"

"Do you have a HUD? You know... H-U-D... heads up display... like words that display in your vision but no one else can see?" she asked excitedly.

He blinked again, not sure he'd heard the woman correctly. Gage scrutinized her up in his display again.

Heather Moore
Human
Rogue / Infiltrator
Level 5 / 4

"You do, don't you?" Heather said, eyes still wide. "Are you from Earth too? Or another planet?"

Gage rocked back as if struck. He was trying to understand why her stats had changed in his... what had she called it? Heads up display? HUD? His display had never lied to him before but a couple of minutes ago, it had said she was a different person. Now she mentioned Earth!

He shook his head, his head full of questions. "Wait. Go back. You know about Earth?"

She jumped up and down in excitement and clapped her hands together. "You are from Earth!"

"Yes," he said cautiously. Part of him was excited but the other part was skeptical. Could she really be from Earth?

"What part?" she asked, her voice still bubbly.

"What part of what?" he retorted.

"What part of Earth were you from? I'm from Chelmsford, just north and east of London, in the UK," she blurted out. Her voice had changed, or rather, her accent had changed. Previously, he would have sworn she was a native of the city. Now, her accent was unrecognizable.

"London?" he echoed. He wracked his brain. He remembered that from school. London was the capital of England, right? "London, England?"

"Yes!" she replied, practically bursting with excitement.

Gage was still trying to take it all in, but his practical side re-exerted itself. "You'd better let me down before we attract the two guards in the hall—if they're still there." He made eye contact with her and asked the question that was really on his mind. "Assuming you're here to free me and not kill me."

The thought had crossed his mind since she'd killed Arteen and had implied that Aeg Derg had sent her. His old mentor might look the other way while he killed Ruy, but now that Gage was captured, he could be a liability to the Shadowed Fist.

"Kill you?" Heather screwed up her face. "If I wanted that, I could have just let big and hairy here finish what he was about to do."

"Some sort of knock out poison?" Gage asked. Arteen's chest was still going up and down. He was still alive.

She nodded as she unlocked the shackle around his left wrist. "That's what he said. The old man heard you'd been captured. He also heard you might have information that could compromise the guild. So, he sent me to free you."

"Just free me?" Gage raised an eyebrow as his left arm came free. His arm was sore and stiff from being in the same position for so long.

"Yeah," she replied, working on the shackle still holding his right wrist. "I'm not an assassin, I'm just doing him a favor. I'll let you out of here and then I'm gone."

Gage groaned as his right arm came out of the shackles and fell to his side. He rotated shoulders and stretched his arms to loosen them while Heather ducked down to start on his ankles. He caught her staring at his nakedness and cleared his throat again.

"Sorry," she said without the slightest hint of apology in her voice. She quickly freed his left ankle and then his right.

When she was done, she handed him the keys and stepped back. "There you go, Gage." She cocked her head.

"I can't believe you're from Earth. Wait. Where were you from? You never said."

"North Carolina in the United States," he replied. He remembered that much at least.

"That's in the southern part of the United States, right?" she asked.

"I... I think so," he replied. He thought it was the south, but he really couldn't remember anymore. It'd just been too long.

"You don't know?" she asked, cocking her head. "When were you taken?"

"When I was ten... no, eleven, I had a birthday the week before," he replied.

"Wow," she replied. "You've been here a long time. You're like what... thirty or something, right?"

"Forty," he replied. He wasn't sure exactly how old he was any longer. The calendar here was different from Earth so he'd lost track of the years when he'd first arrived. But he guessed he was within a few years.

"Wow! Forty!" she replied with a grin. "You're almost twice my age. You look pretty good for an old guy." She gave him a teasing grin.

He looked at her more closely and saw how young she looked. She was right, he could probably very nearly be her dad. But the mention of dad reminded him of Alani and Shaunna, and he frowned, remembering he still had a mission.

"Did I say something wrong?" she asked. She looked back at the door. "I guess we should be going, right? We can talk more when we get back to the guild."

Gage shook his head. "I'm not going back to the guild. Not until I kill Ruy."

Heather's eyes opened wide. "That's what you were trying to do? Kill the Archmage? Are you mad?"

"He killed my family," Gage snapped. "My wife and little girl. I can't just let that go."

"Oh, sorry." Heather bit her lip. "But do you really think you'll make it up there, past all his guards? You're not an infiltrator like me."

Her eyes went glassy as she looked at him. She cocked her head. "You've got levels in assassin, witch hunter and … wait… what's shadow master?"

"It would take too long for me to explain," he told her as he moved past her and stopped at the doorway. He looked down the hallway. It was clear. "If we meet again in this life, I'll tell you all about it and you can tell me more about Earth. I've forgotten so much."

Heather half-frowned-half-pouted. "It sounds like you aren't expecting to survive your attempt on the Archmage."

Gage shrugged. He wasn't sure he'd survive afterwards, but he was certainly going to do his best to survive long enough to stick his dagger into Ruy's heart. If he died afterwards, so be it.

"Are you sure you want to throw your life away?" she asked, coming up beside him.

Her proximity and his own nakedness made the situation a bit awkward, but he didn't look away from her. She smiled up at him. "I hope you make it. It would be terrible if I finally met another person from Earth, only to have them die right away."

"In case I don't get to tell you later," he said, returning her smile. "Thanks for getting me out of there."

She smirked. "When the old man asks you to do something..."

"... you just do it," he finished.

"Exactly," she agreed. She straightened her posture and her demeanor changed.

He felt a slight magic from her but it wasn't like anything he'd felt before. It was some sort of new magic. Something he hadn't encountered. Looking at her, Heather was no longer the excited young woman with dark hair, she was now the battle-hardened blonde, warrior woman. He scanned her in his display.

Terina
Human
Fighter
Level 13

Gage couldn't believe that his display was telling him something different now. He'd always thought it was infallible and he'd never even given its truthfulness a second thought. Now, he realized it could have been wrong before and he never would have known it.

"Good luck," Heather said gruffly and started to walk back towards the entrance of the dungeon. She stopped after a few steps and looked over her shoulder. "I hope you make it."

With that, she turned back around and continued walking down the hall. Gage watched her go until she turned left and disappeared. If he did make it out of this alive, he definitely wanted to talk with her some more.

He sighed and spun around, looking at Arteen's keys in his hand. It was time to find his gear and finish what he'd come here to do.

CHAPTER 48

*A*fter Heather disappeared, he stepped back into the cell. Gage looked down at the torturer. The man had taken great pleasure in making him suffer and he would have liked nothing more than to return the favor.

Unfortunately, he didn't have the luxury of time. He reached down, grabbed and twisted the man's large head. A simple snap and he received some experience for killing the dungeon master.

He turned over Arteen's body and searched the man's pouches. He found three vials of red liquid. Healing potions. One was cracked and leaking from the dungeon's master's collapse, but the other two were still intact. He took them, along with the dagger the man had been about to use on him.

Going back outside the cell, he stopped. He glanced at the open cell and looked down at himself. He was still completely naked and covered in dried blood from his healed injuries. He looked down at Arteen's clothes but dismissed them quickly. The big man's outfit would never fit him.

Gage frowned down at the body of the torturer. Anyone who walked this way would see the dead torturer and instantly know Gage had escaped. He smirked. No reason to make it easy on them. Pulling the door shut, he fished through the keys until he found the one fitting the lock.

He then scraped some small stones from one of the bricks in the wall and shoved them into the lock. He smiled. Even if they had the key, no one was going to open the door without breaking it down.

With the door locked and jammed, Gage quickly checked the other doors around the main torture area, looking for Arteen's room. If his gear was still around, it would be there. Most likely the torturer sold any equipment he took from prisoners to supplement his income. Or perhaps he kept some items as "trophies" of his victims.

The other two rooms off the main chamber led to cells nearly identical to the one he'd been locked in. Like his, they were also magic nullifying rooms. He noted that the stonework in the other rooms looked newer. Most likely, they had been enchanted somewhat recently. But why?

Gage looked around the main chamber. When he'd been the House's master of assassins, there had only been one wizard proof room. Now there were three. Did they really have the need for them? Could it be because of the influx of new channelers and warlocks?

Pushing the question out of his mind, Gage padded barefoot down the hallway. He stopped in front of the first two doors. Next to the one on the right was a wood sign identifying it as the storage. The opposite door's sign told him it was the office.

He decided to search the storage first. Gage tried each key in the lock until he found the one that fit. The door unlocked with an audible click. Checking the hall for any sign of the two guards, he slipped inside and shut the door behind him.

The storage room was pitch black and Gage activated his *Shadow Vision*. As the world dissolved into shades of gray, he could make out simple wooden shelves lining the wall. The shelves had a variety of items. The closest shelf on his left contained a small metal coffer, similar to the ones merchants used to keep their gold and other valuables.

Curious, Gage tried to open the lid but found it locked. He eyed the keyhole, which was much smaller than a door lock and then held up the keyring. He'd seen a small key on the ring and had thought it odd. Trying the key, the lock clicked.

Gage opened the lid to find a velvet lining with three more vials. With his Shadow Vision, he couldn't see what color the liquid was but since the vials were exactly like the two vials he'd taken from Arteen, he thought it a safe bet they were healing draughts. He'd double check later to be certain.

For now, he dropped his own vials into the soft interior. He glanced around the room at the sacks and wooden boxes that populated the shelves. Knowing he'd need both hands to go through the belongings quickly, he set his dagger next to the coffer.

He grabbed the nearest sack and opened it. As he'd hoped, Gage found clothes and a few personal items. Unfortunately, they weren't his. They belonged to another prisoner and judging by the dust that had come off the sack, the person was either long dead, or they'd been in the dungeon for a very long time.

Knowing his stuff must be stored in one of the crates or sacks, Gage systematically searched the shelves. He spent the next hour tearing through the containers but came up empty handed. He cursed. His gear wasn't here.

Gage grabbed the coffer of potions and the dagger and exited the room. He locked it to prevent anyone from seeing his handiwork, then turned to the opposite door. The office. Quickly finding the correct key, he opened the lock and slipped inside.

The office was almost identical in size to the storage room. Judging by the large, unmade bed against the far wall and the open chest of clothes, the room doubled as Arteen's bedroom as well.

The office portion of the room consisted of a large worn oak desk behind which was a single wooden chair that didn't match. Although the varnish was now faded and scratched in many places, the desk had been made by a master craftsman. The chair was the same. It looked extremely well made but was faded and had a scorch mark on the back. If Gage had to guess, the torturer had likely inherited hand-me-downs from the main keep after they had become damaged.

A few feet beyond the chair sat an iron-bound wooden chest without a lid. It appeared someone had ripped the lid off the chest and then discarded it, only to have the Torturer claim it.

Against the far wall was Arteen's bed. Of all the furniture in the room, it appeared to be the only one not of quality. It was barely more than a few boards nailed together, with what appeared to be a straw mattress.

It was a very spartan and utilitarian room. There was nothing decorating the walls, no shelves with personal items, and nothing personal on the desk. It was the room of a man who had been obsessed with his job. Obsessed with hurting others.

Unable to spare time to ponder the man's life and fate, Gage moved into the middle of the room. A quick glance didn't reveal anything appearing to be his equipment and Gage scowled.

If he had to, he'd kill Ruy naked—with his bare hands if necessary—but having his gear would make things much easier. Gage glanced between the bed area and the office. If Arteen had kept the gear, where would he have left it?

Given how obsessed the man seemed to be with his job, Gage moved to the desk. He riffled through the desk drawers and let out a sigh of relief when he found a familiar looking bundle in the bottom right-hand drawer. It was his gear.

Taking his things, he found something unexpected underneath. A delicate tiara of gold set with a large crystal lay on a folded white cloth.

He examined the crystal. Gage couldn't see color with his *Shadow Vision*, but he was certain he knew what it was. A Chymera crystal. Gage guessed it must have been a captured wizardess. He shook his head as he thought what Arteen might do to a female prisoner.

Out of curiosity, he scanned the golden tiara.

Exquisite Wizard Tiara
Type: Headgear
Range: Special
Damage: Special
Durability: 37 of 40
Special: Like a wizard's wand, the tiara allows the wizardess to focus their Mana through the Chymera crystal embedded in the center to cast spells.

He'd been right. It was a Chymera crystal and the tiara was obviously meant for a wizardess. Given its quality, the tiara must have been meant for a noble. It was probably worth thousands of gold, but he'd never find a buyer for it. In street talk, it was simply too hot.

Leaving the tiara in the bottom of the drawer, he looked at his gear. In stark contrast to the man's desk and bed, Gage's gear was neatly folded, with the daggers laid atop the gear. It seemed an odd thing for the dungeon master to do. Had it been some form of respect Arteen had for Gage that he'd stored it separately? Or had the man simply considered this some sort of trophy? He'd never know.

Gage carefully pulled his gear out and set it on the desk, inventorying everything. He was happily surprised to find it all there. In addition to his clothes, he found his healing potions, the vial of poison and even the antidote he'd hidden in his sleeve.

He didn't particularly enjoy being naked and while he did want to get some clothes on, there was something more important he had to check first.

The poison on his blades had long since lost its potency. Prolonged exposure to air did that. But even bottled, Wizard's Folly and Widow's Tears both began to lose their potency after a few days. Gage had no idea how long he'd been in the dungeon, so checking the poison was his top priority.

Most alchemists would sniff the poison and make a judgement call on whether the poison was still viable based on the scent. After years of doing so, many alchemists developed health issues from inhaling the toxins.

Luckily, Gage had a better method. Taking the stopper off the poison vial, he poured a tiny amount onto one of the many parchments scattered around the desk. Bringing up his HUD, as Heather had called it, he examined the drop of liquid.

Draiocht-neim / Wizard's Folly
Type: Poison
Duration: 60 seconds
Effect: 20 Mana Damage Per Second
Description: This poison reduces the victim's Mana by 20 every second until it reaches 0. Cannot reduce Mana below 0.

Widuwe-fertriet / Widow's Tears
Type: Poison
Duration: 30 seconds

Effect: 5 Health Damage Per Second
Description: This poison reduces the victim's Health by 5 every second. Secondary effect, paralyzation onset after 5 seconds. Paralyzation moves from extremities, inward to heart.

His display always told him whether the poison was viable. If it wasn't, nothing showed in his display when he examined it.

Gage paused, cocking his head. He'd always depended on his display. Had always believed in its complete infallibility. His recent experience with Heather had proven the information from the display might not always be correct.

He realized it didn't matter. If he didn't kill Ruy with the poison, he'd kill him the old-fashioned way. He was a Witch Hunter, after all. He could still *Suppress Magic* long enough to kill the Archmage. Without his magic, he was physically no match for Gage.

And if suppressing magic meant he couldn't use his own magic to escape, then so be it. He was willing to sacrifice himself to kill the man who had been responsible for his family's death.

Quickly re-applying the poisons to his daggers, Gage replaced the cork in the bottle and replaced it in his pouch. He made one last check of his gear before stepping out of the room and locking the door.

It was time to get his revenge.

CHAPTER 49

Gage stalked towards the exit of the dungeon, intent on finally taking his revenge on the Archmage, but distracted and suspicious. Just before he reached the intersection of the corridor, he remembered the guards he'd seen on his way in.

The distraction came from the girl, he knew. Heather. She claimed to have a display, like him. She claimed to be from Earth, also like him. But her description in his display had changed. That had never happened before. It made him suspicious and he couldn't quite push her from his mind.

Pausing at the intersection, he peeked around the corner. Just like before, he spotted two elite guards about halfway down the stone corridor. They were different guards, but they were stationed on either side of the same door. He knew he could *Shadow Slide* past them, but his curiosity was aroused.

There hadn't been guards outside Gage's door and he

was an assassin who had tried to kill the Archmage himself. He was extremely curious just who would warrant a double guard when he didn't.

He slid the curved dagger he'd taken from the dungeon master out of his belt. His own daggers were once again coated in poison and Gage didn't want to waste poison on two guards, even elite guards.

Using his ability to manipulate shadows to completely obscure the light from the nearby torches, plunging the corridor into darkness. The guards let out curses, hands going to weapons even as they turned their heads from side to side trying to see in the sudden blackness. Unfortunately for them, Gage's *Shadow Vision* allowed him to see perfectly.

He didn't waste any time. He *Shadow Slid* to the first guard, appearing next to him. The curved dagger struck the guard across the back of his calf which was unprotected by his armor. The man cried out and stumbled back against the wall.

You critically slash Elite Guard for 21 damage.

The man, probably unsure exactly what had happened, fell against the wall and reached back towards his damaged calf. As he did, Gage ducked low and brought his dagger up sideways under the man's unprotected armpit, pushing the dagger through the man's ribs and puncturing his lung.

You critically pierce Elite Guard for 25 damage.

The man tried to gasp in pain, but with the dagger in his lung, the most he could manage was a weak gurgle. Gage reached around the man and grabbed the strap of his helmet with his other hand. Letting go of the dagger, he reached up and grabbed the back of the man's head. With a savage twist, he snapped the man's neck.

You kill Elite Guard.
You have gained experience.

The guard's body went limp, and as it fell, Gage reached down and plucked a dagger from the man's belt. He turned to the second guard who looked terrified in the dark. The man had his sword out, but looked side to side, eyes open wide.

"Rhogget?" the man croaked. "You okay? What was that? What happened to the god's-blasted torches?"

Gage didn't answer the man. Instead, he stepped over the body, ducked under the man's sword, and came up on the opposite side of him. He shoved the guard hard, sending him stumbling over the body of his former comrade. As he expected, the second guard tripped over the dead man and went sprawling onto the floor.

Stepping towards the man before he could recover, Gage slammed his newly acquired dagger into the man's back, just under his breastplate. It was an awkward angle, but Gage still thought he hit the man's kidney.

You critically pierce Elite Guard for 27 damage.

The man arched his back, letting out a cry of pain and

surprise. Gage showed the man no mercy. He withdrew the dagger, eliciting another yelp from the injured man. The guard tried to spin around and grab at him, but Gage had his weight on the man now.

He slid his weight up onto the man's back as the man struggled. Gage waited until the man's head was turned, exposing his throat and then struck out. He slid the blade of the dagger across the guard's windpipe.

You critically slash Elite Guard for 31 damage.
You kill Elite Guard.
You have gained experience

The man struggled for a few seconds before he went limp. Gage waited until the guard's movement had ceased completely before standing up. As he stood, he released his control of the shadows, and the torchlight flooded the corridor.

Gage looked down at the two bodies and the blood covering the floor of the dungeon corridor. There was no way anyone would miss what happened here, even if he dragged the bodies into one of the cells. He sighed. So be it. Hopefully, by the time they were discovered, he would have already killed the Archmage.

Turning to the cell, Gage took the dungeon master's keyring from his pouch. He tried several of the keys until he found the right one. Once the lock clicked open, he swung the door open to a room of complete darkness.

He frowned. His Shadow Vision didn't penetrate the cell and that could only mean there was a nullification field inside. That meant, a magical prisoner. He dropped his Shadow Vision and blinked at the sudden torchlight.

As his eyes adjusted to the light and the figure chained to the wall came into focus, Gage couldn't help but let out a small gasp.

The figure was that of a woman and she was perhaps the most beautiful woman he'd ever seen. Her voluptuous figure was perfect in every way, and even the dirt and grime of the dungeon couldn't dull her beauty.

The woman's long blonde hair fell down over her chest, barely covering her large, firm breasts. Her slim waist gave way to round, feminine hips and tapered down to long, slim legs. Just seeing her caused his mind to wander to thoughts he knew he shouldn't be thinking after so recently losing his wife.

Shoving the lustful thoughts from his mind, Gage realized he knew exactly who the woman was without even scanning her. He'd seen her once before during a mission, though, admittedly, she'd been wearing much more then. Her name was Aphrodite of the House of Olympus, one of the southern Houses.

Aphrodite was the daughter of Zeus, the Archmage of the house, and a powerful wizardess in her own right. He wasn't sure exactly what sort of magic she could do but he was curious how Ruy had captured her.

The woman hadn't bothered to look up and probably expected either Ruy or Arteen. He wondered if they tortured her for information. He frowned. Gage was sure Arteen would have enjoyed that.

"Aphrodite," he said in a low tone.

The woman stirred and slowly raised her head to look

at Gage. Like her body, her face was practically perfect. In fact, both her and her face were almost too perfect. He guessed magic altered or enhanced her somehow.

Aphrodite looked him up and down and then stared into his eyes. Gage swallowed involuntarily when their eyes met. This was a dangerous woman.

"You're short for an elite guard," she remarked.

Gage snorted. "Nice try. I'm here to kill Ruy."

The beautiful woman looked suddenly hopeful. "Did my father send you? Let me out, now!"

Crossing his arms over his chest, Gage smirked. "No. Your father didn't send me. And tell me one good reason I should release you."

Aphrodite furrowed her brow. "If my father didn't send you. Who did?"

"I'm here for my own reasons," he replied.

The woman looked him up and down and then flashed a brilliant smile. "If you release me, I can reward you."

Gage just shook his head, knowing the woman was trying to use her femine wiles to get him to do her bidding. Despite the woman's innate sexuality, the memory of his wife and daughter allowed him to ignore her charms. He frowned at her.

The woman's face became pleading. "Please. I will do anything. My father will reward you. I will reward you. Just get me out of this cell."

At that moment, a quest appeared in his display.

You have received a new quest "Free Aphrodite, Part I" Aphrodite of House Zeus is being held prisoner by House Cernunnos. She has begged you to free her.

Free Aphrodite (0/1).
Reward: 5,000 experience, Unknown.
Accept quest (yes or no)?

He looked at the new quest and considered the situation. He didn't trust any of the nobility of any House, especially not the daughter of an Archmage. On the other hand, she might just be telling the truth about rewarding him and if he didn't die, the south might be a place he could retreat to.

Another idea occurred to him too. If he released her and helped her find her wand—or whatever she used to do her magic—she might make a handy distraction. If she fought her way out of the compound, it would divert some of the guards to her and make it easier for him to reach Ruy.

Smiling, he nodded, accepting the quest. "Sure. I'll let you out."

CHAPTER 50

Using the dungeon master's keys, Gage quickly released the woman. He unfastened the shackles around her feet first, then those on her hands. When her final hand was freed, the woman slumped and would have fallen if he hadn't reached out and caught her.

She wrapped her arms around him, though he suspected it was more to keep herself from sliding to the floor than out of any sort of affection. At the same time, Gage saw a new message pop-up on his HUD.

Quest Complete.
Free Aphrodite—Part I
Aphrodite of House Zeus is being held prisoner by
House Cernunnos. She has begged you to free her.
Free Aphrodite (1/1).
Reward: 5000 experience.

She tried to manage a seductive smile, but it was weak. "Thank you! My father will give you anything you want!"

Gage stared down at her. "Can you walk?"

The woman bit her lip for a second, pushing herself off him. Aphrodite grimaced and she swayed for a moment but managed to maintain her balance. As soon as she'd steadied, one hand went to cover the space between her legs while the other arm covered her breasts.

"Shy?" he mused.

Aphrodite glared at him for a moment but then gave him a crooked smile and a wink. "I don't mind nudity, when it's my choice."

He nodded. "Fair enough."

The woman looked at him. "I need to find my clothes and tiara. Mostly, my tiara"

You have received a new quest "Free Aphrodite, Part II" You have freed Aphrodite, but to escape, she will need her clothes and her tiara. She has asked you to help her find both items but her tiara is the most important. Find Aphrodite's Tiara (0/1). Optional: Find Aphrodite's Clothes (0/1). Reward: 2,000 experience, Unknown. Accept quest (yes or no)?

"Tiara?" he repeated, remembering the tiara he'd found with his equipment.

"It's like a thin crown..." She started with a slight tone of condescension, but Gage raised his hand.

"I know WHAT it is," he said flatly and accepted the new quest. "And I think I know WHERE it is. Follow me."

Not waiting for the wizardess, he spun and stalked out of the cell. He stepped over the bodies of the guards and the pool of blood that now covered the hallway.

"A little help, please?" the woman's voice said from behind him.

Gage sighed and turned around. The woman was standing on the opposite side of the crimson puddle, looking at it in disgust. He took the opportunity to scan her.

Aphrodite
Human
Wizard
Level 16

Impressed, he raised an eyebrow. The woman was powerful. Aphrodite was easily one of the highest-level wizards he'd met. Gage wondered if freeing her was such a good idea.

"What? What's wrong with your eyes?" The woman's eyes were wide, and he realized his Shadow Vision was still active, making his eyes black. Her mouth twisted in disgust. "Are you a channeler?"

He cursed and let his vision fade back to normal. Reaching to the wall sconce, he took one of the torches and held it up to his face. He hoped he could Bluff his way out of it. "Nothing's wrong with my eyes. Why do you ask?"

Aphrodite looked at him with narrowed eyes. "Your eyes were black a second ago."

Gage shook his head. "Must have been a trick of the light."

The wizardess continued to eye him suspiciously for a long moment. While she did, Gage's eyes were drawn to her chest. In her shock at seeing his eyes, she had let her arm fall to her side.

She caught him looking and smirked. "See something you like after all?"

Feeling himself flush, Gage realized he'd been staring at his display but for Aphrodite, it had seemed like he was staring at her. He cleared his throat and held out his free hand to help her hop across the blood.

She eyed his hand for a moment, removed the arm over her breasts, pushed out her chest, and took his outstretched hand.

Trying not to stare at Aphrodite's chest, he took her hand and pulled her across the pool. As he did, she purposely didn't catch herself and stumbled into him. She pressed herself against him and winked. "Thank you."

Aphrodite lingered there and Gage was forced to take a step back to untangle himself from the nude woman. He blanked his face. "We should hurry."

"Fine. Keep your secrets." The wizardess pouted for a moment but then shrugged. She cocked an eyebrow. "You said you thought you knew where my tiara was?"

"Follow me," he told her. Turning, he retraced his steps to the dungeon's master office and unlocked it again with the keyring. Walking around the desk, Gage pulled the bottom drawer open.

Coming around the corner, Aphrodite stopped in the doorway and sneered. "What is this place?"

"This was Arteen's office," he responded, gesturing at the desk with the torch. He twisted his body and motioned to the bed with it, illuminating the back of the room. "And his bedroom."

Aphrodite furrowed her brow. "Who?"

"Arteen," he retorted. "The torturer."

The woman shuddered, wrapping her arms around herself. "That disgusting pig."

Trying not to imagine what horrors the dungeon master had inflicted on her, Gage reached into the drawer and pulled out the tiara.

Instantly, the woman's eyes gleamed and she reached for it. Gage let her take it and his eyes dropped back to the drawer. With the tiara out, he could see that the folded cloth it had been lying on was silk. Reaching down, he picked up the silk and revealed a set of golden sandals and a braided gold belt.

"You found my chiton too!" the woman cried out and snatched the short dress from him. She slipped it over her head and let the thin, silk garment settle over her shoulders.

Gage picked up the sandals and silk rope, handing them to the woman.

Quest Complete.

Free Aphrodite—Part II

You have freed Aphrodite, but to escape, she will need her clothes and her tiara. She has asked you to help her find both items but her tiara is the most important.

Reward: 2000 experience.

Bonus Reward: 1000 experience.

Aphrodite grabbed the golden cord and girded it around her waist. She then walked around the desk, pushing Gage into the wooden chair, before sitting on his lap. She began strapping on her sandals. As she did, she wiggled her butt against him ever so slowly.

He felt awkward with the woman's butt on him and couldn't help the reaction it effected. Gage tried to squirm out from under her, but without tossing her bodily onto the floor, he couldn't get free. The woman seemed to sense his discomfort and wiggled even more as she put her second sandal on.

The moment she put her foot down, Gage gently pushed her off him and quickly stood up. He adjusted his trousers before Aphrodite could turn around.

"I am getting out of this hell hole," the woman said as she faced him, hands on hips. "I do owe you, so I can take you with me."

"I have someone to kill," he replied.

Aphrodite's face twisted in disgust. "I can't say I will be sorry to see that abomination killed! If you don't succeed, I'm sure my father will order it!"

"How did he capture you?" Gage asked. Given her level, he'd been curious since he scanned her.

Aphrodite's face became hard. "I can't tell you the specifics, only that I came here to negotiate with him, and he took me prisoner with some sort of string that wrapped around me and stole my magic! He's been holding me hostage this entire time to keep my father from..."

Gage raised an eyebrow but the woman frowned. "From what?"

"I can't speak of it," she replied.

Gage opened his mouth to point out that he'd saved her and that she owed him a better explanation, but Aphrodite put a finger to his lips.

She shook her head. "I can't tell you anymore."

Without even a glance back, a pool of blue/white light appeared that showed a swirling vortex of rainbow colors. A portal! Aphrodite knew portal magic! It was unexpected and made her even more formidable.

"Are you sure you won't come with me?" she asked. The wizardess gave him a seductive look. "I do owe you and I ALWAYS pay my debts."

He couldn't go. His course was set. He was going to kill Ruy Cernunnos. Gage shook his head.

"Sorry to hear that." Aphrodite seemed to look genuinely sorry as she took a step back. She took another step backwards, towards her portal and smiled. "I hope you kill him. And I hope you don't die."

With that, she stepped back into the portal and disappeared. Gage watched the shimmering colors of the portal for a moment longer and then it winked out of existence.

Gage let out a disappointed breath. He had hoped the woman's escape would be more traditional and would have provided a distraction. That wouldn't be the case now. He'd likely have to fight his way back up to Ruy's bedroom. So be it.

Not bothering to lock the door this time, Gage stalked back towards the entrance of the dungeon. He had a mission to complete.

CHAPTER 51

Gage ran into the first patrol on the staircase out of the dungeon. There were only two of them and he wondered briefly if they might be replacements for the two sentries who had been guarding Aphrodite.

It didn't matter. They were headed to the dungeon. While he could have blended into the shadows and avoided notice, he couldn't risk it. If these guards entered the dungeon and discovered the bodies, they would raise the alarm. He couldn't allow that. He pulled the two daggers he'd taken from the dead guards.

Staying partially in the shadows as the guards came down the steps, Gage *Shadow Slid* behind them. As soon as he appeared, he sprang. Grabbing the sentry on his right, he slammed him into his companion. The two guards collided, lost balance, and tumbled down the stairs.

Following them down, Gage pounced atop the guards.

He grabbed the first guard's head, pulled it back and then sliced the dagger across his exposed neck.

You critically slash Elite Guard for 131 damage.
You kill Elite Guard.
You have gained experience.

He didn't wait for the first guard to stop moving. Gage tumbled onto the second man. Gage plunged both his daggers between the front of his cuirass and the back. The blades slipped through the man's ribs and into his heart. He gave both daggers a twist at the end and then pulled them out.

You critically pierce Elite Guard for 43 damage.
You critically pierce Elite Guard for 47 damage.
You kill Elite Guard.
You have gained experience.

The first man struggled weakly for a moment before going limp. Gage didn't bother wiping the daggers off. He discarded them and grabbed the clean daggers from the guards he'd just killed.

Between the blood and the bodies, there was no way to hide what he'd done. The clock was now ticking. As soon as someone discovered these bodies, the alarm would be raised. He had to make it up to Ruy before that happened. If not, the Archmage might use a portal to escape. Gage couldn't let that happen.

Sprinting up the stairs, he made it to the third floor

before stumbling into a trio of guards. These guards were relaxed, and Gage guessed they had just come off duty.

Off duty or not, a hyena beast-kin's ears rotated his way and a moment later, the guard howled and pointed to him.

Gage didn't give them a chance to pull their weapons free. He *Shadow Slid* just behind them and slashed his dagger across the neck of one of the human guards just as he turned. The large gout of blood told him he'd hit the carotid artery. The man tried to bring his hand up to his throat, but a moment later he collapsed.

You critically slash Elite Guard for 131 damage.
You kill Elite Guard.
You have gained experience.

The other human guard stared wide-eyed at his dying companion instead of going for his weapon. Gage kicked the man on the inside of the thigh, throwing him off balance.

You kick Elite Guard for 4 damage.

As he fell towards the side of the stairs, Gage shoved him over the banister. The man windmilled for a moment before plummeting down the center of the stairwell. The man screamed for the few seconds it took him to reach the bottom.

You slam Elite Guard for 3 damage.
Elite Guard has died.

You have gained experience.

Gage turned just as the beast-kin pulled his sword from his belt. Bad move. In the confined area of the stairs, the sword was unwieldy.

Moving in with his daggers, Gage cursed as the hyena-like head thrust forward and bit down on his shoulder.

Elite Guard bites you for 4 damage.

He'd forgotten how some of the beast-kin still used their more feral parts in combat. He gritted his teeth. At least the thing couldn't bring its sword to bear.

Another miscalculation on the beast-kin's part was how biting an opponent exposed his neck. Gage didn't let the opportunity go to waste. He struck both daggers into the guard's neck once, then twice.

You critically pierce Elite Guard for 31 damage.
You critically pierce Elite Guard for 35 damage.
You critically pierce Elite Guard for 34 damage.
You critically pierce Elite Guard for 31 damage.
You kill Elite Guard.
You have gained experience.

Strength withered from the hyena's mouth first, with the rest of its body followed soon after. It collapsed onto the staircase as the sword slid from lifeless hands.

Dropping his bloody daggers, he grabbed two fresh ones from the bodies. He brought up his display and checked his stats.

Health: 26
Stamina: 53
Mana: 26

He swore as he saw he was almost at half *Mana*. Neither the dungeon nor the staircase had any windows, but given the extra cost of his *Shadow Slide*, he knew it must be day.

And yet, the cost hadn't been as high as he would expect during full daylight. Perhaps it was close to dusk or just after dawn. Gage had no way of knowing and at this point it didn't matter. He couldn't just wait around until it was dark.

Gage looked down at the bodies of the guards. He didn't even have time to wait to let his *Mana* regenerate. Any moment, another group of guards would enter the stairwell, see the bodies, and the alarm would be sounded.

Looking up, he knew there were still four more floors before Ruy. Gage set his jaw. He couldn't afford to waste a single second. Spinning, he raced up the stairs.

By the time he reached the seventh floor, he was out of breath. Worse, his *Mana* had only regenerated a single point.

Health: 26
Stamina: 48
Mana: 27

He stared at the door leading to the seventh floor and then looked at his display again. He didn't like the idea of going up against the Archmage without full *Mana*. He briefly considered waiting at the door until it regenerated fully but then he heard a door opening below him and the sound of men talking.

A moment later, everything went abruptly quiet. He closed his eyes, knowing what would come next. Gage only had to wait a second until the expected cry filled the stairwell.

"Alarm!" yelled a man's voice. "Alarm!"

Gage swore as he heard more shouting and the sound of armored men moving on the floors below. The man's cries had been heard. The cries were starting to be echoed by other voices and it would only spread.

He knew what happened next. In a few minutes, the entire guard would mobilize. Any off-duty or sleeping guards would be roused. Channelers, warlocks, and the few remaining wizards would be roused and join in the effort. The keep would be searched floor by floor until they found him.

Looking down at himself, Gage cursed. He was sweating from the exertion and still stank of being in the dungeon for days. While he could use his Shadow abilities to hide from normal humans, his Dog's Bane had long since worn off. The first beast-kin who came near him would smell him. No, he couldn't hide or sneak past the guards.

Gage opened his eyes. His only choice was to get to Ruy before the guards on the other floors and out in the courtyard were mobilized. He had to move now and move fast. He checked his stats.

Health: 26

Stamina: 48
Mana: 27

He'd have to conserve as much *Mana* as possible for the fight with the Archmage and any other mages that might be with him. That meant he'd have to rely on his other skills. He nodded grimly. So be it.

The sound of men yelling was now accompanied by the commotion of soldiers in the stairwell. They were climbing up, no doubt to protect the Archmage and the other mages on the floors below. His time was running out.

Gage activated his *Uncanny Dodge* and his *Improved Uncanny Dodge*. He had three charges of each; he'd have to make the best use of them. Once they were gone, he'd be forced to either go completely hand-to-hand or use his Shadow abilities.

Taking a deep breath, he reached for the door leading to the seventh floor—to Ruy. Gage let out the breath he'd been holding. Crouching down, he grabbed the door handle and pulled open the door.

Even as Gage saw the hallway full of guards, he heard the twang of crossbows as the closest guards fired into the doorway.

CHAPTER 52

Because he was crouched, three of the crossbow bolts flew harmlessly over him, though he did hear the buzz of one that passed an inch from his ear. His Uncanny Dodge kicked in and he deftly avoided another two.

Elite guard shoots you but you Dodge.
Elite guard shoots you but you Dodge.

The last bolt didn't impact him directly. The barbed tip of the bolt sliced across his shoulder, opening up a gash.

Elite guard shoots you for 2 damage.

It was a shallow wound and Gage ignored it. Instead, he did a quick count of the guards in the hallway. Eight. There were eight Elite Guards, and both his Dodge abilities were now on cooldown. Not good odds.

Gage's experienced mind took in the scene before him. While it was true he was outnumbered, the guards had made a mistake. They'd piled together, probably to optimize the number who could fire their crossbows as soon as the door opened.

They were packed in close. Too close. The guards had gambled on taking down the intruder with their opening volley and hadn't even left enough room to reload their crossbows, let alone draw their swords. They'd made a mistake. Their last mistake.

Leaping forward at the startled guards, Gage struck two kneeling guards in the throat before they could even decide whether to reload their crossbows or drop them. He twisted savagely as he withdrew the daggers, knowing they would bleed out in seconds.

You critically pierce Elite Guard for 87 damage.
You critically pierce Elite Guard for 79 damage.

The other four crossbowmen reacted, but they were much too slow. The third kneeling guard wasted time gawking at his dying companions. It was the last thing he'd ever do.

Gage spun, building up momentum and placing himself directly in front of the crossbowman. As he came around, he flipped the dagger in his hand and rammed the point through the man's eye and into his brain.

You critically pierce Elite Guard for 102 damage.
You kill Elite Guard.
You have gained experience.

The man's body spasmed and jerked and Gage ripped the dagger back out before it was pulled from his hand.

Two guards were behind the three standing crossbowmen. They had swords drawn but they couldn't swing them without hitting their comrades in front of them. The crossbowmen themselves realized their predicament but all three reacted in different ways.

The crossbowman on Gage's left hoisted his weapon, intending to use it as a bludgeon. His companions both dropped their crossbows and went for their weapons. The one on the right went for his sword while the one in the center went for his dagger.

Gage sidestepped the crossbow the guard was using as a cudgel, putting him directly in front of the center man. He sliced his left dagger across the guard's right wrist, while bringing his other dagger up at the man's throat. The guard managed to move his head at the last second but still took a deep gash along his neck.

You critically slash Elite Guard for 19 damage.
You slash Elite Guard for 4 damage.

The guard howled in pain, pulling his injured wrist back away from his dagger and bringing his left hand up to his bleeding neck.

Dropping down, Gage tumbled to his right. The guard above him looked down, still trying to get his sword free of its scabbard. In the confines of the hallway, with a wall on one side and his comrade on the other, it proved impossible in the time he had.

Gage grabbed the man's leg and brought his dagger

across his calf, just below the knee, slicing muscle and tendon.

You critically slash Elite Guard for 24 damage.
Elite Guard is hamstrung.

The man howled in pain and fell. Standing up quickly, Gage shoved the man back against the swordsmen behind him.

As the man tumbled back, Gage threw his left dagger at the crossbowman on the left who had tried to bludgeon him. His aim was true and the dagger lodged itself into the man's throat.

You critically hit Elite Guard for 81 damage.
You kill Elite Guard.
You have gained experience.

Almost at the same time, the guards he'd stabbed in the throat expired with another message.

Elite Guard dies.
You have gained experience.
Elite Guard dies.
You have gained experience.

Reaching out, Gage pulled the hamstrung guard's dagger from his sheath as he fell back against his companions. Turning to the last standing crossbowman, he wasn't quick enough to avoid the man as he charged Gage.

Bleeding and unable to use his right wrist, the guard

had attacked him with the only weapon he had available—his body. The man was a good foot taller than Gage and outweighed him by at least fifty pounds. He slammed into Gage and drove him back into the wall with bone jarring force.

Elite guard slams you for 5 damage.

Gage felt the breath leave him as his back was slammed into the wall, but he managed to retain his daggers. He stabbed both daggers into the man's unprotected sides, just under his armpits. Once, twice, three times before the man slid off him to the floor.

You pierce Elite Guard for 7 damage.
You pierce Elite Guard for 8 damage.
You pierce Elite Guard for 8 damage.
You pierce Elite Guard for 5 damage.
You pierce Elite Guard for 7 damage.
You pierce Elite Guard for 6 damage.
You kill Elite Guard.
You have gained experience.

No sooner had the man slid off him than the two swordsmen attacked. They'd let their hamstrung companion fall to the floor in order to get to Gage. Both men came at him with their swords, one slashing high, the other low.

Still struggling to catch his breath, Gage barely managed to tumble out of the way before the blades sparked off the wall he'd just been in front of. Somersaulting across the hall, he came up behind the two men and forced himself to take a deep breath.

The pair of elite guards spun and moved in, not giving him the time he needed to recover. He started to roll out of the way again when he felt something grab his foot. A momentary glance down told him it was the hamstrung guard.

Seeing their comrade trying to immobilize their adversary, the swordsmen stepped forward and swung at him from different angles.

Gage considered his possibilities. At the last second, he threw himself bodily atop the hamstrung guard. The two swords cut through the air above him, one barely missing him by inches.

His full weight coming down on the hamstrung guard, Gage heard a gasp as the wind was knocked out of the man. Not giving the man time to recover, he sliced his dagger across the guard's throat as he rolled off him.

You critically slash Elite Guard for 81 damage.
You kill Elite Guard.
You have gained experience.

Rolling up to a fighting crouch, he squared off against the two swordsmen. The two looked at him warily and one cried out.

"We have him! In the hall! We need help!" the swordsman on the left called out.

The other man grinned wickedly at Gage, eyes darting to the door at the end of the hallway. "You're dead now, assassin!"

Gage shot a quick glance towards the door, knowing there were more guards behind it. The door slipped open and he knew he needed to act now.

Feinting at the guard on his left, he ducked under the sword swipe meant to hold him at bay, slipped to the side and spun around to the back of the man. He grabbed the man by the back of his breastplate and kept the man between himself and the other guard.

At the same time, he stabbed the man in the kidney, coming up under the breastplate. The man jerked and tried to free himself, but Gage continued stabbing until the man weakened.

You critically pierce Elite Guard for 19 damage.
You critically pierce Elite Guard for 17 damage.
You critically pierce Elite Guard for 20 damage.
You critically pierce Elite Guard for 23 damage.
You kill Elite Guard.
You have gained experience.

Feeling the man go limp, Gage kicked the body at his companion, forcing the dead man's companion to sidestep.

Gage, already moving, intercepted the man. He pushed the man's sword arm out of the way with his right hand, then stabbed his left dagger into the man's bicep, between the armor plating. The guard's sword clanged to the floor as his arm became useless.

The elite guard tried to headbutt him, but Gage moved his head and took the impact on his shoulder. He grimaced as it struck the same place the beast-kin had bitten him.

Elite guard slams you for 3 damage.

With the man's head so close, Gage brought his dagger up from behind and shoved it under the man's helmet and into the base of his skull. The man's body jerked and then went limp.

You critically pierce Elite Guard for 55 damage.
You kill Elite Guard.
You have gained experience.

"I should have known it would be you!" Ruy Cernunnos boomed from the open doorway.

Gage let the body slide off him and turned to face the Archmage. Ruy stood just behind another half dozen guards, smirking at him from the safety of his office.

"You never did know when to die!" The Archmage chuckled. He raised a hand. "But now I get the pleasure of killing you myself."

A ball of fire shot from the Archmage's hand, growing larger as it rocketed down the hallway, directly at Gage.

CHAPTER 53

Gage had only a fraction of a second to react as the fireball grew larger. He knew from experience the fireball would explode as soon as it touched something—whether it be him or the wall.

He could easily negate it with his *Suppress Magic*, but that would leave him without magic for a minute. Gage would be at a severe disadvantage and wouldn't be able to suppress the next magical attack.

Cursing, Gage did the only thing he could. He waited until just before the fireball hit him, now two feet wide, and then activated his *Shadow Slide* ability. Instantly, he disappeared and reappeared just past Ruy.

The moment he appeared, he activated his *Dodge* ability and then *Suppress Magic* ability, effectively robbing both Ruy and himself of any magic for a minute. That still left six more guards to deal with—all elite bodyguards. He set his jaw. Gage was too close to his revenge to let a few guards get in the way.

One of the guards must have caught the glimmer of movement and turned his head. Gage wasted no time. He spun around and buried the dagger in the man's opening mouth, causing him to recoil and drop his pike to clutch at his face.

You critically pierce Elite Guard for 24 damage.

Gage reached forward and drew the man's dagger as he struggled, pulling it free and across the unprotected hip of the man next to him, just under the guard's breastplate.

You critically pierce Elite Guard for 13 damage.

He was about to stab one of the other guards in the back when the Archmage suddenly unfurled his wings, knocking Gage back while cancelling one of his *Dodge* abilities.

Ruy Cernunnos slams you but you Dodge.

The strike didn't do any damage but wasted a charge of *Dodge* on what would have been minor damage.

"What's going on?" The Archmage snarled. "What happened to my magic?"

Ruy looked both angry and afraid. Good. He should be afraid. Gage hoped the man spent the last remaining minutes of his life in fear.

"You!" Ruy twisted around and caught sight of Gage. As expected, the Archmage didn't give a thought for the guard with the dagger in his mouth. His only concern was his magic.

The guards had all turned around by this point, with two of them trying to help out their injured comrades. Ruy saw them and his face grew even more red. "Forget them! Kill Gage! He has some sort of magical item suppressing my magic! Kill him!"

The men helping the two injured guards set them down on the floor before bringing their pikes up to bear. Gage narrowed his eyes. The pikes gave them reach—a long reach—but if he got close, they would be unwieldy. The problem was, getting in close.

The four guards came towards him, forcing him to retreat to the center of the room. Behind them, Ruy was holding out his hands, trying to summon his magic. He thought Gage had some sort of magic item—like the one they'd used on him—to suppress magic. He had no idea it was an innate ability. By the time he figured it out, it would be too late.

Gage considered just throwing one of the poisoned daggers at Ruy. He could easily hit the obese man from where he stood, and the poison would make short work of him. No. Gage wanted to be right there when he stabbed the man. He wanted to make sure the Archmage knew exactly why he was dying. But first, he'd have to deal with the bodyguards.

Watching the men carefully, he waited until they had encircled him. They maintained a safe distance, trusting their longer weapons to keep Gage at bay. For the moment, they did.

He watched the guards, taking a quick moment to scan them.

Ferrin
Human
Fighter
Level 14

Brandubh
Human
Fighter
Level 13

Katain
Beast-kin
Fighter
Level 14

Zarkeena
Human
Fighter
Level 14

Ferrin was an older guard with streaks of gray in the hair that fell out from under his helmet. He also sported a thick, salt and pepper mustache. He watched Gage warily, keeping a bit more distance than the others.

Then there were his old friends, Katain and Brandubh. He'd met both of them earlier. He certainly remembered Brandubh, the man who'd spit on him. He smiled at the opportunity to get revenge.

The final guard, Zarkeena, was a woman. She was muscular for a woman and had a scar down her face. He blinked. Was that Terina? Or rather, Heather? Or was this the guard she'd somehow imitated. The resemblance was uncanny.

He cocked his head and raised an eyebrow at the woman but there was no reaction or look of recognition. If this was Heather, she was a great actor. It didn't matter if it was her. If she got in the way, he'd kill her. Gage had come too far.

"What are you waiting for?" screamed Ruy. "Kill him!"

Brandubh, either following orders or just impatient, chose that moment to thrust his pike at Gage. As if on cue, the beast-kin, Katain, across from Brandubh, thrust his pike as well.

Gage sidestepped Brandubh's thrust. As he did, he grabbed the shaft of Brandubh's pike and yanked as hard as he could. He wasn't sure if he could actually move the large man, and normally he might not, but the man had overcommitted his strike and was off-balance. Gage's yank pulled him forward and directly into the path of Katain's strike.

The beast-kin's steel pike had been designed to puncture armor. The sharp tip pierced Brandubh's breastplate just above his abdomen and tore through his sternum. Both guards looked down at the pike sticking into Brandubh's chest. Gage took the opportunity to spit in the guard's face.

A strike narrowly missed him, his *Uncanny Dodge* saving him from being skewered by Zarkeena's pike. He cursed. The woman was fast.

Zarkeena pierces you but you Dodge.

Gage spun under her strike and was nicked along his back by a strike from the mustached man as he began to whirl behind the warrior woman.

Ferrin slashes you for 4 damage.

Snarling out a curse at the gash on his back, Gage came up behind Zarkeena. He cursed and hoped it really wasn't Heather. Then he stabbed both daggers into either side of her neck.

You critically pierce Zarkeena for 41 damage.
You critically pierce Zarkeena for 49 damage.
You kill Zarkeena.
You have gained experience.

He twisted the daggers slightly before pulling them out and the warrior woman collapsed to the floor, hands dropping the pike and trying to reach her ruined neck.

"What are you idiots doing?" screamed the Archmage, spittle flying from his mouth. "Kill him!"

Katain had recovered and leaped at Gage with his pike leading. Gage dropped to the floor. He avoided being skewered by the beast-kin but felt a stinging pain in his leg as Ferrin's pike punctured his thigh.

The man tried to put his weight behind it and pin Gage to the floor. It was a good strategy. If he couldn't move, Gage would be an easy target for the beast-kin as soon as he recovered.

Flipping his right dagger around in his hand, he threw directly at Ferrin's face. The dagger flew perfectly, and the pommel of the dagger hit the mustached man right between the eyes, stunning him.

You crush Ferrin for 6 damage.
Ferrin is stunned.

The older guard stumbled back, blinking. His right hand reflexively came off his pike to touch his face. Gage took advantage of the man's distraction to reach down and pull the pike from his thigh and then roll to the side just in time to avoid a strike from Katain.

As he rolled, his now empty right hand went down to his pouch and retrieved one of the healing potions. He flipped the cork out with his thumb and drank the contents.

You are healed for 24 Health.

The healing potion burned all the way down his throat and continued to burn as it hit his stomach. At the same time, he felt the itching sensation that accompanied the healing of wounds. He also saw a new message.

Brandubh dies.
You have gained experience.

The guard who had spit in his face was dead, skewered by his own comrade. Gage liked the irony of it.

"Morons!" Ruy screamed, his face turning purple in rage. "Don't let him drink a potion!"

Letting the bottle drop from his hand, he rolled back up to his feet, facing Ferrin and Katain. The mustached man was still shaking his head, but his eyes were still focused on Gage. The two guards stalked forward, pikes aimed directly at him.

Gage felt it then. The sensation he got whenever access to his magic returned. His *Suppress Magic* had ended. Along with that, the cooldowns for his *Uncanny Dodges* reset. He quickly activated both abilities.

Light flared in the room and Gage spared a glance at the Archmage. Sure enough, the channeler had felt it too. Ruy had gotten his magic back, and his hands were covered with flame. Gage cursed.

"Ha!" the Archmage bellowed as the flame spread all over his body. "I have my magic back, fool! And now you die!"

Flame wreathed the Archmage, completely obscuring his form. Gage knew exactly what it was: A spell called elemental armor. In this case, fire armor covered the man's entire body and would burn anyone even coming close to him. If anyone actually touched him, it would be like sticking a hand into a campfire.

Light flared again, brighter this time, as a huge ball of fire appeared between his flaming hands. "If these morons can't do their job, then you can all die!"

Ferrin and Katain, hearing the Archmage, turned to see Ruy launch the ball of fire at the trio.

With his two assailants momentarily distracted, Gage

reached down with his right hand, grabbed one of his poisoned daggers and stepped forward.

The two men, staring dumbly at the approaching fireball, reacted too late. Gage ducked under the pikes and came up inside their guard. He brought the two daggers up with all his might, slamming them under the two guards' chins and up into the brains. They died instantly.

You critically pierce Ferrin for 92 damage.
Ferrin is poisoned.
You kill Ferrin.
You have gained experience.
You critically pierce Katain for 101 damage.
You kill Katain.
You have gained experience.

Letting go of both daggers, he activated his *Suppress Magic* ability, a heartbeat before the fireball hit him.

The fireball disappeared instantly, along with his access to magic. Unfortunately, he was slightly too far from Ruy for it to affect the Archmage. He was still wreathed in flame.

"What? How?" came Ruy's voice from inside the cocoon of flame.

Gage didn't hesitate. He sprinted directly at the Archmage, reaching down to take his last poisoned dagger.

Ruy shot a beam of fire from each of his hands. One missed and the other would have hit but for *Uncanny Dodge*.

Ruy burns you but you Dodge.

Screaming his fury, the Archmage tried to unleash another volley of fire beams, but Gage had closed in. He leaped forward, under the Archmage's outstretched arms, hit the floor and somersaulted behind him.

The proximity to the elemental armor burned him but he ignored the pain.

Elemental armor (fire) burns you for 3 damage.

For some reason, proximity to elemental armor bypassed his *Uncanny Dodge*. He never understood why, but it did. Was it because he couldn't dodge something he intentionally stuck his hand into? The question would have to wait for some other time.

Coming to his feet behind the Archmage, Gage gritted his teeth at what he knew would come next. Then he plunged the poisoned blade into the Archmage's back.

Elemental armor (fire) critically burns you for 11 damage.
You pierce Ruy Cernunnos for 7 damage.
Ruy Cernunnos is poisoned.

Ruy arched his back and took a step away. Gage barely pulled his hand away in time to duck under the Archmage's flaming wing. He looked down at his burned hand and winched. The skin was raw and blistered.

The Archmage managed to turn around, even as his fat, flaming arms attempted to reach the wound. "What... what have you done?"

Gage didn't answer. He reached into his pouch and

took one of the healing potions and quickly downed it, watching as his hand healed itself in front of his eyes.

Ruy staggered towards him, flaming armor starting to flicker. He took one more step before the flames disappeared completely and the Archmage collapsed onto the floor.

CHAPTER 54

Gage stood over the demonic archmage, blood dripping from the dagger in his hand. He glared down at Ruy Cernunnos, the soon to be former archmage, as the man lay on the floor. The Archmage's right arm desperately clawed for the wound in his back, not quite able to reach it, as the blood continued to spurt from the wound.

He let the empty vial drop to the floor. It hit with a clang and rolled into the crimson puddle which was already forming under the dying archmage. The blood seeped into the floor, staining the ancient white and gold marble tiles of the Archmage's office. Not that it mattered to Gage. The entire place could burn for all he cared.

"That's for my wife and daughter," Gage spat down at the Archmage. "You spawn of demons!"

Ruy's red-skinned left arm pointed at Gage, taloned fingers spread apart. No doubt, he was trying to channel more fire at Gage and burn him to ash. The Archmage blinked, mouth opening and closing. He guessed the channeler was trying to understand why his power had suddenly abandoned him.

Unlike his *Suppress Magic* ability, which prevented magic in the area for a short time, the Wizard's Folly would keep Ruy's *Mana* at zero while the other poison did its work. The Archmage could sense his magic, but he wouldn't be able to channel it.

"What?" Gage tried to chuckle, but it turned into a cough. "Did you think I forgot how to make draiochtneim?" He gave the man a wicked smile. "The Cichiadamon came from your own garden."

Ruy's face twisted in outrage but also in fear as he realized his fate. Magic would not save him. Not this time.

Ruy turned a hateful glare on Gage. "Gods... take you... Gage!"

"I'm sure they will," Gage retorted with a snarl. "But they'll take you first."

Gage's face contorted with a mixture of hatred, anger, and grief. Ruy had sent assassins to kill Gage, but they'd made a fatal mistake. The assassins hadn't known, or perhaps hadn't been told, the extent of Gage's training. They hadn't been properly prepared to kill him. He survived. His wife and daughter hadn't. "I hope the demon you made a pact with roasts your soul for all eternity for Alani and Shaunna's deaths!"

Gage heard footsteps in the distance. Armored men ran up the steps and down the marble floor of the hallway. He'd always known it was just a matter of time before they reached him. So be it. He was ready to die. Ready to be with his wife and daughter.

The Archmage coughed, then coughed again, this time bringing up blood. He wiped the blood away with his hand, staining the expensive silk of his sleeve. "You... you think this ends with me? You think... I... gave the order?"

Gage perked up. "Lies won't save you? I know it was you."

Ruy coughed. He was getting weaker. His arms no longer moved but lay limply at his sides. "You think I... gave that order... on my own?

Bending down, Gage grabbed the man by his rich, gold embroidered tunic and hauled him close. He was breaking a number of rules by doing so.

Gage didn't care. He was beyond caring. The rules could burn for all he cared. The guards would be here any moment now and then he could join Alani and Shaunna.

He put his face close to Ruy's. There was one question that had been eating at him since it had happened. "Why? Why did you come after me and my family?"

"You know... why," he coughed.

Gage didn't know for certain, but he had a guess. Something was going on. Something mageslayers would be a threat to. But what? What did this idiot have planned?

The archmage's blood-stained teeth formed into a smile. "This... is... bigger... than you know..."

Ruy's eyes started to roll back into his head but Gage shook him. "Was someone else involved, Ruy?" he growled. "Who?""

Gage heard shouts now as the guards caught sight of the bodies Gage had left in his wake. They would be here any moment. He needed answers.

The once great Archmage's eyes looked up at Gage.

They were unfocused. The man was almost dead, blood loss and poison sapping his remaining strength. His lips moved and Gage had to move in closer to hear the channeler's last words. The words came out a rasping whisper. "The... Council... You... can't stop..."

The body went limp in his arms. Gage turned towards Ruy, to see the man's eyes were vacant. The Archmage, leader of House Cernunnos, was dead. And Gage had killed him. His display flashed and he looked at the message.

Ruy Cernunnos dies.
You gain experience.
Quest Complete.
Vengeance is Mine—Part VIII
Get revenge for your wife and child's violent deaths by killing the man who ordered the assassination.
Kill Ruy Cernunnos (1/1).
Reward: 9000 experience.

You gain 9000 experience.
You have gained a level!

You have received a new quest "Vengeance is Mine —Part IX"
You have learned that Ruy Cernunnos was not the only one responsible for the death of your wife and daughter.
With his last words, Ruy Cernunnos informed you that the Council of Houses ordered the assassination. To

gain vengeance, you must kill the remaining House leaders and the Overking.
Kill the Leaders of the Houses (1/7).
Kill the Overking (0/1)
Reward: 100,000 experience, Unknown.

Accept quest (yes or no)?

He thought he would feel a great weight lift from his shoulders once the Archmage was dead. Gage thought he would feel better once justice had been served. But he didn't. The holes in his heart were still there. The pain was still there. Nothing had changed.

Almost nothing had changed. He chuckled mirthlessly. Gage now knew that the Council had been a party to ordering his death and the death of his family. Why? It didn't make any sense.

Gage had earned his freedom. Had earned the right to have a life that wasn't just killing for this House or that House. He was out of the politics and the games the Houses played. He shook his head.

He thought he'd been out. Had that been his mistake? Thinking he was really out? Believing he could have a normal life. A wife. A family.

Snapping his attention back to his display, he looked at the new quest again. The quest wanted him to go against the Council. Mages as powerful, or more powerful, than Ruy. There was no way to go against the Council of Houses all by himself. Such a thing wasn't possible. Not any longer. With Ruy dead, the others would be wary.

They would be on their guard. It would be impossible to get to them.

The footsteps were closer now, seconds away. In a moment, he would be fighting more of the House Cernunnos elite guard. Judging by the sound of the footsteps, there were at least a half dozen. Probably more.

Gage snickered and wiped a hand across his stubbled head. It had been a while since he shaved it, a sign of mourning for his lost family. It had grown out a bit while he was in the dungeon, but it was still bare.

He quickly tried to think of what he wanted to do. He might be able to take the half dozen guards coming to kill him. He was injured, but still an extremely capable fighter. But more could show up at any moment, perhaps even more channelers or warlocks.

There was still another vial of draiocht-neim in his pouch, but without knowing exactly how many there might be or what powers they had, it would be a hard-won battle—if he won. He was injured and his wounds would slow him down. Perhaps enough that one of them would get in a lucky strike.

His training kicked in, Gage decided. He moved quickly to the window leading out to the balcony. It was most likely trapped, so he didn't dare use any magic. Quiet as a shadow, he slipped through the glass doors, and hopped across the balcony onto the marble railing.

It was daytime but dark clouds obscured the sky and the cool, moist air told him it would soon rain. His Shadow magic would be effective in the semi-dark, but not as good as at night. Gage would just have to make do.

He looked down a hundred and fifty feet to a moat. A long way down. Looking around, he saw men scurrying around the battlements, obviously looking for the intruder.

From inside the room, he heard guards clattering in. Then the yelling began. He was out of time.

"The Archmage is dead! Find the assassin!" a strong, deep voice yelled. There was a hint of command and Gage guessed it was a sergeant or captain.

Gage looked around. He could use his Shadow magic to *Slide* to another rooftop, but the entire place was on high alert. They'd be searching everything. His *Mana* was low, and he'd have to wait for it to completely regenerate before he could make an attempt at getting out of the Keep.

"Search the room!" the commanding voice ordered. "Check the balcony!"

Gage was out of time. He looked down, then at the nearby rooftops. Finally, he looked up. The guards would expect him to go down. He'd been taught that early on in his training. People always looked down. Occasionally they looked to the sides. They never looked up.

He picked a place a hundred feet up, then leapt off the balcony and activated his *Shadow Slide* ability. Instantly, he *Slid* through the shadows and up to a large gargoyle at the top of the keep. He grabbed onto the stone statue and hoisted himself up and behind it.

Concealing himself behind the gargoyle, Gage listened to the shouts from below him and others around him. No one pointed up at him or called out that they had seen him. That was good.

He settled back, hidden between the gargoyle's wings.

He'd have to wait for dark before attempting to escape the Keep. Until then, he hoped he'd be safe in his hiding spot.

A bolt of lightning split the sky and thunder boomed across the city. A moment later, a cold rain began falling. As the rain fell, Gage remembered his wife and daughter and how they'd sit outside and watch the thunderstorms. He pretended it was rain drops falling down his cheeks and not tears from the memories of his wife and daughter.

CHAPTER 55

It rained into the night, soaking Gage to the bone. He huddled behind the gargoyle, shivering until the sun finally set. During his teeth-chattering vigil, he watched the guards search the grounds, buildings, and walls of the Keep. No one found him, and the search had been called off an hour ago.

He had taken the last hour to study the movements of the guards. Gritting his teeth against chattering, he jumped from his hiding place and plummeted towards the ground. As soon as he fell within range, he *Shadow Slid* to the top of the barracks.

Arriving at the barracks rooftop, Gage ducked down below the parapet. His entire body ached with stiffness from sitting in his precarious position behind the gargoyle for hours. He needed to stretch out his muscles but that would have to wait. First, he needed to get out of the Keep.

Gage crawled to the far end of the barracks and peeked over. The guards were just passing along the wall, so he ducked back behind the parapet and counted silently. He tried to still the shivering, but it was no good. At this point, only a warm fire would do the trick. Soon, he promised himself. Soon.

After counting to ninety, he peeked over again to see that the guards were now on the far end of the wall. He didn't hesitate. Aiming for the large chimney of one of the outbuildings, he *Slid* and then immediately *Slid* to the wall.

He arrived at the wall instantly and didn't bother glancing to the side. He looked over the edge of the wall, picked an alley between two buildings, and *Slid*. A moment later, he was between the two buildings and out of the Keep.

Glancing back, he scanned the wall for any sign someone had seen him. Gage also tilted his head one way and then the other, listening for any sound of an alarm. Unfortunately, between shivering muscles and chattering teeth, focusing on sounds proved impossible. He cursed the cold autumn rain.

Gage waited for several minutes in the darkness of the alley. Not only did he want to make sure no alarm had been raised, but he also needed to regenerate some *Mana*. The consecutive *Shadow Slides* had drained his *Mana* and he wanted to regain enough for an emergency *Slide* if he needed it.

He had to assume he was a fugitive at this point. Even though Ruy and Arteen were both dead, someone else had to know he'd been in the dungeon. They would have found the dungeon master's body and realized he'd escaped. His description had probably already circulated through the guards and the town watch. He'd need to be careful.

Once his *Mana* had replenished enough for a *Slide*, Gage slipped out of the alleyway. He crept from shadow to shadow all the way to the river. There were no easy hiding spots to avoid the patrols stationed on both sides of the bridge.

Instead, he stalked along the buildings that lined the riverbank until he found a narrow section of river. Making sure no one was watching on either bank, he *Shadow Slid* across the river. From there, he stuck to the shadows until he reached the safehouse.

As he came upon the building, Gage froze. There was a light inside and he knew he hadn't left it on. He scowled, remembering Aeg Derg had mentioned he'd be moving the safehouses after three days. Likely, he had been in the dungeon for longer than three days. Nevertheless, he'd left equipment inside the safehouse. If it was still there, he wanted it back.

Gage crept to one of the shuttered windows and peeked inside. He frowned as he recognized the figure standing in the room, in front of the fireplace. It was his old mentor, Aeg Derg.

Mentor or not, why was the head of the assassin's guild in the safehouse? Aeg Derg rarely left the guild nowadays. Given that Gage was now a wanted fugitive who had killed Archmage Ruy, the man certainly wouldn't want to be seen with him. He paused. Unless his old mentor had come to kill him.

Gage brought up his stats.

Health: 30
Stamina: 30
Mana: 40

His *Mana* had completely regenerated but the cold prevented him from regenerating his *Stamina* over fifty percent. He'd used up all his *Uncanny Dodge* earlier. Even at full capacity, if it came to a fight, he wasn't sure he could beat his old mentor. In his current shape, he knew he stood no chance.

He glanced around the area. His *Spot* was maxed out, and even with his *Shadow Vision*, he didn't see anyone else. Certainly, the head of the assassin's guild wouldn't have come alone if he meant to kill him—he would have brought backup.

Cold and exhausted, Gage made up his mind. He pulled out his remaining dagger and coated it with Wizard's Folly—just in case. He let the poison dry and then slipped it back into its sheath. Hand on his dagger, he walked around to the door and opened it.

Warm air flowed out of the safehouse, and Gage trembled involuntarily. He'd almost forgotten what being warm felt like.

Aeg Derg was still facing the fire. He didn't turn around. "I thought you might be cold when you returned, so I started a fire," his mentor said. Aeg Derg reached his hands out towards the fire and rubbed them together. "It's gotten a bit too toasty for my comfort, but I'm sure you'll find it enjoyable."

Gage stepped into the room, basking in the sudden warmth. He scanned the room with his Shadow Vision. When he was confident there was no one hiding in any of the shadows, he let his Vision fade and shut the door behind him.

"Are you here to kill me?" Gage asked, cutting to the chase.

"Kill you?" Aeg Derg chuckled and then turned around. "Actually, my boy, I'm here to compliment you on a job well done—unofficially of course. Besides, with Ruy dead, his contract is void and the new Archmage hasn't put a contract out for you... yet."

Furrowing his brow, Gage frowned at his mentor. "Yet, huh?"

"Oh yes," his mentor said with a nod. "I'm certain it will be at the top of her list once she consolidates her power."

"Her?" Gage furrowed his brow again. "Who?"

"Sibeal Cernunnos," Aeg replied.

Gage couldn't disguise his shock. "Sibeal? The channeler with Mental magic?"

"Yes," the old man replied with a smile. "The same one Ruy summoned. The one on her way to... interrogate... you."

"You knew about that? Is that why you sent Heather? So Sibeal wouldn't learn you'd helped me?" Gage thought he was getting the picture now. "Did an inside man tip you off?"

Aeg Derg chuckled and shook his head. "Not... quite."

Gage piqued an eyebrow.

"Sibeal sent me a message letting me know you'd been

captured and that she'd been recalled by Ruy to use her skill on you to discover the traitor in the House," he replied with a smile.

"Sibeal told you that? Why..." Gage started but stopped as the pieces started to come together. "Sibeal was the traitor."

His old mentor nodded. "Indeed. She'd been planning to overthrow Ruy for some time now. She just needed... a catalyst."

"A catalyst?" Gage repeated. He was beginning to get a sinking feeling in the pit of his stomach.

Aeg Derg noticed his expression and nodded. "Technically, she couldn't hire the guild to kill Ruy. Instead, she approached me through more... discreet channels."

Gage felt himself getting angry. "So, you used me?!"

The old man sighed. "Let's just say, I took advantage of the situation."

Slamming his fist into the door frame, Gage fumed at his old mentor, his other hand still on his dagger. "Did you have them kill Alani and Shaunna on purpose?"

"No! Of course not!" Aeg Derg looked genuinely hurt. "What I told you earlier was the truth. Ruy hired the guild to kill you. I sent the novices after you, knowing they would fail."

"So, the entire time, you knew I'd go after Ruy," Gage snarled. "You used me."

Aeg Derg shrugged. "The contract was the contract. I knew, when they failed, you'd come here and..."

"And you'd point me at Ruy," Gage interrupted.

His mentor shrugged. "I knew you'd never rejoin the guild. And the only other thing you could do..."

"... was kill the Archmage," Gage finished.

He was angry for being manipulated but he couldn't fault the old man. He was right. Once Ruy had put the contract out on him, even if his wife and daughter hadn't been killed, Gage would still have come for the Archmage. It would have been the only way to protect his family from future attacks.

Aeg Derg went for something on his belt and Gage tensed, ready to pull his dagger on his old mentor. Instead of a weapon, the man pulled a pouch from his belt and tossed it on the bed. Gage heard the clink of coins as it bounced on the mattress.

"What's that?" he asked, eyes narrowed.

"We were paid a lot to kill Ruy," Aeg Derg replied, glancing from the pouch to Gage. "I thought you should have a share."

"I didn't do it for money," Gage growled, remembering the last time he'd seen Alani and Shaunna. "I did it for them."

"I know, but take it," the old man told him. "You're going to need it. I wasn't exaggerating. Sibeal will be putting a contract out on you tomorrow, the day after at the latest. You need to be out of the province before that happens. Go somewhere safe and live out your life."

Gage scowled. "I can't. Not yet."

"Why not?" Aeg Derg frowned at him. "There's more than enough to..."

"It wasn't just Ruy," he told the old man. "It was the whole Council."

Aeg Derg closed his mouth and looked troubled, but

thoughtful. After a long pause, he spoke. "You're going after them?"

"Every single one," Gage replied.

"You're certain you want to go down that road?" his old mentor asked, concern etched on his weathered features. "I can't protect or help you once you start down that path."

"I understand." Gage nodded. He wanted to say he appreciated the help the man had given him so far, but it seemed his old mentor had really just been pointing him towards Ruy the entire time.

"Do you know who you'll go after first?" The old man asked, but then held up a hand. "No, don't tell me. I don't want to know."

Gage said nothing. In truth, he hadn't thought about it.

Aeg Derg looked at Gage and bit his lip. Different emotions played across his features before he finally nodded, seeming more to himself than to Gage.

"If you're going after the Council," Aeg said finally. "You should know that they are planning something—something big. None of my normal spies know what, but it is big, and it involves magic. I believe it's one of the reasons they wanted any unaffiliated mage slayers off the table."

Gage raised an eyebrow. "But you don't know what?"

Thinking back to his encounter with Aphrodite, he cocked his head. "Does it have anything to do with House Olympus?"

Aeg Derg piqued an eyebrow. "What makes you say that?"

"I found Aphrodite locked up in the dungeon. I let her

go and there was something she was sent here to nego-tiate but she wouldn't say exactly what. Then Ruy captured her and was holding her as a political hostage," he explained.

"My intelligence on this is very sketchy," the old man told him. "They are using mages with Mental magic to make sure no one slips into their meeting. Several of my spies were caught before we knew this."

"That's interesting," Gage said. It was extremely rare to use mental mages in that way. He wondered what was so secretive and important they had to go to such extreme measures.

His old mentor shook his head and then turned thoughtful. "If you find out what it is, I would appreciate it if you'd send word back."

"Unofficially, of course," Gage smirked, realizing his old mentor was trying to turn him into one of his spies.

"Unofficially." Aeg Derg agreed with a nod. He cleared his throat. "You have things to do, and I need to get back to the hall." He paused. "Good luck, my boy."

His old mentor walked past him to the door. He turned and nodded to Gage. "Gage."

"Master," he nodded back.

Aeg Derg went out the door, closing it behind him. Once again, Gage was alone. He walked over to the bed and picked up the pouch. He poured the contents onto the bed and gasped. There was a small fortune in platinum trade bars.

His mentor hadn't been lying. It was enough for him to disappear somewhere and live a comfortable life. Only—

Gage couldn't. Not until he made those responsible for the death of his family pay.

Stripping off his wet clothes, Gage laid them out in front of the fire and changed into his spare set. He sat down on the floor in front of the fire and stared into the flames.

His mind turned to plans for the rest of his revenge.

EPILOGUE

Sibeal Cernunnos slipped into the cushioned chair and smiled. Or rather, she would have smiled if that were still possible. Instead, the tentacles that hung from what used to be her mouth wiggled happily.

The new Archmage looked down at her body. She had never been a pretty woman, had never caught the eye of any men who weren't trying to use her for her position and connections in House Cernunnos. She hadn't even been born with magic—something her parents and peers had never let her forget.

Her tentacles shifted from the pleased wiggle to an angry flex at the thought of her treatment as a second-class citizen. The wizards in the House had mocked her, ridiculed her. Until she'd made the pact.

She ran her thin, clawed hand across her hairless head. Sibeal had made the bargain with a demon. A Cthulhuian . It had promised her power. Power over others. And it had been right. She had more power than she'd ever dreamed. And now, she was Archmage!

Sibeal looked out at the office that had recently been Ruy's and chuckled. Or rather, she tried to chuckle. Because of the changes to her body, she wasn't able to laugh any longer—or even speak. At least, not with her mouth. Then again, she didn't need to speak.

Finally, she thought. She could project her thoughts into anyone's mind now. With enough *Mana*, she could even manipulate their thoughts. If she really focused, Sibeal could even make them see things that weren't real. It was great fun.

While she couldn't control people outright—not yet, at least, she could nudge them in the direction she wanted. Make them think something was their idea. Her tentacles wiggled happily again.

Not only could she communicate to others with her mind, she was able to communicate with her Cthulhu as well, just like a warlock. When the voice spoke to her at first, she'd been afraid—afraid she was going mad. But the more she listened to it, the more it led her to greater power.

Things are going according to your plan, the voice in her head stated without emotion.

Sibeal frowned. Rather, her tentacles twitched in annoyance. She wasn't sure any longer if it really was her plan. She thought it was, but sometimes... sometimes, she wasn't certain. Could her demon be manipulating her like she manipulated others? She didn't think so, but it was possible.

Ruy is out of the way, she agreed. *His little games are ended.*

Her cousin, Ruy, implemented maneuvers towards the other Houses to gain more power once the ritual was complete. He'd been holding up House Cernunnos's support, so her demon had suggested that Sibeal get rid of him and take over the House.

Given the mistreatment before her powers manifested, Sibeal had been quick to agree. It was fitting recompense for the injustices she'd suffered.

And now you will lend House Cernunnos's support? Although the Cthulhu phrased it as a question, its emotionless tone made it sound more like a command.

Not for the first time, Sibeal wondered if she were really in charge.

Of course, you are in charge, the voice said.

Her tentacles wriggled in surprise. She hadn't projected her thoughts to the demon, but it had heard them anyway. Alarming, but so far the demon hadn't steered her wrong. But was it telling the truth?

Am I really? She asked the Cthulhu. *In charge?*

Of course, the demon told her. *I am but... an advisor. I am here to help you realize your true potential.*

My true potential? She repeated. It was a familiar phrase the demon used. The demon told her reaching her true potential would unlock power she couldn't even imagine. It was the same thing the demons in the other Houses told their hosts. They could all reach their true potential—if they performed the ritual.

More power than you can imagine will be yours, the voice

promised her. *The ability to manipulate hundreds—even thousands—of minds. Armies will be yours to command.*

Sibeal sighed. She could still do that, at least. It all sounded so good. Being able to delve into anyone's mind, dig out their secrets, and use them for her purposes. Twist and wrap people in her will and have them obey her every whim.

All they had to do was complete the ritual. Complete the ritual to open the portal and then all the demon's magic would be hers, not just this little trickle she experienced now.

Once the ritual was complete, channelers and warlocks would dominate the world. Wizards would take a backseat. THEY would become the servants while she and others like her would become the masters!

What about Gage? She asked, remembering the assassin. *And the Shadowed Fist?*

The plan is still the same, the demon replied. *Kill them. Kill them all.*

But we've used the assassin's guild for... well... hundreds of years, she objected. It was true. The Houses had employed the various guilds to do the dirty work, rather than risk open confrontation with each other. The thought of wiping them out was foreign to her.

The wizards, they would use them against us, the Cthulhu reminded her. *It is the same in all the Houses. They must all be eliminated.*

Sibeal wiggled her tentacles in annoyance. She knew the plan, but actually giving the order was difficult. And yet, what had tradition done for her? Nothing! When she hadn't been born with magic, she'd become little better than a servant to those wizards who did have magic.

She growled—a noise that sounded like a rumbling in her throat—at the memories. She pushed aside her doubts. Sibeal would not let the wizards treat her like a second-class citizen again! She wouldn't let them use the assassins against her.

Captain, she sent into the mind of the man in front of the door.

The man jerked but recovered quickly. He looked her way and saluted. "Archmage!"

Proceed with the plan, she ordered. *Find and kill the assassin, Gage. And then, wipe out the Shadowed Fist.*

"As you command, Archmage," the captain said with a salute. He spun, and, for a second, she thought she saw relief on the man's face. He was afraid of her. Good. He should be.

The guards at the double doors opened them and allowed the Captain of the House Guard to leave. They shut them as soon as he was gone.

Sibeal sat back and her tentacles wiggled happily. Soon, very soon, the ritual would be complete, and she would have unlimited power. And then... she would be a god!

JOIN THE ADVENTURE

Thank you for reading this book! If you enjoyed it, please consider leaving a review on Amazon or tagging me on social media.

Reviews help readers like you find this book. More readers means more sales, and more sales help independent authors like me to be able to write more books!

To learn more about the author and his other books and projects, visit the author's website at:
https://www.johnecressman.com
Or visit our Facebook Page
https://www.facebook.com/authorjohncressman/

It started as just a game for Madison, but now the entire virtual world may hinge on her decisions!

Madison only joined the Koyesta Online's early access because her brother begged her. Of course, the fact that they're awarding brand new crytocurrency to the early players for in game actions might have something to do with it too.

Thrust inside the world's most immersive fantasy VRMMORPG, Madison, her brother and two cousins find themselves in some backwater little town, far away from other players and the main action of the game.

Determined to make the most of it, they set out on a series of adventures and stumble upon hidden ruins and a secret epic quest capable of reshaping the face of the game before it's even been officially released.

Join a dragon girl, a barbarian, an elf druid and a beastmaster with a big cat named Buddy as they explore the boundless world of Koyesta Online, battle monsters of all shapes and sizes and find out whether they have what it takes to become true epic heroes.

***

The Veil Online Trilogy (Second Edition) - Books 1-3

Check Out The Series on Amazon

Junior programmer Jace Burton is your average computer geek. By day he works on the most popular VR game in the world and by night, he slay dragons and saves damsels.

Not any more.

Today he woke up inside the game and there's no way out. Worse, he's not even his high level avatar. He's a monster. And every time he dies, he jumps into another monster body.

Something is wrong. Seriously wrong.

Join Jace on a mind-blowing adventure as he desperately tries to unravel the mystery of what has happened to him and most importantly, is he even alive any more?

LITRPG

To learn more about LitRPG, talk to authors including myself, and just have an awesome time, please join the LitRPG Group.

MORE LITRPG

For more information on this book and other exciting LitRPG/GameLit books, please visit the following Facebook groups:
LitRPG Books
https://www.facebook.com/groups/LitRPG.books/

and

GameLit Society
https://www.facebook.com/groups/LitRPGsociety/

ACKNOWLEDGMENTS

I'd like to acknowledge all the members of the LitRPG Authors' Guild who helped me in so many ways! Without your help, I could never have gotten this far!

I also want to acknowledge the 20Booksto50K Facebook group! I've received lots of help and inspiration from them and I recommend the group to new and experienced authors.

Also, a big thank you for everyone who had bought one of my books. Your support really means a lot to me.

ABOUT THE AUTHOR

John E. Cressman is an author, magician, mentalist, hypnotist, programmer, and longtime lover of roleplaying games and fantasy/sci-fi books.

He enjoys computer RPGs and MMORPGs, with his current favorite being Elder Scrolls Online. He used to play Skyrim, but then he took an arrow to the knee.